Dancing with the Ferryman

Frankie Valente

Copyright © 2011 Frankie Valente

All rights reserved.

ISBN: 1466297360
ISBN-13: 9781466297364

For Franklin and Ian,
with love x

ACKNOWLEDGMENTS

This story was inspired by Shetland; the amazingly beautiful landscape, but more importantly the people – my friends, neighbours and colleagues. Thanks to everyone who read early drafts and gave helpful feedback – especially Colleen, Kim, Stephanie, Melanie P and Melanie B. Thanks to Jenny for the help with dialect and for her company during our creative writing classes. And grateful thanks to my creative writing tutors Carl MacDougall and Sue Moorcroft, who were both so helpful with their critiques.

Thanks also to Dave Wheeler from Fair Isle for allowing me to use his photograph of the Northern Lights over Shetland for the cover. You can see more of his lovely photographs on his website: www.davewheelerphotography.com

CHAPTER ONE

It was positive. They stared at the word 'pregnant' that had just materialised in the window of the plastic wand. Jo giggled nervously. She dropped the stick into the bin, hesitated for a moment, then bent down to retrieve it. 'Do you think I should keep this to show David?'

'Oh yuk! Do you really think he needs to see your old pee on a stick? I think he'll take your word for it, don't you?' Megan said, wrinkling her nose in disgust.

'Perhaps you're right. Oh God, what am I going to tell him? Should I ring him? It'll be after eleven in Germany now; he's probably gone to bed. Maybe I should just send a text'.

'Seriously Jo? I don't think it's good manners to tell your man he's gonna become a dad by text. Why don't you just ring and see what kind of mood he's in. He might be up for such a surprise.'

'Good idea!' Jo replied, reaching for the kitchen phone. She dialled David's mobile phone and listened to it ringing. There was no reply, and eventually the call went to voicemail. She was about to leave a message, when a thought occurred to her. She hung up in surprise.

'What's wrong?' Megan asked.

'That's funny, earlier when I rang him it rang like it does when you ring a foreign number, but just now it rang like it does back in England.'

'Maybe you dialled the wrong number, try again,' Megan said.

'No, it was definitely his number; it went to his voicemail,' she replied, but nevertheless she pressed the speed dial button for David's mobile.

This time the phone did not ring, but instead an automated voice said the mobile phone was currently unavailable.

'That's even more bizarre; David never switches off his phone.' She looked at Megan and smiled. 'He must have caught an earlier flight home, perhaps he's on the tube. I guess that means I'll be able to tell him in person after all.'

'Well I don't suppose you want any more of this wine then?' Megan said, as she drained the last of the bottle of Pinot Grigio into her glass.

'Oh God no. I'll be giving up that for a while. If only I had realised earlier today I wouldn't have drunk half the bottle already. I've had so much on my mind these last few weeks; I never even noticed I was late.

'Ah, sure; it will be fine, don't worry. And at least you've nearly packed up the house already. There isn't that much more to do now, and David will be home soon, so he can do the rest, eh, and you can relax and put your feet up. Isn't that what they say in the movies?'

Jo made herself a cup of tea, while Megan finished her glass of wine. They chatted and laughed about babies for a while.

'I've missed evenings like this, haven't you?' Jo said, after a moment of companionable silence had lapsed.

'Definitely! So many late nights talking, and then up at the crack of dawn for work the next day. I think I'm getting old; I'm hopeless at late nights now, at least during term time anyway. Thank heavens for the school holidays; I can stay up all night without worrying.'

'I'm going to miss you not living just around the corner. It was bad enough when you got your own place, but at least you were still nearby.'

'Jo, come on, Dulwich is just the other side of London; it's hardly another planet. We can still meet up,' Megan said, reaching over and squeezing her friend's hand.

'I know, but it feels like the end of an era. I've lived in this house so long, and some of the best times of my life have been here.'

'Yeah; know how you feel, I loved living here too. You're so lucky to have bought this place when you did, I'll never afford my own place on a crappy teacher's salary.'

'Why don't you stay over tonight? You can have your old room again, and neither of us has work tomorrow.'

Megan laughed. 'That would be great, but I'm going to

feel a bit gooseberryish when David turns up and you tell him your news. I'll just wait until he gets here. But we'll have one more sleepover before you move, promise.'

'That's a point, where is David? It's a bit late for flights to be coming in from Berlin now isn't it?' Jo stared at the clock on the wall. 'I thought the last flight was four hours ago.'

'Have a look at *Ceefax*, there might be some delays.'

Jo switched on the TV and checked the flights in to Heathrow, and then Gatwick. There were no delays to any flights coming in from Germany and they had all arrived hours ago. The next flights would be in the morning. She tried ringing David again, but his phone was switched off. She rang the hotel in Berlin he had been staying in and was informed that he had checked out after breakfast that morning. He had not been booked to stay until the weekend, as Jo had thought.

'I wonder what's going on.' Jo said, although she did not feel particularly worried about his mysterious absence. It was strange that she could not reach him by phone, but she remained convinced that he would turn up soon with some explanation. She even wondered whether he had travelled on from Germany to somewhere else in Europe, and that she had simply forgotten. With their pending house move she had been losing track of what was going on in their lives.

Megan looked at her watch and noticed it was now 1.30am. She picked up her handbag with a view to heading off home.

'Jo, it's getting late, I'd better go. Ring me if you need me eh?'

Jo yawned and stretched, and then stood up.

'Yeah, you're right, I'd better get to bed, David must have gone somewhere else, I'm so forgetful these days; he probably told me.'

'Of course! Anyway, come round to mine tomorrow after you've had a nice long lie-in. We can hang out in the park if the weather's good again.'

Jo said goodnight at the front door and watched Megan walk down the road towards her flat. A fox slunk along the pavement and crossed over the road to avoid Megan. It stopped for a moment, sniffing the warm night air and then slipped through a gate into the neighbour's garden.

Jo shut the front door, secured the deadlocks and then the chain. David would just have to wake her up if he came home now. She switched off the TV and carried mugs and glasses into the kitchen and loaded up the dishwasher.

She was about to go to bed, but a nagging doubt crept into her mind and she knew she wouldn't get to sleep yet. David had definitely said he would be in Berlin until Saturday morning. He had droned on about the boring meetings he had set up with clients and colleagues. In fact, now that she thought about it, he had talked far too much about this trip. It was almost as if he had something to hide.

She went to the spare bedroom where most of David's suits were hanging in the wardrobe. She started searching through his pockets with the anticipation she would find some evidence in the form of a receipt for a florist, jewellery or lingerie shop, or other stereotypical sign that he had been up to mischief. But David, being the neat freak he was, had absolutely nothing in his pockets.

At the back of the wardrobe was the large black leather briefcase David stored all his personal papers in. She pulled it out and tried to open it. It was secured with two three-digit combination locks. Jo lifted it onto the bed and started to twiddle with the dials. It was bound to be a memorable number and, since it was made up of six digits, it was probably a date. Jo tried lots of numbers that might be meaningful to David. She hoped it would be her birthday or the date on which they had met. It was not; nor was it any other significant date she could think of.

Jo put the bag back in the wardrobe and silently reprimanded herself for being so paranoid. Of course David was not having an affair; it was only six weeks ago that they had got engaged.

Jo got into bed and switched off her bedside lamp, but as tired as she was from spending the day packing up her house, she was wide awake. She was so excited about the baby and desperately wanted to share the news with David. She picked up her mobile phone and considered sending a text; thinking that maybe it would prompt him to ring her. She looked at the clock and put the phone down again, it seemed a bit too late to expect David to respond.

Jo snuggled down under the duvet, but after a few moments shucked it off again as it was too hot. She could not get comfortable and she certainly could not relax. Her thoughts drifted from elation at the unexpected pregnancy, to anxiety about David. It was clear he had lied about his whereabouts that night, and although he probably would have a plausible explanation, Jo became increasingly uncomfortable with the realisation that David had not been his normal happy self recently. She had put it down to the pressure of work, and moving house; but now she was not so sure. They were buying their dream house and planning their wedding; what was not to be happy about?

By 4.00am tiredness, frustration and paranoia clouded her judgement and she began to feel she had every right to find out whether David was hiding something from her. She fetched a screwdriver from her toolbox, and retrieved his briefcase from the wardrobe. It took a while to prise open the locks and she did irreparable damage to the briefcase, but she was beyond caring by then.

The briefcase contained neat bundles of bank statements, payslips and other documents, held together with thick elastic bands. She picked up the bank statements and started to look through them.

Jo was stunned. There were huge numbers of debits and credits going in and out of his account on an almost daily basis. She always imagined David earned much more money than she did, but she had guessed he earned around £70,000 a year. Even that seemed like a lot of money to Jo. But she was staggered to see that his salary was over £200,000 a year, with regular bonuses too, which had brought his income up to almost half a million over the last year. However, what she could not work out was why his most recent statement showed he was £25,000 overdrawn. Jo had never earned anywhere near as much money, and she had never been overdrawn, or even used a credit card in her life.

But as worrying as this information was, there was worse to come. In a large brown envelope was a contract for a long-term lease on the house in Dulwich they had recently made an offer on to purchase. She stared at the document thinking there must be some mistake. But no, it was definitely a long-term lease, for a minimum of one year, with a rental of £2500 per month, and the lease was only in David's name. Jo wondered what had happened to the mortgage application she signed recently. A minute later she found it in another envelope. It would appear David never intended to apply for the mortgage. She looked closely at the form and noticed he had not completed any of his half. Jo could not work out what was going on, but was filled with the cold fear that this situation was far worse than finding out David was with another woman.

She looked again at the bank statements. She still could not comprehend why someone who earned so much did not already own a house, or could be so overdrawn. What could he have been spending the money on? He hadn't even been contributing to Jo's mortgage recently, as he was allegedly "saving" for a deposit on their new joint property. There seemed to be so much money going in and out of his account from the same reference on the statement. It didn't make any sense. On one day last month he spent £35,000 and appeared to have received £12,000 from the same account on the same day. Similar patterns appeared throughout the statements. Jo couldn't work it out but decided that perhaps the Internet might shed light on the company David seemed to be paying so much money to.

Jo went downstairs and switched on her computer, and went into the kitchen to make a cup of tea while she waited for it to boot up.

A quick search on Google revealed that *Texas-Zero* was an online gambling service. Obvious really, she thought, with hindsight. She had heard the expression Texas Hold 'Em in connection with poker games. She just hadn't connected David with gambling, because in her own narrow experience, gambling meant horse racing or greyhounds, and to her knowledge David didn't even bet on the Grand National. This website however, didn't cater for sports betting; just international poker games with no limits on how much could be bet.

The fact he had so little money left from his salary each month indicated he was obviously both unlucky and addicted. Jo reasoned that no bank would give such a reckless gambler a mortgage, which explained why he must have secretly arranged to rent the house instead. But in that case it would be crazy to suggest selling Jo's house; unless of course he had plans for the equity she had built up over the last 15 years.

CHAPTER TWO

Jo curled up on her bed feeling sick. She thought about ringing Megan but it was too early in the morning. She hugged the pillow and tried to calm herself down by working out what to do next.

Jo had been dreaming about having a baby since David had first moved in with her. She had a secure, reasonably well-paid job in the Home Office. She was fit and healthy, and had a good social life. She also owned her own house, which thankfully David had no legal claim over, and if she pulled out of the sale she would be left with a miniscule mortgage, by most people's standards. She could survive financially without David's help if need be.

But Jo loved David and knew she would find it difficult to confront him about his gambling, and she was not sure how she would be able to break up with him if he was sincerely apologetic and promised to change. Was this an unforgiveable act? Should she stay with him? There were too many questions in her head, and at this point in time, still reeling from shock, she did not have the strength to face him. She wanted to run away and hide for a while, but there really wasn't anywhere to run to.

Two hours later, after Jo had dozed off, her mobile phone bleeped, and woke her up. She was still sprawled on top of the duvet, wearing her dressing gown.

Sorry missed your call had late dinner with clients very busy today try call tonight otherwise see you tomorrow. xxx

Jo would not have thought anything of the text a couple of days ago, but now she wanted to reply LIAR LIAR LIAR! She flung the phone down in a rage and wondered how many other times he had not been where she thought he was.

She was relieved not to speak to him just yet. This matter really needed to be dealt with face to face, although the prospect filled her with dread. She decided to go round to see Megan again, who was usually the voice of reason when it came to man trouble.

Jo arrived at the flat just after ten. Megan had not long been up and opened the door with a towel wrapped around her hair. She took in Jo's grim-faced misery and headed straight for the kettle to make some tea. As she pottered around finding mugs and biscuits, Jo explained what she had discovered about David in the early hours of the morning.

'That's not all' Jo said, slumping over the kitchen counter with her head in her hands.

'Seriously? What else could he be hiding; a wife and five kids?' Megan asked.

Jo sat up straight and sighed. 'I wouldn't be surprised actually, but no, from my point of view this was the worst bit. The other day he suggested I gave him the proceeds from the sale of my house so he could add his savings and pay the deposit to the solicitor in one go. But he doesn't have any savings, and there's no mortgage. So really, the worst bit is I think he was intending to con me out of my money. What other explanation could there be?'

Megan shrugged helplessly. 'What are you going to say to him when he gets back?'

'I have absolutely no idea. I don't really want to say anything at all. I need to get my head straight before I see him. I'm worried he'll be able to talk me into thinking there's nothing wrong in what he did. You know David, I feel certain he has a perfectly plausible explanation waiting for the time he gets found out. But I just don't want to hear it'.

'I do,' exclaimed Megan furiously. 'Maybe *I* should be waiting for him when he gets back. I'd love to hear how he explains this. But one thing is certain, there's no way you should be going through with the house sale now. You must ring your solicitor today and stop it before it's too late.'

'I was thinking about that this morning. I'm not so sure I want to stay in the house now. Being pregnant kind of changes everything.' She picked out a biscuit from the packet and sat holding it indecisively for a while, until the chocolate melted and she put it down again. 'Actually, I was thinking of trawling the estate agents to find somewhere I can afford that won't use up all the money I would have left over from the sale,' Jo explained, sitting up straight and feeling a little more energetic now she had hit upon a plan of action. 'I know it sounds crazy, but when I was little we always used to go on holiday to Ireland, to the place where my Dad was born. His parents had this little old cottage near Kinsale, and it was really gorgeous. It was painted white and had a little bit of land and it overlooked the sea. It wasn't a huge house, but it was so cosy. I thought it was just perfect and I always dreamed of living somewhere like that,' Jo said, thinking back to the happiest days of her childhood.

'Are you telling me you're thinking of moving to Ireland? Because you might find it's just as expensive as here these days. And I think you have to pay for healthcare, so now might not be the best time to go,' Megan said.

'No, not Ireland,' Jo replied sadly, as she put down her mug of tea. 'My grandparents are dead now, and I don't really know anyone over there anymore. No, I was wondering where in Britain I might be able to find my dream house. The idea of moving somewhere more affordable like Walthamstow or Peckham is just too depressing for words, and I keep thinking that I'll never again have the opportunity of having so much money in my account, and I should think about making the most of it. Once I've sold my house I should have around £230,000, which is a huge amount of money isn't it? I've always wanted to go to University, or at least to do an Open University degree. Maybe I should take a five year career break from work, have the baby and get a degree.'

Megan did her best to talk Jo into speaking to David before she did anything rash like sell her house and move somewhere else. She offered to move in with her again, to help her out with the mortgage while she had her baby. She calmly listened to Jo rant and rage about David's betrayal. She understood Jo's obsession with security and independence and eventually gave in to Jo's demands to help her find her perfect new home, in the hope that this displacement activity would buy some time before she came to her senses. She could see that Jo was panicking, and with good reason. But Jo was the most sensible and responsible person she knew, and it would not be long before her level-headedness returned. David would be kicked out and life would continue as before, but with the addition of a little baby. It was hardly the end of the world.

They spent hours taking it in turns to trawl the internet through the endless lists of houses for sale, starting in London and gradually moving out to the remoter parts of Britain, as the intricacies of the internet drew them in to more and more property websites. In some ways it was fun, and they laughed about the idea of moving to Grimsby or Wigan, Biggleswade or Pontefract. They fantasised about new lives in France or Spain. There were endless possibilities and Megan was confident that Jo was regaining her sense of perspective on the problem. She had certainly found her sense of humour again.

But then Jo found what she was looking for. The picture of the house on the website seemed to be exactly the same as the one in her memory of her grandparent's house in Ireland. But this little white cottage was in a place called Unst, which she had never heard of. A quick interrogation of the atlas revealed it was the most northerly of all the Shetland Isles.

'Trust you to find the most inaccessible place in Britain.' Megan groaned as she studied the details of the house. 'Mind you, it does seem like a lovely cottage. But what else is in Shetland? I don't really know much about the place, other than their ponies are kind of on the small side.'

They turned their attention to the tourist sites of Shetland. It appeared to be wild and rugged, but absolutely stunning. There were photos of sandy beaches, wild moors, otters, puffins, seals, whales, and of course, the obligatory Shetland ponies. The website suggested there was quite a lot going on in Shetland, particularly in the bustling harbour town of Lerwick. Jo clicked on the local property websites and was amazed to find there were a quite a number of nice houses all well within her budget. Setting aside the idea of quite how far away Shetland was, she was determined to see for herself what it was like.

'Do you fancy a last minute holiday to Shetland, before school starts again? Jo asked, as she clicked the link to the travel websites.

'You're kidding me,' Megan shrieked, doubling over with laughter. 'Seriously Jo, Shetland is miles away. Look at the map; it's so far off the page they have to put it in a little box on its own.' Megan turned to another page in the atlas, which showed a clearer representation of where Shetland was in relation to the rest of Scotland. She prodded the page as if to say *I rest my case.*

'I know; it's probably a dreadful place, freezing cold and swarming with polar bears in the winter, but that cottage does have everything I want in a home,' Jo said as she stretched upwards in the chair, rubbing her aching back. 'And it's cheap, beautiful and there's even a college in Shetland where I could study for a degree. How cool is that?' she continued, trying to restore Megan's enthusiasm.

'I was planning a last minute break to somewhere sunny in the Mediterranean, not somewhere where I would need to pack my ski suit.'

'Look, I know this is kind of nuts,' Jo said, turning to face Megan. 'But I feel seriously stressed out and unhappy. I have some momentous decisions to make about my life, and I'm really scared of making the wrong move. I know you think I should sit tight and do nothing, except stop the house sale. And if it were not for the baby then I would definitely do that. But there's so much more to consider here. I don't want to have to deal with David just yet. I want to get away from him for a while until I get my head together, and in so many ways Shetland still isn't far enough away.' She paused and took a deep breath. 'This was a man I thought I was going to marry and settle down with. And within hours of finding out I'm pregnant I've found out he's a duplicitous double-crossing bastard who wants to scam me out of my money so he can spend it on a poker game.' Jo said, her voice becoming increasingly taut with anger.

'You don't really know that for sure do you? You need to give him a chance to explain himself; and how will running away to Shetland solve anything? I just think you need to slow down,' Megan pleaded.

'And I think I need a holiday. Somewhere completely away from it all, just to think about what I'm going to do next, and quite frankly, Shetland looks like a brilliant place to visit. I'm not saying I'm going to go up there to buy the first place I see. I might hate it. But at least I would have ruled it out,' she said decisively, and quite persuasively.

'I suppose so,' Megan said, groaning. 'I guess I could

forgo a week on a beach in the sun, for a week in the windswept isles of Shetland. I don't suppose it will be worth packing our bikinis then eh?'

CHAPTER THREE

'I can't believe how much there is to do. We'll never see it all in five days,' Jo said, admiring the glossy photographs of beaches and wildlife in the Shetland guide book. Megan looked up from her *Cosmopolitan* where she had been reading an article on fashionable holiday destinations for the rich and famous. Naturally Shetland didn't get a mention, and she looked across at the book Jo was holding and faked an enthusiastic smile in reply.

Twenty minutes before landing the plane started to descend a little, and they noticed the rain clouds had cleared, leaving behind a beautifully sunny afternoon. They peered down at the sea below them, and after a few minutes they could see white crests on the waves below, whipped up by a fresh breeze.

As the plane continued its descent they strained to look out of the window to see what they would be landing on. They hadn't seen any land yet, but as the plane banked they saw the islands stretched out beneath them. The plane raced towards a lighthouse on top of a hill, veered sharply to the left and headed towards the runway that looked like it ran straight into the sea. The airport was almost entirely surrounded by water, or so it seemed from the sky. Jo caught a glimpse of a white sandy bay and turquoise sea, in which a couple of yachts were moored.

***

'I optimistically packed my sunglasses, but I didn't think we'd really need them,' Jo said, as she scrabbled around in her handbag to find them, as they walked across the airport car park to the hired car.

They drove north towards Lerwick, passing the gorgeous

scenery they had seen from the air.

'If it was just a bit warmer here, this would be like the Caribbean,' Megan observed as they drove by. 'Well I guess a few palm trees might help as well, but it's lovely isn't it.'

Jo didn't say much as she drove. She was completely absorbed by the view. The winding road opened up to an ever-changing vista of rugged cliffs, sandy beaches, open farmland, and heather and peat covered hills. A few houses were strewn about the countryside. Some were traditional old croft houses, similar to the picture Jo had seen on the estate agent's website. Others were modern detached houses, with large windows oriented to the sea views.

'This is amazing, I'm so glad we came here, even if we don't find you the perfect place to live. It certainly beats being in London, or at work eh?' Megan said happily, apparently having forgotten all her misgivings about Shetland being the perfect tourist destination.

A few miles further North they stopped at a lay-by which had been hewn into the side of a hill overlooking the sea. Jo got her mobile out of her handbag and switched it on. There were seven text messages from David and one rather irate voicemail. They all said much the same thing, only getting progressively curt. She played back the voicemail on speakerphone.

'Jo, it's me again. What's going on? Why haven't you called me, this is ridiculous? Just what have I done to upset you? I'm staying at my parents' house. Call me now; we really need to talk. You owe me that much at least. You can't just lock me out of my home without an explanation. Call me now!'

'He sounds kind of mad. Whoops!' Megan giggled. 'Shame he doesn't say how much he loves you or misses you, or even that he's sorry he tried to screw you out of your money.'

'Perhaps he hasn't worked out why I left yet?' Jo said quietly, remembering how they had got up at the crack of dawn on Saturday morning and dumped all of David's possessions in the boot of his Audi, left the car keys with a neighbour, and then changed the locks to the front door. Jo had caught a glimpse of David arriving home in a cab, just as she had driven her old Fiesta round to Megan's flat, to hide out for a while. It still made her feel sick at how close her escape was. She had not returned to the house to pack for the holiday until early Sunday morning when she had felt as nervous as a burglar, fearful that David would return at any moment. She still could not work out why she was so afraid of confronting him. It was not as if she would have been alone with him, and David was not the violent type, but even so she just could not bear the thought of speaking to him just yet.

'I think I'll leave this off and just check it a couple of times a day for messages, maybe David will get the hint and stop trying to contact me.'

They sat for a while and stared at the view. Jo was deep in thought. Hearing David's voice had jolted her nerves. She could happily ignore his text messages, but his voice sounded so harsh and unlike him. It was like listening to a stranger, which was how she was starting to feel he was.

'Let's go for a walk. According to this guidebook we're just a few miles away from an amazing beach,' Jo said as she started the engine again.

They drove a couple more miles then turned off the main road and headed to St Ninian's Isle. Minutes later they came across the turn-off to a narrow winding lane leading towards the beach. It was only wide enough for one car to pass at a time, so they hesitated for a moment; unsure whether it was suitable to drive down. Another car pulled round them and headed down the lane so Jo plucked up the courage to follow, terrified of meeting another car coming in the opposite direction, as she couldn't see any passing places.

Half a mile later the lane opened up to a parking area with a footpath leading through the sand dunes to the sea. A wide tombolo of sand joined another little island to the mainland, with the sea lapping gently on both sides.

The car they followed down to the beach was parked beside them. Three children, two dogs and two women got out and headed down to the beach, loaded up with picnic boxes and beach toys. The children and dogs set off running through the sand dunes, obviously determined to find the best spot, ahead of everyone else.

There were a few other people on the beach, including

two small boys who were paddling along the shore wearing wetsuits and carrying surfboards.

Jo and Megan walked along the strand of shingly sand over to the other island, which they discovered was uninhabited, except for sheep. Jo started to feel calmer and more composed in the tranquil surroundings. It was so far away from all of her troubles. She was exhausted after the manic weekend spent packing and avoiding David, whilst thinking of nothing else but him. The sound of children playing, the cry of seagulls, and the waves breaking softly on the beach were hypnotically soothing. She could almost have drifted off to sleep when they sat down for a rest on the beach.

Later that afternoon after checking in to the guesthouse they went out in search of a restaurant. The shops were all closed, but there were still plenty of people milling around the main street, walking between the harbour and the numerous bars and restaurants. They were surprised at the variety of languages they heard as they passed by fellow tourists. Most of them were Norwegian or Danish, although there were quite a few French and Americans too. As they approached the harbour they discovered the provenance of some of the tourists. The harbour was crammed with foreign yachts.

The sea breeze dropped considerably during the evening, and the sun was still quite high in the sky as they ambled along the street, pausing frequently to look in the shop windows. As they reached the end of a parade of shops they came across the estate agents they had seen online.

'It's sold,' Jo exclaimed, pointing to the picture of the little white croft house with its bold red SOLD sticker pasted over it.

'That's a shame,' Megan replied, but secretly feeling rather relieved.

The next morning Jo woke up to hear rain and wind rattling the windows of her bedroom in the hotel. She opened the curtains and looked down towards the sea, entranced by the sight of fat grey seals lounging on the rocks, just over the wall from the Tesco's car park. And even as the rain was hitting the window she could see bright blue sky and sunshine in the distance, with a vibrant rainbow arcing over the town and tumbling into the sea.

The town centre was fully open for business when Jo and Megan wandered down to it after breakfast. The main street was heaving with tourists and they could see a huge cruise ship moored in the harbour. It had arrived first thing, and was now spilling hundreds more visitors into the town. Most of them seemed to be in the knitwear shops admiring the Fair Isle jumpers.

After an hour of pottering around Jo spotted the estate agents they had looked at the previous evening. She caught Megan's arm and dragged her inside. The receptionist confirmed the house in Unst had definitely been sold and apologised that the website hadn't been updated quickly enough. Jo was disappointed, and realised she should have rung them before booking their flights; it was so obviously the sensible thing to have done. When she looked at the details of the other properties for sale she didn't see anything quite like the house she had fallen in love with.

'I'm just typing up the details of a property that went on the market yesterday. If you liked the house in Unst you might like this one.' The receptionist picked up some papers from her desk and looked at them. 'I don't have any photos yet,' she said, 'but the information I have so far is it's an old cottage on Whalsay, very close to the sea. It has three bedrooms, new kitchen; new roof and central heating. I believe the owners recently did it up intending to live in it themselves, but have since emigrated to New Zealand.'

'That sounds interesting, would we be able to see it?'

After a quick study of the inter-isle ferry timetable they made an appointment to see the house around four o'clock.

They left Lerwick and meandered around the country roads, stopping occasionally to look at the views. After lunch at an art gallery in a converted Mill they drove through a little stretch of woodland that appeared like a fleeting glimpse of Surrey in the middle of the open moorland, and also served to make the otherwise largely treeless landscape even more obvious. Shortly afterwards they arrived at the Laxo ferry terminal and stopped behind other cars in the queue.

'I've never driven a car onto a boat before. It looks a bit scary,' Jo said, as she watched the car ferry spin 180 degrees in the water to line up with the quay.

'Maybe you should turn off the sat-nav, it might get confused. Help, help, I'm drowning!' Megan squealed in a squeaky impression.

'Shut up! Don't make me laugh now, we're going on.'

'Just follow everyone else and do what they do, it can't be that difficult,' Megan said encouragingly.

'And you've been driving how long?' Jo replied, as she started the engine and got ready to drive up the ramp and onto the boat.

It was easier than Jo thought. The ferry crew guided the cars and lorries on-board quickly and efficiently. Jo turned off the engine and sighed with relief.

'I wonder how we pay for this. Maybe we should have bought tickets somewhere before we got on,' she said, anxiously looking around for signs that would explain what to do.

A moment later they spotted one of the ferrymen weaving between the cars with a ticket machine. As he approached their car Jo had to quickly fiddle with the keys to get the electric window to wind down.

'Is there anywhere we can go to see the view?' Jo asked, as she handed him the money and took the tickets.

'Of course, there's a passenger deck upstairs with some vending machines for drinks and snacks. And you're welcome to open up the back door if you want to go outside on deck.'

Jo grabbed her bag to go upstairs. They appeared to be the only people bothering to get out of their cars. Everyone else seemed to be occupied with reading, knitting, or catching up on some sleep.

They found the door to the deck and went outside. The air was sharp with salt, but because they were sheltered behind the wheelhouse from the breeze, it was still quite warm. Cerulean sea sparkled in contrast to the surrounding brown suede and olive green hills. It was too bright to face the direction of the sun so they stood with their backs to the sun, leaning over the side rails watching the changing landscape as they sailed past. Birds swirled and swooped close to the cliffs. Every so often huge white gannets would plummet into the sea, resurfacing within seconds with a fish.

'What a way to travel! Do you suppose many people do

this every day for work? It sure beats the Underground,' Megan mused; leaning over the rail to look down at the white surf the boat was creating.

'Well I guess there must be some people using it every day. It's certainly busy enough now, and it isn't even the rush hour.'

'Rush hour? I don't suppose such a thing exists here. I bet it's not much fun in the winter though. Do you get sea sick?' Megan asked.

'I don't know; I haven't been on many boats before. I don't feel sick now, but then again it's perfectly calm,' Jo replied thoughtfully, reminded of the fact that she didn't even appear to be suffering from morning sickness; and not sure whether to feel relieved or anxious about that.

They sat down on the steps leading up to wheelhouse. Jo started to feel a nervous apprehension about the prospect of seeing the house, which made her realise how much she was pinning her hopes on finding her dream home. It was very unlikely that she would find what she wanted on this short holiday, and she had to remind herself to relax and enjoy this trip for what it was. A holiday.

As the ferry approached Whalsay they could see land stretching out either side of the harbour with a surprising number of houses sprawling along the lower hillsides. The outer harbour contained a couple of large modern trawlers, and the marina was crammed full of little boats and yachts.

'What a lot of boats for such a small place. Surely everyone must own one here,' Megan remarked as they made their way back downstairs to the car deck.

They drove off the ferry following the line of cars towards the village and passed houses, a shop, a petrol station, and a small grey stone church. The directions the estate agent gave them were to follow the road for around three miles until they saw a sign saying West Voe.

The houses gradually became more spaced out and the road narrowed to a single carriageway with passing places. There were quite a few cars about and they stopped frequently to allow others to pass by. Everyone they passed gave them a friendly wave or a nod. They saw two teenage boys walking along the road; they too lifted a hand in greeting.

'How weird is this? It's like everyone knows us,' Megan said, as she turned to look at the boys in surprise, more used to rude gestures from the teenagers she taught in London. She cautiously waved back and smiled when they did.

They turned into a narrow side road, passing a large modern house on the corner. A young boy kicked a football around in the garden, and two girls bounced on a trampoline. A bit further on there was a derelict cottage.

'Look, there it is!' Megan said giggling, pointing at the forlorn little house that was missing half its roof and windows. 'How bijou?'

'Shut up!' Jo said good-humouredly, elbowing Megan in the ribs.

They approached the end of the road, and two almost identical houses appeared before them, with the sea as a backdrop. 'Oh my God, this is it,' she said, slowing down as they approached the driveway. 'So far so good. This one doesn't look like it's about to fall down,' she added gratefully, as she switched off the engine.

They stood for a moment looking across to the house where they were told they would be able to get the key. The front door opened almost immediately, and an old woman waved at them.

'Aye aye Lasses! Would you mind coming over here for a minute?'

They crossed over to her house and the woman introduced herself as Ruby.

'The door's unlocked actually. My daughter dropped by and opened the house for you earlier.' Ruby said, looking at them with open curiosity. 'I hope you like it. It was my sister's before she died, a few years ago. My nephew and his wife lived there for a while, and they've made it really bonny and modern inside. But he was offered a job in New Zealand, so they've gone away, which is a shame. Well for me it is; I do miss them. They're selling this house so they can buy somewhere in Wellington.'

Jo got the impression Ruby would like to stop and chat for a while, but she was keen to see the house and tried not to fidget with impatience.

'Anyway I'm sure you just want to go over and see it. Take your time; and I'll put the kettle on and make some tea and you can come and tell me what you think in a while.'

CHAPTER FOUR

The outside of the house was freshly painted white, with a bright blue outline framing the windows. The garden was neatly tended with a few shrubs and some newly planted trees in the shelter of a dry-stone wall. Jo hesitated at the front door and looked down towards the beach. The sea was alarmingly close but the house was reassuringly high up the hill from the shoreline. Jo opened the front door and stepped into the porch.

The kitchen was a large square room with two windows, one looking out to the front with a window seat and another one facing east with a white Belfast sink under it. Despite the traditional looking sink, the rest of the kitchen was fitted out with an obviously new set of pale oak units with a glossy black granite worktop.

Jo knelt up on the padded window seat and looked at the sea. She couldn't imagine ever getting bored with staring out of the window.

'Nice neighbours!' Megan said, pointing at the sheep, one of which was peering enviously over the garden wall at the lush lawn. 'Wouldn't be surprised if you get them in the garden nibbling the grass. At least you wouldn't need a lawn mower.'

The lounge was large, newly decorated, with sanded wooden floors and an open fire, and with two windows that overlooked the sea. Upstairs they found two large rooms immediately above the kitchen and lounge, with a large dormer window in each one, and with even better views of the beach from the higher perspective. One room was painted in a pale lilac colour and had a new dove grey carpet. The other was pale blue with the same carpet. Both rooms were larger than Jo's bedroom in London and she mentally pictured her bed up against the wall. She walked over to the spot where she imagined her bed would be and crouched down a bit.

'I'd be able to see the beach from my bed,' she exclaimed, imagining how nice it would be waking up each morning and seeing such a gorgeous view.

'I have to say it's so much nicer than I imagined it would be. But surely there's a catch somewhere. How's it so cheap?' Megan asked.

They went back down the stairs and wandered back into the kitchen.

'I want this house!' Jo declared emphatically, sitting down at the window seat. 'This is so perfect; it's exactly like my dream house. I can't let this go, it's sure to get snapped up.' Jo had a stubborn decisiveness written over her face, and the way she held on to the edge of the seat it looked as if she intended to chain herself to it.

'I know what you mean, but this is such a big step to make,' Megan warned. 'You should take a bit more time to make such a decision. It's less than a week since you found out about the baby, and David. And don't you think you might find it a bit lonely up here on your own?'

'I think I stand a good chance of being lonely wherever I move to, especially being a single mother and not working for a while. But it's only going to be for a few years. I'm sure I'll tire of the quiet life eventually, and be desperate for the city again.'

'Maybe,' Megan said doubtfully. 'This does seem like a friendly place though. Maybe we should go over and talk to Ruby and find out more before you go jumping in and offering to buy it. And don't forget there are other nice houses for sale in Britain, you don't have to confine yourself just to this one.'

They took another quick look around the house and the neat and tidy garden, and looked inside the garage at the side of the house. There was nothing to disappoint, so they turned back to Ruby's house where she appeared at the doorway again. She was obviously looking out for them.

'Did you like it?' she asked, as she stepped back to let them in. 'Come in, make yourself at home.'

'We loved it!' Jo said as she went into the lounge.

Ruby's house was similar in size and layout to the one they had just seen, but it was decorated in a more old fashioned way. The walls had a style of heavily embossed cream wallpaper Jo hadn't seen since her childhood. The carpet was a riot of swirly brown and gold patterns, which clashed alarmingly with the pink chintzy curtains.

They sat down on an ancient tweedy sofa and were faintly embarrassed to see three tins of homemade cakes and biscuits set out on the coffee table, along with bone china cups, saucers and side plates. There was enough food for a tea party.

Ruby returned from the kitchen carrying a teapot. She poured out tea and eased herself down into an armchair.

'Help yourself to the cakes. I do love my baking. That and knitting are my only vices.'

'I didn't think baking and knitting were normally considered to be vices,' Megan said giggling, as she reached over to help herself to a slice of chocolate cake.

'Maybe not, but eating cakes certainly is. I try to pretend I make them for visitors, but my daughter always seems to be on a diet, and my grandchildren only eat shop bought cakes; little heathens. At least my son still enjoys my baking. Just as well, or I would be even rounder.'

'This is lush; I wish I could bake, but I'm hopeless,' Megan said, as she eyed up the other cakes in the tins.

Jo envied Megan's ability to fit in so comfortably around new people. She imagined that being a teacher and having to stand up and talk to a classroom of children was good for boosting your ability to speak to strangers.

'We loved the house.' Megan continued. 'Your nephew and his wife have done a brilliant job in doing it up. It's such a shame they won't get the benefit of living there themselves.'

'I would love to live in a house like that. I'll be having a baby next year and need a nice place that I can afford,' Jo said, seeing Megan had her mouth full of cake, and she finally had a chance to speak for herself.

'A baby, oh that is lovely. Congratulations my dear. That's just what we want for that house; a nice young family to move in. Do you think your husband would like living up here? What does he do?' Ruby asked enthusiastically, eyeing Jo up with renewed interest.

'Unfortunately I'm on my own. That's why I'm looking for somewhere a bit cheaper than London, so that I can afford it by myself. And I wanted a nicer environment for a baby to grow up in, not some noisy dirty city,' Jo said. Although, it was the first time she had thought about it like that. London would not be a good place to be a single mother. It was bad enough having to watch out for your own personal safety, let alone worrying about a small child. It would be nice to live in a more relaxing atmosphere where her neighbours all knew each other. She imagined it would probably be more like that here.

'You're absolutely right,' Ruby said proudly. 'Nothing beats Shetland as a place to raise bairns. My grandchildren have a great life here.' She paused and waved her hand in the direction of a wall full of family photographs. 'My grandson Callum is representing Shetland in a fiddle competition soon, he's off to Inverness next week; he has a great music teacher at the school.'

'Wow that's good. My parents had to pay a fortune for my violin lessons. We didn't get any music tuition at my school.' Megan interrupted.

'You play too? We all play the fiddle in this family, and my son Magnus, he's really good. I used to play as well, but not so much nowadays. My fiddle's over in the corner. Go and have a look if you like, it's very old now.'

Megan picked up the black fiddle box. Inside was a well-worn but beautiful fiddle, fully strung and only slightly out of tune through lack of use. She put it to her chin and adjusted the strings to tune it correctly, and cautiously drew the bow against them. It had a beautiful tone.

'Would you mind if I had a go?' Megan asked politely.

Ruby nodded enthusiastically, and leant back in her chair. Megan started to play a classical piece she loved. She hadn't played for a few weeks, but she was a very talented musician and it sounded perfect. Ruby smiled with pleasure and also a little bit of amusement. Her fiddle had never been used for classical music.

'Play us some of the music you like,' Megan said, handing the fiddle to Ruby.

'OK then, if you insist. But it won't sound anything like that.'

She started to play a slow plaintive melody, which suddenly speeded up into a fast paced jig, something they could imagine people dancing to. To their untrained ears the music sounded Irish. When she finished playing she told them what it was called, but it was meaningless to them.

'I think I'll have to buy some sheet music for some of the local songs and try this for myself,' Megan said, as Ruby handed her the fiddle to put back in its box.

Jo worried they were getting a little side-tracked from the conversation about the house. Ruby poured out some more tea, clearly in no hurry for them to leave.

'What's that you're knitting? It looks really difficult,' Jo said spying the multi coloured Fair Isle garment that was lying unfinished on top of Ruby's knitting basket.

'Oh this is a gansie, or jumper as you would call it. It's for an order from one of the gift shops in Lerwick. I sell quite a few gansies, gloves and hats to them, and to another one over on Orkney,' Ruby explained as she picked up the knitting and starting working on it.

'I'd love to be able to knit. But I've never seen that technique before,' Megan said, looking curiously at the strange padded leather belt Ruby was wearing, that she had pushed one end of a thin metal knitting needle into. With another needle in her hand and two different coloured yarns wrapped around her fingers she knitted at such a speed they could not keep track of how she was doing it. Ruby explained that using a knitting belt made it easier to knit quickly as there was much less wasted movement of the hands, and it was easier to work with the wool. She slowed down a bit to show them what she was doing, talking all the while.

'I make at least two of these a month, and normally a box of gloves.' She reached down beside her chair and lifted up a cardboard box. Inside were dozens of pairs of gloves in clear plastic bags. 'Go on, have a look if you like. It doesn't pay particularly well, but I have never been one to sit around just watching TV. This way I can earn money while I watch my soaps.'

They tried on the bright colourful gloves. They were soft and warm with such pretty designs; no two pairs looked the same. Ruby explained she used up the scraps of wool left over from the jumpers to make the gloves, and that was why every pattern changed. They were amazed to find out she never knitted from a written pattern, but just from memory, from designs she had learned as a child.

'I used to teach knitting at the school, but when I got to 70 they made me retire.'

'Do they still teach knitting at this school?' Jo asked incredulously. It seemed such a bizarre subject to teach in the 21st century.

'Of course. They take all the traditional skills very seriously here. Although nowadays the boys also learn to knit, and the girls get to learn how to sail,' Ruby explained proudly.

'My goodness, it's another world up here. Imagine learning to knit and sail at school,' Jo said.

Jo looked at her watch; it was after six. They had spent over two hours here and she had no idea which ferry they would be going back on. She thought she ought to say something but could see Ruby and Megan were getting on famously, chatting about the local dialect. Megan taught French and German and she took a professional interest in any type of language and Ruby was explaining where some of the words came from and what they meant. Naturally Megan picked it up quickly and already knew some of the origins of the words from her linguistics studies.

'Ruby, do you happen to know what time the ferries go back at this time? I forgot to check,' Jo interrupted.

'Of course dear. The next one's at seven and the one after is at nine-fifteen, and you wouldn't want to miss that one as it might be the last of the evening, depending on the bookings.'

'We'd better go now then if we want to catch the seven o'clock ferry.'

'Actually, Jo, I was thinking we should have a drive around the rest of the island and see what else is here. I'd like to see the school. Why don't we catch the ferry at nine-fifteen? We would get back to Lerwick just after ten. That's not too late is it?'

'That's a good idea,' Jo replied to Megan. 'Thanks ever so much for showing us the house, and the knitting lesson. Maybe the next time I see you, it will be as neighbours,' she added to Ruby as they stood up to leave.

'That would be splendid. I hope you enjoy the rest of your holiday,' Ruby said kindly.

Ruby stood in her doorway to wave them off. Jo looked back at the house she had fallen in love with. It would be lovely to sit in that window seat and watch the sun setting over the sea.

Megan was keen to see the school, so after touring around the island they stopped the car in the school car park and got out to wander around. The primary school was a long single-storey modern building with a glass roof and lots of windows. They peered in and looked at the cheerful well-equipped classrooms.

'Look at how small the classes must be. I can only count 15 chairs in this room. I wonder if these teachers know how lucky they are. I have to teach classes of over 30 at a time,' Megan said in awe, with her face pressed up to the window shielding her eyes from the glare from the evening sun,

'It certainly looks like a nice place to go to school,' Jo agreed, turning round at the sound of children's voices. Three young boys on bikes cycled past, towards the playground, where they circled around a few times before heading off back up the hill to another play area. Jo and Megan walked back to the car. They could hear the boys talking in the playground. It appeared to be about football, but their accents made it difficult to understand exactly what was being said.

One of them leaned over the wall and grinned cheekily at them.

'Aye aye!' He dropped back down behind the wall giggling.

'Hiya!' Megan replied. The boy bobbed up again smiling shyly. Jo and Megan smiled back, and with that he appeared to grow more confident and clambered up to sit on the wall. The other two boys peeped over and stared at them.

'Do you go to this school? What's it like?' Megan asked the braver of the boys.

'It's okay,' he said, shrugging his shoulders. 'We go back to school on Monday and I'm going to be in P5. Are you a teacher?'

'Yes I am; how did you guess?'

'Dunno; you just sound like one I suppose.'

Megan turned to Jo and pulled a wry face. 'What makes me sound like a teacher?' she said, turning back to the boy.

'You talk funny; you're not from here,' he replied, shrugging again as if it was an obvious matter of fact.

'I see; do lots of the teachers come from other places then?' Megan asked.

'Some do; most of them actually,' he replied climbing off the wall again. 'Are you on holiday? We went to Norway for ours, we just got back yesterday.'

'Norway eh? That's a cool place to go on holiday.' Jo said, joining in the conversation.

'We go nearly every year. My uncle lives there,' he said flatly, and then turned and ran off to the climbing frame; obviously the conversation was no longer interesting enough for him.

'Isn't it nice to see kids outside playing like we used to when we were little,' Jo said, thinking back to her early childhood and looking around in wonderment. She listened for a moment to the happy chatter of children playing in the back garden of a nearby house. It seemed like an idyllic place to grow up, and Jo felt less like she was fleeing from disaster and more like she was arriving at something better than she had before.

They crossed the road to the High School building and stood for a while leaning against an old stone wall, looking down the hill at the hive of activity in the harbour. A curlew strutted around on the school lawn piercing the ground at regular intervals with its unfeasibly large bill. Two oystercatchers flew past, screeching loudly, and came to rest on the lawn as well. Unseen birds chirruped in the background adding a restful feel to the atmosphere. The sun was dipping lower in the sky and cast an orange glow over the distant hills of the mainland. A small fishing boat chugged into the harbour with a couple of figures standing up at the helm. Jo and Megan watched as the boat moored up in the marina, and two men got off carrying their catch in yellow plastic crates to a nearby pickup truck. A flock of seagulls squealed expectantly around a larger boat just making its way back into the harbour. A couple of joggers ran along the road below them and two old men stood on the pier passing the time of day.

'That looks like our ferry coming back,' Jo said, pointing

to the blue and white vessel that had just appeared around the cliffs jutting out from the mainland. 'I guess we'd better go back to the car and get in the queue. I didn't see any hotels here so we'd better not get stranded eh?'

By the time they boarded the ferry the sun had set. They went upstairs to the passenger lounge and sat looking out at the darkening sky with the harbour lights growing ever more distant as the ferry headed back to the mainland. The sun had sunk behind the hills leaving behind a pink blush of colour.

'So do you still think I'm making the wrong decision?' Jo asked, looking directly at Megan to be sure of assessing how honest her reaction was.

Megan put down her cup of vending machine coffee and smiled broadly at Jo.

'No, I haven't thought that since we saw the house and spoke to Ruby. And everything else we have seen since then makes me believe this could be a very nice place to stay for a while. Maybe not forever though,' Megan replied.

'Nothing's forever! I know it looks like I'm trying to run away from my problems, but now I'm here and have seen it for myself I really love this place. I think I can make it work,' Jo said, with renewed confidence in her decision.

'Well it certainly beats some inner city high-rise. If it wasn't so far away from Cardiff, I think even I might be tempted to move here. It seems as if most teachers are incomers anyway, so I might fit in very well. But my parents would kill me if I moved so far away. Ealing is bad enough for them, even though it's only two hours away on the motorway.'

Jo stared out of the window moodily contemplating her own parents. She was sure they wouldn't make any comment on where she lived. They probably wouldn't even come to visit. Megan saw the frown appearing on her face and reached over and grabbed her hand. She guessed what was going through her mind. Whenever the subject of parents came up Jo became miserable, although she never seemed to talk about them much, even to complain.

'Don't worry about them. It's not your fault they're too wrapped up in their own lives to notice they have a fabulous daughter. Maybe things will improve when you produce a grandchild,' Megan said at last, trying to snap her out of the mood.

Jo leaned back in the seat and raised her arms above her head, stretched out and yawned.

'Maybe! ......Oh Lord, I'm so tired now I could just fall asleep right here, but I'm kind of hungry too,'

'We might find a takeaway open when we get back. I'm starving, and you should eat, after all you are eating for two now,' Megan said, whilst looking over her shoulder and watching a group of young men sitting at another table. She could see their presence was causing a stir. Megan sat up straighter under their curious gaze and sub consciously flicked out her long blonde hair.

'I know; I can't get used to the idea of being pregnant. I just don't feel it yet. I keep thinking I imagined it?' Jo said sighing and looking down at her tummy. It seemed impossible not to have any symptoms, it went against every stereotypical idea she had about pregnancy. There should be vomiting and bizarre food cravings at the very least, although she was kind of glad there wasn't vomiting.

'Well you didn't. I saw the result too. I wonder what David will say when you tell him. You are going to tell him aren't you?' Megan said noticing the way Jo had shifted uncomfortably in her seat as if she had wanted to change the subject.

'Not yet I'm not. Not until I have got myself settled somewhere. He would use this as a good excuse to stay together, and I just don't think I can trust him enough now. But on the other hand, I don't trust myself not to go back to him,' she said sadly. 'Why? Do you think I should?' she added.

'Absolutely not!' said Megan. 'Maybe one day when he has proven he can give up gambling, but then again he tried to take your money; well at least we think that's what he was planning.'

Jo looked unhappy again. Aware of Megan's scrutiny she crossed her arms across her body and slumped further down in the seat.

'Hey you, it's going to be fine. Don't worry about David for the time being. Tell him when you're ready. He doesn't exactly deserve to be kept informed of everything, since he hasn't been totally honest with you.'

The ferry started to slow down as it approached the terminal. Jo got up from her seat and threw her empty cup in the bin.

'Let's get some fish and chips; everything's better after food.'

CHAPTER FIVE

In the first week of October Jo moved into Hamnavoe Cottage, West Voe, Whalsay. The sale had gone through within three weeks thanks to the streamlined and efficient system of buying property in Scotland, but Jo had worked another few weeks' notice at work.

She managed to avoid David all this time, ignoring his phone calls, text messages and emails, which thankfully had tailed off recently. He sounded so angry; she hadn't had the courage to face him before leaving London. She had radically changed her working pattern during the last few weeks to avoid the possibility of bumping into him, and had changed her normal route for the same reason. And now it was too late.

Jo drove off the Northlink ferry at seven-thirty on Monday morning, bleary eyed with exhaustion. Despite the comfy ensuite cabin she had not slept much. The voyage had been smoother than anticipated, but she had felt too nervous and jittery to sleep for most of the journey.

Lerwick was quiet at this time of day; hardly any cars or people were around. The sky was dark grey and heavy with the promise of rain. A few minutes later on the road travelling north, that promise was delivered. The windscreen wipers struggled to keep the screen clear of the deluge. On the open road Jo's little Fiesta was buffeted around by strong gusts of wind. It was a dismal start to her new life. She tried the radio but it failed to pick up any of her normal pre-set stations. She put on a CD instead and sang along to the music in an attempt to raise her spirits. By the time she reached the inter-isle ferry terminal she was starting to feel more positive and excited. She had half an hour to wait for the Whalsay ferry so she sat and re-programmed her radio. She caught the end of the news and weather on the local station.

'The weather today will be cloudy with heavy rain showers in the morning, brightening by the afternoon. The temperature will be around 10 degrees. The wind will be variable, blowing south-westerly force 4 to force 5, gusting higher at force 6 to 7. Later it will blow northerly at force 2 to 3 and temperatures will drop to around 5 degrees overnight,' the radio announcer said before music once again filled the car.

Jo had no absolutely no idea what most of the forecast meant. She had never noticed a weatherman give information on wind speeds before, and the Beaufort scale numbers were meaningless. However, she was cheered by the thought that the weather would apparently brighten up later. It was getting cool in the car with the engine switched off. She watched the ferry appear around the headland and grow larger as it approached the terminal. It was fully loaded with commuter traffic and she watched with interest as cars rolled off, followed by a few foot passengers who got on to the waiting bus.

When it was time to drive on Jo started the engine and approached the ferry with a little more confidence than the last time. The passenger lounge was empty and she sat alone feeling a growing sense of trepidation and excitement. She worried the house would not live up to her memory. Her memories of Whalsay were of blue skies and sunshine, and today it was raining hard with little rivulets of rainwater doing their best to wash away the grainy salt frosted onto the cabin windows. But in the distance she noticed a glimpse of blue sky flirting with the rain clouds.

She had butterflies in her tummy when it was time to get back in the car and drive off and was relieved to see that the rain stopped during the five-minute drive to her house.

Jo parked in her new driveway and switched off the engine. She sat for a moment looking at the house finding it hard to believe it was all hers now. As she got out she caught sight of Ruby across the road, walking towards her with the aid of a stick.

'Hello Jo! I've been looking out for you; the solicitor said you would be arriving today. Here's your key, although I opened the house up earlier this morning in case I missed you. I hope you don't mind but I put the central heating on for you as well, it's been a bit chilly recently, so I thought I'd better warm it up for you.'

'Oh thanks so much! I'd noticed it was a bit colder up here than I'm used to; it's been really warm in London for the past few weeks. I would ask you in for a cup of tea, but I won't be able to find anything for a few hours.'

'Why don't you pop over later for a bite to eat? My daughter's coming round about one, and she's dying to meet you.'

'That would be lovely; thank you. I expect I'll need a break after unpacking,' Jo said gratefully.

'Don't overdo it will you dear. If you need anything heavy moving I'll get my son Magnus to come over later. I think the removal men put the furniture in logical places for you, so it shouldn't be too bad. Anyway, off you go, I'll see you about one o'clock then.'

It felt strange walking in to the house alone; she missed Megan's cheerful presence. She opened the kitchen door. In her memory it was one of the rooms she imagined spending the most time in. It was just as she remembered, although the sea view didn't look quite so inviting today. She took off her coat and laid it down on the window seat and knelt on the padded cushion and looked out. The sky matched the sea's gloomy shade of grey. White crested waves scudded across the bay and seagulls screeched overhead, oblivious to the weather.

A couple of cardboard boxes labelled *kitchen* sat on the worktops. Jo peered in at the sad assemblage of pots and pans. Regrettably she had given away so much to charity before she moved, thinking she would be buying new stuff with David.

She found her favourite armchair in the lounge sitting all alone, as her battered old sofas had gone to the tip. She noticed the satellite receiver box left behind in the corner of the room and remembered she no longer possessed a TV either. She momentarily regretted putting David's new LCD TV in the boot of his Audi and wished she had kept it for herself. She went upstairs to the bedrooms and found one of the double beds but the other one appeared to be missing. Curious, she thought, as she stood in the middle of the empty bedroom wondering what had happened to the bed.

She went downstairs again and found the missing bed in one of the back rooms that she had decided would be her office. Why on earth was it in here, she thought. There was no way she would be able to move it on her own. There was also no way she would feel able to ask Ruby's son to help her. She had lived in her road in Ealing for 15 years without asking for so much as the time of day from her neighbours. It had been embarrassing enough leaving the set of keys to David's car with them. The bed would just have to stay there for now. At least it wasn't in the way.

In the bigger house her furniture seemed very lost. She realised she would need to buy quite a bit just to make it comfortable to live in. She chewed her lip anxiously. In all the rush of moving and leaving work, she hadn't really considered how much she would have to spend on furnishing the house. It would certainly eat in to her savings. She had just shy of £105,000 in her account. Surely this would last her for at least five years until she went back to work. It seemed like a huge amount of money, especially as there was no mortgage to pay, and no expensive commuting. She relaxed and sighed, so long as she didn't go mad she would be fine.

She found a stack of packing boxes and nylon laundry sacks in a room that led out to the utility room and back door. She decided to make this her office instead. She found her portable stereo in one of the boxes and carried it into the kitchen and plugged it in. The lively sound of *The Cranberries* filled the room. It was nearly ten and so far Jo hadn't even unloaded her car.

She went out to the car where her bedding and clothes had been stashed away on the back seat in plastic rubbish sacks. She dragged them out, and carried them upstairs to the bedroom. She made her bed and hung up her clothes in the built-in wardrobe. The room was warm and rather stuffy, and she looked round for the source of the heat. The small radiator was cranked up to the highest level, presumably by Ruby. Jo smiled to herself as she turned it down. She doubted she would need it that warm.

She went back downstairs and started putting away the kitchen equipment. It didn't take long. She emptied the car of the remaining bags and put the rest of her clothes away and filled the waiting bathroom cabinets with her cosmetics and shampoos, and stacked up a pile of towels on a shelf above the heated towel rail. Away in the kitchen Dolores O'Riorden was singing her heart out and Jo joined in. The house was quickly taking shape, despite the lack of furniture. Before too long it was time for lunch. Jo was desperately hungry and in need of a cup of tea, but was confident this would not be in short supply at Ruby's.

Ruby was delighted that Jo was happy with her progress in unpacking and settling in.

'Jeannie will be here in a while. I've made some soup and sandwiches. We'll eat in the kitchen, I think. Will you help me lay the table? My hip is playing up again.' She lifted her cane to show Jo. 'I hate this damn thing. In my head I'm only 21, but this thing keeps reminding me I'm a lot older.'

While they were in the kitchen Jo heard the front door open and close. She turned round to see a slim, pretty, dark haired woman, roughly the same age as herself, standing in the kitchen doorway.

'Hello, I'm Jeannie.' She held out her hand to Jo and smiled.

'Hi, I'm Jo, pleased to meet you,' she said shaking Jeannie's hand.

'Mam, how's your hip today? Have you been taking your medication like I told you? Jeannie asked, turning her attention to her mother.

As Jeannie shrugged off her jacket, Jo saw she was wearing a navy blue nurse's tunic with her name Mrs Jeanne Anderson, Community Nurse/Midwife, etched on a plastic badge. Before Ruby even had a chance to answer her daughter, Jeannie directed a question at Jo.

'Mam says you're having a baby, how many weeks are you?'

'14 or 15, I think. I haven't had a dating scan yet as I was in the middle of moving, so I couldn't get it organised.'

Jeannie frowned. 'You'd better come and see me in the next couple of days then. We'll need to book you in for an appointment and give you a check-up,' she said seriously, but promptly lightened up. 'It'll be great to add another baby to my list. We're expecting another six on the island over the next few months.'

After lunch, Ruby brought over some metal cake tins and opened them up to take out a selection of homemade cakes. Jeannie refused to have one but insisted Jo did.

'I'm still trying to lose my baby weight from seven years ago. It doesn't help having a mother that force-feeds you homebakes whenever you call round. But you go ahead; you must be starving after your long journey.'

Jo talked about her journey. Jeannie shook her head and tutted when Jo explained she had left London at three in the morning on Sunday, arriving in Aberdeen at four later that afternoon, with just a couple of stops for food along the way.

'No wonder you look so worn out. You mustn't do this to yourself,' she said, putting down her cup and looking at Jo closely, with a professional interest in her well-being.

'I was too afraid to stop on the way, nearly everything I have of value was in my car, and I didn't think it would be a good idea to stay in a strange hotel and risk getting it broken into.'

'I suppose so.' Jeannie said. 'But promise me you won't do anything as crazy again. I want to see you in the surgery tomorrow morning. I'd better get going Mam; I have some visits to make around the isle.'

With Jeannie gone, Ruby poured out some more tea for Jo. She obviously was in no hurry to get rid of her. 'She's a lovely lass, my Jeannie, but very bossy.'

'I think she's right though, I have been overdoing it these past few weeks. I do feel tired,' Jo said, starting to feel quite weary now.

'Well that's only to be expected, the first few months are the worst, and you don't expect it either, as you always imagine you would feel more tired when you start to get bigger,' Ruby said.

'Well I have plenty of time to recover now.'

CHAPTER SIX

On the first morning in her new home Jo awoke early. It was still dark outside, and for a brief moment she couldn't remember where she was. She was struck by the silence, so different to what she was used to in London, but as she stretched out in the bed and listened, she realised it wasn't silent at all. There was a gentle, rhythmic murmur of waves breaking on the beach and the subsequent dragging reply as they pulled back over the sand and shingle.

She opened the window to hear it better and cool air hit her face as she leaned out. The stars were still visible in the sky, although when she looked towards the east she could see a cold blue light emerging over the hills, where the sun would soon rise. She heard something rustling around in the field next to her garden. In the moonlight she could see a couple of sheep shuffling around looking for shelter against the wall. A car's headlights appeared along the main road travelling in the direction of the harbour. Jo picked up her mobile phone and peered at the time. It was nearly six. She closed the window and got back into bed. She was still tired, but it was hard to get back to sleep now, so she reached out and put the bedside light on and stared up at the sloping roof. Her first full day in her new home and her head was buzzing with things she wanted to achieve. She curled up in the bed, pulling the duvet up around her shoulders and wondered what David was doing and where he was.

Jo studied the dark purple paisley pattern of the bed linen and remembered the shopping trip to Lille where she had bought it. It was hard to believe it was only a few months ago she had travelled over to France on the Eurostar with David. They had spent a long weekend in the city, wandering around the shops and markets, captivated by the marvellous bakeries and decadent chocolate shops. It had been a perfect weekend, not least because David had booked it as a surprise for her birthday. He met her after work one Friday afternoon, carrying a suitcase and her weekend bag. Arriving at the Eurostar terminal Jo had presumed they were heading off to Paris, but David had declared that was too much of a cliché. Lille was closer and by all accounts charming and rather quaint.

They had spent a fortune in the shops, which were a mixture of unique boutiques, French chain stores and a surprising number of British household names. Jo had particularly admired the beautiful household linens, china and cutlery, that were a fraction of the cost back home.

David had proposed to Jo that weekend, over dinner in a very smart restaurant. He had obviously planned it in advance as the waiter had appeared with Champagne and glasses within seconds of Jo saying yes. She had been speechless with joy, and had blushed with pride as the other diners in the restaurant had broken into spontaneous applause when David had produced a diamond ring and put it on her finger.

Lying in her bed, swaddled in the duvet cover they had chosen together, it was hard to believe that the David she knew, who could be so romantic and thoughtful, could also be so deceptive. Her engagement to David had made her so happy, but thinking of it now filled her with misery and confusion.

Three hours later Jo woke up again to the sound of a dog barking outside the house. She peeped out of the window and watched a man striding past, following a black and white sheep dog that was scampering ahead towards the beach. The man wore a fluorescent yellow and blue jacket with FERRY CREW printed on the back. He whistled at the dog and it stopped instantly and waited for him. Jo watched their progress along the beach until they disappeared from sight, although she could still hear the dog yap occasionally.

She looked at the time and rushed to the bathroom to get ready for her visit to the health centre, it was later than she had expected.

When she arrived at the health centre she was greeted by the receptionist who already seemed to know who she was. Within a couple of minutes the doctor called her in.

'Hello Jo, I'm Maureen Kelly, have a seat over here and tell me how you are today.

Jo was momentarily surprised by the Doctor's strong Dublin accent, and her informal way of introducing herself. When Jo told her she was pregnant Maureen went through the formalities of Jo's full name, date of birth, and health history, including the method of contraception and date of last period. Jo said she had been on the pill for a few years but had given up the previous year, due to her worries about her age and the fact she wanted to have a baby at some stage.

'I didn't expect to get pregnant quite so soon. We weren't really trying for a baby. We had just stopped trying not to, if you see what I mean. I thought it would take ages at my age,' Jo explained.

'It sometimes does. But you're one of the lucky ones. Now let's just check your heart and blood pressure.'

'Your blood pressure is a little high,' she said solemnly, as she unwrapped the cuff from Jo's arm. 'Have you been under any stress at all recently?'

'Well, what with from moving from London to Shetland, and splitting up with my fiancé, I guess you could say I was a little bit stressed out, although to be honest I haven't really been feeling that bad.'

'Well I think it's showing in your blood pressure even if you don't feel it in your head. Are you getting enough rest and eating properly?'

Jo felt herself blushing at the memory of her rushed breakfast of tea and two chocolate Hobnobs.

'Well I'm not working now, so I suppose I'll be resting more than a week or so ago, and I do try to eat properly, but I could probably do a bit better,' she replied.

'Just because you've given up work, it doesn't naturally follow that you've been resting. When did you move up here?' Maureen asked, as she scribbled some notes on a form.

'I arrived yesterday. I finished work on Friday and I drove up to Aberdeen on Sunday. Now I think of it, I suppose it is a bit much.' Jo shifted uncomfortably in the chair. Seen through the eyes of the doctor she probably sounded a bit nutty. No wonder her blood pressure was a bit high, she hadn't really had one stress-free day in the last six weeks, and barely a decent night's sleep. Who was she trying to kid?

'Right, well it's early days at the moment, so hopefully you'll have plenty of time now to take it easy and look after yourself. I'm writing down your estimated date of delivery as 3rd April. That might change depending on how the scan looks. I'll get a request in today for that and you'll probably get an appointment sometime next week. I'll need to send for your previous medical history so can I have details of your last GP?'

Jo watched Maureen recording the details on a fresh file. As she gave her new doctor all the information she needed she started to feel she was making a complete fool of herself. What must Maureen think? Jo's colleagues and some of her friends had been brutally frank in their opinions about her sudden decision to move to Shetland, even going as far as to say they thought she was being irresponsible and stupid. She had never done anything impulsive in her life before, but she now wondered whether she had made a monumental and expensive error. She felt tears welling up, and dropped her head so Maureen wouldn't notice. She sat completely still, willing them to dry up, as she didn't want to draw attention by wiping her eyes. But then her nose started to run, and she was forced to delve into her handbag quickly to find a tissue. Maureen beat her to it and passed a box of tissues to her without even seeming to hesitate in her writing.

'OK then. Is there something else you want to talk to me about, as you don't seem very happy at the moment? I know it can be quite an adjustment to make when you find out you're having a baby. Are you having doubts about that?' Maureen asked kindly, as she put down her pen and turned to face Jo.

'No, not at all. I'm delighted to be pregnant. I just wonder if I've done the right thing in moving up here. Everyone thinks I'm crazy for giving up my job and my house in London on a whim.'

'Well, was it on a whim, or did you put a great deal of thought and planning into it?' Maureen asked, as she sat back in her chair and looked at Jo who was hunched over as if she was trying to disappear inside herself.

'It was kind of both,' she replied, whilst trying to regain

some composure. 'I discovered my fiancé had a problem with gambling. And because I had just found out I was pregnant I wanted to get away from London, and him, and go somewhere new where I could start again. I came to Shetland by chance, and fell in love with it and so I bought my house. But I still have my job to go back to if I want, and in the meantime, I can now afford to take some time off and have a baby.' Jo hadn't intended to tell the whole story, but it just seemed to pour out of her and she felt slightly breathless when she finished.

'Well that maybe slightly impulsive, but it doesn't meet the textbook definition of crazy I'm afraid. Actually, what you seem to have done is instinctively acted to look after your new family. Not so crazy eh?' Maureen said reassuringly. 'And Shetland's not such a bad place to raise a family. That's why I'm here; well that and getting away from my cheating ex-husband who's now shacked up with a student nurse back in Dublin - Eejit!' She smiled conspiratorially at Jo, who looked up in surprise at this disclosure. 'It's going to take a bit of getting used to, you have lots of new things to deal with, but your first priority is to relax and take care of yourself and your baby. Don't worry about what other people think. It's your life. I'm sure they'll be very jealous of you the next time they get stuck in a traffic jam on the M25.'

Jo smiled in gratitude, relieved that Maureen seemed so understanding about her situation.

Jo checked the ferry timetable when she went back to the car after leaving the health centre. Perhaps she should have had a more restful day planned, but she really needed to stock up the cupboard with groceries, and to order some new furniture. Then she would be able to relax.

It was nearly lunchtime by the time Jo arrived in Lerwick, and she headed straight for a café, as she was famished. It was the same café she had visited with Megan a few weeks ago. She got out her phone and sent Megan a text.

Jo looked at her watch. Megan would be teaching now, and probably wouldn't reply for a while. Jo was about to switch the phone off but decided that as David hadn't sent any messages for over a week, perhaps she could risk keeping the phone on for a while.

The café started filling up and soon two women asked if they could share her table. Jo nodded and shifted along the bench and moved her handbag out of the way.

'Okay, now we're sitting down, can you please tell me the big secret?' One of the women said as she unbuttoned her coat and leaned across the table to hear the reply.

'I'm pregnant!' Her friend shrieked, jiggling up and down in the seat next to Jo. 'Thirteen weeks today. I've been dying to tell you, but Alasdair swore me to secrecy.'

'I knew it! So that's why you weren't drinking at Vaila's hen night. Antibiotics; you little liar. Ohmigod! I'm so excited for you? What did Alasdair say when you found out.'

'Oh he was so sweet; I thought he was going to cry. Look, look what he bought me the next day,' she said flashing a diamond-studded ring.

Jo couldn't help but look across at the woman's hand. The next minute the pregnant woman drew out a black and white photograph from her bag and proceeded to tell her friend about her recent scan. It was difficult not to listen and Jo wished she had a magazine to retreat behind.

'So sorry, here you are trying to have a nice quiet lunch, and I'm shouting in your ear about being pregnant.'

Jo looked up in surprise when she realised she was being spoken to.

'Oh that's okay. I'm pregnant too, so I know just how excited you are. Congratulations!'

Jo thought that would be the end of the conversation.

'Really, what a co-incidence. How many weeks?'

'About 15. I haven't had a scan yet, I'm having one next week I think,' Jo replied.

After that Jo found herself included in the discussion about babies and hospital appointments. Although Jo thought it was odd to strike up a conversation with complete strangers about such an intimate subject, the other two women were behaving as though it was perfectly normal. Jo could only assume that in Shetland it probably was.

When she finished her sandwich Jo thought she ought to excuse herself from the table and get on with her shopping. She said goodbye to the women, who wished her well with the baby. Jo smiled and said 'you too' and went out to the street feeling curiously uplifted.

She spent a couple of hours wandering around the shops. She bought some new saucepans, cutlery and a television from a small department store. The young man who served her kindly carried the heavy boxes out to her car and loaded them into the boot for her. After that Jo drove out to the trading estate on the edge of town in search of the furniture shops. She had a long list of items she needed for the home.

After a long afternoon of shopping she set off back to Whalsay. It was starting to get dark and it seemed ages since her lunch in the café. Jo mentally added up how much she had spent since she had arrived in Shetland. It was nearly £5000. Apart from her house, she had never spent so much in such a short space of time. Not even her car had cost that much. She consoled herself with the fact she wouldn't need to spend much more money; now most of the furniture was ordered and paid for. Well, all except for the cot, the pushchair, car seat and every other nursery essential. Jo sighed; she would have to be more careful, especially if she was going to keep hold of a decent reserve of cash in case it didn't work out in Shetland and she had to return to London.

CHAPTER SEVEN

After the second night in her new house Jo woke up to find her bedroom flooded with sunlight. She looked at her watch and was surprised to see it was already after ten. After drawing open the curtains and a quick visit to the bathroom she got back into bed. She had nothing planned for the day and she still felt sleepy. She lay in her cosy warm bed and watched feathery white clouds drifting across the blue sky. It was not really a day for lazing around in bed, but Jo lacked the motivation to do anything else. She couldn't even be bothered to get up for breakfast. This was the first day in weeks she hadn't got a plan of action for the day. She had run out of steam.

Two hours later, Jo woke up again. She ached all over and felt even more wretched. Her sleep had been disturbed by horrible dreams where she was either being swept out to sea or unable to find her way out of a dark and scary building. She still could not bring herself to get up, despite the dry mouth and dull headache. Not just yet, just a few minutes more, she told herself. Overwhelmed by the events of the past few weeks, it was as if by finally having nothing to do she had begun to absorb how deeply unhappy she was. Yesterday's shopping expedition now seemed like a sticking plaster stuck on a severed artery. She could not believe she had felt anything close to happiness, less than 24 hours ago.

She now had nearly six months with nothing of any consequence to do before she had her baby. Six months in a lovely house, in a beautiful place, but nobody to share it with. Getting a job would be one way to make friends, but it was hardly going to be possible in her condition. She wouldn't be able to start a college course either for the same reason. In fact she couldn't think of any kind of activity she could do where she stood any chance of getting out and meeting anyone other than her immediate neighbours. She knew herself well enough to know that her natural inclination towards shyness would only get worse if she got out of the habit of speaking to people. By the time she had this baby she would end up like some sad old hermit, she thought moodily.

Finally, Jo's bladder forced her out of bed. She still felt exhausted but decided to have a long hot bath to ease the aches and pains she felt from her over-indulgent sleep. When she finally emerged from the bathroom she had missed the sunshine, and rain was now coursing down the windows, and the sky had turned black. So much for her half-hearted plan of going for a walk along the beach.

As Jo was getting dressed she heard the front door open and close. She jumped with fright, and frantically threw on the rest of her clothes. She heard a car pulling away and as she looked out of the window she was relieved to see it was just the Royal Mail van. Jo ran downstairs to see what had been delivered, and as she opened the door to the porch she realised for the first time there was no letterbox in the front door, which explained why the postman had opened the door to drop the mail on the mat. She couldn't believe she had not locked the front door last night. She had always been so careful in London to bolt every window and door in the house, and set the alarm before going to bed. Oh well, she thought, as she picked up the pink envelope, it was hardly a hotbed of crime here.

The envelope had Megan's neat calligraphy styled writing on the front. It was a card wishing her happiness in her new home. She took it into the kitchen and put it on the windowsill feeling slightly more cheerful, and set about making some breakfast, even though it was now lunch time.

Jo put on the radio in the kitchen and listened to the unfamiliar accent of the Shetland Radio presenter, reciting the news in his rather pedantic slow style. It was a strange mixture of national and local news, with rather a lot of items from Norway and the Faroe Islands, mostly about fishing. At the end of the bulletin there was an announcement about a missing cat. It was odd, this combination of news about what the Prime Minister had said about the war in Afghanistan, how many boxes of fish had been landed in Lerwick, and then ending up with a missing cat in Scalloway. The weather forecast came next with a warning about a storm for the end of the week. Jo didn't take much notice of that; she loved thunderstorms.

She mooched around the house for the rest of the afternoon. Her headache vanished after a few cups of tea, and her aching limbs eased as she tackled more of the unpacking. She set about transporting things around the house trying to find homes for her possessions. She went into the back room, which the removal men had decided was one of the bedrooms. The unmade bed was positioned facing the window. Being at the back of the house the view was of the grassy hill that stretched upwards and obscured the sky from where she sat on the bed. Sheep wandered past and the only other signs of life were a couple of large rabbits sitting in her garden, oblivious to the presence of the new occupant in the house.

Jo decided that it would make quite a nice spare bedroom after all, so she dug out the duvet and sheets and made up the bed, even though she knew it would be a long time before anyone would need it. She finished off the room with two of the bedside cabinets that she had brought with her and put some books onto the shelves above the fireplace. The room looked a bit more lived in now, which gave Jo a sense of accomplishment, which lasted for all of an hour.

Back in the kitchen making more tea, Jo caught sight of a sheepdog running past the window; followed by the same man she had seen the day before. They were heading off towards the beach, despite the rain. She watched the dog approach the edge of the sea. It was prancing around on the shore barking at something in the water that Jo couldn't see. As they disappeared from view Jo realised she still hadn't seen the beach properly. She cursed herself for missing the early morning sunshine, and vowed not to let the next opportunity go by.

It was getting darker now and she looked out at the sky and across the fields towards the main road, where in the distance the lights of other houses twinkled in the twilight. The day was ending already and she hadn't so much as spoken to a single person. But just as she thought that the phone rang.

'Hiya, it's me. How's it going? Sorry I didn't reply to your text yesterday. I left my phone at home and then I went straight out after work.' Megan sounded breathless, as if she was doing something strenuous as she talked.

'Hi, what are you up to? You sound busy.'

'Sorry, I've just got home after a crazy day at school where I didn't get a lunch break, so I'm just trying to find something to eat in the kitchen and sort out the washing machine at the same time. Sorry I'll stop and give you my full attention. So how's the baby and when's she due?' Megan asked.

'April 3rd. Knowing my luck it will be born on April Fool's day though. Everything's fine. The doctor thinks my blood pressure is a bit high and I have been told to rest a bit. But you know what, I've done absolutely nothing all day and I feel more tired than ever?' Jo complained as she carried the phone over to the chair and sat down.

'Well it's no surprise really, after all that's happened. What were you doing in Lerwick yesterday?'

'I went shopping and spent a fortune. I didn't really mean to, but now I'm here the house seems really bare, and I needed a lot more than I thought.'

Jo went on at length about her shopping trip to Lerwick, she was vaguely conscious that she was being boring on the subject but couldn't stop herself from rambling on, grateful for someone to talk to at last.

'That's brilliant. So anyway how's our Ruby?' Megan interrupted after a while.

'I haven't seen her since Monday. Her daughter Jeannie invited me round for coffee one day but I don't know whether she was just being polite.'

'No I bet she really meant it. You should go. You'll need to make some new friends you know. Nobody will be as perfect as me of course, but you have to get out there and make an effort,' Megan teased.

Jo laughed. 'No of course nobody's as perfect as you. If only you could get a job up here life would be brilliant.'

'No chance of that I'm afraid. I'm just about to apply for a promotion to Head of Modern Languages. If I get that I might be able to think about buying my own place too.'

'Really? Oh you're bound to get it. I don't know anyone

who speaks as many languages as you,' Jo said enthusiastically.

'If only it was that simple,' Megan replied. 'But I should stand a good chance I guess, I've been at that school for ages now so they know what I'm like. The only down side is it means slightly less teaching, but a lot more boring paperwork. But the pay's much better, so fingers crossed.'

'Well I suppose I'll have to go and find some new friends then, but you'll be a tough act to follow,' Jo said.

'Perhaps you should get dog.'

'A dog?' Jo replied in surprise. 'I know they are supposed to be man's best friend, but I hardly think that I'll find one that is going to sit around drinking Pinot Grigio and gossiping about their love life.'

'No, silly!' Megan said, laughing. 'I mean if you get a dog you'll get out and about and so you'll get to meet people. Apparently this is the perfect way of meeting men in London now. Buy a dog, go for a walk, and let your dog chat up theirs and bingo, true love or an unexpected litter of puppies will surely follow.'

Jo thought about the man she had seen walking with his dog. Not that she particularly wanted to meet him, but she was struck by the idea that having an animal to care for might stop her becoming miserable on her own. It would also force her out of the house whatever the weather; which might be a mixed blessing of course.

'Actually I think that might be a good idea, but not for that reason,' she said thoughtfully. 'I think I need a purpose in my life as I realised today I don't have anything to do, which I'm not really used to. I'm going to investigate getting a dog tomorrow. Thanks for that!'

'No problem. Anyway I'd better get something to eat now; I'm starving. Ring me tomorrow and let me know how you get on with your dog hunt,' Megan said before saying goodbye.

After Jo put the phone down she realised she had just had a whole conversation with Megan without any mention of David. It was like he never existed. The one good thing about moving to such an unfamiliar place was that it was sufficiently disorienting to distract her from her past life. She briefly wondered what he was doing, but then started daydreaming about getting a dog. It was a brilliant idea.

CHAPTER EIGHT

Jo's newly found zest for life did not last long. At the animal rescue centre, she was interviewed by a rather scruffy but well-spoken middle-aged woman, who was singularly unimpressed with Jo's potential as a prospective dog owner. Jo had the right kind of house, but she lost marks for lack of experience with dogs, or indeed any kind of pet, and when the woman found out Jo was pregnant she sighed and put down the clipboard, where she had been filling in an adoption form.

'I'm sorry, but we have a policy of not re-homing our dogs with families who are expecting a new baby. It is not an ideal time to get a dog, as they need lots of love and attention and when a baby comes along the dog is often pushed out. Quite literally sometimes. I suggest you wait a couple of years before getting any kind of pet,' the woman said as she stood up, abruptly signalling the end of interview.

Jo didn't attempt to argue her position. She drove into Lerwick and wandered aimlessly around the shops for a while, feeling more and more miserable by the minute. She hadn't realised just how lonely she was until her attempts to adopt a dog had failed. She felt utterly foolish, and thought back to some of the harsh criticism she had received from people when they first heard of her plan to move to Shetland. She started to consider they might have been right after all. Being turned down at the dog rescue centre was just a minor setback, but it felt like the straw that broke the camel's back.

She hurried away from the busy street back to her car, keeping her head down to avoid making eye contact with anyone. Jo hadn't really let herself cry about David. She had buried the pain of his deception in desperate activity, and now she finally had nothing to do, she had to face the truth. It hurt. A great weight pressed upon her lungs, hindering her ability to breathe freely.

But the pain of it all would be more bearable if she didn't feel quite so lonely. She dried her eyes and pulled out a pack of cleansing wipes from her handbag and removed the final vestiges of smudged mascara from her eyes. She started the car, intending to drive back home. Maybe she would speak to Megan again who was guaranteed to come up with another bright idea to cheer her up. Then again, she though moodily, she was almost embarrassed to speak to Megan today. She wondered whether her friend was holding back her true thoughts about her move.

By the time she got back home it was late afternoon and she was tired and hungry. She put the kettle on and rummaged around the newly stocked cupboards and fridge for something to eat. Nothing appealed. It was all too boringly healthy. Chips, pizza, pasta, or sticky toffee pudding would have been perfect. Salad was no way to mend a broken heart; but the phone interrupted her search for comfort food.

'Hello Jo, its Ruby. Are you busy?'

'Er, no, not really. I was just thinking of making something to eat. How can I help you?' Jo sensed Ruby had some kind of request to make. She carried the phone over to the window and looked across at Ruby's house wondering what her neighbour wanted.

'I was wondering if you would like to come along to a meeting tonight, at the Scottish Women's Rural Institute, a bit like the Women's Institute you have down in England.'

Jo was momentarily stunned into silence, and sat down heavily on the window seat wondering how to respond.

'Um, thanks, I don't really know. I've never been to a Women's Institute meeting before. I don't mean to be rude, but aren't I a bit too young for that?'

'That's what my daughter thinks too. But we're not all ancient fuddy duddies at the Institute. It's great fun and it might be a nice way for you to meet folk. I'm helping to make the supper tonight and I've made some lovely chocolate brownies,' Ruby argued persuasively.

The mention of chocolate brownies piqued Jo's interest.

'What time is the meeting?' she asked hesitantly.

'It's at seven. I normally get the bus but if you want to go we could take your car, and then you could leave early if you really didn't think it was your cup of tea. I thought you might enjoy the slide show on Africa. One of our members was working over there, helping to build a school, and she's going to talk about the charity she was working for.'

Jo thought this sounded vaguely more interesting than watching soap operas on TV. A slide show on Africa and the promise of Ruby's chocolate brownies wouldn't be such a bad way to spend an evening.

'OK, I'll give it a go. Thanks for asking me. Shall I pick you up around ten to seven?

'That's splendid, I'm sure you'll have fun. I'll ask Jeannie if she wants to come along too, but she'll probably say no. She thinks it's all too competitive. She doesn't do as much knitting and baking as I do, and doesn't see any point in craft competitions. But it's just a bit of harmless fun.'

Jo was alarmed by the last comment. But then Ruby went on to explain that at every meeting there were usually two competitions, one of which would be cookery or another homemade craft and the other something that could be bought.

'I know it's short notice but tonight's competitions are a "ladies emergency kit" and a sparkly necklace,' Ruby added.

'What do you mean by ladies emergency kit?' Jo asked, puzzled.

'Well, I'm going to take my little embroidered sewing kit that contains a variety of needles, and threads, but it could be any kind of kit that you make up for an emergency.'

Jo wondered what kind of emergency she would ever have that required getting out a needle and thread. Surely that was what safety pins were invented for. If she had ever lost a button on an item of clothing she normally just went out and bought something new.

'I'll see what I can come up with then,' Jo said, looking at her watch, frowning at how little time she had to be creative.

She made a toasted cheese sandwich, and ate it sitting in the kitchen, mulling over the competition. The closest she had come to having any kind of emergency was during her minor meltdown in town that afternoon.

That prompted an idea, and she rummaged around one of the kitchen drawers where she kept a small first aid box.

She emptied out the box of the plasters and antiseptic wipes and replaced them with a small pack of tissues, a large bar of milk chocolate, her mobile phone and a debit card. The first aid leaflet she had discarded caught her eye and inspired another idea, so she went to her computer and quickly typed up her own instructions on what to do in any emergency.

'In the event of an emotional trauma or similar domestic emergency, open the pack of tissues. Pick up mobile phone and ring best friend for advice, rescue or comfort. While you wait for the emergency services to arrive, use chocolate for immediate first aid. When help arrives, share remaining chocolate with the rescue worker and discuss the trauma until it feels better. In the event of severe drama, usually where a man is involved, use the debit card to go shopping. Warning: Do not overdose on this rescue therapy as the side effects range from weight gain to an unhappy bank balance.'

Satisfied with her creation she rifled through her jewellery box and found a crystal necklace. She was all set for her very first Women's Institute meeting. She found herself giggling at the thought, and picked up the phone to call Megan.

'You'll never guess where I'm going tonight,' she said trying to control the laughter and then going on to explain before Megan could attempt a guess.

'You're not serious! The Scottish WI? When have you been in to making jam or flower arranging, or whatever it is they do there?'

'Ruby asked me to go tonight, and I've had such a shite day and I was on the verge of ringing David, and feeling so awful on my own that suddenly it seemed like a good idea.' As she said it, she started to see how pathetic it sounded.

'You know what; maybe it's not such a bonkers idea. I mean, Ruby's a lovely person; maybe all the other old dears will be like her too. At least it's one way to get to meet people,' she said encouragingly. 'And you never know, they might have tall dark handsome single sons, or maybe make that grandsons.'

'Shut up! I'm not going just to meet men or get introduced to somebody. Honestly, you have a one-track mind. Anyway, now that I'm about to become a mother, perhaps it's time to learn to cook and do fabulous domestic goddess stuff, like arrange flowers and make patchwork quilts from recycled old frocks,' Jo said, managing to raise a smile at this alien concept.

Megan made her promise to ring her and tell her all about it tomorrow night.

Jo went upstairs to make an effort to look presentable. Her eyes were still a little puffy from the afternoon's crying session. She pressed a cold wet flannel over her face and put on some make up, managing quite successfully to hide the evidence. Looking better made her feel a little more cheerful. She opened her wardrobe to see whether there was anything in there that might be considered appropriate for a Women's Institute meeting. She pulled out her favourite vintage floral tea dress. It was pale green cotton with tiny pink flower sprigs. She put it on and was pleasantly surprised to see it still fitted – just. At just over three months pregnant, Jo hadn't really put on much weight although she seemed to be expanding around her chest. The dress buttoned up the front and had a fitted bodice and flared skirt, that Jo normally wore a full petticoat with. She found the petticoat and put it on too. The skirt stood out better and with a pair of flat ballet pumps she looked like an extra out of 'Grease'.

She wondered briefly whether it was a little excessive to dress up for this occasion, but she knew she would feel a little more confident dressed up than if she just turned up in a pair of jeans and a jumper, and she could hardly wear one of her old work suits. She looked at her watch, it was almost time to go so she collected her emergency kit, sparkly necklace and her handbag, and left the house. She started up the car and as she looked in the mirror to reverse out of the drive she saw that Ruby was already at her door waiting. She appeared to be laden down with bags and tins, so Jo hurried out of the car to help her put them into the boot.

Ruby exclaimed enthusiastically about the dress.

'What a bonny frock, where did get that? I used to have something very similar.'

Jo told Ruby all about her passion for vintage clothes and how she found they suited her figure better than modern styles, the only problem being they were hard to find and expensive.

'Good heavens. Didn't you ever think about making them yourself?' Ruby said when Jo told her some of the prices she had paid for her second hand dresses.'

'Unfortunately, I never learned to sew, bake, or knit, or anything much. I'll probably be kicked out of your meeting in the first half hour for being an incompetent housewife,' Jo joked, but almost feeling that could actually be her fate in the long run. She doubted her ability to knock up the perfect curry would be a valued skill.

'Don't be daft my dear. We're not all brilliant at these things. That's why we always have something in the competition that you can just pick up and bring along, like the sparkly necklace. That way everyone can join in,' Ruby explained cheerfully.

'Oh, I see,' said Jo. She felt a little bit more confident now, and as they arrived at the hall she prepared herself to meet some new people. Most of the ladies seemed to know who she was already. She was the newest of the incomers to the island and word had got around. Ruby introduced her to some of her friends, who seemed genuinely interested and pleased to meet her.

Just before the meeting started, the members handed in their competition items, which were numbered and spread out on display ready to be judged later. Jo glanced over nervously at the selection of beautifully made kits presented in hand embroidered bags or hand painted wooden boxes. She saw one of the women opening the battered first aid box and smirking.

The woman presenting the slide show on Africa was at least 70 years old. She had not long returned from a small town in a previously war torn area, which was trying to rebuild the community. She showed slides of children dressed in ragged clothing, sitting in their open-air classroom. At the end of the presentation she was able to show the same children wearing smart new uniforms in a new building which the charity for which she worked had built. It was an amazing transformation for the children's lives. But the fascinating part, at least for Jo, was how this woman still had the energy at her age to get involved in such activities, and in what was quite a hostile environment. Jo was completely captivated by the story and really pleased that she had decided to come along to the meeting.

While the supper was served Jo heard some women giggling over at the display. She felt sure it had to be her entry that was causing the commotion, and wished she had had time to put together something more conventional, or not bothered at all.

She was therefore, stunned to find out a few minutes later she had won first prize for her emergency kit. The guest speaker who had been asked to judge the competition thought it was tremendously funny and original. Jo grinned with relief and wished Megan could have been there to witness her first success at the Institute.

CHAPTER NINE

As Friday afternoon approached Jo had yet to get out on to the beach that lay tantalisingly just a few yards away from her front door. It had been such a busy week already. She promised herself that she would get out and go for a walk to explore her new surroundings. She didn't really need a dog to take for a walk; she just needed a fine day and some willpower. She would do it tomorrow.

She switched on her computer and logged on to her email account. It was difficult using the computer without a desk to put it on so she sat on the floor and rested the keyboard on her lap. There were a few emails from ex-colleagues, asking how she was getting on and all of them asking about the weather. She sighed to herself; what was the obsession with the weather? She decided to reply to them later, and to concentrate for the time being on writing to David.

Dear David,

I think that it's time that I explained why I moved away. You have probably worked out by now that I found out about your gambling addiction, although this wasn't the main reason I left. Even though I was shocked and hurt that you had kept this from me, and you had led me to believe that your job was not quite so well paid as it obviously is, the reason I left was because I found the rental contract for the house that I thought we were going to buy. I could not believe that you had no intention of buying that house with me, but were going to rent it instead. How on earth did you think you would be able to keep that a secret from me?

It was the combination of these two things that made me leave, but there was something else too. I had been trying to ring you in Germany and you weren't there, I knew you were somewhere in Britain because of the ringing tone, and when I called the hotel they had said you had checked out. So I waited for you to come home and you didn't. I tried lots of times to ring you but your phone was switched off, which it never normally is, so I panicked. I imagined that you had met someone else. I would never have tried to open your briefcase otherwise. It was the early hours of the morning and I was going nuts with worry.

I want to give you a chance to explain yourself. I have moved out of London and for the time being I would rather not say where I am, so please reply by email.

Regards Jo

She sent it off to David's work address. It was only just after five so there was every chance he would see it this evening. Jo leaned back against the wall and stared at the screen, almost anticipating an immediate response. But this was unlikely. David, even if he had seen it already, would doubtless take his time to compose a reply. She left the computer on, and headed off to the kitchen to make dinner. But in between putting on the pasta and chopping up vegetables she couldn't help walking back frequently to see if David had replied. He hadn't, and even her mobile phone remained silent on the windowsill. Jo felt slighted; in her imagination David had been sitting by his computer just waiting for her to contact him.

Jo ate her dinner in front of the television. She remembered her promise to ring Megan, and looked at her watch to see what time it was. She was bored, but it was just a bit too early to ring any of her friends, as they would only just be getting home from work. She watched the local news and the weather forecast. A severe weather warning was given for Orkney and Shetland. Jo didn't take too much notice of this, as Ruby had already mentioned the storm that was due to arrive later and she hadn't seemed unduly concerned about it.

An hour later Jo had to turn up the volume on the television, to compete against the roaring sound outside. She hadn't got around to ringing anyone as she had started to watch a film, but halfway through, the picture began breaking up, accompanied by annoying static crackles. She gave up and turned it off when it became apparent the reception was not going to improve.

Without the noise of the television, she could hear the house creaking and groaning under the force of the wind. She walked around the downstairs and discovered it was worse at the back where it faced south. In the spare bedroom the noise was truly awful; like the roar of a jumbo jet taking off in the back garden. She touched the window pane and was shocked by the vibration she felt through her fingertips. As she peered out into the darkness she could just see the edge of the satellite dish juddering on the wall outside, which did at least explain the poor television reception.

It was now too noisy to ring Megan so she checked her emails instead. There was nothing from David so she switched off the computer as it was getting too late to expect a reply from his office email address. Just as she reached down to the plug socket the entire room went dark. She stood up carefully, and waited for her eyes to adjust to the almost pitch-black darkness, and then felt her way back to the kitchen. The whole house had lost its power. She looked across at Ruby's; her house was also in darkness and the lights she could normally see a mile or so away were out.

She made her way over to the window seat and sat down, considering the logic of going to bed early and waiting until the morning when the storm would have passed. There was nothing she could do now, but she was afraid of the darkness in the still unfamiliar house. The deafening noise added a curious claustrophobic feeling to the darkness, as there was no escaping from the sound. She remembered there were candles under the sink and scrabbled around blindly for them. But although she found a bag of tea-lights, she could not find any matches. In fact she couldn't even recall having seen a box in the house. There was nothing she could light a candle with. Even the gas hob was useless, as it needed the electric ignition to light it.

She was about to give up and go to bed in the dark, when she remembered the torch in the glove compartment of her car, and possibly a small souvenir matchbook from a restaurant she had been to with David. She recalled seeing it on the floor of the backseat. With the dim light from her mobile phone she found her way out to the front door and put on her coat. As she opened the door she was pleasantly surprised to discover it didn't seem too bad outside. It certainly wasn't cold; just extremely loud. As she stepped outside she noticed a car driving slowly along the road towards her.

A moment later she gasped with surprise as the full force of the wind hit her as she moved away from the shelter of the house. She was propelled down the drive, her long coat lifting up in the wind and acting like a sail, and she stopped only because her car was in the way. She caught hold of the bonnet in relief and kept a hold of the car as she moved round to the passenger door.

She opened the door, yanking it with all of her strength against the wind, and jumped into the seat, yelping with fright as the door slammed shut. Her hands shook as she opened up the glove compartment and located the torch. 'Thank God.' she said aloud as the light came on, at least it was worth it. She felt around on the floor for the matchbook and found it. Inside were ten fragile looking matches. She shoved the torch and matchbook deep into her coat pocket, and sat for a moment preparing to go back outside. She watched as the moon appeared from behind the clouds, momentarily shining down on her house, before more clouds raced across the sky and obscured it again, and she was once more in darkness. She looked round to see where the other car had gone, just making out the dark shape of a pickup truck parked on Ruby's drive, and she figured it would be someone who had come along to check on her. Her own car was trembling violently, and Jo knew she would have to get out soon and back inside the house where it would be safer.

She fumbled for the door release and leaned all her weight against the door. She cautiously put her feet down on the ground, pushing the door away with her arms, nervous about it slamming against her shins. With a determined shove she stood up, facing the direction of the wind. As she turned to move away the squally wind raged harder, and she yelped as the door jolted into her. Jo spun out of its way, instinctively snatching her hands free, but the door caught her left shoulder and the side of her head, before it finally slammed shut. She screamed out in pain and leaned against the car holding her head, feeling dizzy and disoriented.

Jo was about to make a run for the house when she became aware of headlights shining on her. She hadn't heard the pickup moving but it had suddenly appeared on the driveway behind her car and as she looked up she saw a man get out and hurry towards her.

'Are you hurt?' He yelled above the noise. He caught hold of her shoulders, keeping her steady against the onslaught of another gust of wind. She nodded, still clutching her head. He gently pulled her hand away from her head, and looked closely, frowning at the sight of blood trickling down the side of her face.

'You're bleeding! I'll take you to my sister's house; she's a nurse. You need that looked at.'

He steered her firmly to the pickup and opened the passenger door and leaned back against the door to keep it open, then he grasped Jo's elbow and bundled her up into the cabin. Jo waited while he ran round to his side and got in. Despite the pain radiating from her head she was slightly anxious about being in a stranger's car and was running through every possible scenario of danger in her mind. It was hard to shake off the years of ingrained caution, despite her calculated guess that this man was probably Ruby's son Magnus.

Jo fumbled with the seatbelt, her hands still trembling with shock. 'I'll get it,' he said kindly, as he leaned across her and pulled the seat belt and fastened it. She glanced at his face as he did, making eye contact briefly just before the pickup's internal light went off. He smelled vaguely of diesel oil. She became aware of something snuffling around in the back seat, and she looked around to see a familiar sheepdog leaning between the seats and sniffing at her.

'Ben, sit!' He said sharply to the dog. Ben turned around obediently and slumped back down on the back seat.

He started up the engine and reversed out into the road. Magnus didn't speak again which Jo was quite relieved at, as she was not up to making polite conversation. He didn't drive very far before pulling up outside Jeannie's house.

'Wait there, I'll get the door,' he ordered, as he switched

off the engine. He got out of the car and let Ben out first, before coming round to open Jo's door. He held his hand up to Jo as she swung her legs out unsteadily, and stumbled forward, surprised by the height of the cabin. He caught hold of Jo and led her safely away from the vehicle and guided her towards the front door with one arm shielding her shoulders.

'Watch the step!' he cautioned, as they reached the porch.

Through the glazed doors Jo could see a warm light glowing from deep inside the house. Ben scampered ahead of them into the kitchen, and a second later Jeannie appeared.

'Hi Magnie, come on in. Who's this? Oh it's you Jo. What on earth happened to you?' Jeannie said in surprise as Jo stepped forward into the light.

Jeannie took Jo's arm and led her into the warm kitchen, which was remarkably well lit with a variety of candles and ancient glass Tilly lamps.

'Sit down here; let's get a better look at you'. She said kindly, indicating the kitchen stools at the end of the breakfast bar.

Two children burst loudly into the kitchen followed by Ben, who had gone in search of them.

'Magnie, can you put the kettle on for me? And you two can take Ben into the lounge. I won't be long, I'm just going to sort out our new neighbour,' Jeannie said briskly.

Magnus got busy setting an old fashioned whistling kettle onto the gas hob, which he lit with a long handled gas lighter. Jeannie was obviously well prepared for the weather, thought Jo. There was a large box of matches on the worktop and the glass lamps and candles were throwing enough light into the room to be able to see quite well. Jo wondered whether power-cuts were common here and made a mental note to get her own house better prepared.

'What happened to you then?' Jeannie asked as she lifted a large medical case out from a cupboard under the stairs.

'I caught my head on the side of the car door when the wind blew it shut. I went out to get a torch and some matches I'd left in the car,' Jo explained. Jeannie shook her head and tutted, as if she had heard this story a thousand times before.

'OK, let's see what the damage is?' Jeannie said, as she stood next to Jo, pushing her curly dark hair away from her ear where the blood seemed to be originating from. 'Did you lose consciousness at all? Do you feel nauseous?' she asked, as she inspected the cut and looked for signs of bruising.

'No, but it does hurt a lot.

'I'm not surprised. You're quite lucky not to have been knocked out. It just missed your temple by a whisker. Luckily your ear has taken most of the blow. Which is good as it is quite soft and fleshy, although I imagine it must sting a bit,' Jeannie explained, as she cleaned away some of the blood and applied some steri-strips to the cut.

'The door hit my shoulder too,' Jo said, as she shifted uncomfortably on the stool, gradually becoming aware of a burning sensation in her shoulder.

'Let's have a look at that too then. Can you take your cardi off?'

Jo pulled her cardigan off carefully, grimacing as she did. Her shoulder was really starting to feel sore and stiff.

'Magnie, would you mind going into the other room for a minute?' Jeannie said as she helped Jo pull her arm out of the tee shirt to reveal her shoulder.

'Ouch!' Jeannie said, in sympathy. 'That's going to be a nasty bruise.' She got some ointment out of her case, and applied it gently. 'That should help relieve it a little, and I think I'll dig out an ice-pack to put on it for a while.'

She called Magnus back into the kitchen after Jo had made herself decent, just as the kettle started whistling.

'I think a cup of tea is in order here, don't you, or would you prefer some coffee or hot chocolate?'

'Tea would be perfect, thanks' Jo murmured gratefully.

'How was Mam?' Jeannie asked Magnus as he brought over some mugs of tea. He handed one to Jo and smiled shyly at her, before replying to his sister.

'She was just going to bed. I thought I'd drop in and make sure she was ok, I rang earlier and she didn't answer the phone. But she hadn't heard it ringing with all the noise.'

'Well I guess it was lucky you were just passing Jo's house when you did. Have you two been introduced yet?' Jeannie asked as she put away her medical case and rummaged around in the freezer for an ice-pack which she wrapped in a tea towel and then handed to Jo.

Jo shook her head. 'I'm Jo McMorrow, nice to meet you!' she said, holding out her hand to Magnus.

'Magnus Inkster,' he replied, shaking her hand. 'I've heard all about you from our mother. She's delighted to have such a friendly neighbour.'

'It's even nicer for me. I've never got to know my neighbours before. People are a bit more reserved in London. In fact if somebody had come along like you did and dragged me off in his truck I would have been screaming for the police,' Jo said, which made them both laugh.

'I can just imagine,' Jeannie replied. 'I only spent a few years living in Edinburgh while I did my nursing degree, but I hated living in the city. It was so unfriendly compared with Shetland,' she added, as she opened up one of the kitchen cupboards in search of a packet of chocolate biscuits.

'The power will be off until at least tomorrow morning. Do you want to go back to your house tonight? I'm sure we can fix you up with plenty of candles and matches,' Magnus said to Jo.

Before she had a chance to reply, Jeannie invited Jo to stay at her house.

'I absolutely insist! There's plenty of room. Fraser's away at the fishing this week so it will be nice to have some company. The kids will be going off to bed soon, so we can just cosy in by the fire and eat lots of biscuits with our tea.' Jeannie led Jo into the large lounge where a fire was lit in the solid fuel burner in the corner of the room.

'That sounds better than going back to my house on my own. I don't imagine I'll get any sleep with this racket.' Jo was relieved not to be on her own in the dark, and it overrode her natural inclination not to intrude upon people. The hospitality appeared to be genuine, so she relaxed a bit and took a seat in one of the armchairs by the fire and sipped at her tea.

Magnus volunteered to get his nephew and niece off to bed and there were loud shrieks of laughter from the children as he chased them up the stairs.

'Not exactly the best way to get them to calm down before bed, thankfully it's Saturday tomorrow so I won't have to get them up too early. Still they love having their uncle around. I think it makes up for their Dad being away at the fishing so much,' Jeannie grumbled good-humouredly. She was sitting on the sofa with her feet tucked up under her, looking across at Jo. The only times Jo had seen Jeannie before she had been wearing her nurse's uniform. This evening she was wearing a pair of faded blue jeans and a chunky hand knitted jumper, it made her seem both younger and more approachable.

'It must be quite hard for you too I imagine' Jo said sympathetically.'

'You get used to it. Fraser was working on the fishing boats when we started going together, so it's always been like this. But he always tries to make sure he's home for special occasions. He gets quite a bit of time off, especially with the new fishing quotas nowadays; they are only allowed a set amount of days at sea each month.'

'I see, well that's not so bad then,' Jo said, although as she spoke she realised it was probably the wrong thing to say as she contemplated the fact that reduced fishing quotas possibly meant reduced income as well.

'How's your head now?' Jeannie asked, ignoring Jo's naïve remark.

'It's not too bad; it's my shoulder that hurts more now.' She shifted the ice pack to a different spot. She didn't know what was worse, the cold or the quickly maturing bruise.

'You'll be fine, unfortunately I can't give you anything for the pain, but I'm sure it will ease off by tomorrow. I'll get us some more tea and dig out some of Mam's homemade cakes.'

'Your mum was teaching me to knit earlier today. It was fun actually; I've never tried before.' Jo said as she followed Jeannie into the kitchen.

They sat down again with their drinks talking about Ruby and her passion for knitting and baking until Magnus came downstairs. Anya and Callum had finally quietened down after the excitement of playing with their uncle, and the added drama of the power cut. Ben followed him into the room and immediately took up a position as close to the fire as possible, so close in fact that Jo worried whether the dog would end up with a scorched tail. Magnus went over to a large wicker basket next to the hearth and threw some more peat into the fire, releasing a fresh burst of smoky sweetness into the room.

Jeannie stretched her legs out on the sofa as if she was getting comfortable for a long evening. Jo slipped her shoes off and curled up in the armchair and stared at the fire. Magnus didn't say much, but he didn't seem in a hurry to leave either. Jo found herself glancing across the room at him where he sat quietly. He looked nothing like his sister or even Ruby for that matter. He was about six feet tall and of fairly indeterminate shape, due to the bulky clothing he had on. He was wearing an old blue boiler suit with the hem of his jeans poking out underneath. Underneath the boiler suit he also wore a colourful Fair Isle jumper, presumably knitted by Ruby. It was a strange combination; he could only have been in his mid-thirties, but his clothes gave him the appearance of someone who was either much older or from another era. She found herself comparing him unfavourably to David who was always so immaculately and fashionably dressed, even when he wasn't working.

When Jeannie started talking to Magnus about one of their neighbours, Jo realised she could hardly follow what they were talking about. She had overheard the Shetland dialect before, but had never really tried to understand it. She realised that whenever they talked directly to her they seemed to revert naturally to English, just with a fairly strong accent, which still took some getting used to.

Jeannie turned to Jo, observing the look of incomprehension on her face. 'I'm sorry; I bet you didn't catch any of that. It takes a bit of time to pick up the dialect, not to mention the accent, but you soon will. In fact I think I have something that might help.' She got up and walked over to a bookcase and picked out a paperback book.

'Shame it's a bit too dim to read at the moment. Take it with you tomorrow, and then you can have a proper look at it.'

'Thanks, I will,' Jo said, just about making out the words *Shetland Dictionary* on the front cover.

Magnus stood up. 'I'd better get back home; I'm on the early shift tomorrow. It was nice to meet you Jo; I'll see you around no doubt.'

After he had gone Jo wondered whether she ought to go

to bed too, she worried she was keeping Jeannie up.

'My brother is nothing like the rest of the family is he?' Jeannie said, as she came back to the room and resumed her comfortable lounging position on the sofa. She didn't look like she was in a hurry to go to bed.

'Well, he certainly looks different; does he take after your Dad?' Jo asked politely.

'No, that's the strange thing. Dad was kind of short like Mam and me, and he had black hair too, so we don't know where Magnie's red hair and freckles come from. But Dad was also really loud and sociable, especially after a whisky or two. Magnie's a bit on the shy side; mind you it didn't help when his wife left him. He's been even quieter since then, poor lamb.'

'That's a shame; when did that happen?' Jo replied, surprised at the way Jeannie had started divulging so much personal information about her brother.

'Oh it must be over three years ago, but he's never really got over it. I don't think he's even been out with anyone since, which is stupid really, he's such a nice kind person and I know loads of single women who would love a man like him,' Jeannie said fondly, as she leaned over and set her empty mug down on the floor.

'I don't know really, sometimes it takes a while for you to get over things like that. I can't imagine ever going out with anyone else again. I know it's only been a few weeks, and David and I weren't even married, but I think I would find it hard to trust someone else again.'

'Yeah I suppose so, and Lynne really did a number on him, the evil bitch,' Jeannie said, with an edge of sourness in her voice, and then proceeding to recount the whole story.

Jo listened quietly; soberly considering the fact that she wasn't the only person who had been put through hell, in fact she figured Magnus had fared much worse than she had.

'Oh my God, no wonder he doesn't ever want to start again. I don't think I would get over something like that either,' she said at last.

'I know, it was awful, but not all women are like that, are they?' Jeannie asked sadly. 'I hate to think of him giving up just because he had such a bad experience.'

'No, but it is kind of hard to tell who is going to break

your heart or not at the beginning.'

The rain clattered suddenly on the window as if someone had just thrown a bucket of fine gravel at the glass. The wind rumbled on, although it appeared to be easing gradually.

Jeannie continued to stare into the glowing embers of the peat fire. 'You'll soon make new friends up here,' she said after a while. 'That reminds me I'm starting up a new antenatal class at the health centre. We normally just do the appointments as individuals, but at the moment I have four first timers and two other mums who are new to the island so it would be a good time to have a little group that can meet up and get to know each other. I also spoke to the manager of the leisure centre and she's planning to organise some aqua-natal classes in the swimming pool. It will be fun. I'll come along too; I could certainly do with the exercise.'

'That sounds brilliant. Isn't it funny, I have only been here since Monday and already I've done so much? And there were so many people saying that I was mad for coming here and would be setting off back to London within a few weeks.'

Jeannie laughed. 'Well to be fair, you haven't made it through your first winter yet. Imagine a whole week of days like today, only with snow and freezing cold winds.

'I guess so, but then again, if I hadn't gone outside it wouldn't have been so bad. I just need to be better prepared for power cuts like you obviously are.'

'Actually the power cuts don't happen that often, I think we were unlucky today. But it does pay to be well prepared for any eventuality. But if you hadn't bumped your head you wouldn't be sitting here now would you? This has been lightsome. But I think we'd better get to bed now, I promised to take the kids to town tomorrow. They want to go to the cinema...... Do you fancy coming too?'

CHAPTER TEN

On Sunday morning Jo finally managed to find time to visit the beach. She looked out of the kitchen window at the sea. It was glassy smooth, indicating there wasn't a breath of wind outside. It would be a perfect day to go for a walk, and she was determined not to let another opportunity pass by.

Below her house was a wide bay, surrounded by rocky cliffs, that revealed a long stretch of white sand when the tide was out. The cliffs dipped down around the beach as if they had been neatly carved out with a giant ice cream scoop. At the lowest level, near to Jo's house, fields rose up gently from the shoreline. Sheep roamed all over and were also occasionally spotted on the beach grazing on the seaweed. Apart from the small turning space between the two houses the beach was pretty much inaccessible by road, as there was nowhere to park for visitors. It was almost like having a private beach Jo thought smugly as she wandered along the shore.

The tide was out, exposing little islets of rocks in the water. Jo stood for a moment watching a small gang of seals sunbathing on the rocks. They turned their heads lazily to watch but were otherwise undaunted by her presence. She wandered along to the far edge of the beach and followed a well-worn footpath leading up between the rocks to the fields above the beach. She guessed this was the route that Magnus took with his dog. She clambered up the steep path and found herself in a field behind Ruby's house, and face to face with a little huddle of sheep that stared morosely at her as she started to walk across the grass in the direction of the road. They dispersed swiftly stopping only when they reached a safe distance and turned to observe what she did next.

Jo stopped in alarm. It had just occurred to her that she

might be trespassing, and as she was afraid of disturbing the sheep anymore she turned round and went back down the path to the beach. It was too lovely to go back home so she settled down on some dry flattish rocks and gazed out to sea. Across the bay she could see two small uninhabited islands; that is to say they were uninhabited by people. She was surprised to spot sheep roaming around happily in their own little universe, with no dogs or humans to bother them. Beyond that she could see the mainland stretching out in both directions. Little white houses nestled on the slopes of the shore directly opposite to where she sat, but too far away to see whether there were any signs of life in them.

It was beautiful and very peaceful, but Jo was not quite at ease. She was still fretting about David and the absence of a reply to her email. She contemplated whether she should ring him, but she had no idea where he would be this Sunday morning and felt a twinge of guilt, and wished she had taken Megan's advice to speak to him straight away. Burying her head in the sand had only put off dealing with the problem, and running away to Shetland had also failed to resolve anything satisfactorily.

The bark of a dog further up the beach startled her. She thought at first it was Ben barking at the seals on the rocks, but as there were now two black and white sheepdogs wandering around on the beach she was less certain. One of the dogs was limping and wore a white bandage around its foreleg. It hung back from the sea, watching the other one energetically splashing around at the water's edge. The seals stared back from the security of their rocky outpost, although a couple of them slid slowly off and disappeared under the water. They surfaced again further out to sea, keeping their eyes on the dogs.

Jo was amused by the action of the barking dog, which appeared to want to join the seals in the water, but at the same time seemed a little nervous of them. It was funny really, since the seals in the water looked just like dogs when they bobbed up to the surface. She was so busy watching the scene she didn't notice Magnus walking along the beach towards her until he spoke.

'Aye aye, it's a better day than the last time I saw you isn't it? How are you getting on today?'

'Oh fine, thanks. I didn't see you there, I was watching the dogs, I didn't realise you had two of them,' Jo said looking up at him, noticing that he was still dressed in an old boiler suit.

'One of the dogs is Mam's. Jess had an accident a few weeks ago and has been nursing a nasty infection ever since, she's only just got back from the vet's. I've been looking after her as Mam is not so bright on her feet at the moment, and Jess has a tendency to trip her up since the accident. She follows Mam around the house as if she is afraid to let her out of her sight. Poor old lass, this is her first walk outside today.' He turned, and whistled sharply to Ben who promptly stopped harassing the seals and raced across the beach towards Magnus. Jess ambled along behind.

'Ben's really well behaved isn't he? I wish I could whistle like that,' Jo said, impressed with how Magnus seemed to be able to control the dog with just a short sharp whistle.

'He's not as well behaved as his mother. Jess was a brilliant working dog. Ben has an obsession with the seals for some reason; it's the one thing I can't get him to stop barking at.'

'Oh they're mother and son, how sweet,' Jo said as she ruffled the head of Jess, who had come along to sniff curiously at Jo.

'You shouldn't really stroke working dogs.' Magnus warned gently.

'Oh sorry, I didn't know that,' Jo said stuffing her hand quickly back into her pocket.

'That's OK; Jess enjoys being made a fuss off. What I meant was you should be careful of the other sheep dogs you might meet around here. They're not always kept as pets and they'd be more likely to snap at you too. I'd hate for you to get bitten,' he explained kindly.

'What about Ben then, is he a working dog?' Jo asked, remembering how Ben had seemed to enjoy playing with Anya and Callum at Jeannie's house.

'I trained him as one, but I don't keep many sheep these days so I guess he only works part time. He has a kennel and a run at my house for when I'm working, but he does come in the house quite a bit. He loves people, especially children for some reason, and he behaves like one too.' Magnus bent down and picked up a well-chewed plastic ball and threw it along the sand, which set Ben running off after it.

'I wanted to get a dog and I went along to the rescue centre but they wouldn't let me have one. Apparently I should wait until the baby is at least two before getting a pet. It's a shame really as I thought having a dog might give me a reason to get out and about more,' Jo said, watching Ben running back with the ball in his mouth, looking delighted with himself.

'Yeah, I don't suppose I would do quite so much walking without Ben around for company. We get out in all weathers, although it's much nicer on a day like today. Have you been across the park yet?' Magnus asked.

'What park?' Jo asked, wondering whether she had missed something on the island.

'I mean the fields up there,' he said, pointing towards the place that Jo had just tried walking across.

'Oh that, well I did try, but the sheep went running off and I was afraid I might be trespassing, or I would upset the sheep, so I came back down here,' Jo said.

Magnus laughed, and Jo couldn't help thinking how nice and friendly he looked when he smiled. In the sunshine his brown eyes had a warm amber glint to them.

'You're allowed to walk in any of the fields up here,' Magnus explained, interrupting Jo's thoughts. 'The trespass laws aren't the same as in England. And as for the sheep, you needn't worry about them, stupid creatures. I walk through there everyday with Ben and they don't take any notice of us now. They belong to our family anyhow.'

'Oh right, that's good to know, I was going to walk across to the road and then back along to my house.' Jo felt relieved that she hadn't been committing some kind of blunder by walking on the land, but she did feel a little silly that she hadn't known this fact. He probably thought she was really ignorant.

'That's the route I usually take, so you can come along too if you want,' Magnus said casually to Jo, not really expecting her to want to walk with him.

'Are you sure?' Jo asked, standing up and brushing off the sand from her clothes.

'Yeah of course, we don't often get company on our

walks do we Ben?'

They set off along the beach, as Ben ran on ahead, scouting for rabbits. Jess plodded along beside Magnus and as they got to the steeper path leading up to the fields he scooped her up in his arms and carried her up to the higher ground and set her down again.

'What do you think of Shetland so far then?' Magnus asked as they proceeded across the field.

'I like it. It's really beautiful and peaceful and everyone seems very friendly. I think I'm going to be happy here,' Jo replied as she hurried along, struggling to keep up with his longer stride.

They walked on in silence for a while, Jo could see her house in the distance behind Ruby's and when she looked in the other direction she could see another small settlement of houses at the bottom of the hill, grouped around a loch. Three Shetland ponies grazed in a field that ran alongside Ruby's land. Two girls were in the field with the ponies, preparing to catch them and go for a ride. Jo watched in fascination as one of them cornered a pony and attempted to get a halter over its head.

'Sorry, am I walking too fast for you?' Magnus said slowing down for her. 'I think Jess is getting a bit tired too.' Jess flopped down on the ground as if she had suddenly had enough for the day.

'Oh, I'm not tired, it's just I don't have such long legs as you,' Jo retorted indignantly, trying to conceal the fact she did feel a little puffed out.

Magnus looked down at her, smiling as if he didn't quite believe her.

'Look, would you mind doing me a favour? I think Jess is finding it a bit challenging for her first outing. Do you think you could escort her back to your house and I'll come by with the pickup when I get home and collect her? Mam's at the Kirk, otherwise you could have taken her there.' He said, crouching down to pet Jess who panted with exhaustion.

'Will she come with me do you think?' Jo asked cautiously, thinking it was rather strange of him to try to palm off the dog on her. Although since it was Ruby's dog she thought she should at least try and help, and after all Jess seemed docile enough.

'I think she would if you called her, but here's her lead if you need it. It's my fault, I shouldn't have been so ambitious, but it's such a nice day and as I'm not working today I fancied a long walk,' he said apologetically. He clipped the lead onto Jess' collar and handed the end to Jo.

'OK, I'll give it a go,' Jo said cautiously, turning to walk back to the beach, the shorter route back to her house. 'Jess, come on, Jess,' she called, gratified that the dog had started to follow her, albeit at a snail's pace.

'See you later then, and thanks!' Magnus called.

At the sound of his voice Jess paused, and looked perplexed. Magnus whistled at her and she appeared to understand what he meant and plodded on after Jo.

'What did that mean?' Jo said softly to the dog. 'Was that whistle language for follow the city girl and make sure she doesn't get lost?'

Jo was convinced that Magnus saw her as some naïve creature who did not understand much of Shetland life. It was true she didn't, but she was embarrassed it was him that had pointed out her misunderstandings about dogs, sheep and trespass laws. And after almost getting knocked out by her car door the other night, he really must think she was brainless.

Jo and Jess meandered along the beach. Jo sat back down on the rock for a little while, and Jess lay down beside her on the sand, seemingly glad of the respite. Jo figured it would be ages before Magnus would get back to her house to pick up the dog.

The tide was coming in fast and the rocks that the seals had rested on were almost submerged. The seals had departed and a stiff breeze had started to blow soft white clouds across the sky. The mirror like surface of the water had broken up. A raft of Eider ducks bobbed along on the sea. Jo stood up, shivering from the sudden coolness, called Jess and set off back to her house.

The dog obediently followed her indoors and headed straight for the kitchen after Jo had unclipped her lead. The dog seemed familiar with the layout of the house and Jo figured she had probably been inside before when she watched the dog flop down beside the radiator with an audible sigh of relief.

It was getting on for lunchtime, so Jo made a sandwich and sat eating it in the kitchen. It was nice to have company, and she again regretted that she had been unable to get her own dog. She felt much less lonely and enjoyed sharing her biscuits with the very appreciative Jess, although Jo quickly wondered whether she had committed some other faux pas by doing so. Luckily the evidence disappeared quickly and Jess was soon snoring in the corner.

Magnus did not seem to be in any hurry to collect her and after a while Jo decided to check her emails again, even though it was Sunday and she didn't have any real expectation of a reply. However, when she logged on to her email account she was surprised to see there was a message from David's private email account. Her heart raced as she clicked it open.

Jo,

At last you have had the decency to get in touch with me after your hasty departure and appalling lack of manners in failing to give me any explanation for why you left.

I discovered you had broken open and ruined my briefcase, which as you know was a much-loved graduation present from my father, and I realised you had jumped to a conclusion that was wholly inaccurate. I cannot imagine why you felt the need to do something so underhand as to look through my private papers, and once you had done so, I cannot understand why you did not give me the opportunity to explain myself. It was the lack of trust, which offended me the most.

However, I now have the opportunity to explain myself and I am only doing so to ensure that you do not slander me around the city for being a gambling addict. I am no such thing. I am a semi-professional poker player, which I combine with my work at the bank. I am sure you will appreciate that the same skills are required for both types of work and I make a successful living at it. So much so that I have now bought outright the house in Dulwich, you accused me of trying to rent. The rental agreement was only drawn up, as there was a small possibility that my bonus payment might be delayed and I agreed to rent the house until I had the full funds available, rather than lose it to another buyer. It would have been pointless taking out a mortgage for such a small period of time and you seemed to have your heart set so much on buying it.

I had not confided in you about my plans, as I wanted it to be a nice surprise, so I got you to complete the mortgage application so you would not know what was going on.

I am sure that you will now be wondering why I had not told you about my real work. I took up professional poker whilst I was married and my wife Hannah was very unhappy about this. She felt that it was not a respectable way to make a living and after a while she left me, taking our two sons with her. However, in recent months she has discovered that professional poker is now quite respectable, if not fashionable, and the fact that I have become successful and quite well known in the game has changed her attitude.

The day you tried to call me I was at Hannah's house seeing the boys and she was trying to persuade me to consider reconciliation. Naturally I turned her down because of you. However, now that you have decided to opt out of our relationship I have taken her up on that offer. My sons need a father and I have decided it is in their best interests if Hannah and I live together. Therefore, she will shortly be moving into the house in Dulwich.

I realise you will probably be shocked I am married and that will be just another thing for you to hold against me. However, when we first met you made it very clear indeed you would not consider going out with a married man, so I kept it quiet. I was legally separated and had intended to get a divorce. As it happens I did not get around to divorcing my wife, which now seems quite fortuitous.

I hope you are happy in your new home. I also hope that you will respect my privacy and not try to contact me again. My wife knows I had a relationship with you and this is a *sensitive area for us.*

Kind regards
David

Jo sat at the computer for ages staring at the screen. It was too much to take in. Megan had been right; there was a plausible explanation for what she had found in David's briefcase. She felt sick. This whole move had been for nothing. Torn between wanting to howl or throw the computer out of the window Jo decided instead to pour her heart out to Megan

'Hi there, how are you today? Any more adventures? Megan asked brightly when she answered the phone.

'I'm just sitting here reading an email from David. You were right; I should have given him a chance to explain himself. He isn't a gambling addict; he's a professional poker player. And he's married with two children.'

'What? 'Married, so quickly, how did that happen?'

'He's always been married apparently, here, listen to this,' she replied. She proceeded to read the email, despite constant interruption from Megan who interjected outraged expletives as David's news was revealed.

'I got it all wrong didn't I? I feel so stupid,' Jo said despondently, when she had finished.

'No Honey, I think you're missing the point. David has been deceiving you the whole time and now he has turned it around to make it seem as if you're the guilty partner. He's an arrogant, pompous bastard who has turned everything into your fault. And it is *so* not your fault. How dare he hide the fact that he was married from you! Didn't he only just ask you to marry him back in June? What was all that about?' Megan ranted furiously.

'I don't know. I don't know what to think anymore,' she replied staring at the screen wondering how she could have been so blinkered to everything.

'Well I think that you absolutely did the right thing in getting a million miles away from him. I feel sorry for his wife too; he isn't exactly flattering about her either. And I can't imagine there is much conceivable difference between a professional gambler and an addict. His whole weird behaviour points to someone who has some very serious problems. I wouldn't be surprised if most of this turns out to be a pack of lies anyway.'

'I suppose so,' Jo said quietly. 'But he doesn't want to hear from me ever again though, so what am I to do about telling him about the baby?'

'Well I still think he needs to know,' Megan replied seriously. 'It's not just about him is it? There's his parents to consider too, and one day you might need support from him, so it would be best if you told him before the baby was born. Tough shit if he doesn't want to hear about it.' She paused for a moment. 'By the way, what's that strange noise in the background?'

'Oh that, it's a dog I'm looking after,' Jo said fondling Jess who had put her head on her lap and was making funny snuffling and whimpering noises.

'You're babysitting a dog now? Whose is it?'

'It's actually Ruby's sheepdog, called Jess, but Magnus has been nursing her back to health after an infection. I met him out walking on the beach and Jess got tired so he asked whether I could bring her back home with me. He's going to pick her up soon,' Jo explained.

'Well there's an unusual chat up line I must say,' Megan said.

'Don't be silly, he was not chatting me up or even flirting with me in any way whatsoever. In fact I'm sure he thinks I'm perfectly dense. And he knows I'm pregnant so I'm hardly the world's greatest catch now am I?'

'Sorry! I was just trying to cheer you up, but I bet if you weren't pregnant he would have asked you out by now?' she said mischievously.

'I don't think so! Anyway I get the impression that he's not keen on women at the moment. His sister told me about his ex-wife running off with another man, and taking their daughter with her.'

'Yeah well, who can blame him then? Still it won't do you any harm to be friends. After all his mum and his sister seem really nice don't they?' Megan suggested.

'I suppose so, anyway I'd better go and get this dog something to eat or let her outside for a pee, I'm not sure what she wants.' Jo walked with the phone to her ear and opened up the front door for Jess, whilst worrying at the same time she might run off somewhere.

'OK, but you take care now and don't let what David said upset you. God, if I ever run into that man, so help me I'll have something to say to him,' Megan said.

The dog pottered around the garden for a bit and then found a shrub to pee beside. After that she limped back indoors and headed straight for the kitchen. Jo looked at her watch, it was ages since Magnus had left them and she wondered what was keeping him. Not that she really minded, since Jess was good company.

Jo got the dog a bowl of water and then searched her cupboards and fridge for something to feed her. All she could find was some thin slices of cold roast beef she had bought to go with a salad later. She sighed and took the beef out of the fridge and cut it up into another bowl for Jess.

Jo was feeling weary after the latest upset with David so she decided to go and lie down in the downstairs bedroom so she could be ready quickly when Magnus came to fetch the dog. Jess followed her into the room and circled around on the floor for a moment before settling down for a snooze. Jo pulled up the duvet and within minutes she had dozed off.

CHAPTER ELEVEN

The house was in darkness when she woke up to the sound of Jess scratching at the bedroom door. Jo got off the bed to let her out and fumbled around for the light switch. She heard someone calling her from the porch.

'Ah there you are. I've been knocking for ages. I thought you might have gone out again,' Magnus said, as Jo emerged into the hall, blinking in the sudden bright light.

'No sorry, I was lying down, I felt a bit sleepy this afternoon. So did Jess,' she said bending down and rubbing the dog's head.

'I'm really sorry I took so long. I got called out to fix a boat. Two of my friends had taken their boat out to the salmon cages and broke down. I had to tow them back in and help them fix the engine. I didn't think it would take so long, sorry,' he said apologetically. 'Has Jess behaved herself?' he added.

'Yes, she's been great company. I didn't mind looking after her at all. I did wonder whether I should take her to your mum's. But it looks like she has been out all day.'

'Yeah, she always goes to the Kirk on Sunday, and then usually round to Jeannie's for her dinner. I picked her up and dropped her home just now,'

'Would you like a cup of tea or anything? I'm just going to put the kettle on.' Jo thought she ought to be polite and offer, since it was obviously the customary thing to do here.

Magnus followed Jo into the kitchen. 'Do you have coffee, otherwise tea is fine?'

Jo noticed Magnus was carrying a large package wrapped in newspaper, which he put down onto the kitchen counter.

'Do you like salmon? This was my payment for fixing the

boat,' he said, unwrapping the package and revealing a large fish. 'I've got tons in my freezer already, so you can have this if you want.'

Jo stared at it in horror. Although she quite liked salmon she had never attempted to cook anything like a whole one. She was used to buying it from Sainsbury's in nice conveniently filleted portions. Or better still, from Marks and Spencer's Food Hall, pre-marinated and ready to throw in the oven.

'I do like salmon actually, but I'm not sure what to do with something like this, still with its head on and everything,' she confessed, expecting, indeed hoping, for him to take it away again.

'That's OK. I can fillet it for you if you want. Do you have a sharp knife and a chopping board? You can have some fresh now and freeze the rest. Do you like scallops too?' he asked, pulling out a handful of creamy white shells from the package, and seemingly oblivious to Jo's anxiety over the bizarre gift.

'I'm not sure; I don't think I've ever eaten them before.' She looked at the shells lying on her kitchen counter and wondered what she should say. She remembered seeing similar shells on a market stall in Camden, only then they were being sold as soap dishes.

'Really? Then I don't suppose you would know what to do with these either?' he said, grinning at her.

'No I don't. You can just add that to the list of things I don't know,' she said, picking up a scallop and turning it over in her hand, trying to remember if she had even eaten one before. 'But I'm sure you can show me that too,' she said. He obviously wanted to show off his seafood expertise and she was curious to know what a scallop looked like inside, for all she knew she might have had them before. She fetched a chopping board and a sharp knife over for him.

'Have you eaten yet? I could cook you up something nice if you want.' Magnus smiled hopefully at her.

Jo looked at him and weighed up what to say. Part of her just wanted to be left alone to sulk about David's email. But she also felt she should accept all overtures of friendship. Magnus seemed friendly enough. It would be harmless enough to have a lesson in cooking fish from one of her neighbours.

'That's sounds good! Are you Shetland's answer to Jamie Oliver then?' she said, injecting some much needed warmth into her voice.

'Maybe, you'll have to wait and see,' he teased. 'Do you have any white wine?'

'No, afraid not, I do have some diet coke and some orange juice, but I'm not drinking at the moment,' she said, walking over to the fridge.

'No of course, I didn't mean to drink it actually, just to cook the scallops in it. What about lemon juice?' he asked.

'I do have that!' Jo said proudly, taking out a bottle of juice from the fridge.

'That'll be perfect! How about garlic, coriander, black pepper, olive oil?'

'Yes, I have all that too.' Jo collected all the ingredients he asked for, and setting them on the worktop.

'Excellent, so you obviously like cooking too,' he said, impressed with what she had got stocked in her kitchen so quickly after moving in.

'Sort of, I'm only really good at cooking certain things, like Indian food. I can't seem to get my head around ordinary English food and I'm hopeless at making anything like cakes or pastry,' she said, watching him handle the salmon and grimacing when he cut the head off, which made him laugh.

Jo watched in squeamish fascination as he expertly gutted and filleted the fish and cut it into portions. He wrapped the spare salmon steaks into polythene bags for Jo to freeze for another day. He moved confidently around the kitchen, chopping up garlic and coriander and putting together a salad to go with the fish. Jo put on some new potatoes to boil and made some tea and coffee.

'Where's Ben?' Jo asked after a while.

'He's still in the pickup, I didn't think I would be stopping long, so I left him there,' he said, glancing up at Jo as he cracked open a scallop shell with the sharp point of a knife.

'I'll go and get him shall I?' Jo offered, seeing that he had his hands full.

'If you don't mind two dogs in your house, that would be great thanks, I expect he's bored by now.'

Jo went outside and opened up the driver's door of the pickup, which was already unlocked, with the keys hanging in the ignition. It was another reminder of how different this place was from London. Ben was sat in the passenger seat and looked at Jo with anticipation.

'Come on Ben, do you want to come inside?' she asked the dog, and then felt foolish for speaking to him like that.

Ben hopped over to the driver's seat and jumped down and bolted in through the open front door. She followed him and found him nuzzling up to Jess by the radiator.

'Something tells me these dogs have been in this house before. They seem really comfortable here,' she said with amusement, as Ben pushed past his mother to get closer to the radiator.

'They've been here many times before. I spent a lot of time here with my cousin Lowrie; in fact, I helped renovate the house with him after my aunt died. I put this kitchen in actually,' he said proudly, gesturing around the room with the knife.

'Really, no wonder you seem to know your way around it so well,' Jo said in surprise. 'Weren't you tempted to emigrate to New Zealand too? I always imagined it would be a nice place to move to.'

'I still am tempted, to tell you the truth. But it wouldn't be fair to leave Jeannie on her own with Mam. My mother's getting on a bit, and if her hip operation isn't a success she's going to take more and more looking after. Who knows, one day I might go over there. It would be easy enough getting work as a marine engineer, according to Lowrie.'

Jo sat down at the window seat and watched Magnus cooking. It was oddly relaxing. David had never cooked anything for her before, his idea of providing a meal would be to go out to a restaurant or ring for a takeaway.

'What's Jo short for then? Josephine or Joanne?' Magnus asked, after a minute or two of silence.

'Neither!' Jo said sharply.

Magnus looked at her quizzically. Jo was staring down at her feet with embarrassment.

'Come on, it can't be that bad?'

'I'll tell you if you promise not to sing,' she said at last.

'Sing? Now I'm really curious.' He was occupied with

making up a salad dressing but she could see he had made the connection already. He grinned wickedly.

'Jolene? Oh no you poor thing. Were your parents big Dolly Parton fans then?' he asked, trying hard not to laugh out loud, when Jo's face showed he had guessed correctly.

'No, not at all, in fact I was born two years before that song was released. But it's been the scourge of my life. I hate telling people what my full name is and I have lost count of how many people have burst into song when I tell them, which I usually try to avoid.'

'Jolene, Jolene, Jolene, Joleeeeeeene, please don't take him just because you can!' Magnus sang tauntingly.

'You promised not to sing!' she said, laughing despite herself.

'No I didn't. Anyway, Magnus isn't exactly the best name in the world either, especially outside of Shetland where the only Magnus anyone has ever heard of is Magnus Magnusson. For some bizarre reason people seem to think I must have a burning ambition to go on Mastermind. And my nickname is even worse,' he confided.

'Tell me then.'

'Minke, as in the whale. It started at school, but I still haven't shaken it off yet, although thankfully my family don't call me that.' He sipped at his coffee, which had now gone cold. He put the kettle on to make some more, and then wondered whether he was making himself too much at home. He had to keep reminding himself that this house did not belong to his family now, which was hard as he had spent all of his childhood and a good few adult years running in and out of it on an almost daily basis.

'Minke? I don't get it, why would anyone call you that?' Jo asked completely mystified by the name and not really paying attention to what he was doing.

'Well my name is Magnus Inkster, so at first it got shortened to Minkster and then it just became Minke. Jeannie used to get called Jinks but she seems to have outgrown that now,' he explained.

'Minke's not that bad, it's kind of sweet,' she said sympathetically. 'I love whales, and I can't wait to see one.' She smiled in amusement at the face he was pulling in disagreement.

'No it's not! My hair used to be even more red when I was younger, so I used to get called Ginger Whale, like ginger ale, if you see what I mean. The whole whale and red haired thing made my life hell at school,' he said, delighted to make her laugh, even if it was at him.

Magnus had finished serving up the dinner on to the plates.

'I've just thought, I don't think I'm supposed to eat shellfish while I'm pregnant,' Jo said, regretfully as she breathed in the sweet garlicky scent of the stir friend scallops.

'Damn, you're right! Sorry I didn't think about that.' He quickly removed the scallops from Jo's plate and put them on his own, and gave a couple to the dogs that seemed to enjoy them immensely.

'Where do you want to eat this?' Have you got a dining table stashed away somewhere?'

'Not yet, it arrives tomorrow, and there's only one chair in the lounge, or this window seat.'

'Well in that case maybe we'll go in the lounge, and I'll sit on the floor.'

Jo fetched some pillows from the spare room for Magnus to sit on, and they settled down to eat in the lounge. The dogs followed and stretched out on the floor beside Magnus.

Jo usually felt uncomfortable eating in front of people she didn't know but she quickly found she could relax with Magnus, as there was no pressure on her. She found herself thinking about Megan who she knew would tease her about her first 'date'.

'This is really delicious,' she said approvingly of the salmon. 'I wish I could try the scallops too, they smell lovely. Where do you find them?'

'These were dredged up by one of my friends who has a shellfish dredger on his boat. You don't catch them in a net like you do fish,' he explained politely.

'Oh I thought you might find them on rocks on the beach. I have so much to learn about this place, don't I?' Jo mused out loud.

'Not as much as I'd have to learn if I moved to London! I once spent a whole afternoon going round and round on the

Circle Line, as I missed my stop and didn't realise it went in both directions,' he said.

'You did not! I don't believe you!' Jo replied, in mock horror. Surely nobody was that stupid, she thought.

'Okay, you're right, but I did go on for two more stops before I realised and had to go back again. I was tempted just to keep on going round though. Jeez, what a way to travel,' he said shaking his head at the memory.

Jo really enjoyed the evening, and was sad when Magnus said he ought to get back home. She was just as reluctant to see Jess get up to leave.

'Jess could stay here you know, while she gets better, I like having her here,' she offered suddenly, not wanting to be left on her own.

Magnus studied Jess for a moment. The dog stood quietly under his appraisal, slowly wagging her tail.

'Well, if you're sure, but what about food, she'll be needing her supper soon?' Magnus asked.

'That's true, I already gave her some slices of roast beef earlier but I don't have any left now,' Jo replied.

'Roast beef? No wonder she's in no hurry to leave. Wait there!' He said. 'I'll get some dog food from Mam's she'll probably have some in the back porch.'

With that he sprinted across the road and disappeared inside his mother's house. A few minutes later he came back with a carrier bag.

'Here's everything you need for a few days. Now are you sure about this? She'll get you up early in the morning to go outside. Mam said you can bring her over for a visit tomorrow if you like, she hasn't seen her for a few days now,' he said, setting down the bag in the kitchen for Jo. 'I'll come by tomorrow evening to check her wound, if that's OK with you.'

After he had gone, Jo went upstairs to bed. Jess trundled up slowly behind her, obviously finding it difficult to climb the stairs. Jo understood now why Magnus thought it would be difficult for Ruby to manage Jess at the moment. Everywhere Jo went Jess followed, even to the bathroom. It would be easy to trip over her if you weren't very steady on your feet.

As Jo lay in bed thinking about the strange day she'd had, Jess snored quietly on the floor at the foot of the bed. It was nice to have company.

CHAPTER TWELVE

Jess whimpered to go out just before seven in the morning. The sun was barely up and Jo struggled into her dressing gown and crept downstairs to let the dog outside. She stood in the doorway watching in case the dog decided to go back to Ruby's house after she had done her business. She was a little alarmed to see Jess run out of the garden into the field next door, but when she saw what the dog was doing she was relieved.

'Well done, Jess, at least I won't have to clear up the garden after you,' she whispered.

Jess trotted straight back to the kitchen and sat expectantly beside her bowls on the floor.

'OK, OK, I get the hint; it's time for breakfast is it? Well I can't say he didn't warn me you were an early riser,' Jo muttered out loud, as she poured out dried dog food into the dish and put some fresh water down.

Jess ate noisily and quickly, while Jo poured herself a glass of orange juice. She fully intended going back to bed for an hour or so, but as soon as Jess had finished her food she sat expectantly by the front door again.

'What do you want now? Another trip to the doggie bathroom or is it time for a walk?'

At the mention of the word walk Jess got very excited and started wagging her tail frantically and danced around making a clattering noise on the hard tiles with her claws.

'Oh dear, I think I said the wrong thing. Look I'm not dressed yet, so you'll have to wait here till I throw on my jeans.'

Jo ran upstairs to her bedroom, resisting the temptation to get back into her still-warm bed.

A few minutes later they set off to the beach. It was another calm day. The sun had just risen, casting a silvery glow over the hills. Dark clouds loomed in the west but in the east there were cheerful patches of blue sky. The tide was out again but there were no seals lounging around on the rocks this morning. Jo wondered where else they hung out.

Jess set off along the sand sniffing along the edges of the shore. She seemed to be a little bit steadier on her feet today. Jo noticed footprints in the wet sand, indicating a man and a dog had visited the beach ahead of them.

'It seems like you're not the only one that likes to get up early,' Jo said quietly to Jess. 'Am I going nuts, talking to you like this?' she added, smiling to herself. Whenever she spoke Jess would look up at her, but she seemed content to play the role of quiet companion and they wandered happily up and down the beach for a while before Jo could see Jess getting tired.

'Let's go back and then you can have a snooze and I can have a shower and get dressed properly. I'm going to have to find some jeans that fit me, these are getting uncomfortably tight.'

Back home Jo found that the fresh air had woken her up properly and she no longer felt inclined to go back to bed. She had a shower and spent a long time looking through her wardrobe to find something to wear. All her trousers and jeans were just a bit too snug now, although when she looked in the mirror she couldn't really see any change in her shape. Eventually she put on a dress that felt a little too grand to be wearing around the house but it was comfortable. It was a bold pink vintage tea dress from the sixties. She put on a pink cashmere cardigan that she had bought to go with the dress. When she had first bought the outfit from a trendy boutique in Notting Hill she felt like Sarah Jessica Parker, who always seemed to look so fabulous in her trademark mixture of vintage and new designer clothes. Today, Jo thought she looked like Mrs Frumpy Housewife.

She pulled out her flat ballet pumps and some bold costume jewellery and put them on, and then after she had dried her hair she tied a pink chiffon scarf in her hair. Finally she put on some makeup, realising it was the first time she had done so for a few days, when normally she would never have stepped outside the door without the full works.

She looked in the full-length mirror. 'Oh dear, what a state,' she said sadly to herself, as she took off the excessive jewellery and the scarf. 'I think I need to do some shopping.' Jo stroked her tummy and tried to imagine what she was going to look like soon. She couldn't recall having seen any maternity clothes shops in Lerwick so she decided she would do some shopping online after breakfast.

In the afternoon sun she got out her digital camera and wandered around the house and garden taking pictures to send to friends who had asked for them. Jess followed her and subsequently appeared in many of them. Jo thought she would nip down to the beach to capture some of the fabulous views. She figured she would hear a van with her furniture delivery pulling up outside her house, if they didn't go too far away.

Jess was delighted at the bonus of going for another walk. This time the tide was coming back in and the rocks were almost covered again. A solitary fat grey seal sat on the last remaining rock and stared balefully at Jo and Jess. Jo zoomed in with the camera and got a brilliant shot of him in full sunlight with another seal having just bobbed up in the water beside him.

She felt a rush of pleasure at being here on the beach on this lovely day. It was kind of chilly though and she wrapped her long black woollen coat around her, thinking as she did she would also have to buy something more suitable for walking on the beach.

The combination of sunshine, fresh sea air and the sounds of birds all around her made her feel glad to be alive.

'Did you know Jess; I've only been here one week? Imagine that! It seems like a whole other lifetime ago I was down in London,' she said out loud to the dog. After a while she headed back to the house to download the photographs onto the computer. She was delighted with the results and emailed some of them to her friends.

A sharp rap at the front door caught Jo and Jess by surprise. The dog followed Jo to the front door and when Jo opened it there were two young men carrying large flat pack boxes.

'Shall we bring these in the house for you? They're quite heavy.'

'Yes please,' Jo said gratefully. She pointed out the study for the bookcases, desk and office chair and the kitchen for the dining table and chairs.

'It looks like your husband is going to have busy evening putting all this lot together. Sign here please love.' He smiled as he handed over a clipboard and waited for Jo to sign the receipt.

Jo stood at the front door as the van backed down the driveway and turned to the dog.

'Well Jess, since I'm sadly lacking a husband, it looks like it's just you and me putting all this lot together. But how about if we go over and see Ruby first; I said I would take you over there today. I bet she's missing you!'

'Come in! Hello Jessie, come here lass!' Ruby said to the dog, as they entered the lounge. 'That's another bonny frock you have on,' she said to Jo looking admiringly at her pink flowery outfit.

Ruby made some tea and they sat in her kitchen chatting for a while.

'How's your head now, after that accident? Jeannie told me you hit your head on the car door. I did feel bad about that, I should have warned you about how strong the wind can get. But I didn't want to patronise you,' Ruby said.

'Oh crumbs, it wasn't your fault. And anyway please patronise me as much as you like, I think I have lots to learn about this place. Well Magnus certainly seems to think so,' Jo replied.

'Yes I saw he came to see you yesterday. Thanks for offering to look after Jess for me. She can be a bit of a handful. I noticed she got you up early this morning. Actually that was quite late for her; she's normally up at six.'

'You don't miss a thing over here do you?' Jo remarked, as she helped herself to a slice of Whalsay huffsie. 'Magnus brought me a salmon and some scallops when he came over to collect Jess but I didn't know what to do with them so he stayed and cooked me some dinner. It was lovely. I've never bought a whole fish before; only fillets.'

'Goodness me, fancy that. The price they charge in shops for a fillet of fish is extraordinary. I don't think I've bought fish from the shops for years and years, not since Jeannie decided she wanted to try some fish fingers when she was a peerie lass.'

'Ah well, you don't get so much choice in London, given the lack of fisherman around,' Jo said, 'and it is seriously expensive in the supermarkets.'

'I suppose so. Well it will do Magnus good to make some new friends. I do worry about that boy. He works far too hard and never has time to just sit and relax,' Ruby said, as she picked up her knitting again, and gestured for Jo to join in.

'I wonder where he gets that from?' Jo said laughing. 'I mean when do you sit and just do nothing either?'

'I know, I guess it is in our genes. But I don't think of knitting as work, even if it is making money. But Magnus works two out of every three weeks on the ferry and during the other week he is usually helping out his friends on their boats, or mending fences on the croft, cutting hay or feeding the sheep. He's been helping one of his cousins build a house, not to mention he did a lot of the work over at your house, and on top of all that he works as a volunteer fireman.'

'That is busy!' Jo agreed, delving in to Ruby's knitting basket to find the baby blanket she had started, under the expert supervision of her neighbour.

'Yes indeed, and next week he'll be playing the fiddle at a wedding so he won't even get a chance to just have some fun and have a drink.'

'October's a strange time for a wedding isn't it?' Jo said thinking about the recent weather.

'Actually the winter months are a traditional time for weddings in Shetland. It used to be the only time when people had any chance of getting time off in the past. The weather would be too coarse for fishing and the harvest would be in, so a wedding would be the perfect opportunity to have a spree. They tend to take place over two or three days as well, so it is like a mini holiday for families to get together over.'

'Three days, wow, that must be expensive to organise,' Jo said, thinking of the very vague research she had done for her own wedding.

'Oh not at all, well at least not like it would be in the rest of the country. We celebrate in a much more low-key way and everyone helps with the catering and the preparations. I've donated some of my sheep for the mutton supper on the first night.'

'Sheep?' Jo was astounded at the idea of using home reared sheep for a wedding meal; it was a million miles away from her experience of catered affairs in large hotels.

'Oh yes, well I'm running down the flock a bit now; it's getting too much work for me. And the bride is my cousin's daughter Morag, so that'll be their wedding present from me.'

'So they'll be having roast mutton for their reception then?' Jo asked as she started knitting, concentrating hard on every stitch, unable to look away from what she was doing, unlike Ruby who could cheerfully multi-task.

'Oh no, the cooks will make a big stew with the mutton and that eaten with bannocks, and then they'll be tea and fancies.'

'Is the mutton stew like an Irish stew? My Dad used to make that when I was little.'

'A bit, and it's the men who cook it too, in the old cookhouse that has a big open fire for the iron cauldrons. You should go along and see it one day it is very interesting. A lot of whisky gets drunk on the day and the musicians go along and entertain them while they are cooking.'

'It sounds fascinating,' Jo said, trying to imagine a group of drunken men cooking up stew in a cauldron. It defied belief.

'It is; in fact I think you should come along to the wedding, I think you'll enjoy it,' Ruby suggested suddenly.

'Oh no, I couldn't possibly go, I don't even know the bride or groom,' Jo exclaimed with embarrassment.

'Nonsense, what better way to get to know people than at a wedding? Morag won't mind at all. You can come along to keep me company; I don't suppose I'll be doing any dancing.'

'But...' Jo started to protest but Ruby wouldn't hear of it. She picked up her phone and dialled a number.

'Alice, I'm just sitting here with my new neighbour Jo, and I've invited her along to Morag's wedding. She wanted me to check that it was fine with you,' she said, grinning over at Jo as she spoke. 'I know, that's what I told her, that'll be great; then I'll have someone to take me home if I can't last the distance eh? ...... I know, I wish I were young again too!'

'See, I told you it would be fine,' Ruby said as she put the phone down. 'You'll be doing everyone a favour by coming along with me. Otherwise they'll all worry about whether I'm getting too tired and wanting to go home,' Ruby explained.

'Well that's great then, I would love to go to the wedding,' Jo said, thinking that it would be a good opportunity to get to know more people. She was also curious to know what Magnus' band would sound like.

They sat and chatted about the wedding for a while longer before Jo thought she had better get home for her dinner.

'I just got my dining table and chairs delivered today and when I've put it together, you can come over and have tea at my house for a change.'

'That'll be splendid. See you later Jessie. You be good,' she said, fondly patting the dog on the head as Jo got up to go.

Jo examined the pile of boxes in the kitchen and wondered where to start. She opened up one of the boxes and took out the instructions, which were the usual meaningless diagrams with precious few words of explanation. She put on her CD player and was just thinking about abandoning the task until the next day when Magnus appeared at the kitchen door. Jo still wasn't used to the way people just walked into the house, and looked up in alarm.

'Sorry I did knock, but I don't think you heard me,' he said, nodding towards the stereo. 'How's Jess today?'

'I think she's a bit better than yesterday. We've been out for two little walks on the beach and we just got back from your mum's,' Jo replied, turning down the music.

'Splendid, I'll just have a quick look at her leg then,' he said, kneeling down on the kitchen floor and calling Jess over.

'What's that you're building?' he asked, looking at the opened flat-packed furniture box. 'Do you need a hand?'

'It's my new table and chairs so my dinner guests don't

have to eat off the floor from now on,' Jo replied laughing. 'But I think I can manage to put them together, thanks.'

'Really? Well I can see you're dressed for the occasion. I always put on my party clothes when I'm doing DIY,' he teased.

Jo looked down at her pink dress and shrugged.

'It's not a party dress! Well I don't think it is anyway, but it's all that fitted me this morning. I'm getting too fat for my jeans.' Jo regretted saying anything when she noticed Magnus staring at her tummy. She turned away and picked up the kettle feeling self-conscious in her ludicrous outfit.

He stood up, having finished with Jess. 'Seriously, let me help you, I'm not doing anything else this evening and I have all the tools you'll need in the pick-up.'

'I've got a tool box too, somewhere,' she retorted, although she couldn't quite remember where it was at the moment. 'But OK then, if you put together my furniture I'll cook you a curry. How's that?'

'Perfect, so long as it isn't salmon curry, that would taste braaly weird,' Magnus said, delighted she had accepted his offer of help.

'How about chicken?' Jo offered.

'Perfect!' Magnus replied, and went out to the pick-up and returned with a large metal toolbox, and Ben trotting along behind him.

'Hope you don't mind if he comes too,' Magnus said, as Ben resumed his favourite spot cuddled up to the radiator and Jess.

'No of course not,' Jo said, as she started pulling things out of the fridge to make dinner.

Magnus proved to be an expert at putting together flat packed furniture. He had the table and chairs set up remarkably quickly and then took all of the packaging out to the pick-up and said he would offload it at the community skip for her on the way home.

'Is that everything? He lifted the table into place by the window seat, and set the chairs underneath. It was the first time he had spoken in a while as the noise of power tools had made it impossible to have a conversation.

'Actually, I hate to say this but there are some

bookcases and a desk and a typing chair in the other room. I wouldn't like to ask, but I can see you are obviously much better at doing this than me,' Jo said cheekily, as she stirred the curry.

'No problem at all, and that dinner smells really nice by the way.'

Magnus disappeared into the office and shortly after Jo could hear the electric screwdriver buzzing away again. She smiled to herself. She hadn't intended to ask for help but he really seemed to enjoy being useful. In return Jo was making a supreme effort with the curry.

While he was still working in the other room Jo set her new table and got some plates and glasses out. She hoped he would be impressed with the dinner. She had been out of practice of cooking Indian food, as David hadn't liked spicy stuff much.

She fried some poppadoms and made a yoghurt and mint dip for a starter and put them on the table. Everything was ready for dinner so she went to fetch Magnus.

He had assembled the bookcases, which were now leaning up against the wall and he had just started on the desk.

'I think I'd better fix the bookcases against the wall for you, the floor's not quite level and they might tip over once you start loading them up with books. Is that where you want them?' he asked as he put the electric screwdriver down.

'Yes thanks, it is. Er, dinner's ready now if you want to stop.'

'Thank heavens; I'm starving now. That smell's been driving me mad,' he said as he stood up. 'I'd better go and wash my hands first.'

Jo sat at the table and waited for him to return from the bathroom. It was weird having dinner with him for a second night in a row. Well, weird but kind of unremarkable too since it occurred in such a casual way.

'This looks very impressive,' he said, snapping off a piece of poppadom as he sat down opposite Jo.

'Thanks, help yourself; this is just a starter.'

'Mam tells me that she's invited you to Morag's wedding. That'll be an experience for you. Whalsay weddings are famous throughout Shetland,' Magnus said, spooning the yoghurt dip onto his plate.

'I don't think I'll be able to party all weekend. It's not quite the same when you can't drink I guess,' Jo said ruefully.

'No, I don't suppose it is. Not that I want you to get the idea that we are all raging alcoholics who need a dram or two of whisky to have a good time, but in fairness there'll be quite a lot consumed.'

When they had finished the poppadoms Jo stood up to clear the plates and then served up the curry. She set a plate before Magnus who looked very impressed. He scooped up a forkful into his mouth.

'Wow, this is good! What sauce did you use, I've never tasted anything as nice as this, even in a restaurant,' he exclaimed enthusiastically.

'I do hope you're not implying I used a jar of curry sauce,' Jo said, pretending to be affronted. 'This is entirely homemade.'

'Really, where did you learn to cook like this?'

'I was adopted by an Indian family,' Jo said enigmatically. 'OK, it's only partly true,' she conceded, registering the surprise in his expression. 'When I was younger I worked every evening after school for an Indian family who owned a grocery shop in Shepherds Bush. I used to help their kids with their homework sometimes, as they had only lived in England for a couple of years so they struggled with the written language for a little while. The wife used to giving me lessons in how to cook, and quite often I had my dinner with them. She was kind of like a second mother to me really. I even called her Auntie.'

'Didn't your parents mind you working such long hours?' he asked.

'I didn't live with them, I lived with my Gran after my parents split up, so I think Auntie felt a bit sorry for me,' Jo explained.

'I'm not surprised, that must have been tough on you,' he said sympathetically.

Jo shrugged. 'I don't know really, I made the best of it at the time. I can't imagine any other life now.'

'You really are full of surprises. What else can you cook?' he asked thoughtfully.

'Pretty much the whole range of Indian food really, certainly anything you can get in a restaurant, although to be fair most Indian people don't eat quite like that at home. They eat a lot more salads and a lot less heavy sauces,' Jo said.

Magnus ate in silence for a while but Jo could tell he was mulling something over.

'I don't suppose you would be willing to do me a huge favour would you?'

'Ha, ha, I suppose you want me to cater you a fancy dinner party so you can impress your friends?' Jo asked, as she got up to refill their glasses with water.

'Not exactly; Jeannie, Fraser and I are planning to hold a charity event at the golf club in a few weeks. It will be the 10th anniversary of my dad passing away, and we thought we would mark the occasion by raising money for cancer research. We were just going to lay on soup, sandwiches and fancies for the supper, but if you would be able to do something a bit more exotic that would be really special.'

'So you'd like me to cater for a golf match, what happens if the weather's really bad?' Jo asked, remembering the recent stormy weather.

'No no, it won't be a golf match; we'll just be using the clubhouse which isn't used much during the winter. We're planning a charity poker tournament. Hopefully for around 70 people, who would each buy a place at the tables for £10 each. We would set aside some money for the prizes, and some for the cost of catering and venue, but the rest will go to charity. We'll also be raising money through a raffle of donated prizes and from bar sales,'

Jo was momentarily stunned by the extraordinary coincidence. Her face fell and she shifted in her chair with discomfort.

'I'm sorry, don't you approve of gambling?' It was Magnus's turn to look uncomfortable.

'Oh no, it's not that, it's just a surprise that's all.' Jo didn't want to have to explain herself at this stage.

'Jeannie and I would help you get set up and there's a huge professional kitchen at the clubhouse. It's all for a good cause,' he pleaded.

'Wouldn't soup and sandwiches be cheaper than

cooking up an Indian supper, I mean, it could be quite expensive depending on what you had in mind?' Jo asked, calculating how she could possibly do this on a tight budget.

'Well here's what I was thinking. I have a couple of lambs in my freezer and I'm sure Jeannie has too, plus fish of course, and I dug up tons of potatoes, onions and garlic from my garden which are in storage for the winter, so if we provided all that for nothing, just buying rice, spices and other vegetables might not be so expensive. What do you think?' Magnus asked hopefully.

'I guess I could make up some pakoras and onion bhajees and if I got some spinach I could also make some sag aloo. I could make lamb curry, maybe a lamb pasanda or if I bought lentils I could make a lamb dhansak. And with some fish I could make some spicy fish kebabs depending on what kind of fish it is, white fish would be best,' Jo said, thinking aloud.

'OK, what about monkfish? I can get loads of that,' Magnus suggested.

'Wow, that's really expensive! I've only ever cooked it once but it made a brilliant fish curry.'

'Well I can get it for nothing.'

Jo drummed her fingers thoughtfully on the table wondering whether she was up to the challenge of cooking for such an event.

'I think it could be possible, but I've never cooked for more than 10 people in my life before, and certainly nobody was paying for it,' Jo said apprehensively.

'Don't worry; we'll help you get everything sorted during the day. I imagine some things can be left to marinade for hours before cooking, or we could just heat it up later,' he said.

'Yeah, you're right, and some things taste even better when they have rested for a few hours. I would just have to make the rice fresh and heat up the nan bread, and I bet if I showed your mum how to make nan bread she could probably help. I bet it's no harder than bannocks,' Jo said, starting to get enthusiastic about the project.

'Now you're talking! This is going to be brilliant. We'll sell out and I'd love to raise at least £1000,' he said, smiling broadly at the prospect of a successful evening.

'OK then, it's a deal!'

Jo finished her dinner contemplating what she would need to do for the poker night.

'Would you like some coffee now or anything else to eat? I don't have any pudding as your evil sister banned me from junk food, but there is some fruit,' Jo said after Magnus had finished his second helping of curry.

'Typical Jeannie! But just for the record she got as big as a house when she was pregnant. But a black coffee would be lovely thanks, I'll just go and finish putting your desk together, so you can set your computer up a bit more comfortably,' he said, standing up from the table.

Jo loaded up the dishwasher and took the coffee through to the office and sat on her new typing chair and watched Magnus work, whilst trying to resist the urge to spin her chair round like a five year old.

'I've nearly finished, but I need some wall fixings for the bookcase which I haven't got on me. I'll come back tomorrow if that's alright.'

'That's fine, thanks so much; do you need some money for them?' Jo said, wondering whether he would be back in the evening, conveniently in time for dinner again.

'No, no, I've got loads at home in the workshop. It'll probably be early in the morning as I'm out later on and I'm playing darts tomorrow night at the boating club,' he explained.

'I've got my antenatal appointment with Jeannie so I might not be home in the morning.'

Magnus jumped up and pushed the desk against the wall and started lifting the computer into place, expertly disconnecting cables and reconnecting them again keeping the untidy wiring out of sight.

'If you leave the door unlocked I'll just come in and do it, it won't take ten minutes. Nobody keys their doors around here, there's no need,' he said, starting to pack the tools away.

'So I noticed, yeah, that'll be fine then.' Jo felt vaguely disappointed that he might come around when she wasn't in.

Magnus stood drinking his coffee and surveying the boxes and bags of books that were sat waiting to be put away.

'I thought Jeannie liked reading, but I think you have even more books than her and it looks like you have the same taste in romantic fiction,' he said, smirking at her.

'There's nothing wrong with that is there? I used to spend hours every day on the underground and as I get claustrophobic I had to have a book to read to take my mind off it. I actually gave loads away to Oxfam before I moved up here, these are just my favourites and some that I haven't got around to reading yet,' she said defensively.

'I wasn't criticising your taste. I even read Bridget Jones' Diary when I was away at sea for a few weeks. I wanted to see what all the fuss was about. I thought it was quite funny actually.' He drained his cup and moved towards the door as if he was about to leave, then hesitated in the doorway. 'I was an engineer in the Merchant Navy. I used to sail all over the place, mostly to Malaysia and the Middle East but I gave that up a few years ago for the quiet life on Whalsay,' he added, looking deep in thought.

'That's quite a change,' Jo said, hoping that he would tell her more.

'Anyway I'd best get home, it's getting late. I might see you tomorrow morning when I come round to do the shelves. Otherwise I'll be in touch about going shopping for the curry and poker night. Maybe you could write a list of everything we'll need?'

Jo watched from the front door as he left with Ben. Jess pottered around the garden for a few moments then headed back inside. It was bitterly cold outside but the sky was crystal clear. Jo grabbed her coat and stepped out into the garden to get a better look. She had never seen such a clear night sky before. The absence of streetlights made the moon and stars stand out dramatically against the velvet black. Jess wandered back outside and sat down patiently beside her. The waves crashed on the beach and unseen creatures shuffled around in the field next to her. She knew without looking they would be sheep. It was peculiar standing here late at night but not being the least bit scared about what might be out there in the dark.

CHAPTER THIRTEEN

Jo took Jess out for an early morning stroll on the beach and then set off for her antenatal appointment. Jeannie was pleased to see her again and even more pleased after taking her blood pressure.

'That's much better than last week. Not perfect though, so you still need to take it easy. I hear you're looking after Jess now, that'll be the perfect cure for stress. I'm sure she will love going out for some gentle walks along the beach with you,' Jeannie said, as she uncuffed Jo's arm.

'Actually it's great having her around, I shall miss her when she is well enough to go back to your mum's.' Jo said, as she watched Jeannie scribbling down the notes in her antenatal folder.

'Actually Magnie and I think that Jess shouldn't live with her again. You've probably noticed already how Jess follows you around the house wherever you go, well she does that with Mam too, and I really worry about her tripping over. She is getting more and more frail and Jess doesn't seem to realise, but then I guess she's getting older too and having been injured she seems to be more insecure. Really she should just live outdoors like other working dogs but Mam won't hear of it. She's too soft and thinks Jess deserves a comfortable retirement,' Jeannie explained.

'Well I agree, and I would be more than willing to keep her; if she's good with babies, that is?'

'Of course, no, she's an absolute angel with children, my two have jumped all over her, pulled her ears and tail, and she has never so much as growled at them,' Jeannie said reassuringly.

Jo walked out to her car feeling more cheerful about her health. Her BP was down and the baby's heartbeat was still ticking away nicely, she couldn't wait until Friday when she would be having her first scan. She hurried to the car to get out of the rain and looked at her watch. She had decided to drive to Lerwick to do some shopping but she had just missed the ferry, so she turned the car in the direction of home thinking that she would have a while to wait for the next one, denying to herself it was to see whether Magnus had called round yet.

As she set off she put on the radio and started singing along. As usual a number of sheep roamed along the verges, and on the road, trekking from one field to another. One of them darted across the road and Jo braked hard as she approached the rest of the flock. They all seemed to be safely across and she watched them plodding up the hill looking dejected and soggy. Jo eased her foot off the brake. She started to accelerate along the clear stretch of road, but as she did, another straggler hopped out of the ditch at the side of the road, hesitated for a moment, then sprinted across her path. Jo slammed her foot on the brake and swerved to avoid it, and subsequently hit another sheep she hadn't seen just emerging from the ditch.

The impact was sickeningly loud, and the injured sheep squealed in agony. Jo clenched the steering wheel in bewilderment; terrified of what she would see when she got out. However, before she could open the door she felt the car slip and jolt to one side, as the wheels slid over the edge of the waterlogged grass verge she had stopped on. Her faithful old Fiesta tipped over the edge and slid down the embankment coming to rest heavily at a 45-degree angle on the opposing bank of the ditch. Jo shrieked in alarm, and was horrified to see water starting to seep in through the passenger door. She grabbed her handbag away from the muddy puddle with one hand, whilst clutching the steering wheel to stay in her seat. The seat belt fastener dug into her hipbone, and her left knee was pinned uncomfortably against the gear stick. The engine had stalled, but the radio continued to blare out until she turned off the ignition.

She swore out lout, and looked around the car for a sensible way to get out. Her door now opened skywards and there appeared to be at least a three-foot drop from the doorsill to solid ground. As she tried opening the door with one hand its weight pushed down heavily against her. She unfastened the seatbelt in order to be able to move more freely and was relieved to hear another vehicle stop, followed by the sound of a door slamming. A second later her driver's door opened from the outside.

'Jesus Christ, are you OK?' Magnus asked as he looked down at her.

Jo could not believe Magnus had been the first to arrive on the scene. She felt a mixture of pure relief and huge embarrassment.

'I hit a sheep and then the road collapsed, well that's what it felt like anyway. But I think I'm OK.'

'Come on let's get you out of there; are you sure you're not hurt?' he said, pushing the door up as far as it would go.

Jo handed Magnus her handbag and then pushed the seat back as far as possible to give herself more space and then levered herself into the awkward position of standing on the handbrake whilst holding on to the muddy doorsill for support. As she stood up she saw a police van had also stopped and another man ran towards her car. He wasn't in uniform, but he still maintained an air of calm authority.

'Is everyone ok?' he said. 'Here, I'll hold the door, Magnus, can you help her out?'

Jo scrambled onto the edge of the seat and knelt painfully onto the doorsill. Magnus reached up and caught hold of her and swung her on to the ground, and as he did she heard her coat ripping where it had snagged on the seat adjuster. Jo stepped away from him and as she did she saw the body of the sheep a few feet away from the car. One leg was twitching and she could see it was still panting for breath, although it was now morbidly silent.

'Oh my God, it's still alive; will it be all right? I'm so sorry,' Jo exclaimed, horrified by what she done to the sheep.

'Don't worry about the sheep, are you all right? I'm PC Mark Ashcroft by the way.'

'I'm fine,' Jo whispered, although she didn't feel it. She felt like she was going to cry at any minute and the very last thing she needed was sympathy.

'Come here, it's just a silly old sheep, everything's going to be OK,' Mark said, putting his arm around her shoulders and leading her away from the carnage. 'Let's go and get in my car out of the rain. I think I should take you along to the surgery to make sure you haven't hurt yourself, you look a bit shaken up,' he said as he opened the passenger door for Jo.

'Magnus, will you take care of that sheep or shall I call someone?' Mark called out as Jo climbed into the police van.

'No problem, I'll sort it out and I'll come back later and winch the car out the ditch.'

'So much for being off duty eh?' Mark said, cheerfully as he started the engine. 'What's your name? I don't recall seeing you before; you must be that new English girl that's just arrived.'

'I'm Jo McMorrow, and yes I've just moved here. Am I in trouble?'

'What for maliciously running down a sheep and destroying that lovely grass verge?' he said chuckling. 'Not unless you've been drinking or doing something else you shouldn't have been!'

'I haven't been drinking; I'm pregnant,' Jo said, but thinking that the way her hands were shaking it would be easy to assume she was hung-over.

'Really? Well I definitely think the Doc should take a quick look at you then.'

'I feel so stupid, I saw those sheep from a long way off so I slowed right down, and I thought they'd all crossed over, I didn't see one of them jumping out of the ditch until the last second.'

'Yep, there a bloody nuisance those sheep, between you and me I wish they could be fenced them in. Although to be honest they're crafty buggers, I've seen them jumping over stone walls to get to another field. Sometimes the grass really is greener eh?'

He stopped the car in the surgery car park, and scooted round quickly to open the door for Jo.

'I'll come in and wait with you; I expect you'll need a lift home afterwards. And I might as well take a statement from you; you'll probably want to make a claim on your insurance won't you?'

Jo shrugged. She was too stunned to take it all in. The receptionist looked up in surprise at the sight of Jo looking considerably more bedraggled than when she had been in a few minutes earlier. Her hair was dripping wet and the ripped edge of her coat was trailing mud on the floor.

Jeannie appeared out of her office, just about to call her next patient.

'Jo! Jesus, what's happened to you?' she asked, taking in her shaken appearance and the policeman standing beside her.

'This young lady had a mishap with a sheep. I brought her along just to make sure she's hasn't hurt herself, but I think she'll be fine,' Mark explained to Jeannie.

'Come and take a seat, Maureen will see you as soon as she's free,' Jeannie said, signalling to the receptionist to let the doctor know. She came over and gave Jo a quick hug, which was just the thing to send her over the edge.

'Ah come on now, don't be upset, it's just a nasty shock that's all. You'll be fine,' Jeannie said, as Jo started to cry.

Mark grabbed a box of tissues from the receptionist and steered Jo towards a seat in the waiting room.

'Here, take one of these,' he said, offering her a tissue.

Jeannie crouched down in front of her and took her hand.

'Cheer up, it's just one of the hazards of living up here, sheep are terminally stupid and have no road sense whatsoever. I think everyone up here must have had at least one accident or near miss, don't you think so Mark?'

Jo had a quick check up with Maureen who said that there were no signs of any serious injuries, but she did warn that she would probably feel a few aches and pains over the next few days.

'I don't expect you'll feel like doing anything much tomorrow, but it would be a good idea to at least go for a walk or something and take a long soak in the bath to relax.'

Mark drove her home, past her car that was still lying in the ditch, although there was no sign of the dead sheep. He wrote down some details about the accident but promised nothing would come of it. Before he left he suggested she should call in to see his wife Sarah who was also expecting their first baby and who would appreciate getting to know another new mother.

After he had gone Jo made herself a cup of tea and sat

down at the window seat in the kitchen. Jess came over and laid her head on Jo's knee.

'Now what Jess? I've crashed my car, ruined my best coat and made such a fool of myself. What else can go wrong? What on earth have I done to deserve all of this?' She stroked the dog's head absentmindedly and sipped her drink.

She felt miserable and pathetic. Magnus had hardly said anything to her after the accident. He probably thought she was a complete idiot for running down the sheep.

'Oh God!' she whispered. 'It must have been one of his. Oh Jessie! I want to go home!'

The sound of the front door opening made Jess jump up and skitter out to greet the visitor.

'I think your car's going to be a write off, I'm sorry,' Magnus said, as he appeared in the kitchen doorway.

Jo fought the temptation to shriek 'Don't you people ever knock?'

Jo couldn't think what to say to him, she was suddenly aware of what a sight she must look, still wearing her ripped coat and the likelihood of her makeup streaking down her face.

'What happened to the sheep?'

'It got put down,' he replied quietly, and walking over to the table to sit down next to her. 'Look I know you probably don't feel up to it, but would you like a drive in to town with me to buy a new car? You certainly won't feel like it tomorrow, at least I didn't the last time I was in a car accident.'

'A new car?' Jo said. 'I hadn't really thought that far ahead yet.'

'Maybe not, but I expect you'll need one fairly soon. I suppose it depends on whether you want to claim on your insurance first, although if I were you I would just write that car off as you would probably lose more from losing your no claims bonus than your car was worth,' he said bluntly.

Jo contemplated her little Fiesta. It was ten years old and probably wasn't worth that much. 'I expect you're right; but I thought you were doing something today though.'

'Yeah, I was going in to Lerwick to do some shopping. I have some stuff to get for Mam.'

'I look like a right state though, I can't go like this,' Jo said, looking down with shame at her appearance.

'Definitely not! I'd be embarrassed to be seen with you,' he replied. 'Why don't you go and get cleaned up and I'll sit here with Jess and have a cup of coffee while we wait.'

Jo hesitated. She didn't want to be any trouble to anyone, but couldn't reasonably see how else she was going to buy another car. She certainly couldn't do without one living here. It was over three miles to the ferry terminal and the local shops.

'Okay, just give me a few minutes to get ready. Are you sure you don't mind?'

'Nae bother; it's hardly going out of my way is it?'

Jo went upstairs to the bathroom and looked in the mirror.

'Oh my God!' she muttered out loud to herself, shocked at the hideous reflection. She grabbed a face wipe and scrubbed furiously at her face, wiping away the streaks of mascara from her eyes and cheeks; then quickly reapplied some more make up to cover up the blotchiness.

She took off her coat and looked at the ripped lining and hem with dismay and threw it over the chair in the bedroom to deal with later. Her dress was streaked with grime after climbing out of the car, so she took that off too. Her wardrobe did not immediately offer up anything else suitable to wear. In the end she put on some black trousers and left the top button undone, as they were now uncomfortably tight. She found a floral linen shirt, which was a bit too summery and needed ironing, but at least it was baggy and long enough to cover up the gaping waistband. She layered a long purple cardigan over the top in lieu of a coat. This will have to do she thought sadly, as she caught sight of the bag lady in the mirror.

Magnus was sitting contentedly in the kitchen with Jess when she came downstairs. If he was surprised by her odd outfit he didn't show it, but then again she thought to herself, he was hardly the world's best-dressed man himself. Although for once he wasn't wearing a boiler suit; he wore black jeans and a grey and blue Fair Isle jumper and black work boots. Magnus grabbed his jacket from the back of the chair and stood up, looking at his watch.

'Best go if we want to catch the next ferry,' he said.

'Shall I put Jess out in the utility room?'

Jo nodded and picked up her handbag. It was still a bit muddy and damp so she quickly wiped it down with some paper towels, checked her purse was dry inside and walked out to the front door.

'Aren't you taking a coat?'

'My only coat got ripped and dirty this morning and my other jacket is suede, so I don't want to ruin that in the rain.'

'Never mind, I've got an oilskin in the pickup you can borrow.'

'Fabulous!' Jo muttered to herself, as she climbed in the front seat.

'You're not having a good day are you?' he said, grinning at her as he switched the engine on.

'It's an absolute fecking nightmare, I can't believe I'm having such bad luck,' Jo fumed. 'My life is worse than an episode of Coronation Street.'

'I wouldn't know, I don't watch Corrie; I'll ask Mam for her opinion,' Magnus said, doing his best to tease her out of her grumpy mood. 'What kind of car would you like?' he said suddenly changing the subject.

'How about a sheep proof one, with rubber doors so I don't get concussed the next time the wind blows?' Jo replied, resolving to cheer up, at least until she could comfortably sulk all alone in her bed that night.

'Sadly they aren't available on the market yet, although I think you make a good case for Ford to create one.'

'I don't know really. I guess I'll just buy another little hatchback, I don't care what make it is.'

'Maybe you should go for something just a bit bigger, what with the baby coming, you'll need a heap of space in the boot for a pushchair, travel cot and baby stuff if you ever go anywhere to visit, not to mention the additional groceries and nappies you'll be buying each week,' he suggested helpfully.

'Mmm, I take your point; I imagine you have more experience about these things than me.'

Magnus frowned, but didn't reply, and continued on to the ferry in gloomy silence. Once on-board he switched off the engine and shoved his seat back as far as it would go and reclined it a little. He shut his eyes as if he intended to go to sleep.

Jo glanced over at him. For once she didn't particularly want to get out of the car and go upstairs to the lounge. She felt scruffy and wanted to stay away from the scrutiny of fellow travellers.

The ferry started to bob around in the sea, which had become quite rough as she moved out of the harbour and into the open body of water. Jo felt a bit alarmed at the unexpected bumpiness of the journey.

'Lie back and shut your eyes, then you won't feel sick, it will calm down in a minute,' Magnus reassured her.

Jo did as instructed. She hadn't felt sick at all but it had been slightly disturbing for the journey to be so rough when she had only ever experienced flat calm before.

'What kind of car shall I buy then?' Jo asked, in an effort to break the uncomfortable silence.

'I would suggest a larger hatchback, probably with a diesel engine for fuel economy, maybe even a small four wheel drive, might be handy in the winter.' Magnus said, still lying back in the seat with his eyes shut.

'Really? I hate four-wheel drives; they clog up the streets and are a real nuisance. I never imagined getting one of them,' Jo replied emphatically, thinking back to where she lived in Ealing, where all the middle class mothers seemed to drive huge 4x4's, and more annoyingly never seemed to grasp how to park them.

'When have you ever seen a road clogged up in Shetland?' Magnus opened his eyes and looked at her in amusement.

'Fair point! But I've never driven one before, is it hard?' Jo asked.

'Not in the least! Here, you can drive this one, that'll give you an idea of what it feels like before you get to the garage.' Before she could respond he got out and hurried round to her side and opened up the door.

'But I'm not insured to drive this,' Jo protested, making no attempt to move from her seat.

'Are you fully comp?'

Jo nodded.

'Then you're insured to drive this, and what are the chances of you hitting two sheep in one day?'

'OK if you insist!' Jo stepped down from the cabin and

walked around to the driver's side and sat behind the steering wheel studying the unfamiliar dashboard. The seat was still tilted back so Magnus adjusted it upright again for her. She fished around under the seat for the lever to pull it forward.

'I didn't realise how short you are, can you even reach the brakes?' he said, laughing at how far the seat needed to go forward.

'This feels huge compared with my car, and so high up too,' Jo muttered, feeling a little inadequate for the job of driving it off the ferry.

She adjusted the mirrors and fiddled with the seat back again, until she was comfortable. She noticed a couple of the ferrymen giving her a strange look. One of them raised a hand at Magnus, who wound down the window and shouted out something in dialect she couldn't understand. The ferryman laughed and cowered back in mock fear of Jo.

'Shut up, you're so mean to me,' she said, slapping Magnus on the leg but giggling anyway.

Jo drove off the ferry painfully slowly and set off up the hill to join the main road.

'You can go a bit faster you know. The speed limit is 60 here.'

'Shsh, I'm concentrating. It feels so weird up here.'

But Jo quickly got the hang of it and speeded up. It wasn't so different really, the gearshift was a little stiffer, but then again it was much newer than her car.

'I quite like this, it's so high up, you can see much more of the road ahead of you. I don't think I would have hit the sheep this morning if I'd been driving this,' she said, as she started to enjoy the drive.

'Maybe, but I don't think a pick-up is the perfect car for a housewife though, do you?' Magnus said.

'Oh my God! That's an outrageously sexist thing to say. And I'm not a housewife, I'm a...' Jo stopped mid-sentence. She didn't really know what she was anymore.

'OK, sorry, it was a little bit sexist, but if you are not a housewife, what are you?' Magnus turned and stared at Jo who was contemplating how to defend her position.

'I don't know. I used to be a civil servant until two weeks ago. Now I guess I'm a lady of leisure,' Jo replied doubtfully, feeling the enormity of losing her occupational status after such a long time of taking it for granted.

'Exactly; a housewife!'

She smiled at his attempt to wind her up.

'Seriously though, I quite like this driving position, but I don't want to drive a pickup, not because I'm a housewife, but because I don't want to look like I just stepped out of *The Dukes of Hazzard.*'

'Is that how you see me then, some Redneck country bumpkin?' Magnus asked, narrowing his eyes suspiciously at her.

'No, of course not, I just...' Jo paused again, not knowing how to justify her comment, and thinking that she might unintentionally cause further offence.

Magnus studied her intently as if he was remembering something. 'Anyway you don't need to buy anything as big as this; we'll have a look around the showrooms and see what you do like. We've plenty of time and you don't need to make a decision today do you?'

Jo drove on in silence.

CHAPTER FOURTEEN

Magnus directed her to a large car dealership that sold a wide range of makes, both new and second hand. It was still raining quite heavily so Magnus leant over to the back seat and grabbed a bright yellow rubberised jacket and handed it to Jo.

'What's that?' Jo asked, unable to mask her disgust at the rather ugly oilskin. 'It smells vile!'

'It's waterproof and it will keep you warm, what's wrong with it?'

'I'd look like Captain Birdseye in it,' Jo said, wrinkling her nose in displeasure.

Magnus rolled his eyes to heaven and shook his head in disbelief. He unzipped his own jacket and shrugged it off.

'Wear this one then, and I'll go out as Captain Birdseye then, I'm not proud,' he said in good-humoured exasperation.

'That's better, this is all lovely and warm, and smells a whole lot nicer too,' Jo said gratefully, pulling on his Helly Hansen jacket and breathing in the unfamiliar but rather pleasant woody scent of his aftershave.

'Thank you, I'm relieved to hear that. Now shall we go and get you some new sheep-proof wheels then?'

Magnus walked over to the selection of second hand cars parked on the forecourt. Jo watched him for a moment and studied the cars from a distance. She didn't see anything that appealed to her. She had been considering her options during the drive to town. She could either splash out on her first ever brand new car, with the expectation that it would give her no expensive maintenance problems for the next few years, or she could save on the initial outlay and get a cheaper second hand car and keep her fingers crossed. Buoyed up with a sudden flush of recklessness she decided to opt for a new car.

'Oi Captain Birdseye! I'm going inside to look at the shiny new cars. They're much prettier than these ones.'

Magnus turned round in surprise and followed her into the showroom. He took off the oilskin and dropped it onto a chair inside the door.

Jo walked over to a smart looking Toyota Yaris and peered inside, ostensibly to check out the CD player.

'This looks nice!' Jo said looking to him for approval.

'It's a bit small. Look at the boot, you won't fit a pushchair in there very easily, as well as all your groceries. You might find it a bit limiting.'

She moved away quickly towards a larger hatchback.

'That's much more practical,' he said, opening up the boot and looking in. 'Better leg room inside as well, so you'll be able to access the baby-seat in the back more easily.'

Jo examined the car. It was definitely a practical choice and looked quite nice; she supposed. But after studying the colour charts she found them disappointingly dull. She looked around the showroom at what else was available. There was one car that was even smaller than the Yaris and a huge executive style saloon. Very boring, she thought. She walked through to another wing of the showroom and spotted a four-wheel drive, Toyota Rav4, in the corner. It was shiny metallic turquoise and gleamed delightfully under the bright showroom lighting.

She marched straight over to it, followed by Magnus and the sales assistant, who came out of his office when he saw them.

'Look, look, this is lovely isn't it?' Jo enthused, running her hand along the bonnet and peering in through the windscreen. She opened the door and climbed in to the driver's seat, adjusted the seat and mirror and fiddled with some of the controls. She loved the feeling of being a little bit higher up than her old Fiesta had been. She turned round and admired the legroom in the back seat. It had ample space, and there were more luxury refinements than she had ever had before. Air conditioning, CD Multi-changer, docking station for her iPod, eight airbags, cruise control - whatever that was, and a built-in hands-free mobile phone. Quite simply, it was fabulous.

'Can I help you with anything?' the salesman asked Magnus.

Jo glared at the young salesman through the open door. Magnus explained that it was Jo that was looking for a new car and the salesman swiftly turned his attention to her.

'Sorry love? What kind of car are *you* looking for?' he asked politely.

'One like this actually! How much is it?' Jo replied coolly as she got out of the car and inspected the outside of it.

The salesman proceeded to rattle off the costs of the various models in the range and what extras could be purchased.

'No, I just want to know how much *this* actual car would cost,' she demanded sulkily, still annoyed with the way the salesman had taken it for granted that Magnus was the one to speak to.

'Right, well actually this is a demonstrator that we've had for just over a year, it's about to be replaced by a newer model so there would be a discount on it from the normal list price,' he said nervously.

'Yes?' Jo replied impatiently. 'So how much can I buy this car for?'

'I'll have to go and ask the manager for you, we haven't priced it for sale yet,' he replied.

'If it's the right price, tell the manager I'll buy it today for cash,' she said loudly, as he scuttled off to the office.

'Jo, don't you want to look at any other cars first?' Magnus asked, concerned at her hastiness.

'But I like this car, and don't you think it would be perfect, I've seen lots of these on the ferry, so they must be popular eh?'

'Yes they are, but they're kind of expensive too,' he said.

'Don't you believe in love at first sight?' Jo asked flirtatiously, as she stroked the steering wheel lovingly, having climbed back inside for another look.

'Are we still talking about cars?' Magnus replied, although he looked deeply embarrassed at Jo's comment,

'Of course; but seriously though, this car meets all of the practical requirements that you suggested to me earlier, and it's a beautiful colour isn't it?'

'It's not a colour I would choose,' he said, stepping back

to look at it.

'No, but then you've got that big black and chrome macho thing with silver tattoos all over it, that would look a bit silly in this colour. Although it might make it a bit more housewifely eh?'

Magnus folded his arms and at frowned at her. 'At least take it for a test drive first, you might not like the feel of it on the road,' he pleaded.

'Aye, aye Captain!' She said, saluting him and getting back out of the car and walking around to open up the boot.

The salesman came back, accompanied by the manager, who sensed an easy sale, even though he had been warned he would be dealing with a stroppy little soothmoother.

'We can give you a two thousand pound discount on the list price, which is very good value since there are less than 300 miles on the clock,' the manager said, looking very proud at the exceptional bargain he was offering her.

'You've got to be kidding! It might have only done 300 miles but it has less than two years left before I have to MOT it, and your assistant has just said that another model with new features has been launched, so in effect this car is not much good to you as a demonstrator is it? It's just another second hand car. I think you can do better than that, don't you?' Jo said, looking the manager straight in the eye.

'I'm not sure we can actually, this is the lowest price we can go to at the moment, and we fully expect to be able to sell it at that price,' he replied, avoiding Jo's gaze and looking at Magnus as if he was really the one who would eventually make the decision.

'Well do so then, but it won't be to me,' Jo replied. 'I could just as easily get one on the Internet for less than that.' Jo was losing patience with the fact that neither of the salesmen were taking her seriously enough, and she believed that Magnus probably wasn't either.

All three men stared at Jo apparently not really knowing what to make of her. Jo marched towards the exit, then turned and smiled sweetly at Magnus.

'Honey, would you mind taking me back to the Subaru garage, I think you might be right about that estate car?'

Magnus looked down at the ground so that nobody could see him smile.

'Yeah of course Pumpkin, no problem,' he replied. He walked over to the chair and picked up his oilskin, and stood aside to let her out the door.

"Just a minute Madam, perhaps we can try and knock a little bit more off the price, as I believe you did say you would be paying cash. Can we talk about this in my office?' The Manager called after her.

'Bingo!' Jo whispered, winking at Magnus before turning back to the salesmen.

Jo negotiated a substantially larger discount from the original retail price. It was still a little more than she was wanted to pay for a new car, but after she had taken it out on a test drive she decided it was worth it. She was delighted with her purchase, the only disappointment being she would not be able to collect it until Friday, when she would have the new insurance policy in place, but she would be coming in to Lerwick again anyway for her hospital appointment.

'Pumpkin?' Jo said later on, turning to Magnus, when he had parked his car on the pier. 'Pumpkin? What kind of name is that?

'Hey listen; you caught me off guard! One minute you're rudely calling me Captain Birdseye, the next you're calling me Honey. It was the first thing that came to mind. I wasn't expecting to be drawn into your cunning little plan to defraud the salesman.'

'Gee, thanks, but that's not what I need to hear on the first day I can't do up my trousers.'

'My apologies; you're nothing like a pumpkin,' he replied insincerely.

'That's OK; you're nothing like a honey. Gosh I'm starving now, can I buy you a very late lunch?' she added, looking at her watch, surprised at where the time had gone.

Jo had to insist loudly on paying the bill in the cafe where she took Magnus for coffee and sandwiches. He relented only when it looked like she was going to create another scene.

'Where to next?' Jo asked as she put her purse back in her handbag.

'I just have to go to the supermarket. What about you?'

'Nah, I'm good, I just need some groceries too.'

'You know, I was just thinking, maybe you should buy

yourself a decent winter coat while you are here. There's going to be a real cold snap next week and you won't survive in just a cardigan.'

'Good point, perhaps I had; this old thing is too big for me,' she said, tugging at his jacket she was still wearing.

'Sounds like it's the only thing that's too big for you at the moment Pumpkin,' he declared, jumping out of her reach as she attempted to slap him.

Jo followed him out into the street and they walked along the harbour to a shop she had never noticed before.

'You'll be able to get a good weather-proof jacket in here,' Magnus said opening the door for her.

Jo stood in the entrance and glanced around the shop confused at the sight of fishing tackle and boat paraphernalia.

'It's a fishing shop,' she exclaimed loudly, rather stating the obvious.

'This way,' he sighed, taking her arm and propelling her towards the back of the shop. He stopped by a large rack of outdoor clothing, mostly in the form of sailing gear.

Jo stared with obvious dismay at the range of hideous jackets in the most outlandish colour combinations; light blue with ecru, salmon pink with grey, maroon with beige. She ran her hand over the fabrics that were cold and unyielding to touch, and even worse made an alarming rustling sound when she sifted through the rail to get a better look.

'What awful colours they are, why don't they have anything that's just one colour, and a decent one at that, like black? Whoever would have thought to put these two colours together?'

Jo picked up an apricot and sky blue parka and scrutinised it in horror, even more so when she saw the price. 'My God look at the price; and it's ghastly.'

'What does it matter what colour they are, they're just supposed to keep you warm and dry?' Magnus shrugged.

'Maybe, but even so, they just feel so nasty and why would anyone want to wear a noisy coat? This one isn't,' she said referring to Magnus's Helly Hanson jacket which she now thought was the height of good taste by comparison. 'Where did you get this from?'

'Norway. A few years ago, but you can them here or on the Internet, however they're even more expensive than this brand,' he said, examining the label of the jacket she had rejected. 'There's another shop that might have something more suitable for you though. I don't suppose you'll have been in there before either,' he said.

Jo walked along beside him wondering which shop she could possibly have missed from the rather limited range in the high street. Magnus stopped outside a very old-fashioned "outfitters". The shop front looked as if it had been created for a wartime street scene in a film. The décor and signage were ancient, without any redeeming vintage chic. Jo realised that she had indeed passed the shop before, and had dismissed it immediately for its drab exterior, before even checking what it sold inside.

Magnus went in and held the door open for her. She hesitated briefly and then followed him in, pausing to look around at the display of men's clothing which seemed as dated as the exterior of the shop. It was curious; the displays showed a variety of tweedy sporting jackets and formal suits, the like of which she had never seen any local men wear. The only man she had ever noticed wearing so much as a tie was one of the bank clerks. She wondered where all the formally dressed men were hiding in Shetland, as boiler suits or jeans seemed to be de rigueur here.

The women's section was upstairs. Jo perused the glazed display cabinets hanging on the wall of the stair well in an ambitious attempt to draw customers into the shop. What she could see so far made *Country Casuals* or *Windsmoor* look like cutting edge street fashion. Her heart sank when she got to the top of the stairs and surveyed the crammed racks of clothing, where everything was a variation of beige or cautious navy blue. A row of coats and outdoor jackets hung on a rail in the corner, but Jo was rooted to the top of the stairs unwilling to venture further into the place that fashion had forsaken.

'Look, normal coats,' Magnus said cheerfully, and stood aside to let her look at them.

Jo walked over slowly and scanned the section of trench coats that looked neither warm nor waterproof, and the frumpy tweedy coats like her Gran used to wear, which obviously weren't waterproof either. There were some decent looking long wool coats much like the one she had ruined earlier, but they didn't seem to be the practical choice for walking the dog on the beach. She turned to look quizzically at Magnus who had now sat down on a chair. She turned back to the coats for a final look. Tucked in between the end of the row of semi decent coats and the start of the short waterproof jackets similar to the ones in the fishing shop, Jo spotted something different. She pulled it out to get a better look. It felt soft and silky to the touch. The swing tag on the sleeve declared it was shower proof. Jo took it off the hanger and felt a quick buzz of elation, as she tried on the long black quilted puffa coat. It was light as a feather, and soft and warm to the touch and Jo knew it would be toasty warm to wear. It did up with poppers and by the time she had done them all up she was fairly glowing with heat. Perfect, she thought, admiring herself in the antique cheval mirror. Warm and waterproof, a little on the expensive side mind, but it will have to do.

She turned round in triumph to face Magnus. He looked like he was trying very hard to keep a straight face.

'What? What's wrong with this?' she demanded huffily.

'Nothing, nothing at all, just don't ask me whether your bum looks big in it that's all,' he said, unable to hold back the laughter any longer.

Jo spun round to look at her rear view. She had been too busy looking at the detail of the coat to take in the overall effect of what it looked like. It made her look enormous, and this was before the effects of being pregnant were starting to show.

'I'm sorry Jo, but you look like you're wearing a giant sleeping bag.'

Jo ripped open the poppers and quickly shrugged off the coat in disgust. Magnus bent down and picked up the coat patiently and hung it up again.

'Let's go,' she said crossly, 'I'll buy something online.'

'No wait, you haven't seen them all properly,' he said, rummaging through the rail. He examined a couple of the tags and after a moment pulled out a knee length black wool coat.

'Teflon? Isn't that for frying pans?' Jo queried, pulling at the label for a closer look.

'It also makes fabric resistant. I think this looks like a nice coat, what do you think?' He handed it to her to try on. She noticed he had chosen a size 14; he was either very lucky or very observant.

She tried it on and looked in the mirror. It was made of a soft expensive-feeling wool fabric and had a luxurious fake fur collar. The coat fastened with two large velvet covered buttons. It hung beautifully in an Empire line style and Jo could see it would be suitable for when she got a bit bigger too. The sleeves were just the right length, and there were two deep pockets in the side seam, which she put her hands into. The quilted layer of thermal lining added to the cosy warmth.

'That really suits you,' Magnus said sincerely. 'It might not be brilliant when it's braaly windy, but it's very bonny and would be fine on a day like today.'

'Do you think so?' Jo asked.

The sales assistant had finished with another customer and came over to offer assistance.

'That's a lovely coat on you. Is this the kind of thing you were looking for, or can I show you anything else?' she asked Jo.

'No I think this one will be fine, thanks.' Jo turned round to check the back view, mindful of Magnus's joke about her bottom.

'It's perfect,' he reassured her. 'Sorry, I shouldn't have been so rude before,'

Jo took off the coat and handed it to the sales assistant.

'Is there anything else I can help you with?'

'Not unless you sell maternity clothes,' Jo said doubtfully, feeling the minor discomfort of her overly tight trousers.

'We don't have a large stock, as you can see we normally cater for the more mature ladies,' she said, almost in a whisper. She led Jo over to a small selection of clothes tucked away by the window.

Jo rifled through the rail looking for a pair of jeans or trousers that she could wear until her Internet order arrived. She found just one pair of dark blue jeans in her size. She examined the odd side zip fastening at the waistband, trying to figure out how it worked.

'Do you want to try these on?'

'Yes please, but I'll just see if there is anything else here I might like first.'

She skimmed through the tops and pulled out a silky pink paisley top for a closer look.

Jo took the two items into the changing room and tried them on. It was a relief to be able to do up the jeans comfortably. She didn't really need a new top as well but she wanted to try on the whole new maternity outfit, out of curiosity as much as anything else.

She stepped shyly out of the changing room looking for the mirror.

'What do think?' Jo asked, looking directly at the sales assistant.

'That's a lovely colour on you dear. It looks very nice,' she said genuinely.

The wide scooped neckline flattered Jo's curvy figure, and the fluid fabric skimmed neatly over the bust and flowed gently down to her hips.

'I think I'll buy them both,' she said impulsively, not waiting to hear Magnus' opinion.

'Can I wear them home now?' Jo asked the assistant. 'I'm so fed up with these trousers that won't button up now.'

'Of course you can dear, let me just remove the tags for you,' she replied, picking up a tiny pair of scissors from the counter. 'Do you want to wear your new coat too?'

'Ooh, yes please.'

Jo went back to the dressing room to retrieve her old clothes and brought them back to the counter to put in the carrier bag.

'Here, you can have your jacket back now, thanks,' Jo said to Magnus. 'Which means you can stop showing me up in that nasty old yellow thing.'

'Cheers!' Magnus replied, taking back his jacket and putting it on in place of the oilskin. The assistant handed him the carrier bag while Jo was busy putting on her new coat.

'That comes to £294 please,' the assistant said, looking at Magnus expectantly. Jo bent down to pick up her handbag off the floor. When stood up she was mortified to see Magnus' hand reaching for his wallet.

'Ohmigod! No, don't be silly!' She cried, handing over her card to the assistant, and glaring at him.

'Sorry, I was miles away,' he said, hurriedly putting his wallet back in his pocket.

The assistant swiped Jo's card through the till and waited for the computer to respond.

'I wouldn't say no to my husband treating me to new clothes. You young lasses are so independent now eh?'

Magnus opened the shop door to let her out into the street. It was dark now and much cooler.

'Right, *Mrs* Birdseye, where to now?'

'Very funny! Why do sales assistants always expect the man to be paying for everything up here? That's never happened to me before and yet twice in one day people have assumed I'm your wife or something.'

'I know, I don't think I'll ever live this down,' Magnus said, hanging his head in shame. 'It's OK for you, nobody knows you yet, but I have a reputation to keep up.'

'That's not the point is it?' Jo protested, slapping him gently on the arm and then realising that this was the third time she had done this in one day, and really she ought to stop behaving like a teenage girl.

'What is your point then? What would be the harm in a man buying a new car or clothes for his wife? I probably would have been buying them if I was *unlucky* enough to be married to you,' he replied, clearly enjoying the opportunity to wind her up again.

'Yes, but it is the assumption that gets me. I'm just not used to this,' she said, smiling at the barbed comment.

'Well, if you're going to stay up here, you'd better get used to it; things are a little bit more traditional. That's not to say we don't think women are equal or anything, before you jump down my throat and accuse me of being a male chauvinist pig.'

There was something in the way he said this that gave Jo the impression that he was getting a little exasperated with her. She wanted to make amends quickly; after all he had been nothing less than helpful and generous the entire day. Her first impulse was to ask whether she could treat him to dinner, but after that discussion she figured it might make things worse.

'I'm sorry Captain, I've taken up your whole day with my shopping and we haven't got around to getting the things you need. What would you like to do now?' She took his arm, intending to flirt with him and make him laugh again, but suddenly the gesture felt a bit too intimate, and she felt him recoil at her touch. He didn't seem the touchy-feely type, given to spontaneous hugs and kisses, like most of her other male and female friends. She dropped his arm slowly, as if that was her intention from the start.

'It's getting kind of late now. I think we had better get going to the supermarket. If we go now we can catch the six thirty ferry, otherwise there isn't another one until half eight,' he said, heading back towards the car park. Jo followed him back to the car, feeling faintly embarrassed.

Inside the supermarket they both took a trolley and went their separate ways inside the shop. Jo headed off in search of fruit and vegetables.

Magnus was a few aisles away stocking up on teabags for his mother when he heard the theme tune to *Sex in the City* and felt something vibrating in his jacket pocket. He fished around and pulled out a shocking pink phone. A photo of a pretty blonde girl accompanied by the name Megan appeared on the screen. As he was glanced around the shop in search of Jo he realised he had accidentally answered the phone and put it on loud speaker.

'Hi, Jo, it's me, are you there? I can't hear you,' a strong Welsh accent said.

'It's not Jo, she's somewhere else in the shop; I'll try and find her for you. She left her phone in my coat pocket,' he explained.

'Oh!' Megan said in surprise. 'Who are you? I'm Megan by the way.'

'Magnus; I was just taking Jo shopping as she wrote off her car this morning. But don't worry, she's fine.'

'What happened? Are you sure she's ok, she's pregnant you know?' Megan asked anxiously.

'Nah, really she's OK, she's just been buying a new car, I think she's forgotten all about the poor sheep she hit earlier, nothing like a bit of retail therapy eh?' he replied, as he wandered up the aisle in search of Jo.

'So you're Magnus then? I met your mum when we came up to Shetland; she's lovely. I hear Jo's been getting to know all your family. I'm so relieved she's making friends up there. I really didn't want her to move that far away, although I can't say I blame her after what happened. You will take care of her for me won't you; she's my dearest friend? Anyway where is the crazy mare? I haven't spoken to her in days. She's obviously dumped me already,' Megan gushed, in her usual quick delivery, and lilting Welsh accent, which made it difficult for Magnus to follow everything she said.

'Hold on, I can see her now,' he replied, relieved to see Jo pushing her trolley around the corner.

'Lovely to talk to you Cariad, Bye!' Megan said sweetly.

'It's Megan for you; sorry I answered your phone by mistake.'

'Hey it's me, what's new Honey?' Jo said to Megan, whilst pulling a silly face at Magnus. Jo switched the speakerphone off before Megan said anything out loud that she wouldn't want Magnus to hear.

'What's new? How can you ask *me* that? Sounds like the drama queen has been pulling yet another stunt. I thought you moved up there for a quiet life? God, he sounds lush!'

'I think I might have to get back to you on that one,' Jo said, choosing to ignore the comment about Magnus. 'It's a long and sad story involving a sheep and I know how you Welsh get sentimental over sheep, so I'll have to break it to you gently another time. Can I ring you later this evening, or maybe tomorrow?'

'Yeah, tomorrow will be better, I have a date with the new geeky, but rather gorgeous science teacher, so wish me luck,' Megan said cheerfully.

'You don't need luck; you're a total babe, he'd be lucky to have you. Speak to you tomorrow then, take care!'

Jo hung up the phone, and noticed that Magnus was still hovering nearby.

'What does Cariad mean?' Magnus asked.

'It's Welsh for darling, but don't flatter yourself, she calls everyone that all the time.'

'And so I shouldn't be flattered you called me Honey earlier then. You city girls are so fickle!'

Jo started to push her trolley away and looked over her

shoulder at him and smiled coyly.

'You'll just have to settle for being Captain Birdseye,' she said.

Jo walked away feeling cheerful; delighted that Megan was out on a date. She felt guilty for moving away from her. Even though they both had lots of other friends in London, they had always been particularly close, and despite the miles between them now, they seemed closer still.

She turned her attention to the shopping since they didn't have too much time left. She picked up some more candles, matches and a gas lighter for the cooker, mindful of last week's power-cut and the fact that winter hadn't even got going yet. She stocked up on cleaning products and then turned the trolley into the pet food aisle remembering she now had a dog to feed. She scanned the shelves looking at the bewildering array of dog food. She caught sight of Magnus at the end of the aisle and was about to go and ask his advice when she noticed he was speaking to someone.

An attractive tall brunette woman in her early thirties was standing proprietarily close to him, and laughing at something he said. She ran her hand through her long glossy straight hair in a boldly flirtatious gesture. As a final measure, when they had finished the conversation the woman leaned in close and touched Magnus' face with one hand and kissed him on the cheek.

Jo turned back swiftly to the display of dog food hoping to look like she hadn't seen anything. Her heart was thumping and she was conscious of a sudden pang of jealousy, although she had no right to feel that way, she told herself furiously. She had never reacted like that in the past, when other women flirted with David, which had happened frequently.

She picked up a sack of dog food that looked vaguely similar to the type Jess ate.

'You don't need to buy that, I get it from a wholesale place, it's much cheaper, I'll bring some more round for Jess later,' Magnus said cheerfully, as he strode towards Jo.

Jo didn't trust herself to speak yet, so she just smiled in what she thought was a cool and casual way, and proceeded to move on.

'Jo, I've been thinking, why don't we take our time doing

the shopping and we can catch the later ferry. Do you fancy going to get a Chinese or something? It will save cooking later.'

Jo looked at him in surprise and felt herself blushing.

'Yes please Captain,' she replied in her best attempt to sound nonchalantly grateful.

'Great, just don't buy anything frozen then, or it will defrost before you get home.'

CHAPTER FIFTEEN

They finished their shopping and loaded the bags into the pickup. Jo stepped up into the passenger seat and closed the door. She suddenly felt rather tired now and her muscles were starting to ache in her back and around her ribs. She guessed it was the delayed reaction from the accident, which now seemed ages ago.

'What's up? Are you getting the spaegie?' Magnus asked, as he started the engine.

'The what?' Jo replied; not understanding the dialect.

'Spaegie. I don't know the English equivalent for it. It means the muscle ache you get when you have over exerted yourself.'

'I see; spaegie, what a great word. I think it sounds highly appropriate for what I'm starting to feel.'

Magnus laughed. 'It sounds funny when you say it. But then again Shetland words always sound funny when soothmoothers say them.'

'What's a soothmoother?' Jo raised an eyebrow at him quizzically, knowing that whatever the word meant, it had been used to describe her.

'It's a word used to describe folk who move up to Shetland. It comes from the fact that people used to arrive in Shetland from the south mouth of the harbour in Lerwick. It used to be kind of a derogatory term but not so much nowadays; it's usually said in jest.'

'I suppose I must sound a bit funny to you. Everything's pronounced so differently here. Sometimes I just don't understand people when they are talking to each other. Don't you get exhausted speaking to me in plain English all the time?' Jo asked, as they drove back towards the town centre.

'Of course not! Don't be daft. Don't you speak differently

to people sometimes, like when you're at work? I bet you spoke in a posh telephone voice without even realising it. And I heard your accent change when you spoke to your friend, you sounded like someone out of Eastenders. Ah fort you was gonna start singin roll aat da barrol,' he said in a mock cockney accent.

'I don't sound like that,' Jo protested, giggling at his unflattering impersonation of her.

Magnus parked outside the Chinese restaurant and turned to Jo.

'Now before we go inside, I'm paying okay? So no more tantrums when the waiter deliberately ignores you and hands me the bill,' Magnus said grinning provocatively at her.

'Fine by me! If you have such a sad life you have to pretend to be my husband, then I'm more than happy to fleece you out of your money,' she retorted. 'Shame I'm pregnant or I would have ordered Champagne cocktails.' She got out of the car and grinned cheekily at him.

'Thank God the divorce will be cheaper,' Magnus muttered, as he locked the car.

'No way, I'm a Catholic, I don't believe in divorce, so you're stuck with me,' She put her arm through his as they crossed the road to the restaurant, and this time she was pleased to notice he didn't flinch quite so alarmingly when she touched him.

They sat down at a table and studied the menus in silence for a while, until the waiter came along to take their order for drinks.

'Can I have a diet coke please?' Jo asked.

Magnus looked up from the menu and leaned across the table to her.

'Jo, would you mind driving home? I feel in desperate need of a cold beer.'

'Yeah, of course! No problem, what else are wives for?'

'A pint of lager then please,' he said turning to the waiter.

When the waiter had gone Jo sat and looked around the restaurant at the typical Chinese décor. She listened to the sound of the oriental music playing softly in the background, and thought how strange it was that being in an ethnic restaurant made her feel more at home. It was more familiar to her and reminiscent of London than any other place she had been to in Shetland. She felt a moment's pang of homesickness as she remembered the many evenings she had spent in Chinatown, trying out different restaurants over the years.

'Are you really a Catholic?' Magnus asked, waking Jo up from her daydream.

'Well kind of, I was brought up as one, but I'm really an atheistic now I suppose. A Catholic atheistic of course,' Jo explained, as the waiter returned with their drinks.

'What on earth's a Catholic atheistic?' Magnus picked up his glass and looked at Jo for further explanation.

'Well, you don't really believe in God anymore, but you spend your whole life feeling guilty about it, and wondering how many Hail Mary's it's gonna cost you one day when the priest finds out. Why, what religion are you?'

'That would make me a Church of Scotland atheist,' Magnus replied.

'Blimey, you really are screwed, cos if there is a God, then your protestant butt is gonna to burn in hell.'

'Good! At least you won't be there then,' he teased back.

The food arrived and they started eating. Jo regarded him thoughtfully when he wasn't looking.

'You're nothing like Jeannie described you. She said you were really shy, especially around women. That's not true at all is it?'

'That kind of depends on the situation,' he replied cryptically.

'Well you didn't seem shy in the supermarket when that gorgeous woman launched herself at you. I expected to see you running out screaming,' Jo said, as she helped herself to some more egg fried rice.

'Believe me, I was tempted, but not because I'm shy,' he said. 'Fiona's definitely not my type of woman, and she's married anyway.'

'I see, so when you're with women you don't fancy then you're not shy at all, just with the ones you do,' she suggested innocently.

'Something like that yes,' he said. 'But Jeannie doesn't often see me out socially, so she doesn't really know me like that at all, although she likes to think she does obviously.

But she bases all her assumptions on the fact that I've never taken anyone home to meet them since Lynne.'

'That makes it sound like there's been millions of women since then,' Jo said, eyeing him suspiciously, but trying hard to sound casually interested.

'Not really, just a couple, nothing of any consequence,' he replied sombrely.

Jo got the impression he didn't want to persist along this line of questioning, but at least she had found out what she wanted to know. He most certainly didn't fancy her, which was good, because it would be weird if he did. She ate in silence for a moment, hoping that he would introduce the next conversational subject. But after a while Jo started to feel uncomfortable.

'Now we've discussed religion and sex, I guess all that's left of the conversational taboos is politics. Are you a secret communist or maybe even a member of the British National Party?' Jo asked, having given up waiting for him to speak, although she had observed that he didn't appear to find the silence as awkward as she did.

'Liberal Democrat, but I don't really pay a lot of attention to politics. Most people vote LibDem up here, although the SNP are picking up more votes these days; anything to get rid of the soothmoothers.'

'Really? Is that what they want?' Jo asked in alarm, 'I thought they just wanted Scottish Independence.'

'They do, I was just joking,' he replied, laughing at her seriousness. He shook his head with amusement and picked up his glass.

Jo watched another couple enter the restaurant and sit down at a table by the window. As soon as they sat down the man reached across and took the woman's hand and held it, even when the waiter approached them with menus. Jo looked away, reminded briefly of her old life with David.

'My work was so tied up in politics and yet here I am less than two weeks after quitting my job, and I haven't so much as picked up a newspaper. There could have been a cabinet reshuffle and I wouldn't have known. It all used to be so important and now it's all so far away,' she said thoughtfully. She sipped her drink thinking how strange it was not to be caught up in what was happening in the world.

'That's the beauty of this place,' Magnus replied. 'You can escape from everything that goes on down south. Crime; traffic; politics; terrorism; it's all reassuringly far away.'

'You forgot fashion.' Jo grinned provocatively at him.

'Excuse me?'

'You forgot to add fashion to the list of things that are reassuringly far away from here.'

'You can't judge the whole of Shetland based on the shopping experience you had today,' Magnus said defensively.

'I didn't mean to insult the place. What I meant was all that fuss over style. What's hot and what's not, crap. It's all such a long way from here too; and that's a good thing isn't it? Somehow it all seems so shallow to be obsessed with appearance and I've noticed that even more since I moved here,' Jo said hastily, realising she had accidentally ruffled his feathers.

'It's hard to care about what you look like in a force nine gale,' he conceded. 'But you seemed to care very much about what you looked like in your coat.'

'But it wasn't because I wanted to be the height of fashion; I just don't want to look like the back end of a bus, or a bag lady. I have enough insecurity about my appearance already.' Under Magnus' careful scrutiny Jo started to feel uncomfortable so she tried to change the subject. 'By the way, thanks for taking me shopping today! I would never have gone in to that shop on my own. I suppose you used to get dragged in there by your wife eh?'

'No, actually, she wouldn't have been seen dead in that shop, or any other clothes shop in Shetland,' he replied, picking up his glass and finishing the beer. He signalled to the waiter for another one, and another coke for Jo.

Jo noticed an edge of bitterness to his voice when he spoke, and it crossed her mind that perhaps taking her to the shop today was some kind of test. It didn't seem appropriate to enquire about his ex-wife's taste in clothes; it sounded like a sore subject. They ate in silence for a while. Jo glanced over at the lovebirds on the other table, amused that they were still holding hands whilst attempting to eat their dinner.

'I like that outfit you bought, it suits you,' Magnus said suddenly.

'Thanks!' she said, shifting uncomfortably in her chair. 'Gosh, I really am feeling the spaegie now.'

'I don't think you should plan on doing much for a couple of days, it will be worse tomorrow. Chill out and read a book or something. Oh, I fixed your bookcases to the wall by the way, so you can safely put your books away now. I was just driving away from your house when I saw you had landed in the ditch.'

'Oh, thanks, you know that feels like such a long time ago now, it's been quite a day,' Jo replied, suddenly feeling tired.

'Yes, I think we had best get you home to bed,' he said sympathetically.

'I'm all right. I'll be fine to drive anyway,' Jo said, trying to look a bit more energetic, she was enjoying the evening and was in no rush to end it.

'I meant to tell you earlier; I won't be able to give you a lift in to town on Friday to pick up your new car. I've swapped a shift with someone so I'll be working.' He hesitated for a moment as if he had just remembered something important. 'Shit, excuse me, sorry, I forgot I was supposed to be playing darts tonight.'

He fished his phone out of his jacket pocket and dialled a number.

'Aye aye Jimmy, joost tae let de ken I'm still idda toon, I missed da bloody ferry... I'm at da muckle dyke haen me tae... yeah, aha... nah boy, dunna be coarse...she's bonnier dan de onywye...Aye, see de later boy. Cheers ee noo.' He put the phone back in his pocket. 'I'm sorry, I should warn you that the current gossip is that you and I are stepping out together.'

'Stepping out? I thought that was just an Irish expression,' Jo said looking surprised at the expression, rather than what it implied.

'Aye, well, I didn't want to convey the exact message, it was a bit crude. It's what passes for humour here,' he said.

'What's does muckle dyke mean? I think I followed the rest of your conversation,' Jo asked, changing the subject; she could imagine only too well what might have been said.

'Big wall, as in Great Wall of China, the name of the restaurant,' he explained.

'I've learnt so much today already,' she said proudly.

'Doesn't it worry you, the thought of people talking about you?' he asked as he put down his empty glass and signalled for the bill.

'Not really, it's not like I'm Madonna is it? I'm not a very interesting person so I can't imagine what people would find to say about me.' Jo shrugged and finished her drink.

'Well at the moment your presence has certainly not gone unnoticed. It's not often we get attractive single women moving to the island,' he explained.

'Yeah well, it will soon die down when the baby arrives. I'm not exactly the world's most eligible spinster am I?' Jo replied, reaching for her handbag.

'I couldn't possibly comment,' he said.

CHAPTER SIXTEEN

Jess woke Jo up by jumping up at the bedroom window and whimpering. The dog stuck her head through the curtains and wagged her tailed vigorously, then turned and limped heavily down the stairs. Jo opened her eyes and groaned. She tried to turn over to see the clock, but this was difficult, as she seemed to have been beaten up in her sleep. Every muscle in her back screamed in pain when she tried to move, and her neck was so stiff she could hardly turn her head.

The thought of poor Jess needing to go outside finally persuaded Jo to get out of bed. She dragged on her dressing gown and hobbled down the stairs and found Jess scratching at the front door. Jo was just about to open it, when it opened from the outside.

'Sorry, Jo, didn't mean to wake you, I just came by to get the pickup, and I heard Jess at the door. I thought I'd let her out for you. Are you OK, you look done in?' Magnus asked. He stood on the doorstep wearing his old boiler suit and hi-viz jacket, with Ben running around behind him.

'I feel like I've been beaten up. I can hardly move.'

'You poor thing, what you need is a hot bath and lots of rest. I'll take Jess off your hands today so you don't need to be getting up and down for her. Go on, go back to bed! Take care now,' he said kindly, and closed the front door behind him.

Jo turned and went upstairs. She felt dreadful and wished she could take something for the pain. A hot bath didn't seem entirely adequate for what she felt. She went back to bed and tried to sleep. She wondered what Ruby must have thought seeing Magnus' pickup parked outside her house all night. She couldn't have known she had dropped him off at his own house after driving home from the restaurant. Or perhaps she did, Ruby didn't seem to miss much.

She thought about how she had overreacted the day before to the way the sales people had assumed she was with Magnus. What did it matter anyway? But the truth was that now that Jo had given up her job she felt she had lost part of her identity and status, and the confidence that came with it. At this moment she wasn't quite a mother, and although she was a newly single woman, she wasn't exactly on the hunt for a new man. She was in a strange limbo land, single, jobless, and with no direction. No wonder she had been so paranoid about being overlooked. She was starting to feel invisible.

She had enjoyed her day out with Magnus. The running joke about being married had been funny. He was easy to tease and good humoured. But after a while she started to see the situation differently. Throughout the light-hearted banter they had never actually lingered on anything meaningful. She hadn't felt able to ask him anything about his past or his ex-wife and daughter. He hadn't asked anything personal about her either, even after she had volunteered information. Was he just being polite or was he completely disinterested?

Jo felt her spirits fall and she got annoyed with herself. It was stupid to be upset about this. If she had met him in a different situation she probably wouldn't even have looked twice at him. Not that he wasn't nice looking or anything, but she had always been drawn to tall, dark, good looking, skinny men, who were well groomed and intellectual. Magnus was a red-haired, freckly, rather scruffy outdoorsy type, vaguely smelling of diesel oil and kept his own sheep. Not only that but he clearly thought that women should be looked after by their husbands. This was the 21st century, Jo thought crossly; not even her dad was that old fashioned.

She got up after a while and decided to follow the advice of having a long soak in a hot bath. She poured a generous measure of *Chanel No 5* bubble bath into the tub and turned on the taps. She wouldn't be getting any more gifts like this from David she thought sadly. For all his faults he had always been generous and regularly brought her flowers, perfume, Champagne and other trinkets from his regular trips away. She realised gloomily that these were probably guilt induced presents, bought quickly at the airport or train station, without any real thought behind the gesture.

Jo climbed into the bath and slid under the beautifully scented bubbles. It did feel better, and she started to relax a little. As the bath cooled down, she topped it up with more hot water and continued like this until her fingers started to feel uncomfortably wrinkly.

It was silent and lonely in the house without Jess. She took her breakfast into the lounge and switched on the TV. The jolly repartee on the daytime chat shows grated on her nerves, so she was grateful when the phone rang.

'Hello Jo, it's Ruby. I just wanted to check you're all right now. I heard about your accident yesterday. You poor thing!'

'I'm fine, thanks for asking. My back and neck ache a bit, but I'm sure I'll feel better soon,' Jo replied, grateful for the interest in her well-being.

'Do you have a microwave?' Ruby asked.

'Yes...' Jo replied hesitantly, wondering why on earth Ruby wanted to know this.

'That's good, I was just checking.'

Jo put the phone down and thought sadly that perhaps Ruby's mental health wasn't all it should be. A few minutes later she heard the sound of the front door opening and got up to see Ruby entering the hallway, aided by her walking stick and carrying a shopping bag.

'I just thought you might like to try this. It works for me,' she said, holding out the bag to Jo.

'Come in, come and sit down in the kitchen, it's the only place I have more than one chair at the moment," Jo said, taking the bag from Ruby and leading her into the kitchen.

'Are you sure? I don't want to get in your way.'

'Don't be silly, I was just going to put the kettle on anyway and you'll have to explain what to do with this,' Jo said, peering into the bag at the long tartan beanbag.

'Of course; I'll show you.' Ruby followed Jo into the kitchen and sat down at the table. 'You're getting this looking very nice and homely now,' she said, looking around approvingly at the room.

'Thanks. I think this is the only room that's completely done, I still don't have a sofa yet and I haven't unpacked everything in all the other rooms.'

'Oh, you have plenty of time for all that. Anyway you should be taking it easy now and not working too hard. I'm glad you asked Magnus to help you with the furniture, he is always blyde to be useful.'

'I didn't ask him actually, he just kind of took over, bless him, but I really appreciated it anyway,' Jo explained, as she walked over to the sink to fill the kettle.

'I hear you're going to be doing a curry for the poker night. That will be super! I don't like curry much myself, but it seems all the young folk do, I think it will be a great success.'

'I'll tell you what then, I'll make you a special extremely mild curry just for you. I'm sure that will convert you,' Jo said, as she opened up the dishwasher to get some clean mugs out.

Ruby laughed. 'I guess I'm not too old to try new things, I'll give it a go.'

'Ten years is a long time to be on your own isn't it, you must miss him dreadfully,' Jo said, as she made the tea. She was thinking about how hard it must be for Ruby to commemorate the loss of her husband with a social event, even though it would be raising money for charity.

'Yes, time is not the great healer that I hoped it would be, but I'm not really on my own thankfully. It's been lovely having Jeannie and Magnie so close. And Robbie comes up from Aberdeen a fair bit too. I'm very lucky really. Some of my friends have seen their children grow up and move away from Shetland. They hardly get to see them or their grandbairns; I couldn't bear that,' Ruby said.

'That would be tough,' Jo agreed, as she set some plates on the table and a selection of shop-bought cakes and biscuits.

'I know Magnie is itching to get away from here, I think he wants to go and join his cousin down in New Zealand. I've told him he should just go, he really needs to find a new life for himself, but he won't hear of it. I feel bad sometimes; I know he's just waiting until I'm gone. But I'm in no hurry to leave,' she said cheerfully, choosing a cake from the plate Jo had set out.

'No! I don't think he's waiting for that. That's a horrible

thought,' Jo exclaimed.

'Oh, I didn't mean it like that. It's just that he seems to feel so responsible for me. I know he's the eldest and all, but I wish he would feel able to do what he really wants to do, without worrying about me. It makes me feel guilty, but at the same time, I don't really want him to go away either.' She shook her head sadly. 'It's not easy being a mother.'

'I shall be finding that out for myself soon enough eh? Anyway, what do I do with this beanbag thing?' she asked, pulling it out of the bag.

'Put it in the microwave for two minutes on high and then your wrap it around your neck. It helps you relax, and it smells bonny too, it's got lavender in it.'

Jo put the bag in the microwave to try it. When she pulled it out, it felt slightly damp and steamy and it reeked of lavender. She wrapped it around her neck and sat down again. It was surprisingly pleasant.

'Thanks; this is brilliant. It was nice of you to bring it over for me, but I could have come over to get it,' Jo said, thinking of Ruby's difficulty in walking any distance.

'That's OK, I need to get outside sometimes; I'm not used to being indoors so much. I'd rather be out on the croft working. I hate having to get Magnie and Jeannie to do things for me. But I've got my hip replacement operation booked for just after Christmas, so hopefully things will get better then. I'll be like a new woman again!'

That evening after dinner Jo picked up the phone to ring Megan.

'Tell me all about your date then. How was it and where did you go?' she asked Megan, getting comfortable in the armchair ready for a long gossip.

'It was okay... Well actually it was a little bit disappointing,' Megan replied. 'We went out for dinner and it was a bit of a disaster really.'

'Why, what happened?' Jo asked anxiously.

'Well first we took ages deciding where to go. Can you believe this, but he doesn't eat any kind of foreign food and he's a vegetarian? Not that I'm against being a veggie, but really, how can you be a vegetarian and not like Indian,

Chinese, Thai, Italian or any other foreign food? That's just mad isn't it? That rules out 99% of all the decent restaurants in London. So we ended up going to this seriously hip vegan restaurant, which served up miniscule portions of, well basically lettuce, mushrooms and lentils. I was starving afterwards. And then to make matters worse, he doesn't drink either, and the restaurant didn't serve any alcohol. And I *so* needed a rum and coke by then.'

Jo was giggling throughout Megan's indignant description of her night out.

'So what did you talk about?' Jo asked trying hard to stop laughing.

'Oh God, he was so boring. He just seemed to want to convert me to his bizarre veggie ways. You know; no leather shoes, handbags, or jackets. I never realised anything like this about him at work. He always came over as a really sweet, funny and intelligent man, and he is criminally good looking. I wondered if I should persevere in case the shag was worth it, but I just couldn't bring myself to speak to him any longer. So I went home early with a migraine. He said it was because I have too many toxins in my body. I managed to stop myself from saying that it was a fake migraine induced by terminally toxic boredom; after all I still have to work with the freaky geek. Anyway, more to the point, how was your date?' Megan asked.

'It wasn't a date! He just took me shopping to buy a new car and we ended up going for a Chinese afterwards. It was quite nice, but a bit strange too. I don't really know what to make of him really.' Jo told Megan about her unfortunate accident with the sheep and the day out in Lerwick, and then described the two previous evenings she had spent with Magnus.'

'So you don't think it's a date, but yet this man has come round to your house bearing exotic gifts of fresh fish, conveniently at dinner time. He puts together all your furniture while you cook him an Indian then comes round again to finish the work in the morning and dramatically pulls you out of the wreckage after your accident, and takes you shopping and pretends to be your husband all day. What exactly is your understanding of the word date?' Megan asked dramatically.

Jo was laughing at Megan's interpretation and couldn't speak for a bit. 'It wasn't like that at all; he was just being friendly and helpful. You are reading far too much into it.'

'Maybe,' she replied dubiously. 'Did he stare longingly into your eyes and make unnecessary physical contact?'

'No, in fact if you put a gun to his head I bet he couldn't tell you what colour my eyes are, and the only time he ever touched me it was more like the way you would with a naughty child. You know, dragging me along by my elbow to look at the coats in the fish shop. And when I put my arm through his in the street I could feel him freeze as if he was terrified. But he didn't do that when that old slapper kissed him in the supermarket,' Jo protested.

'Jo, don't be ridiculous, I bet you were too far away to see how he reacted. Anyway, what do you think of him? I think he sounds lovely, the perfect gentleman, and he has a seriously sexy voice. I wish I'd seen him when I was up there.'

'I don't know what I think, that's the trouble. I like him, but I haven't thought about what it might be like to kiss him or anything so I don't think I fancy him. I just don't know how to behave anymore. We were flirting and being silly all day yesterday, but I think that just substituted for a real conversation. And I'm not sure it's really appropriate for me to act like that when I'm pregnant with another man's child. It's a bit tacky isn't it?' Jo said mournfully. She sat on the floor in the lounge trying to stretch her back in her best attempt at a yoga pose, whilst holding the phone to her ear.

'Jo, you won't always be pregnant. One day you'll get back to being your normal gorgeous self, only with a lovely daughter named Megan, and then you can see what happens. You might meet someone else up there. I hear there are more single men than single women in Shetland, so if I get desperate enough I might join you.'

'Very funny, and why are you so certain I'm having a girl, which I'm not going to call Megan by the way, well at least not as a first name anyway.'

'Just a feeling, and no, Megan is not a great name to have, I'm sure some of my darling pupils have nicknamed me Smeggy Meggy. Charming little bastards! Have you got any names in mind yet?'

'Not really, although I was thinking of going with

something Irish, kind of getting back to my roots, and it would go nicely with McMorrow. The only trouble is most people have trouble pronouncing some of the prettiest names. Anyway, plenty of time for that; how's your job application going?' Jo asked, determined to turn the conversation back around to Megan's life.

'It's ok, the closing date is on Friday, and the interviews will be during the half term holiday I think. But I've been scouting around the estate agents already, seeing what I might be able to afford if I get it. My dad's going to let me have £30,000 when he retires from his partnership in January. He wants me to have something for a deposit on a flat. They just told me they're thinking of buying a place in Spain, and living there during the winter and coming back to Cardiff in the summer. I think Dad wants to rent out the holiday flat for another income,' Megan explained happily.

Jo could hear the pent up excitement in her voice at the prospect of buying somewhere of her own.

'That's really good news isn't it,' Jo replied. 'And you'll be able to have cheap holidays in Spain now as well. Have you seen any decent flats in Ealing?'

'No way, they're still way too expensive even if I get both the promotion and the deposit. I'm probably going to have to move somewhere cheaper and get the tube in to school. Although I did see one quite nice flat overlooking the park, well studio really. It was just one room with a bathroom and kitchenette in the third floor attic of a converted house. But the view's nice and it's walking distance from school so it would be ideal, and I'd stay nice and fit walking up and down those stairs.'

'I hope it's still on the market when you get around to buying,' Jo said hopefully.

Jo had an early night, going to bed almost as soon as she had finished her call to Megan. It was quiet in the bedroom without Jess snoring, and as she didn't get her early morning alarm call from the dog either, she slept in until after ten.

Rain lashed down the windows and Jo prepared herself for another day in the house. The stiffness had eased a little so she decided to put away her books now that the bookcase was safely in place. She sat in the office most of the day, putting things away or surfing the net now that the computer had a desk, and she had a comfortable chair to sit on. She replied to her emails and edited the events of the previous two weeks to make them sound witty and interesting. She had no intention of letting anyone believe that she had any reason to regret moving here.

Nobody rang her or called around, so other than booking a taxi she had not said a word all day. She hadn't seen Magnus go by for his normal walk on the beach. Growing paranoia made her wonder whether he was trying to avoid her. She sat and watched TV all evening, drinking endless cups of tea and resorting to forbidden chocolate biscuits. During a re-run of one of her favourite sitcoms there was a scene where an expectant couple go to have a scan. There was a nauseatingly cute moment where they gushed over the first sighting of their baby on the monitor. Moments earlier the couple had been bickering but this had been forgotten now and they hugged and kissed joyfully. Jo remembered that she had laughed the first time she watched it. This time she switched off the TV in disgust and stomped off to bed feeling sorry for herself. There would be nobody to kiss and make up with at her own scan tomorrow she thought moodily.

CHAPTER SEVENTEEN

Jo put on her one and only maternity outfit in readiness for her day out. The top smelt vaguely of Chinese food so she liberally sprayed on some perfume to cover it up. The taxi pulled up outside and Jo grabbed her coat and bag and hopped into the passenger seat.

During the five-minute ride to the ferry the driver bombarded her with questions about how she was enjoying her new life. Jo replied as brightly as possible she was having the time of her life. After all, in many ways it was no exaggeration.

Jo boarded the ferry and ran upstairs to the lounge. She sat down and stared out of the window at the harbour. There were lots of other passengers in the lounge. Most of them smiled and said hello to her. She noticed little groups of people sitting together and gossiping, and she thought back to her many journeys on the underground where nobody spoke for the entire journey. The cars started loading on and after a while more passengers came upstairs to get coffee and to take advantage of the warmth.

An older couple sat down at the table next to Jo and immediately started chatting to Jo about the weather and how cold it was turning. They asked whether she was going in to town to go shopping. Jo explained that she was catching the bus for a hospital visit and then she was going to collect her new car.

'Of course! You're the young lady that had the accident with the sheep. What a fine start to island life eh? I'm going in to the hospital too so we can give you a lift if you like, save you walking all the way from the bus station in this cold,' the woman offered kindly.

'Thanks; that would be lovely.'

Jo was becoming accustomed to the generosity of strangers here, and realised that saying no would sound standoffish and unfriendly. She had no idea who these people were but felt sure she would find out by the end of the journey.

That afternoon Jo got into her new car and drove it off the forecourt. It felt great. It was not substantially bigger than an ordinary car, but the extra height and the sturdy design made her feel more confident on the road. Everything was going well again. Healthy baby and a brand new car, what more could a girl ask for? She headed off north towards home

Jo left Lerwick and set off for the Whalsay ferry. She wondered whether she would get Jess back soon, she was feeling so much better now and wanted to get out and stretch her legs on the beach, if it wasn't too dark when she got home.

She sat in the queue and waited, fiddling with the new radio and flicking through the car manual, feeling inordinately proud of her new vehicle. Jo drove on to the ferry and waited in the car until the ticket collector came round. She bought a book of prepaid discount tickets as Magnus had suggested she should do to save money on fares. She felt like a local now, as she tucked the rest of the tickets into the screen visor. As she walked across the car deck to go up to the lounge she saw Magnus standing in the doorway of the engine room, wearing a blue boiler suit and a yellow fluorescent vest with a set of ear defenders slung around his neck. He smiled at her.

Jo wanted to go over and speak but knew that it would be inappropriate as the ferry was about to pull out. Instead she waved and smiled back. She went upstairs and sat down by the window and looked out.

Black and white cattle grazed the low-lying land close to the ferry terminal and a cluster of houses sprawled over the hills. Close to the sandy shore two tiny derelict stone cottages looked like they had been abandoned a century ago. Jo wondered what it would have been like to live in such a pretty place but without the benefit of decent heating and lighting.

She was still daydreaming out of the window when a familiar face appeared beside her, along with a pretty woman who was rather obviously pregnant.

'I thought it was you. How are you doing now?' Mark said to Jo, standing aside to let his wife sit down. 'This is Sarah; we thought we would come over and sit with you if that's alright.'

'Yeah, of course, nice to meet you Sarah, I'm Jo.'

'Hi, it's great to meet someone else who is new to the island; and pregnant too. Are you going to go to that new class that Jeannie is starting up?' Sarah asked.

'Yeah, I'm looking forward to it, I just had my first scan today and it made me realise how little I know when the radiographer was talking to me. I just bought a book on the subject. Jeannie was right, it kind of makes gruesome reading, but then again I just flicked through it in the shop, so I probably just looked at all the wrong things,' Jo explained, feeling an immediate bond with the other pregnant woman.

'I know what you mean. Have you got the scan picture on you?' Sarah asked.

'Yes, here it is,' Jo said, delighted to be able to show someone the photo that she had spent much of the afternoon poring over.

'Isn't it amazing how clear they are these days? My sister had a baby about ten years ago and the photo she brought home from the scan was completely incomprehensible to me. It just looked like two little grey blobs. This is a real baby isn't it? Sarah said.

'I know! I can't believe it's real. I can't feel anything yet and it was only three days ago that I stopped being able to do up the button on my trousers properly. I just don't feel pregnant yet, but at least now I have proof,' Jo said happily.

'You're very lucky then, poor Sarah was throwing up for weeks in the beginning.' Mark said, taking the photo to look at.

'God yes, it was awful, I lost half a stone, they talked about admitting me to hospital as I was getting so ill. But thankfully since then everything is much better,' Sarah said, pulling faces at the memory of it.

'When's yours due?' Jo asked, trying not to stare at

Sarah's bump.

'25th of January, Burns night. What about you?'

'31st March, according to the radiographer,' Jo replied.

They chatted away for the rest of the journey about babies and their recent moves to Shetland, comparing it favourably to life in a city, but also discussing what they missed, which was mainly friends and family. Just as the ferry was docking Sarah invited Jo to come round to see her in the week and also invited her to a jewellery party.

'A jewellery party?' Jo queried, as they walked down the stairs to their cars.

'You know, kind of like a Tupperware party, but for jewellery, it's just an excuse to sit around and gossip and you can buy stuff if you want, no obligation of course, but I thought I would hold one just in time for Christmas,' Sarah explained.

'Of course, I'd love to come! See you soon!' Jo didn't care what kind of party it would be; it was great to be invited to any kind of social event.

She got into the car and started the engine. As she waited for the ramp to drop down, a tap on her window startled her. She fumbled around for the electric window.

'Nice car Mrs Birdseye! Watch out for the sheep won't you, they're after revenge,' Magnus said, grinning at her.

'Thanks for reminding me of my misfortune!' Jo said smiling back. 'I was just wondering when I might get Jess back again, that's if you still want me to look after her for you?' she added hopefully.

'Of course, just stop by on your way home and you can pick her up. I've just finished my shift, I'll be along in a few minutes,' he said.

'Okay!' Jo replied, just as one of Magnus' colleagues was signalling for her to drive off.'

She moved off slowly and as she passed the group of ferrymen gathered around the little office on the pier, one of them jumped back in mock terror of her. Jo pulled a face at him as she drove past, and they all laughed.

CHAPTER EIGHTEEN

Jo had never been to Magnus' house before and was curious to see inside, although she stopped to consider that he might just intend for her to pick up the dog without staying very long. It was Friday evening after all, and he probably had other plans.

She parked on his drive and sat waiting in the car for him to get home. Five minutes later he pulled up next to her.

'Goodness me woman, I thought you would have least have put the kettle on, what are you doing out here?' Magnus joked, as Jo got out of her car.

'I didn't like to just walk in and I thought it might be locked.'

'I hardly ever lock up and you can walk in anytime you like,' he said, opening up the porch door.

'I can't get used to this idea of just walking in to people's houses yet. It seems rude somehow. What if they're doing something?'

'Like what; pole dancing in their front room? Drug dealing in the kitchen?'

'You know what I mean,' she said, amused at the images he had conjured up.

'Well you might find that the front door would be keyed if there was anything like that going on. Which is why sadly, I never feel the need to lock my front door.'

She followed him through to the kitchen trying hard not to appear too nosy. Magnus walked straight across to the French doors that led out to a patio and came back a few seconds later with the two dogs.

They both scampered around the kitchen and came over to greet Jo who crouched down to make a fuss of them.

'I guess *I'll* have to put the kettle on then,' he said,

sighing dramatically and walking over to the sink to wash his hands before filling the kettle. 'Honestly, after a hard day at work, the least I'd expect is a cup of coffee from my wife.'

'Ha, ha, very funny,' Jo replied. 'I've had a busy day too you know. I had my first scan today.'

'Really, did you bring back a photo?' he asked, turning round from the kitchen sink.

Jo dug around in her handbag for the picture; she was surprised by his interest.

'Aw, that's sweet; she looks just like her mother.'

'How do you know it's a girl?' Jo said, snatching the photo back and staring at it, trying to work out what he meant.

'I don't, I was just teasing you. Do they know what it is yet?'

'Not yet, I have to go back in a few weeks for another scan and then possibly another one after that, in case I have something called placenta previa,' Jo explained, as she put the precious photo back in her handbag.

'Well, let's hope not... Are you hungry?' Magnus asked.

Jo hesitated. She didn't want to impose herself on him, and didn't know whether he was just being polite or whether it was a genuine invitation. Magnus leaned back against the kitchen worktop waiting for an answer.

'I don't want to get in your way, aren't you going out tonight?'

'Nah, Julia Roberts couldn't make it.' He passed her a mug of tea and grinned cheekily.

'I see. Well in that case, I suppose I could cancel George Clooney, and keep you company instead.'

'George is way too old for you. Anyway we need to plan this poker gig. Let me just go and get changed, as I can see you're not overly impressed with my boiler suit.'

'It's not your colour!'

'Nothing's my colour with this hair.' He smiled an acknowledgement that he knew she had been teasing him and left the room and ran up the stairs, with Ben following closely.

Jo sat at the dining table drinking her tea and taking advantage of his absence to check out the kitchen. Magnus' house was quite new and seemed enormous compared with her cosy cottage. The kitchen was twice the size of hers, with a large dining area containing a table that would comfortably seat eight. The appliances were all expensive brands, and everything gleamed as if it was brand new. A huge American style fridge hummed quietly in the corner, with a large wine rack beside it. Jo heard a shower running upstairs and stood up to look out of the window but it was dark outside. Moonlight bounced off the sea below the house, and she guessed that there would be a breath-taking view in the daylight. To one side of the garden she could just make out a large fenced off area with a kennel, which she guessed the dogs had been in all day.

One door leading from the kitchen was ajar so she peeked in. It was a utility room and well-stocked larder with a large chest freezer at one end. Jo sat down again at the table quickly as she heard the shower stop above her.

A few minutes later Ben trotted in followed by Jess and Magnus.

'Is this better, Madam?' he asked.

'Much!' she said approvingly; observing the way he seemed to lose three stone just by changing out of the unflattering boiler suit. He was really quite lean and fit looking in the black jeans and tee shirt he was now wearing.

'Good! Where's my dinner then?' he asked cheerfully. 'Good God, you haven't even got started yet. What have you been doing all this time; looking for the family silver?'

Jo blushed guiltily.

'I haven't been anywhere yet. And aren't you supposed to be cooking me dinner, it's your turn?' she replied.

'True, but why don't we start with the grand tour of the house. I know you're dying to see it. And after all I practically grew up in your house, so it's only fair.'

'I'm not...' Jo started to protest, but stood up to follow him anyway.

'Right, well here's the lounge, which you're not seeing at its best as it's dark and you canna see da bonny view.'

Jo walked over to the full-length windows at one end of the room. She could see shadowy outlines of a boundary fence running down towards the sea. She turned away from the window and spotted a piano in the corner of the room, with a fiddle case lying on top, but didn't get a chance to comment before he led her back to the hall. 'Next we have an office... a bathroom... and a bedroom, and through that door is the garage.

Jo's first impression was that everything seemed unnaturally tidy. The décor was neutral and could be considered rather chic with its predominant use of ivory and taupe, but Jo thought it looked somewhat austere, and definitely lacking a feminine touch. She had to stop herself from mentally redecorating each room as she viewed them. In her opinion Magnus needed some more colour in his house.

'Why do you have a bedroom downstairs?' Jo asked curiously.

'Most Shetland homes do, saves moving when you get too ancient to make it up the stairs to bed. Magnus explained, shrugging as if it was an unusual question.

'I see, so that explains why my spare bed ended up downstairs in what I was going to use as my office,' Jo said.

'Probably, that room used to be my Aunt's bedroom. Do you want to see upstairs?'

'Yeah, sure,' Jo said cautiously.

'Another bathroom ... a spare bedroom, and this was Ella's room,' he said, hesitating for a while in the doorway of his daughter's old bedroom.

Jo stood in the doorway and peeked into the child's bedroom. It was unfurnished but still decorated in pink and lilac with a mural of butterflies and flowers on one wall.

'It's pretty, did you decorate it?'

'Most of it, although Lynne painted the mural,' he said, turning off the light and closing the door firmly.

'Wow, she's a good artist,' Jo remarked, almost to herself.

'And this is my room,' he said, walking in to the bedroom and switching on the light.

The room was huge with a large archway leading to an ensuite bathroom and walk-in wardrobe. Jo guessed he had redecorated it after his wife had left, as it seemed rather overtly masculine, decorated in pale blue and ivory, and completely lacking any frippery like cushions and ornaments. The only picture on the wall was a watercolour of an old croft house in the snow. The king size bed was covered in a plain denim blue duvet cover. It was all immaculately tidy.

'Did you build this house all by yourself?' Jo asked in amazement. 'It's huge.'

'Well not exactly by myself; I'm not superhuman. But I did do a lot of it, with help from Fraser, my brother Robbie and some local builders. I drew up the designs for it though... Anyway, what would you like for your tea then?'

'I don't mind,' Jo said, as they walked back downstairs. She was still surprised at how lovely the house was and wasn't thinking about food.

'Well we have a choice of lamb or fish basically, and whatever vegetables I pulled out of the garden.'

'Whatever; you choose,' Jo said, not wishing to sound fussy.

'OK, lamb steaks it is then,' he said, disappearing into the utility room.

'Are they from your own lambs?' Jo asked, staring doubtfully at the two steaks he had put into a microwave dish to defrost.

'Of course, where do you imagine I got them from? Don't tell me you don't want to eat poor old Nelly?' he said, and laughed as Jo's eyes widened in horror. 'I'm kidding, it's not a pet lamb; I'm not that much of a monster. Honestly, a fine crofter's wife you'd make.'

'Sorry, sorry, carry on,' Jo replied. 'I'm just used to seeing meat all neatly packaged in the supermarket and not thinking about where it came from.'

'Do you have any problems with home grown vegetables? Or are you going to get upset about the carrots being pulled up before their time?'

'Stop taking the piss out of me, it's not my fault I didn't grow up in the country,' Jo said, finally feeling the brunt of his humour.

'It's the best entertainment I've had all day, winding you up. I've missed you these past couple of days. Although I must admit the roads have been safer without you?' he said.

'Can I do something to help?' she asked, ignoring the jibe.

'I'll have a glass of red wine please. And I think you'll find some juice or coke in the fridge for yourself, unless you want some more tea.'

Jo went over to the wine rack and selected a bottle of

Australian Shiraz. She opened the glazed cupboard where she noticed the glasses were kept and picked out a wine glass for him and a tumbler for the soft drink. It felt weird making herself so much at home, but he didn't seem to be treating it as a big deal. She helped herself to ice cubes from the dispenser in the fridge, and poured out some orange juice and took the drinks back to the counter. Magnus had defrosted the lamb and was expertly dicing up vegetables.

'Could you get me some blackcurrants from the freezer please? He asked Jo, just as she was about to sit down.

She rooted around in the freezer and pulled out a plastic tub and carried it back to the kitchen.

'Thanks Pumpkin!' He grinned mischievously at her.

'It's not too late for me to go home you know.' Jo made a face at him as she pulled out the barstool from the breakfast bar and sat down where she could watch him cook. She realised she had moved the stool uncomfortably close to where he was standing, so she edged it discreetly away again.

'I'm sorry, I shouldn't call you that,' he said trying unsuccessfully to sound serious, whilst opening the tub and emptying the fruit into a small saucepan. 'It's just you remind me of Ella, and that's what I used to call her.'

'How do I remind you of her?'

'Well you don't look like her obviously, although she had dark curly hair too, but it's more the way you frown, and the way you put your hands on your hips, like this, when you're mad at me. It's really funny and cute, well it was on a three year old, maybe not so much on a thirty year old,' he said, miming Jo's expressions perfectly, which she couldn't help but find funny.'

'I'm not thirty,' Jo said, after she had regained her composure.

'Oh, no don't tell me I've offended you again?' Magnus groaned dramatically.

'No, that's a compliment actually, I'm 35.'

'Really, you have worn well, I'm surprised,' he said, leaning towards her and studying her face intently. 'No lines at all, well I guess all you city girls resort to Botox nowadays.'

'I have not had Botox!' she retorted indignantly, 'And what do you know about such things anyway?'

'I can read you know,' he replied, as he lit the gas under

the vegetables. 'And I have actually been known to watch television occasionally, so I do know something about what goes on in the world.'

'Anyway, how old are you?' Jo asked, noticing she had touched a nerve.

'39, I'll be forty next summer, so if you are still around maybe you can cater for my big party.'

'What do you mean, *if* I'm still around?'

'Well some soothmoothers high tail it out of here after their first winter. They're just too soft for our climate.'

'I have no intention of leaving here; for at least five years anyway,' Jo replied emphatically.

'Why five years? What's going to happen to you then, have you got some strange Cinderella type deadline going on?' He paused in the middle of turning the steaks over under the grill while he waited for her to answer.

'That's how long I've got off work, kind of like a long sabbatical. I have to go back in five years, or resign and find another job. I haven't made up my mind what I would do instead yet. But that's roughly how long my savings will last, so long as I stop buying new cars and expensive new clothes obviously,' Jo explained.

Magnus carried on cooking, wrapped up in his own thoughts. Jo didn't know what else to talk about now. She really wanted to ask him about his wife, but it felt too intrusive. She watched him take a sip of wine as he stirred the blackcurrant sauce on the hob, she would dearly love to have had a glass too. After quite a long silence she finally plucked up the courage to question him.

'How come you still live here all by yourself, you seem like a really nice guy and you have this lovely big house, you must be a bit of a catch surely?' Jo asked boldly, and then instantly wishing she could retract the question when she saw the heavy-hearted look on his face.

'It's not quite that simple is it?' Magnus replied quietly. 'First of all it takes a while to get over having your whole life destroyed by someone you trusted. Then once you get over that, you look around and discover you're fast approaching 40, and all of the lasses you know around your own age are either married, or divorced from one of your best mates, or worse still, related to you in some way. There's not a whole lot to choose from, unless you want to get a mail order bride from Bangkok, or start chasing after really young lasses, who probably wouldn't look twice in my direction.' There was a tiny edge of bitterness in his voice, which made Jo feel uncomfortable.

'Well, if I were you I'd go for the mail order bride then, at least you might get some interesting dinners cooked for you,' she said, in an attempt to lighten the conversation a little.

'That's true,' he conceded, smiling briefly. 'What about you then? Are you going to keep your pal George Clooney on your speed dial, or trawl the net for some Russian hunk who wants a work permit?' he asked as he put the lamb steaks under the grill.

'I don't think I'm in the market for a man right now, Russian hunk or not. Although I will bear that in mind for later, thanks.'

Jo decided that her foray into the personal had not been wise and tried another tack. She sipped at the orange juice in silence and watched him, dredging through the depths of her mind trying to find something interesting to talk about.

'Do you play the piano?' I noticed you had one in the lounge,' she said at last.

'Yeah sometimes, but not as much as the fiddle though. Why, can you?' he replied, not looking up from the stove where he was checking the vegetables.

'No, sadly I'm musically incompetent, I can't even play the tambourine,' she said, getting up from her seat and helping herself to some more orange juice and then topping up his glass with wine.

'Don't be silly, anyone can play a tambourine,' he said, shaking his head in disbelief at her.

'No really, I'm completely uncoordinated and can never get the beat right,' she replied sitting back down at the table.

'Oh dear, that is a tragedy. No wonder you have such strange taste in music.' He turned to face her, grinning from ear to ear.

'What do you know about my taste in music?' Jo watched him serving up the dinner. He appeared to be highly amused at something, but she had no idea what he was finding so funny.

'I meant to tell you, I emptied out your old car of all the

CDs and trash you had in it. It was going to be collected to take to the dump, so I saved them from being crushed,' he explained.

'Crumbs, I forgot all about them!' Jo said, trying to remember what else she had left in the car, and completely neglecting to thank him in her anxiety of what else he might have found.

'It's all in a bag in the hall, I kept meaning to bring it round but I've been busy,' he said, gesturing towards the hallway.

Jo went to fetch the bag. Inside she found her collection of ancient CD's, a couple of lipsticks, a worn looking Jodi Picoult paperback, a road atlas, an assortment of pens, coins, packets of tissues, an unopened packet of tights and another carrier bag inside the first that contained some clean underwear and a toothbrush. Oh shit, how embarrassing, Jo thought, as she walked back to the kitchen.

'Tea's ready when you are,' Magnus said, clearly amused at her discomfiture.

Jo dropped the bag on the floor by the door and walked over to the table.

'Don't worry, I haven't been looking through all your stuff,' he said.

'But you noticed my CD collection enough to pass judgement on my musical taste,' Jo retorted, before taking a sip of her drink.

'Only enough to see I didn't recognise any of it. Other than the Spice Girls, it all seems to be foreign music.' He put the plates down on the table and sat down opposite her.

Jo jumped up again and retrieved one of her CDs from the carrier bag, then loaded up the portable stereo on the windowsill.

'You don't mind do you?' she asked, after she had already pressed play.

'No you go right ahead, I'm all ears,' he said, picking up his wine glass and waiting for her to come back to the table.

A mournful but melodic piece of orchestral music filled the room; Jo turned it down a touch and then sat down again. A few seconds later a woman's voice joined in.

'Who's this?' Magnus asked.

'It's a Lebanese singer called Fairuz,' Jo replied, picking

up her knife and fork.

'Can you speak this language, it's Arabic isn't it?' he asked, frowning in concentration at the unfamiliar voice.

'Yeah it is, and no I can't, but a friend translated some of it for me once; they're just love songs. But I love the sound of it, don't you? It's brilliant background music, as you don't find yourself concentrating on the lyrics, and trying to sing along, although actually sometimes I do try, and you really wouldn't want to hear that,' Jo said.

'I see, well it's very nice, so I take it back about your musical taste, well apart from the Spice Girls that is,' he conceded.

'Oh that, that's just to sing along in the car with my friends, when we're going out,' Jo explained, remembering many a journey with Megan and her other girlfriends, singing along at the tops of their voices to a variety of seriously uncool pop songs.

Jo started tucking into the food, ignoring the pangs of homesickness brought on by thinking about nights out with her friends in London. Magnus had made lamb steaks with a tart blackcurrant sauce, mashed potatoes, carrots and runner beans. Jo thought it was delicious.

'Do you cook like this all the time? It's fabulous!' she said enthusiastically.

'Thanks! Not every day, some weeks I have to work all evening so I don't cook then. But if I have plenty of time I do; after all I have to do something useful with all the lamb I get, not to mention the fish, and the vegetables and blackcurrants that grow in the garden.'

'You're almost self-sufficient aren't you?' Jo said admiringly.

'Well I haven't figured out a way to grow grapes up here so I will always need to buy my own wine, unfortunately. But I'm thinking of putting up a wind turbine to get cheaper electricity, although it's kind of expensive to install so I might wait until I know what I'm doing long term.'

Jo took this to mean the possibility of moving to New Zealand and was going to enquire further but the phone interrupted them.

'Excuse me,' Magnus said, getting up to answer it. 'Aye aye boy! No, no da night I'm kinda busy eenoo, ...Yeah, could be, but den du wid ken dat onywye seein as du's been spyin' on me... Nah, fuck off! ... Yeah,... I'll see de at da ferry da moarn. Cheers eenoo.'

Magnus sighed, sat back down again and picked up his wine glass. 'Sorry about that, maybe you should have hidden your car in my garage. I'm not doing much for your reputation.'

'I don't suppose I'm doing much for yours either,' she said despondently.

'Actually I think you are. The boys I work with all think you're pretty hot stuff,' he said, winking at her.

'I don't suppose they know I'm pregnant then,'

'Course they do, you can't keep secrets like that around here for long.'

'Oh dear, what must people think of me?' Jo asked sadly.

'I thought you didn't care what people thought,' he said, raising an eyebrow at her.

'Well I lied, I do care, I'm not used to being noticed or being the centre of attention,' she said, putting her fork down on the plate. 'Oh shit, I've spilt blackcurrant sauce on my new top!' Jo jumped up from her seat and heading for the roll of paper towels.

'Damn, it will ruin it! Take it off and let me rinse it out for you,' Magnus said looking at the purple stain on her top. 'Run upstairs and get something out of the wardrobe to put on,' he added, looking at the alarm on her face at the idea of taking her top off.

Jo turned and hurried up the stairs. She opened the door to the walk-in wardrobe in his bedroom, and surveyed the row of shirts that looked like the uniform shirts that the ferrymen wore. She pulled an ancient looking Scotland rugby shirt off a hanger and put it on and went downstairs to the kitchen carrying her top.

'Give it here, I've got something that should take the stain out,' he said, holding out his hand to take it from her.

He took it into the utility room and sprayed on some cleaning product. She saw him check the label and then throw it in the washing machine and set it going.

'I seem to be making a habit of wearing your clothes,' Jo said, as she rolled up the overly long sleeves.

'I think it would be more worrying if I started wearing yours,' he replied.

'Can I wash up? Jo asked after they had finished eating. I should at least do something useful after you cooked me that lovely dinner.'

'That's OK; I'll just throw it all in the dishwasher. Maybe you can feed the dogs; I expect their fanting now; starving that is. Their food's in the utility room under the sink.'

Jo went to feed Ben and Jess and Magnus loaded the dishwasher. The kitchen was a cosy scene of domestic harmony, which they both noticed in their own way, and both felt vaguely uncomfortable about. Magnus watched Jo crouching down next to the dogs, making a particular fuss over Jess. Then she stood up and pushed her curly hair back behind her ears and left the dogs to their supper. She caught his eye and smiled shyly at him.

'I was going to offer you some ice cream but I'm not sure I want Ben and Jerry's *Chunky Monkey* dropped down the front of my favourite rugby shirt. Given that you're clearly not a Scotland fan I wouldn't put it past you to ruin it on purpose,' Magnus said,

'*Chunky Monkey*, that's my favourite!' shrieked Jo childishly. 'I promise I won't ruin your shirt. Boy you sure know the way to a woman's heart!'

'Left hand door of the fridge,' he directed, as he reached up to a cupboard to take out two bowls.

'Hey, you've got *Cherry Garcia* too, who were you saving that for?' she demanded cheekily, and went to take the both cartons out of the freezer compartment before it occurred to her that she looked just a tad piggish and put one back.

'Come here, you can have a bit of both. After all there are two of you now.'

Jo looked a bit sheepish and handed the cartons over to him and sat down.

'At least you are not one of those women who never eat anything, that's so annoying,' he said, dishing out a generous helping of ice cream into the bowls.

'I wish I had that kind of willpower,' Jo said quietly, genuinely believing she would rather be annoying and skinny, than chubby but good company at the dinner table.

'Don't be stupid, you're fine as you are,' he said passing

her a bowl and a spoon.

'Are you going to entertain me on the piano or the fiddle later?' Jo asked, inwardly savouring the unexpected compliment.

'Possibly, but you'll hear me at the wedding if not.'

'Yeah, but that's not the same as having your own personal serenade is it?' she said flirtatiously, before tucking into the ice cream.

Magnus wanted to run through the menu and shopping list for the poker night, but Jo pointed out that there was plenty of time for that as it was weeks away. When they finished their dessert she dragged him into the lounge and demanded he played something for her.

'I don't know anything by the Spice Girls,' he said sarcastically, reluctantly picking up his fiddle.

'Of course not, you're too old! Play me something I'll hear at the wedding, I want to know what we're going to be dancing to,' she demanded.

Magnus started playing a traditional piece of Shetland music. Jo took off her shoes and got comfortable on the sofa. At the end he bowed theatrically and put the fiddle back in the case.

'Is that good enough for you?' he asked, as he sat down at the other end of the sofa.

'It was brilliant, you're really good, but I was kind of wondering how you'd dance to this kind of music. It's not like Irish dancing is it?'

'No, but some of it you'll know, as it's just waltzes and other traditional country dancing.'

Jo burst out laughing at the suggestion that she would know how to waltz, or even what a country-dance was.

'I'm sorry, but I've never waltzed in my life. I haven't got a clue. Please will you show me,' she begged.

Magnus sighed heavily and stood up and walked slowly over to the stereo and put a CD. He held his hand out to her. Jo stood up and suddenly felt a little shy, and regretted badgering him to dance. She took a deep breath and stepped forward to take hold of him, which made him snort with laughter.

'Look I know you're a bit of a feminist but it might be better if you let me lead, at least until you know what you're doing.'

'What do you mean, I haven't done anything yet?'

'You were holding me as if you were the man,' he replied still laughing at her. 'You put your *left* hand on my shoulder, and you put you *right* hand in mine and follow me,' he said, taking hold of her hands and placing them correctly then drawing her in towards him with his hand on her back.

Magnus guided her around the spacious lounge floor showing her the moves of the *St Bernard Waltz*, which he thought she ought to be able to pick up quite quickly. Jo found it hard to keep up but after a while she stopped thinking about what to do next and relaxed. They danced through three tunes in a row before she said she needed a break. Jo sat down on the sofa feeling slightly worn out, and dizzy from spinning around the room. After a rest she asked him to show her a different dance. He explained that some of the other dances would be done in groups and he tried to demonstrate how a *Strip the Willow* and an *Eightsome Reel* would work on the dance floor. Jo decided it all sounded too complicated and thought she stood no chance of remembering either the names of the dances or the moves.

'It's OK not to dance you know, you could just watch so that you know for next time,' he said reassuringly, seeing the look of incomprehension on her face.

'What about when the band takes a break, don't they just put on pop music instead?' Jo wondered hopefully.

'No, they don't, everyone sits around chatting or going to the bar until we go back on stage.'

'Well I'm sure it will be fun, I'm looking forward to it. What CD is this anyway, it sounds nice?' Jo said, thinking that she would probably just have to enjoy watching everyone else having fun.

'It's one of mine,' he said modestly.

'Really?' Jo was impressed, but she didn't want to be too gushing with her praise. 'Isn't that a bit strange listening to your own music, that's a bit like reading a book you wrote yourself?'

'I *don't* normally listen to it, but as you wanted a dancing lesson I thought I'd play you something you would hear next week. Take it with you; you can do your homework.' He put the disk back in the box and handed it to her. 'Here, keep it, I have plenty more of these.'

Jo stared at the artwork on the cover. It was very professionally done and showed the band standing on the beach, with all their instruments as if they were about to perform. Magnus looked much younger in the photo, and happier too. She discreetly checked the text on the back to see when it was recorded. It was four years ago, which explained why he looked so cheerful in the picture, as his life hadn't yet fallen apart. She looked at the names of the tracks which all seemed to be written in dialect so she didn't understand much of it. However, the last track on the album was called *Ella's Song*. She wondered whether this was the reason he had turned it off before it had finished.

Jo looked over at Magnus who had sat down on the sofa opposite her. He looked deep in thought, and Jo wondered whether she should just go home. It was getting on for nine now and he was probably tired from starting work at six that morning. But she didn't want to leave him just yet.

If it had been any other of her friends that had just given her a CD of their own music she would have given them a hug and a kiss and said thank you. Jo didn't know what to say or do. Despite having been dancing in his arms just minutes before, it all seemed so tense now, and she didn't understand why.

'You haven't played the piano for me yet! Just one song and I'll leave you in peace, promise!'

Magnus stood up wearily and walked over to the piano and sat down. He lifted the lid and sat for a moment deciding what to play. He turned and looked at her for a second and then broke into a rendition of Dolly Parton's *Jolene*, singing along faultlessly for good measure. Jo felt immense pleasure at the way he had switched back to taking the piss out of her. She got up and marched across to the piano and grabbed the lid as if she intended to slam it down on his fingers.

'If you wanted to get rid of me, you could have just asked me to leave. You didn't have to play the theme tune to my nightmares.'

'Sit down and behave, and I'll play you something nicer then,' he said shifting along the stool to make room for her.

She sat down feeling like a child about to get their first piano lesson. Jo expected him to play something traditional but he starting playing Elton John's *Sorry seems to be the hardest word.*

'I accept your apology,' she said in mock graciousness, when he had finished. 'Now do you have any other musical messages for me before I go?'

Magnus sat for a moment practising scales on the piano, deep in thought. Then he started playing a Bill Withers song, which unknown to him, Jo adored.

"*Aint no sunshine when's she gone. It's not warm when she's away. Aint no sunshine when she's gone, and she's always gone too long, anytime she goes away. Wonder this time where she's gone. Wonder if she's gonna stay. Aint no sunshine when she's gone, and this house just aint no home, anytime she goes away.*"

He had a clear deep voice and Jo was entranced, but started giggling when he changed the refrain, from the longwinded repetition of *I know, I know, I know.....* to *I keen, I keen, I keen* ...... with an exaggeratedly strong Shetland accent.

'Thank you, that was lovely.' Jo said when he had finished. 'But I'd best be getting home now. Thanks for dinner and the CD which I'm sure I'll play to death so I won't feel such an idiot next Friday.' She put her arm around his shoulders in the briefest of hugs and stood up to go.

'Jo, I won't be around much until the wedding as I have the stag night tomorrow, which will go on all weekend, and then I'm working the late shift all next week,' he said regretfully.

'That's OK, I don't expect you to be at my beck and call all the time,' she replied hastily.

Jo wasn't sure she understood his tone; it felt like a polite brush off. She walked over to the sofa and put her shoes back on and picked up the CD.

He followed her out to the front door, not knowing how this simple statement had caused the atmosphere to cool so suddenly.

'Drive carefully, it looks a bit frosty tonight,' he said gently.

'I will. Goodnight!' Jo replied, wondering whether it was another dig at her driving.

***

Jo had just got to her front door when Magnus pulled up behind her car in the drive. He opened up the passenger door of his vehicle and lifted Jess down onto the ground.

'Oh how silly, I forgot all about Jess, which is after all the *only* reason I came round to your house,' she said, bending down to stroke the dog's head.

'Thanks, I thought you came round to see me.'

'Well that too,' she conceded, 'After all, a girl's got to eat and you are a damn fine chef.'

'See you soon; call me if you need anything won't you,' he said kindly, and turning to go home. Jo clicked her fingers at Jess and opened her front door to go indoors. As she did Magnus appeared beside her again, grinning like a lottery winner. He stood close to her, and for one scary moment Jo thought he intended to kiss her.

'Shut your eyes!'

But Jo continued to stare at him a little anxiously. He spun her around and covered up her eyes with his hands, and then turned her round again and led her carefully away from her house towards the beach.

'Where are we going?' Jo whispered. She got the impression he was leading her away from his mother's house, but surely if he wanted to kiss her he could just have easily taken her indoors. She was getting nervous and wondered whether she even wanted him to kiss her. It was all too sudden.

Finally he stopped when they got to the beach. She could hear the gentle lapping of the waves on the sand. There was no wind at all so the cool air was tolerable and fresh.

'You can open your eyes now,' he said, letting go of her and pointing her in the direction of the Northern Lights.

Jo stared at the green and yellow flickering lights that cast an eerie glow across the sky, seemingly suspended above the mainland. It took a while to sink in what it was, as she had only ever heard about them and didn't really appreciate what they would look like.

'Oh wow! That's amazing!' Jo said at last, staring up at the sky. It was hypnotising , and they stood for quite a while in silence watching the lights as they rippled and danced amongst the stars. Jess and Ben took advantage of the unexpected opportunity to explore the beach in the dark, sniffing around for seals and other interesting objects. Jo shivered suddenly as the cool night air finally penetrated her coat.

Magnus wrapped his arms around her and stood behind her looking over her head at the sky. Jo leaned against him enjoying the feeling of warmth from his arms.

'What do you think of the Mirrie Dancers?' he whispered into her ear. Jo simply nodded vigorously not wishing to break the spell by speaking. She would happily have stood there forever, but the lights started to fade away and Jo could not ignore the cold any longer.

'Thanks,' she whispered softly at last. She turned and slipped her arm through his, to walk back up the beach to her house. She squeezed his arm before letting go and called Jess over to the front door.

'See you later Captain,' she said, as he got back into the pickup. She went inside her house and went straight upstairs to bed, looking out of the window to see if the Northern Lights had returned.

CHAPTER NINETEEN

On Saturday morning Jo was disappointed to find it was now raining and windy. She could not get used to the ups and downs of the weather that never stayed the same for more than a day, if that. She had heard the expression from a number of people that you can get all four seasons in one day in Shetland, and she was starting to feel that this could be applied to her life too.

She went downstairs to feed Jess and let her out for a few minutes. The little dog showed no inclination to go out walking in the foul weather, which Jo was relieved at. They both went upstairs back to the bedroom for another snooze. Jess snuffled around at the foot of the bed and Jo listened to the rain clattering against the windowpane.

She thought about Magnus and relived the moment when he put his arms around her. She knew it was just to keep her warm but it had felt so intimate, more so than if he had kissed her. She felt a flutter of excitement inside her, but then started to wonder why he hadn't. After all one couldn't possibly have planned a more romantic setting. Jo's spirits fell swiftly.

She got out of bed determined to stop the pointless fantasising about Magnus. The rain was easing off and she decided to pop across to see Ruby, as she wanted to show her the scan photo. As she went out into the hall she saw that Magnus had delivered her new paisley top, all freshly laundered and ironed and the blackcurrant stain had miraculously vanished. It was hanging up in the porch with a tiny scrap of paper pinned to it with a scrawled *'See you at the wedding Mrs Birdseye, Mx.* She grinned to herself feeling more cheerful at the continuation of the shared joke.

She wondered why he hadn't called in to speak to her

and decided that he must have come round while she was in the bath. She took Jess over to Ruby's and quickly ascertained that Ruby hadn't seen them outside the house as she had gone to bed early with a headache. She didn't seem her usual chatty self. Jo didn't stay too long, before deciding to take Jess back home, after a quick walk down to the beach during a short break in the rain. She stood on the sand near to where she had been with Magnus the night before. She shut her eyes and thought back to the moment when he had held her, but then laughed out loud at her foolishness for standing like an idiot on a cold wet beach. She went home to ring Megan and see what she was up to today.

'Well, Mrs Drama Queen, what have you been doing since we last spoke?' Megan asked, preparing for the next instalment in Jo's life.

'I've just emailed you a copy of my scan photo!' Jo said excitedly.

'Brilliant, I'll look at it now; tell me everything else while I wait for the laptop to wake up.'

Jo told her about the appointment and then the dinner she had later with Magnus.

'JoJo! This is becoming quite a habit, these spontaneous dinner dates with the divine ferryman. I want to hear all the details, don't spare my blushes with anything.'

'Nothing happened I promise!' Jo protested, but then filled Megan in as requested.

'What do you mean nothing happened? Our romantic hero sweeps you off to a deserted moonlit beach to watch the Aurora Borealis, nature's greatest lightshow, and wraps his manly arms around you to keep you warm. It doesn't get more exciting than that. Believe me I was sat indoors watching a re-run of *Friends* for the millionth time. I wish I could have been up there with some gorgeous man. Honestly I thought you were going to be living some deadly dull life on *Craggy Island*, but it's been non-stop since you got there.'

'I know, I'm exhausted!' Jo said with feeling. 'Anyway have you downloaded the email yet?'

'Yes, it's just appearing now,' Megan said, watching her computer screen. 'Oh, wow, Baby Mac, isn't this amazing! I can't wait till the big day. I'm definitely coming up there for the Easter holidays if that's still all right with you?'

'Of course you can. I can't wait either now; it's finally starting to sink in. I haven't felt the baby move yet, but apparently I will fairly soon. But I'm definitely needing to wear maternity jeans now, as my waist is expanding rapidly,' she complained.

'That'll be all those dinners with your new man. I bet you still look beautiful though,' Megan said, sighing with the tiniest bit of jealousy.

They talked some more about Megan's job and her growing excitement at the prospect of finally being able to afford to buy her own place. Megan had another appointment to see a flat that afternoon so Jo let her go and promised to ring in the week.

She sat in the kitchen drinking a cup of tea when she heard a van pull up outside. A woman was walking up to the front door laden down with parcels for Jo. She jumped up and went to the porch to collect them.

She spent the next half hour trying on her new maternity clothes and admiring them in the mirror. She loved the long midnight blue velvet dress, which was even prettier in real life than on the computer screen. She put it on and tried to imagine dancing in it at the wedding. She doubted she would have the nerve to dance, and obviously she would need someone to ask her and the only man she knew would be otherwise engaged. He had promised she would not be short of dancing partners should she wish to dance, and had laughed when he added that most of them would be old enough to be her father. She smiled at the memory and took off the dress carefully to hang it up in the wardrobe. She spotted Magnus' rugby shirt on the back of the door and decided she ought to take it back.

She wondered whether she ought to wash it first, but it still seemed clean and she was afraid of shrinking it. He had stressed it was his favourite shirt so she decided to let him launder it.

She drove around to his house feeling slightly guilty at letting herself in, and looking each way up the road in case she was seen. She stepped in to the porch and picked up the letters that were on the floor and carried them into the kitchen, then instantly worried whether she overstepping the mark. She dropped them down on the counter and laid out the shirt on the table with a note pinned over the Scottish thistle emblem. Jo had drawn an outline of a rose on the paper and written *'An English rose would be prettier'*. She turned and left immediately in case the temptation to snoop around took over her.

Meanwhile Magnus was not having such a fine time on the stag day for his cousin's fiancé. After going out for an early morning walk on the beach he had put Ben out in the kennel and got ready to go out. The boys met at the ferry and travelled over to the mainland to join up with some other friends. They started off with a clay pigeon shoot, which Magnus had enjoyed, not least because there had been very strict instructions not to drink any alcohol before or during the shooting session. That would at least ensure it didn't get rowdy too quickly. He wasn't in the mood for getting blootered and it would be a long night.

Later on the serious drinking got going with a pub-crawl around the town, followed by a meal in an Indian restaurant and then back to the pub. The atmosphere in the group was merry and mischievous. At one point Morag's hen party had collided by accident with the stag party. The girls were all wearing themed outfits from the musical *Cabaret*, with fishnet tights, high heels and outlandishly tarty clothes and elaborate makeup. The boys teased and flirted with them before leaving to go on to another pub, where they could drink away from the prying eyes of their wives and girlfriends. Magnus finally started to relax and enjoy the atmosphere.

After midnight they had found themselves in a nightclub and the party was breaking up a bit. The single men amongst them were chatting to single girls they had met in the club, or who had abandoned the henny. The married men were sitting in a group discussing sport, fishing and building projects. Magnus felt like he was on the outside of both camps. The single men tried to drag him over to a table where a group of young women had joined them.

Tricia sat at one end of the table looking expectantly in his direction. He did not wish to start anything up with her again, although she seemed keen to do so. She came over to where he was sitting, and plonked herself on his lap, draped her arm around his neck and kissed him on the cheek. She had been aiming for his mouth, but he had turned away from her. She reeked of cigarettes as usual. He was conscious that he was snubbing her, and it was probably rude given their history, but it was too noisy to try and explain anything, and in many ways there was nothing to explain. He wouldn't have been interested in Tricia regardless of Jo. She was a lovely girl, prettier without the makeup she had plastered on her face, and a kind and generous person when she wasn't pished. Unfortunately Tricia seemed to enjoy her social life, which revolved around alcohol and smoking cannabis, far too much for Magnus' taste.

'You're wasting your time there Trish! That boy is under the spell of some new soothmoother,' one of his friends shouted across the table. 'Come over here! We'll see you don't have to go home alone,' he added suggestively.

'Is this true, Minke? Are you seeing someone else now?' she asked, clutching on to him even tighter.

'Not exactly, they're just winding me up,' he said gently, sliding her off his lap on to another chair beside him. He didn't want to hurt her feelings, but he didn't want to discuss his personal life either. He hoped she would just go off and rejoin her friends again. After a while she took the hint and got up and went to the ladies, and when she returned she sat back down with her friends. He watched her huddled in a group obviously discussing him. One of his friends leant in to say something and he caught the word *pregnant* before they all started laughing. Tricia looked at him, with a mixture of horror and disappointment.

Magnus picked up his jacket and left the club without saying goodbye. He was annoyed with his friends, although he knew they meant no harm. It was just the usual drunken banter that went on at such events. He was also annoyed at himself for feeling this way. He walked along the busy street full of young people spilling out of the pubs and clubs heading off home, or on to other parties. He was meant to be going to one himself, and as a result of abandoning his friends he no longer had anywhere else to go that night. The next ferry home was not for another six hours and it was too cold and windy to stay out all night. He considered walking along to one of the larger hotels where a night porter might be persuaded to give him a room for the night. But then he remembered that one of the Whalsay trawlers was berthed at the pelagic boat quay, after arriving in Lerwick that evening to unload their catch. He decided to walk along to the boat and see if he could get on-board for the night.

He marched with his head down against the strong wind that blew unhindered off the sea, and stuffed his hands deep into his pockets, drawing his shoulders up against the biting cold. His mood got darker the further away he got from the town centre. He half considered going back to join his friends as they were probably laughing about him even more. Jo would never even know if he went home with Tricia, and it might shut everyone up, he thought. It's not as if Jo had any reason to mind what he did; after all they were not an item, whatever else he thought about her.

He tried to see things from her point of view. She had obviously just left a disastrous relationship and was now facing life as a single mother. Why on earth would she want to start again with someone like him, and for all he knew it was possible that her boyfriend might turn up again and claim her back? He had already been the victim of that situation once, and he was damned if he would let it happen again. He looked at his watch, it was too late to go back to the club and he felt tired now. He arrived at the boat and stood peering up at the wheelhouse to see if there were any signs of life. A dim flickering light inside indicated that someone was up there, probably watching TV. He decided to go up and ask if it was all right to come aboard.

He moved quietly through the large modern trawler and up to the wheelhouse hoping not to wake anyone. He opened up the door and whispered to Dougie who had nodded off in his seat. Dougie jumped and swore when he saw Magnus.

'Fucks sake Minke, you scared the life out of me. What the hell are you doing here? I thought you were on the stag night. Don't tell me you've all come aboard?' He said looking anxiously past Magnus at the door.

'No, course not, I left them all at the club, I must be getting too old for this, I couldn't face going on anywhere, and it's too late to get a hotel.'

'Yeah well, I guess you could sleep in the lounge, just don't go expecting a full Scottish breakfast in the morning.

We're setting off at the back of six so you'll get a free ride home too, ya fuckin' cheapskate!'

'Cheers mate! I see you drew the short straw in staying up tonight, I thought you'd be out with the others,' Magnus replied.

'Yeah right, if I went home shit-faced with a hangover after being away for a week, Vanda would kill me. The bairns are on their October break and they're not giving her any peace. She can't wait until I'm home,' Dougie said moodily.

'Yeah well, I'll leave you to your hard work then Goodnight!'

Magnus went downstairs to the crew lounge and sat down on one of the sofas. He thought about the days when his dad was at sea, and wondered what he would have thought if he could see the luxury of this state of the art boat. On one wall was a large flat screen TV, complete with satellite stations and an X-Box. He went over to a cupboard and pulled out a blanket and a pillow and took them back to the sofa to make himself a bed for the night. The low thrum of the engines feeding the generator lulled him off to sleep quickly, and he only awoke when he felt the boat pulling out of the berth the next morning. The skipper laughed when he saw him later on, calling him a lightweight for leaving the stag do, and threatening to make him work for his passage home.

He arrived at the house just after eight and let Ben back in the kitchen. He didn't notice the rugby shirt immediately, and only saw it when he went to put the kettle on. He picked up the note and smiled. An English rose eh? He wondered how to reply and then he noticed his post stacked neatly on the worktop and wondered how long Jo had spent in the house.

Magnus picked the shirt up and headed upstairs for a shower. He put the rugby shirt on afterwards and recognised the sweet perfume that Jo wore. He was surprised, as he expected her to have washed it before giving it back, but he was kind of pleased she hadn't. He went back to the kitchen and set about doing some washing. He put the stereo on and was momentarily surprised by the Arabic music. She had forgotten to take her CD back. Now he had time to listen properly he found he quite liked the tune. He studied the insert to see if there were any explanations to the lyrics. The only English writing on it was a translation of the song titles. The first song was called *Kifak Inta?* Which translated as *How are you?* He played the track a few times mentally recording the melody. It would convert quite easily to the fiddle and he was curious to know what it would sound like.

Magnus spent an hour repetitively playing along with the first track. As an experienced musician he picked it up quickly and he wondered how he could add it into the play list at the wedding. Jo would find it amusing.

Magnus was feeling decidedly more cheerful now and rang his brother Robbie in Aberdeen. They caught up on the family news and decided to get together soon. Robbie suggested Magnus came down for a long weekend. They worked out that this conveniently meant that they could go and see the Aberdeen v Celtic match. Magnus thought it would be great to take a break from Shetland for a few days. He had spent so many years travelling around the world that sometimes he felt hemmed in by the close familiarity of the place and people. Although even in Aberdeen it was normal to bump into fellow Shetlanders, bustling around the shops and laden down with carrier bags.

Ben was itching to go for a walk, despite the cold wet day, so Magnus put his survival suit on. Not very sexy, he mused but it was too cold for all that. He headed off over the hills with Ben, automatically checking the fencing along his land for wear and tear and mentally noting maintenance work to go back to later. Sheep scattered at the sight of them and Magnus sang quietly to himself, watching the sky and monitoring the approach of another weather front. He hurried along to the beach and noticed with disappointment that Jo's car had gone. He had hoped to stop for a minute or two just to say hello. He intended to use the excuse of warning her about the weather in case the power went again. He hesitated outside her house, before deciding to go in and leave her a note.

He found a pad of paper and a pen in the kitchen, which he helped himself to. He had to think quickly as he didn't want her to come back and find him. Finally he settled on:

English roses don't always transplant so easily to Shetland. Here's hoping for favourable conditions! Mx.
PS. A storm is coming!

He thought it looked suitably enigmatic and slipped out the front door to finish his walk. He hadn't expected to be home so early that day so he went out later to visit an old friend of his dad's and sat and had a dram of whisky with him, talking about old times at sea.

CHAPTER TWENTY

Jo got home from the shop where she had gone to get some bread and found the note on the kitchen table. She smiled to herself. So he thought she was an English rose eh?

She was feeling energetic and she bustled around all afternoon and evening unpacking more boxes and sorting out where to put things. She surveyed the array of formal work suits hanging in the wardrobe and wondered whether she would ever need them again. After careful consideration she decided that in five years, when she might be thinking of going back to work, they would no longer be fashionable, so she would donate them to charity instead. Once she had cleared out the final vestiges of her former career she had very little hanging up in the wardrobe. But she didn't care much. She had noticed there seemed to be far less attention paid to such things up here. The majority of the women she came across were casually dressed and hardly wore any makeup. Jo had barely ever left her house before without putting on mascara and lip gloss at the very least, now she found she was bothering less and less, and nobody was dropping down in a dead faint when they saw her.

The weather outside reminded her to seek out some candles and matches to be on the safe side. As it happened she went to bed that night untroubled by power failures. She didn't seem to notice the wind so much either, and fell asleep even as the house rattled in protest at the storm.

Monday morning brought calmer weather and Jo set off to Lerwick, lacking anything else to do with her time. She drove past Magnus' house on the way to the ferry and noticed the pickup had gone. Further along the road she saw it parked beside a half-built house. She spotted him up on the roof fixing slates. She realised then it had never been a brush off when he said he was busy; he was working flat out and didn't even see her go by.

Jo bought more things for her home to spruce it up. She bought new duvet covers and blankets for the spare room, mindful of the cooler climate. She bought herself some roses from the florist and invested in a large stone pestle and mortar from an Asian grocery store where she also stocked up on useful spices and ingredients for the poker night.

When she got home she made some dinner and plotted how to respond to the note from Magnus. She was keen to try out her new purchases so she cooked up some spicy vegetable pakoras and onion bhajees and took them around to his house in a clear plastic box and put them in the fridge. On the box she stuck on a post-it note that said:

Tell me if it's too hot for you! Jo x

On Tuesday she went to see Sarah while Mark was on duty. She discovered she had a lot in common with Sarah who had worked for the Highland Council's press office. Sarah was intelligent, politically aware, good humoured and was really enjoying her new life in Shetland. It was nice to spend time with someone who had such a sunny positive outlook on life. She reminded her of Megan.

When she got back she discovered, on the kitchen table, a printed page from a website specialising in outdoor clothing for extreme climates including arctic exploration. There was a photograph of a very attractive long parka in a chocolately bronze colour. It was described as lightweight, waterproof, windproof, warm and insulated. It had a fur-trimmed hood and it nipped in at the waist to give a "feminine" shape, and was made with a "non-rustle" fabric. The only thing missing in the description was the price, but it fit the bill perfectly and Jo could imagine wearing it a great deal for walks on the beach with Jess. Magnus had scribbled a note on the page that said.

Saw this and thought of you! Might protect an English rose from frostbite! Mxx

Two kisses, I'm moving up in the world, even if they are just on paper, Jo thought with pleasure. She studied the page again. She couldn't imagine him accidentally coming across this; he must have gone looking on purpose. How very sweet and thoughtful he was, she mused as she made herself some dinner, and wondered what could she do to look just as casually caring? She thought about burning some of her favourite music onto a CD for him, but changed her mind when she realised it would make her seem like a lovesick teenager.

She had a whole evening to kill so she crushed up some spices and made a marinade that would go well with lamb chops. She took it around in a jar to his house and left it on the kitchen counter with a note.

Try this with some lamb, preferably out of your freezer, not straight from the field! Jo xxx
PS. Loved the coat, where can I get it from and how much? Thanks x

Jo got back in her car and noticed one of the neighbours watching her from the nearest house, which was thankfully far enough away that she didn't feel the need to speak. She wondered what they thought of her visiting when he was so obviously out.

On Wednesday morning Jo went to her antenatal class and met the other expectant mothers. They were all very friendly and they all knew who she was, but with the exception of Sarah she knew nobody. Jeannie got everyone to write their names on labels and stick them on their tops so that the newer residents would not be at a disadvantage. For their first class they discussed birthing plans and what to expect in a modern delivery suite. Jo wondered how you could plan something that seemed to run to its own timetable with such varying results, but she sat and listened carefully. She added the numbers of potential friends to her mobile phone and promised to drop by for cups of tea. She hurried home wondering what she would find when she arrived.

There was no obvious note for her and she felt a moment's disappointment, until she noticed the kitchen windowsill. Five terracotta plant pots neatly filled with compost sat on a long terracotta tray. Each one had a tiny flag in it explaining the contents. There were chilli peppers, coriander, mint, parsley and basil. She supposed she had to use her own imagination about what this gift meant but while she was feeding Jess she noticed a piece of paper that had fallen on the floor. She picked it up and read the note that Magnus had left for her.

Dear Mrs Birdseye, thought you might like to make a start on your herb garden. You'll need this if you are going to carry on cooking me curry, which was brilliant by the way. I saw the coat on a Canadian website. I don't think you can buy this make in Britain, but I have a cousin over there who could send you one if you like it. Mxx

Jo grinned to herself, feeling absurdly happy. She made herself a cup of tea and rang Megan to tell her about the latest development.

'It does sound sweet. But isn't it a bit strange going round to each other's houses and leaving random acts of cooking and gardening?' Megan cautioned.

'Yeah, I suppose so, but so far it seems kind of laid back and funny. I'm sure he doesn't mean anything by it,' Jo replied honestly.

'Maybe; but what about you? What are you trying to tell him by cooking him curry and leaving it in his fridge?' Megan enquired.

'I don't know! I'm just practising for the poker night and basically I have nothing better to do with my time,' she said thoughtfully, and wondering how it might be interpreted by Magnus. She spent the rest of the evening worrying whether things were getting out of hand, and resolved to play it cooler from now on.

On Thursday morning she awoke to a bright and breezy day, which was a relief after the heavy rainfall in the night. She got up early and put on some washing and when the machine had finished she decided to make use of the breeze to dry her clothes instead of lazily throwing it in the tumble dryer like she normally did. Then she went off to her first Aqua-natal class, feeling self-conscious in her old swimsuit that seemed to emphasise the now pronounced but tiny bump. But she felt energetic and cheerful when she drove home afterwards.

While she had been at the leisure centre Magnus had gone for a walk down to the beach with Ben. As he passed

Jo's house and the empty driveway he noticed she had pegged out her washing on the line. However, the stiff breeze had pulled off some of the garments and had left them strewn across the lawn. He smiled to himself. Jo obviously hadn't discovered storm pegs yet. Nobody in Shetland used the flimsy plastic spring pegs Jo had used to hang out her washing. Without thinking he stepped over the wall and collected up the assortment of muddy tee shirts, towels and an exotic black and pink lacy bra that had snagged in the pampas grass. He carried them over to the back door and was relieved to find it unlocked. Inside the door was a plastic washing basket. He threw the muddy laundry into it and then looked back at the other stuff on the line. The wind was picking up so he went outside again and quickly retrieved it all and stuffed it in the basket. He intended to leave Jo a note and considered going to buy her a pack of storm pegs as funny gift.

Before he had a chance to do that he noticed a patch of water on the tiled floor near the back door. At first he thought Jess was responsible, but as he looked closer at the little puddle he saw water dripping down from the top of the doorframe. He frowned in annoyance. He had helped Lowrie put in the new door to the utility room and had lectured him about sealing it properly. He obviously hadn't. Magnus traced the leak through to the outside. Even though it was no longer raining the strong wind was blowing water that had settled on top of the doorsill into the crack, and this was now dripping steadily onto the floor. It would only get worse if left unchecked. He looked at his watch. He had just enough time to go and get some mastic and patch up the leak. He set off over the hill to his house and put his toolbox into the pickup and drove back to Jo's.

Jo was pleasantly surprised to see Magnus' pickup in the drive. She got out of her car and hurried inside. He wasn't in the kitchen, which surprised her. She walked through the rest of the downstairs, wondering where he could be, feeling increasingly tense as she did. She found him in the utility room standing on a stepladder with a mastic gun in his hand fixing the leak above the door.

'What are you doing?' Jo asked, feeling rather uncomfortable at seeing him making himself so much at home he was helping himself to DIY tasks she hadn't even noticed needed doing.

'I noticed this doorsill was leaking.' He pointed to the puddle on the floor by way of explanation.

Jo stared at the tiny pool of water not comprehending how he could have known it was there. Magnus looked at her and realised she was annoyed. It had only just occurred to him that he should have asked her whether she wanted his help or not. It had just seemed such a natural thing to do; since he felt partially responsible the door had not been fitted properly in the first place.

'I'm sorry Jo, I should have spoken to you first,' he explained, as he climbed down the stepladder. I was just taking Ben out for a walk and half your washing had blown off the line, so I picked it up for you and brought it inside, and that's when I noticed the door was leaking. It's probably my fault it wasn't sealed properly, I helped Lowrie fit it and I didn't pay enough attention to what he was doing.' He looked at Jo, who was now staring in horror at the washing basket, noticing the rather muddy looking bra trailing over the edge and feeling mortified that he had been handling her underwear.

He apologised again and since he was in a hurry to get back to the house site he was working on, he packed up his toolbox and left immediately. Jo thanked him half-heartedly for helping her, but felt annoyed with him for causing her so much embarrassment. She spent the rest of the day switching between annoyance and shame and then wondering whether she had been too harsh on him. It did seem like he genuinely wanted to help her, but it wasn't as if she couldn't have fixed the leak herself, if she had noticed it.

CHAPTER TWENTY ONE

Jo had offered to drive Ruby and some of her friends to the wedding. She collected the ladies, in all their finery, and set off down to the Kirk. They all wanted to get inside quickly to get a good seat but Jo was going to wait outside to watch the procession. Ruby had promised she would find it entertaining.

She sat in her car facing the ancient grey stone Kirk. More guests came along and hurried inside. Most of them noticed her sitting in the car and smiled or waved at her. Jo wound down the window. Ruby had described the weather as being fine. Jo thought it was dull and grey but the absence of wind and rain made it feel quite pleasant and almost warm. With the window down she could just make out the sound of a fiddle playing in the distance. It got louder and louder and was joined by the sound of giggling and merriment as the procession of the groom and his groomsmen, followed by the bride and her bridesmaids marched down the hill to the Kirk.

She felt a small jolt of excitement when she saw Magnus was leading the procession. He was dressed in an old fashioned black suit with a black cap on his head. Jo couldn't tell whether this was some kind of eccentric costume he was wearing, or whether it was just his normal wedding attire. He was playing a light-hearted jig, which increased in tempo as the wedding party couldn't help but speed up down the fairly steep road to the Kirk. The bride wore a very stylish white wedding dress. Jo couldn't see the detail from the car, but it looked like a strapless silk gown with a white velvet cape around her shoulders, as protection against the cool weather. The groom and his companions were wearing smart dark suits with lilac ties. The bridesmaids were wearing lilac satin gowns with the exception of a little flower girl who wore a white dress with a lilac sash around her waist.

Jo felt a little self-conscious sitting in the car watching them, and wished she had got out quicker and found a seat inside with Ruby. She didn't know what would happen next and realised she might get tangled up in the group of people making their dramatic entrance. She had just made up her mind to stay outside in the car and wait until after the service when Magnus came over to her, still playing the fiddle. Jo looked beyond him at the wedding party, but they seemed not to have noticed his dereliction of duty. The bride was having photographs taken with the bridesmaids and her father. Jo realised that she might have an opportunity to get inside after all.

'Are you coming in? Don't be shy,' he said kindly, studying her face carefully for signs she was still cross with him. Jo could smell whisky on his breath as he leaned slightly towards the open window.

'Won't I get in the way now? It looks like they are getting ready to go in. I don't want to do anything embarrassing like trip up the bride, or be walking down the aisle when the Wedding March starts.' Jo said, smiling at him.

'No, there'll be ages with the photographer. He always takes a long time trying to get the perfect shot,' Magnus said, remembering his own exhausting experience. He stopped playing at the end of the tune, and opened Jo's door for her. She stepped out and stood for a second looking up at him.

Magnus took in the pretty navy velvet dress she was wearing that seemed to match her eyes. She was wearing make-up but not so much that it looked too unnatural. She wore a dark pink lip-gloss, which made him notice her very kissable mouth, and he thought about the missed opportunity on the beach. He should have been bolder then, and she was probably pissed off with him now and he might not get another opportunity like that. Still, she had smiled at him, so perhaps she wasn't holding a grudge.

'I'm going inside now; care to join me, Mrs Birdseye?' he asked, using his favourite nickname for her and watching to see if it annoyed her.

'I was wondering when you'd ask me.' Jo said. 'I thought perhaps you were waiting to assess your chances with the bridesmaids.'

He leaned towards her and whispered whilst looking back towards the gaggle of women queuing up to go inside with the groomsmen. 'Married, married, 2nd cousin, too young, too young, and illegally young,' he said, laughing at Jo. 'Although the peerie one is bonny, maybe I should wait another 15 years; do you think she'll fancy me then?'

'Yuk, you're disgusting!' Jo said, in mock revulsion, and prodded him in the ribs. But they hurried across to the Kirk and slipped in to the last row of seats. It seemed Magnus' role as musician was finished for a while. A few moments later the Minister walked down the aisle to the door to greet the bride and her father, and then the organist started playing the *Trumpet Voluntary* and everyone stood up as the bride entered the Kirk.

Jo studied the bride's face. She had watched this lovely young woman laughing and joking with her friends outside just a few minutes ago, and now she looked serene, if not slightly nervous, as she walked along clutching her father's arm tightly for security.

Jo loved weddings, and she also hated them. She loved the romance, but felt uncomfortable in the types of social settings where families were important. She couldn't ever imagine walking down an aisle like Morag was, and holding on to her own dad like that. They weren't comfortable with physical displays of affection. Jo felt a lump in her throat, which always happened when she attended weddings or even watched them on TV. She kept her eyes fixed firmly on the floor trying to contain her emotion. For some reason she felt worse this time. She knew it was because of all the emotional strain she had been under recently, but she struggled to erase thoughts of David and her own relinquished wedding plans. She felt like she was going to explode.

The Minister was speaking now and everyone sat down again to listen to him. Magnus handed Jo a printed order of service and she occupied herself by reading it. She sat in a distracted daydream trying not to think about her family and her own problems. It was not her day after all.

So much for being a professed atheist, Magnus knew all of the hymns and sang loudly and perfectly beside her. Jo knew none of them, and was too self-conscious to even try to join in. She saw Magnus looking down at her and could see he was amused at her reticence. It made her feel inadequate.

After the service when the congregation had all gone outside for more photographs, Magnus drew Jo aside and spoke to her quietly.

'I'm really glad you came. I want to speak to you later if I get the chance.'

Jo drove Ruby and her friends along to the Hall where the wedding breakfast for close family and friends was taking place. Jo would see them later for the evening reception that was starting at seven.

She drove home feeling drained and decided to go back to bed for a while, to summon up the energy for a long evening. She fell asleep quickly and woke up when it was dark outside, and Jess was whining to go out. Jo was startled by the darkness and wondered what time it was. She had just over an hour to get ready and wasted no time showering, applying make and putting on the blue dress again. She laced up her Victorian style ankle boots that had an elegant but stable low heel. She figured she ought to wear something sensible enough for dancing, but wouldn't look out of place with her long dress. As a final touch she added a sparkly clip to her hair, which would help keep the long curls out of her face. A spray of her favourite perfume *Angel* and she was out the door. She collected Ruby again who had come back home in the late afternoon for a rest and they headed off for the hall.

'That's a very bonny outfit,' Ruby said, brushing the sleeve of Jo's velvet dress. 'They didn't make maternity dresses like that in my day. A sack of tatties would have looked more shapely than I did in those awful smock things. I can't bear to look at some of my photos back then. Mind you I can't bear to see new photos of me, I look at them and think, who's that old granny?' she tutted to herself, half-jokingly but saddened at the same time at how fast time was passing by.

When they arrived at the hall Ruby took Jo's arm and they walked slowly up the steps towards the noisy warmth of the wedding reception. There were a group of young women standing outside smoking and gossiping. Jo noticed a tall skinny blonde woman in a pair of tight black hipster trousers and a jewelled strappy top staring at her. What Jo noticed most about her was the fact that she didn't return Jo's smile. In a short space of time Jo had got used to the open friendliness of strangers, so it struck her as odd.

'You'd think they'd at least put a coat on to go outside; silly things, they'll catch their death,' Ruby muttered, as they passed the women.

Ruby led Jo over to a table on one side of the dance floor and sat down gratefully. She introduced Jo to the other people at the table and soon everyone was chatting happily. They were interested in how Jo was finding her new life in Shetland and how she was enjoying her first Whalsay wedding.

Just after seven the bride's father stood on stage and welcomed everyone to the reception, and then the band started playing. The bride and groom linked arms and marched around the dance floor whilst everyone clapped in time to the music. After one circuit their parents joined in, linking arms with their partners, and followed the newlyweds around the floor. Then the bridesmaids coupled up with the groomsmen, and they too joined in the promenade. The dance floor got increasingly crowded as relatives and friends join in the well-choreographed parade of couples. When the tune ended there was raucous applause and then the band starting play music for a *St Bernard's Waltz*.

Jo looked up at Magnus who was seated to the right of stage next to the accordionist. He winked at her as if encouraging her to look around for a dance partner. Jo visibly, but not deliberately, shrank down in her seat, wanting to become invisible. She needn't have worried; nobody asked her to dance so she started to relax and enjoy the party. Drinks were circulating freely, and the noise of cheerful chatter competed with the band. The tiny flower girl carried a basket of homemade sweeties around and offered them to everyone.

After a while there was a call for supper. Guests started disappearing in batches off to the dining room for the mutton supper. Jo didn't feel like eating so she continued to sit at the table while the other ladies went off. She could smell the mutton stew from where she sat; it smelt cloyingly rich, and not altogether pleasant, although she imagined it would be far more welcome if she had been drinking alcohol and dancing all evening like everyone else. She sat alone and watched the dancing. It was every bit as complicated as she feared but it looked great fun and she wondered whether anyone would ask her to dance. She had noticed people looking at her as she sat on her own, especially the pretty blonde woman who couldn't seem to stop staring at her. Although after a while, Jo noticed the same woman paying quite a lot of attention to Magnus too. It didn't take long for Jo's brain to click into gear. She was obviously very friendly with him. Ah well, she thought, it's not like I have any exclusive rights to his company, but she wondered what the relationship was.

After a few minutes Jeannie dragged her over to join her and Fraser at their table.

'Jo, you shouldn't feel you have to sit with Mam all night, she's fine with her pals, come and chat with us. I'm sure Fraser will be dragging you up on the dance floor later,' Jeannie said, pulling up a chair next to her. Jo sat with her back to the stage getting to know Fraser who she had never met before. He was just home from a fishing trip and was in fine spirits. Jo wondered what he was normally like, as he seemed a little merry.

Jeannie had heard some of the gossip about Jo and her brother, and she was interested to see for herself how they got on. Since the night of the storm she hadn't seen the two of them together and they had hardly spoken then. She found it hard to believe that Magnie was getting involved with her. Not that she had any objections; it just seemed such a long time since he had taken any interest in anyone. It was about time too, as far as she was concerned. Perhaps it wasn't ideal that Jo was about to have a baby, but as a nurse Jeannie liked to pride herself on being unshockable. She had noticed Jo looking up at the stage frequently but she had not been able to see what her brother was doing from where she sat. After a while she prodded Fraser into taking Jo up for a waltz.

'Jo, you really must get up to dance, you have such a super dress on, you can't just sit around like a wallflower, you have to show it off.'

Fraser jumped up quickly, and held his hand out to Jo, who although reluctant to get up and dance, felt like she was obliged to. Jeannie shifted around to a different chair so that she could see both the stage and the dance floor. Fraser was a good dancer, even when he'd had a few drinks, and he moved fluidly around the floor with Jo. He was a natural born flirt too, and she could see her husband laughing and joking with Jo. She also noticed Magnie looking down at them. He seemed completely captivated with Jo and she saw them exchange smiles as Jo twirled past.

They stayed up on the dance floor for two dances before coming back to sit with Jeannie. Jo glowed from the exercise in the rather warm room, but she seemed to sparkle and come alive. Another man approached their table and asked Jo to dance and she was whisked away to take part in an Eightsome reel. This was far more energetic and Jo struggled to keep up, frequently getting it wrong. This caused much good-humoured giggling, with people grabbing her arms and turning her to the right direction, and keeping her going until it ended. She thanked her partner, but politely refused another dance, she felt too worn out.

She flopped down next to Jeannie and picked up her drink. Jeannie appeared to be amused by something, looking at Jo as if she was trying to decide whether to say something to her.

'What's wrong, did I look silly out there?' Jo asked, wondering what the matter was.

'No of course not! I just noticed Magnie watching you while you were dancing. It must be all that cleavage on display. That's a fabulous dress, I don't think I ever looked that sexy when I was pregnant,' Jeannie said innocently, sipping her whisky and lemonade.

Jo looked startled by Jeannie's comment and looked down at her dress, fearful that it was showing more than was decent.

'I'm sorry; I didn't mean to embarrass you. What's wrong with him finding you attractive anyway?' she said, fishing for a response from Jo.'

'Don't be daft, why would anyone fancy me like this?' Jo replied, in genuine horror at the suggestion. She was not enjoying this particular conversation. She certainly didn't wish to speak about Magnus with his sister, or anyone else in this room.

'There'd be no harm in it if he did, you know! But I know you have a lot going on in your life and you've only just moved here, but who knows what will happen in the future, eh?' she said, in a manner that suggested it was no big deal to her what her brother did. She turned and looked around at Magnie who once again was looking down at Jo. Under his sister's scrutiny he shifted slightly in his chair and looked away. He's a guilty man, Jeannie thought to herself, whilst worrying how this might turn out. Who really knew why Jo had ended up in Shetland? She seemed a nice enough lass, and in many ways she would be perfect for Magnie, but not yet, not for a long while, she thought.

Jo was getting tired and she was feeling a little down after her bizarre conversation with Jeannie. She didn't understand what angle she was coming from. It seemed as if she had been trying to warn her that she knew what was going on, insinuating that she wouldn't mind if there was something between them, and then hinting that it was all too soon. It was a very mixed message. But what else was new with this family, she had been getting very mixed messages from Magnus too. She had hoped she would get a chance to speak to him, if only for a few minutes, but he seemed tied to the stage.

She crossed the room to see how Ruby was getting on, as she could see that Ruby looked a little down too. She wondered what was going on with her; she had seemed such a bubbly happy person just a few days ago. She worried it was something to do with her new friendship with Magnus, although she had always seemed to encourage Jo to contact him if she needed anything. Jo felt weary at the lack of understanding she had of her new friends and neighbours.

But Ruby smiled with relief when she saw Jo walk back to her table. She wanted to go home and hoped that Jo wouldn't mind driving her.

'Jo, would you mind if we left soon, I'm not fit for anything but my bed now,' Ruby whispered to Jo, when she sat down.

'I'm so glad you asked, I feel exhausted, and I only had three dances. Do you want to go now?' Jo said with relief, although part of her wanted to stay to see if she got a chance to speak to Magnus, but she thought it would be a bit silly to hang around just for that. She had plenty of time in the next few days to catch up with him. She picked up her handbag from the floor and moved as if she was going to stand up.

'The band will be taking a break soon, perhaps we'll go then, it will be easier to get across the room,' Ruby suggested.

Jo looked at the heaving dance floor and nodded. Couples seemed to be spinning round in all directions. It would be difficult to get across to the door, especially for Ruby. As the tune ended the band announced they were going to take a 15-minute break. Jo was about to stand up to go when she realised Ruby was now in the middle of a conversation with someone. They were making plans for an outing so she sat and waited for them to finish. She noticed the band had left the stage and were heading for the bar, with the exception of Magnus who had jumped off the stage and was now leaning against it. He appeared to be adjusting something on his fiddle. One of the band members turned back to say something to him and Magnus gestured to him to bring back a drink. Jo watched him put the fiddle to his chin and start to play. At first she couldn't hear above the volume of chatter. She looked away for a moment to see if Ruby was getting ready to go, but she was still chatting. Jo fiddled with her bag to check her car keys were there and as she did she found herself humming along to the familiar music, and the foreign lyrics that went with the tune filtered into her head. She looked up in surprise. Magnus was playing one of the tunes from her *Fairuz* album. She hadn't recognised it straight away, as it sounded slightly different without the accompaniment of the Eastern musical instruments and the singing.

'What on earth is he playing?' Ruby said, looking up at her son. I haven't heard that song before; I guess it must be something he's been writing himself. It sounds kind of gypsyish to me.'

Magnus caught Jo's eye and grinned cheekily. She smiled back, wondering whether he knew what the lyrics meant or even what the song title translated as. Whatever he understood it was obviously a direct message of some sort. When he had finished he put down the fiddle and strolled nonchalantly towards her. Jo stood up and helped Ruby to her feet.

Ruby was saying goodbye to her friends and Jo thought she would get a chance to speak to him, to at least acknowledge the song he had just played for her. Ruby, however, intervened by taking Magnus' arm and asking him to see her out to the car. The three of them left the hall. Jo handed Magnus her car keys whilst she went to the cloakroom to fetch her coat. While she was rooting around for it on the overloaded coat pegs she overheard some girls talking in the ladies toilets around the corner. Jo heard the word Minke and froze in the middle of putting on her coat. She could not imagine there was more than one person with that nickname.

'Tricia, don't tell me you're still gonna chase after Minke after what happened last week? Let it go for Christ's sake. There are plenty of other men here, let's go and have some fun and show him what he's missing.'

'I just don't get it, why would he chase after that fat pregnant tart when he could have me. It's not fair; and he was such a great shag,' Tricia slurred angrily.

Jo was repulsed by both the crudity of what she had heard and by what it implied, and she felt sure that the unseen speaker would be the blonde woman who had been staring at her. Jo hurried out; she was deeply embarrassed and did not want to make it worse by bumping into them in the cloakroom. She needed some time to mull over what she had heard, and in the meantime she still had to give Ruby a lift home. She ran down the steps and heard the girls following her outside for another cigarette break. As she crossed the car park Magnus walked towards her grinning expectantly, hoping for a positive response regarding the tune he had played her.

'So? How are you then?' he asked cheerfully. Jo felt the eyes of the girls watching them together and drew on all of her reserves of pride to face him. She smiled as warmly as she could and placed her hand on his chest and reached up and kissed him on the cheek. He reeked of whisky, but he didn't seem otherwise worse the wear for drink. She didn't say anything to him, just hurried over to the car. She looked over her shoulder to see if he was watching. He was, and so were the girls.

Jo started the engine and turned round in the car park to head for home. Magnus was standing on the steps of the hall watching her. He waved at them and glanced down briefly in response to something one of the girls said. He appeared to ignore whatever it was and disappeared inside.

Ruby sat quietly beside her. She seemed very unhappy. She was gazing out of the window into the dark as if she was miles away.

'Ruby, are you ok? You really don't seem to be very happy these days. Is there anything I can do to help?' Jo asked, after plucking up the courage to intrude on her silence.

'Oh no, there's nothing anyone can do, thanks,' she replied, sighing deeply and fiddling inside her handbag looking for some tissues.

'I used to love weddings, all parties actually. George and I used to have some fun on the dance floor. We were always the last to go home,' she continued quietly. 'But nowadays I'm just too tired to have fun, and it's not the same without my man. Oh, my lamb, I just feel so tired.' She sounded it too, and Jo felt very sorry for her.

'Maybe you'll feel better when you've had a good night's sleep. It's been a really long day,' Jo suggested kindly.

'I don't think sleep is the cure for what ails me. I'm just tired of saying good bye to folk.'

Jo didn't really understand what she meant and as they had arrived home she didn't get a chance to ask. She helped Ruby out of the car and into the house and said goodnight.

CHAPTER TWENTY TWO

Jo woke to the sound of a gale blowing outside. Jess very reluctantly went outside for an early morning visit to the garden and it appeared that it was not just the weather that was bothering the dog. Jo watched her anxiously. There was something not quite right today, and she decided to take her around to see Magnus. He would know what to do with her.

Jo was upstairs getting dressed when she heard the front door open and shut loudly. She heard the commotion of Ben running into the kitchen and greeting Jess.

She ran downstairs and in to the kitchen where Magnus was making himself at home, putting the kettle on and making tea and coffee. She stared at him for a second trying to work out what strange outfit he had on today. He wore a padded black and fluorescent orange suit that zipped up the front and had a hood.

'So you finally decided to get up then?' he said cheerily, handing her a mug of tea as she sat down at the window seat.

'I was up ages ago actually, it's just that I didn't get dressed straight away,' Jo said defensively. She was well aware she didn't seem to get up as early as everyone around here. 'Anyway, what on earth are you wearing; it looks like a pram-suit?'

'It's a survival suit; not a pram-suit thanks. I'm sorry I'm not more fashionably dressed for you this morning,' he said unrepentantly.

'What are you trying to survive, a nuclear fallout? Did we declare war on someone while I was in the shower?' she said trying to wind him up further.

'No, but it's braaly windy today and I have a bit of a hangover so I was feeling the cold more than usual,' he said, drinking his coffee, and noticing a tiny drop of water falling off the end of one of her curls. She didn't have any make-up on and her face looked fresh and pretty.

'A hangover eh? I thought I smelt whisky on your breath last night,' she said, recalling the brief kiss she had planted on his cheek. She wondered whether he remembered that. 'I was going to come and see you actually,' she added, noticing the way he looked up hopefully. 'I think there's something the matter with Jess, she doesn't seem to be herself again.'

'Yeah, I noticed when I came in just now; maybe we should take her back to mine so I can have a proper look at her. I may give her another shot of antibiotics and see if that will help. I'm hoping her infection hasn't come back again. Poor old lass' he said sadly, watching the dog sitting quietly by Jo's feet. 'I wanted to talk to you too. Sorry, it's been so busy this week, what with the wedding and everything.'

'That's ok,' Jo said sympathetically. 'I saw you up on somebody's roof the other day. Don't you ever have a real day off?'

'Oh that, I was just trying to help them get it wind and watertight before the worst of the weather sets in,' he explained.

'Thanks, for that song by the way. That was very sweet.' She stood up and walked over to him and put her mug in the sink. She touched his arm briefly with her hand. 'Shall we go and see if there's anything we can do for Jess then?' She pulled her hand back, aware that he seemed slightly nervous of the gesture and she wondered whether he only seemed to be able to warm up and relax when he had been drinking.

Magnus lifted Jess into the back of Jo's car and they set off on the short distance to his house. He carried the dog into the garage and set her down gently on top of a large worktop. Inside the double garage was a car inspection pit, a full engineering workshop for maintaining cars and boats, a sink and cupboards on one wall and on the other wall was a woodworking bench with DIY tools laid out neatly on it. In one corner was a large grey metal cupboard that appeared to have a very sturdy secured padlock on it.

'Is *that* where you keep the family silver then?' Jo asked jokingly, pointing at the cupboard,

'Oh that, no that's got a couple of guns in it, which is

why I keep it so well locked up,' he said casually, concentrating on examining Jess. He reached up to a bank of spotlights on the ceiling and directed one at Jess.

'Damn it, I think the infection has come back. I can't think why though, the wound doesn't seem that bad to look at, but there is a lot of heat around it and her pulse is rather rapid. Something nasty is going on!'

Jo was still trying to deal with the fact that this man kept guns in his garage; it made her feel very uncomfortable. Magnus saw the look of concern on her face and sighed.

'Jo, lots of people have guns here, it doesn't mean anything,' he tried to explain, but sounded a little impatient with her.

'Why would you need to keep a gun, it's not like there are any foxes or anything, is there?' she asked suspiciously.

'I have one air rifle from when I was a teenager and I used to shoot the rabbits on the croft with my Dad, otherwise they ate all our vegetables. They're like vermin here. And then there's a shotgun that used to belong to my dad. That's just there for emergencies. I've never had reason to use it thankfully.'

Jo wondered what kind of emergency involved requiring a shotgun, and the doubt showed on her face. He sighed again and turned to face her properly.

'Jo, think about it, we are a minimum of an hour away from the vet, and in the middle of the night or in bad weather it could be more like 12 hours. If there's a problem with one of the animals we need to be able to deal with it efficiently and quickly and not prolong any suffering.' He seemed exasperated with her and Jo felt embarrassed at her ignorance of rural life in a remote area, although she still couldn't quite reconcile herself to the idea of needing a gun for any reason.

Magnus turned back to Jess and opened up a cupboard, which contained all manner of strange medical products for sheep. He picked up what appeared to be a pre-loaded syringe and checked the label on it. Jo moved closer to see what he was doing.

'Stand back, I don't want her to bite you if this hurts,' he said to Jo raising his arm to guide her backwards a bit.

He gave Jess a shot of antibiotics the vet had left with

him for this eventuality. The dog didn't even whimper, but she was shivering. Magnus picked her up and carried her into the kitchen where it was warmer. Jess lay down on the floor looking very sorry for herself.

'Do you think she'll be OK?' Jo asked anxiously. Magnus fetched an old blanket and a basket from the garage and set them on the floor by the radiator and Jess gratefully lay down in it.

'I don't know. I hope so, but she's getting old now, and she doesn't seem to be fighting it off like she would have done a few years ago. We'll just have to wait and see. I'll take her over to the vet on Monday and see what she thinks.'

Ben went over to Jess and lay down on the floor beside her. He seemed a bit fed up too and Jo felt very worried about the whole situation. In the short space of time she had spent with Jess she had got very attached to her already.

'Did you have breakfast yet?' Magnus said, watching Jo as she crouched down to make a fuss of Jess.

'No, I haven't got around to that yet. I keep being pestered by very strange men in tellytubby outfits.'

'Would you like something to eat then? I fancy a bacon roll, I'm still feeling the effects of last night, and that would be the perfect cure,' he said walking over to the fridge and studying the contents.

Jo sat down at the table. She was thinking about the woman at the wedding.

'Look, I know I have absolutely no right to know this, but who's Tricia?'

Magnus shut the fridge door and looked at her. He could not believe that Jo could have heard about her already. He walked over and sat down at the table opposite her. There was no point lying since Whalsay was too small a place for that kind of tactic. He would be found out very quickly once Jo got to know more people.

'I went out with her a few times, but it all ended a very long time ago. I hadn't seen her for about six months before I met her again on the stag night and then she appeared at the wedding. Why?' he regarded Jo carefully, wondering what she had heard.

'It's just I overheard her talking about you in a very embarrassing way and I just wanted to know what the history was,' Jo said quietly, not wishing to repeat it word for word.

'I don't know what she said, and to be quite frank, I don't really want to either. I stopped seeing her because she's not the kind of woman I want a long-term relationship with. She's a nice enough lass in some ways, but she's too much like hard work. I got fed up with how much she drinks, smokes, swears... I know you'll probably think I'm old fashioned for being this way, but it's just the way I am.' He looked serious and uncomfortable and Jo felt sure he was telling the truth. Tricia hadn't seemed like someone that Magnus would go out with. But what did Jo know really. Tricia was very attractive and after all Magnus was a single man who was free to do what he wanted and with whom.

'I'm sorry, I shouldn't have asked. It's none of my business is it?' Jo said after a moment of uncomfortable silence.

Magnus shrugged. He stood up and put the kettle on for want of anything better to do.

'I should go really. I know you've got this second night of the wedding thing later. Maybe I should take Jess back home with me as you are going out,' Jo said hesitantly.

'Don't you want to come too? You'd be very welcome. It's much less formal tonight and there's a *normal* band so you can dance *your* type of dancing.'

Jo didn't know what to say. She was pleased to be invited along, but she was tired and confused. It was like playing some kind of strange game that she didn't have the rulebook for. He was sending such mixed messages. He was kind, thoughtful, generous and seemingly interested in her in all ways, except sexually. Obviously there was a perfectly good reason for that, but Jo wondered whether he regarded her as some poor lost orphan that needed looking after. She also felt self-conscious about how other people might view their friendship. Did others think of her as a pregnant tart that was hoping to snare some unfortunate man to be her new breadwinner? Jo burned with the shame at the thought.

'Thanks for asking, but I'm kind of worried about Jess, so I think I'll just take her home and I'll call you if I need anything. Although actually I don't have your phone number.'

Magnus wrote down his home number and his mobile

for her.'

'Call me anytime, really,' he stressed, wishing he could persuade her to come out that night.

Back home she tried ringing Megan, who was out, not surprisingly, given that it was a Saturday afternoon and the weather in London was bright and sunny, according to the weatherman. Jo briefly felt a moment of homesickness when she watched the news. Here she was in this wet and windswept island, a million miles away from Megan and the rest of her friends. She decided to email her instead, partly as a way of keeping her up to date, and partly to see how her thoughts looked when they were written down.

Dear Megan

Hope you are having fun somewhere, I tried to ring, but you were out. Feeling a bit confused at the moment and having a crisis of confidence. Here is the latest instalment of the ferryman saga, let me know what you think!

I went to the wedding, which was fab; really interesting, you'd have loved it. Captain Birdseye played the fiddle and led the bridal party down the road to the church. He was wearing this weird old suit which I later worked out was a costume, rather than his wedding suit, but you can never quite tell with him. The dancing was fun, and I even had a dance with a couple of men, one of them being Jeannie's husband. But some blonde slapper seemed to be hanging around the stage watching Magnus and just as I was leaving I heard her talking about how she'd slept with him and that she wasn't going to let "some FAT pregnant tart" get him. I was a bit upset obviously, but I can hardly complain about what he did in the past, but the next day I asked him about it and he said she was some old girlfriend and that it all ended months ago.

But here's my problem. I can't work out whether he likes me as a friend, a neighbour, a prospective girlfriend or even some kind of surrogate daughter. One minute he is all flirty and cute, although usually when alcohol is involved, and the next he is cool and distant. Help, I'm going nuts up here. Oh and by the way he learnt how to play one of my Fairuz songs and played it at the wedding in the interval. How weird is that? It would be romantic, except that he hasn't followed it up with anything else so I'm thinking he is taking the piss out of me. Every time I so much as go near him or touch him he freezes.

I thought being pregnant would give me a much needed break from man-trouble but all that has happened is my rule book has been taken away. I don't know how to interpret anything that man says or does now. Is it because I'm pregnant; is it a cultural thing that's lost in translation, who knows? Hoping you might, Ring me soonest, Jo xxxx PS. Miss you tons!

Jo decided on an early night, given that the night's viewing on TV looked dire. She briefly reconsidered going to the second night of the wedding, but didn't want to look desperate. Jess seemed very weary and Jo was concerned when she didn't follow her upstairs to bed, but chose instead to stay in her basket in the kitchen.

Jo sat in bed reading for a while. Periodically she got up and went downstairs to check on Jess. She lay quietly in the basket and only lifted her head in greeting each time Jo entered the room.

After a while Jo got tired and fell asleep with the bedroom light on, and the book she was reading lying on the pillow beside her.

Meanwhile Magnus was at the hall for the second night's celebration of Morag's wedding. He was relieved not to be performing again and set about catching up with friends and family and trying to have a good time. He was distracted though and kept thinking about Jo. It didn't help when people kept talking about her either.

'Magnie, where's the lovely Jo tonight? I thought you'd want to be dragging her up on the dance floor,' Fraser asked when they were at the bar.

'Minke, where's your new soothmoother girlfriend?' One of his colleagues taunted as he passed by him on the way to the toilets.

'Didn't you invite Jo? I thought she would have enjoyed coming out again?' His mother asked when he sat down next to her for a moment.

'I think she really likes you, she couldn't take her eyes off you last night,' Jeannie whispered to him when they were talking to their friends.

Magnus concentrated on doing what was expected of him. He danced a couple of times, when a female friend or cousin dragged him onto the dance floor. To the average onlooker he was having a good time. To his mother and sister he looked miserable and fed up and they both wondered what was going on. When it got to the end of the party, the bus arrived to take people home, but Magnus got a lift with a friend and stopped off for a nightcap before walking the rest of the way home.

When he approached the house he was surprised to see an upstairs light on. He opened the front door and instantly knew someone else was inside, although it certainly wasn't Jo, which he had optimistically hoped it would be.

Whoever it was smoked, as he could smell the unmistakeably reek of cigarettes in the hall. He guessed who it would be and was furious. He had managed to avoid speaking to Tricia throughout the whole evening. He had deliberately and quite brutally ignored her when she spoke to him when he first arrived. He had turned and walked away before he said something regrettable. He was annoyed she had been mouthing off about him in a way that Jo had overheard, although it could just as easily have been his mother or sister. He resented Tricia's loud-mouthed coarseness and lack of discretion.

He looked around downstairs and didn't find her so he reluctantly went upstairs. He found Tricia lounging on his bed in what she must have assumed was a provocative position.

'Minke, I thought you'd never come home. Come over here, I got us some drams,' Tricia said, patting the bed beside her. He noticed the generous measures of whisky waiting on the bedside tables.

'Tricia, what the fuck are you doing in my bedroom?' he asked caustically. 'Did you not get the hint that I'm not interested?'

'Why not? What's wrong? You certainly don't have some other woman keeping your bed warm,' she said sulkily, but not moving. He guessed she had been drinking a fair bit and he didn't know what to do about getting her to leave. She would have missed the late night ferry and he was in no position to drive her anywhere.

'Tricia, I'm telling you now; I'm just not interested OK. Please don't embarrass yourself anymore like this. I'm going downstairs, you can stay here since there's nowhere else to go tonight, but you're leaving first thing in the morning,' he said coldly, and slammed the door behind him, ignoring the way she swore at him as he walked downstairs to the kitchen.

Magnus let Ben into the house and made himself a black coffee and carried it into the lounge. He wasn't tired now, just pissed off with the world. He sat down and put the TV on and checked his mobile phone. There were no messages from Jo, which he took to be a good sign with regard to Jess. After a while he fell asleep on the sofa with the TV on quietly in the background.

A little after three Jo woke up to the sound of Jess whimpering half way up the stairs, trying to make her way up to the bedroom. Jo went down to meet her and wondered whether she was asking to go out. She seemed really distressed, so Jo picked her up and carried her back down to the front door. Jess didn't seem to want to go outside in the cold. She flopped down on the floor in the hall and lay there crying and whimpering, an eerie high-pitched sound that scared Jo. She knelt down beside the dog and tried to comfort her. She wondered briefly about ringing Magnus but it seemed more sensible to just take Jess there, since in all likelihood Magnus would be over the limit for driving.

When she got to his house she quietly opened up the front door and slipped inside. She had seen the bedroom light on upstairs but she could also hear the TV in the lounge. Magnus was asleep on the sofa, although Ben had woken up and was looking up at her with interest, silently wagging his tail at her.

Jo crouched down beside Magnus and gently touched his shoulder to wake him. He jumped and swore. Jo recoiled in surprise.

'Oh, it's you! Sorry. What's wrong Jo?' he said, sitting up and rubbing his face with his hands.

'I've got Jess in the car; I don't think she's very well at all. I hope you don't mind but I thought you ought to see her,'

Jo explained.

'No, of course I don't mind. I'll come out and get her.'

He swore under his breath while he examined the dog, checking her breathing and running his hands over her, seeing where it hurt. Ben sat next to him, whimpering as if he too was afraid. Eventually Magnus stood up and sighed.

'I think this might be it for her,' he said sadly. Jo followed him out to the garage wondering what he was going to get.

'You're not just going to just shoot her are you?' Jo asked fearfully.

'For Christ's sakes Jo, of course I'm not!' He snapped. He picked up the dog basket and blanket and carried it back into the kitchen. He lifted Jess into the basket and covered her up with the blanket.

'You might want to say goodbye to her. I'm not sure she's going to make it through the night,' he said gently.

'Can't you give her anything?' Jo asked desperately kneeling down to stroke Jess.

'I don't have anything that will help her, and it's impossible to get the vet here now. But I'll call her in the morning and see if she'll come out. All we can do is keep Jess warm and comfortable and hope she has the strength to fight it,' he replied, and sat down on the floor beside the dog and stroked her head gently. Jess whimpered quietly and tried to turn her head to lick his hand.

Jo sat down on the kitchen floor devastated at the thought of losing Jess. They sat without speaking for a while, until the silence was broken by the sound of a toilet flushing upstairs. Jo looked up in surprise.

'It's not what you think Jo,' he said quietly, but with a guilty edge to his voice.

Jo frowned at him. 'I didn't actually think anything until you said that. But let me guess, I bet if I called out *Tricia* some blonde tart will just miraculously appear from your bedroom,' Jo said furiously, standing up and picking her coat up from the kitchen table.

'Don't go. I can explain. She was just here when I got home from the hall. I left her up there because she's pished, and there was nowhere else she could go at this time of night,' he pleaded.

'Yeah sure! That's what all girls do; just throw themselves at someone by turning up in their bed when they get home. I used to do it all the time,' Jo said sarcastically, heading for the door.

She slammed the front door shut and got in her car and started the engine. She drove home rigid with anger and stomped upstairs and burst into tears when she got there.

CHAPTER TWENTY THREE

Magnus sat in the kitchen for most of the night, keeping watch over Jess and brooding over Jo's hasty departure. He was annoyed with her for not believing him, but also was rather surprised by it, as it seemed to indicate that she cared whether he was seeing someone. Nevertheless she should have trusted him.

He heard Tricia moving around upstairs around seven. He went upstairs and told her to call herself a taxi or a friend to collect her. She looked very sorry for herself, so he fetched her some aspirin and coffee before she left. It was a relief to have the house to himself, and he headed straight upstairs again to strip the bedding from his room. When he came down having showered and dressed he went over to see Jess. Ben whimpered beside her with his head on her tummy.

Jess had gone. Magnus shooed Ben out into the garden and carried her body out to the flatbed of the pickup and covered it up with a blanket. It was a bit early to call his mother, although he knew she'd be up already. He wondered about leaving the bad news until after she had got back from the Kirk. He thought about ringing Jo but that seemed a bit cold, given the way they had parted.

He settled on taking Ben for his usual walk along the beach and would decide what to do when he passed Jo's house. If he saw any sign of life he would call in on her. As it happened it was his mother he saw first. She was out in the garden hanging out her washing on the line, fretting about it being a Sunday morning and that she ought not to be doing this, but it was such a fine drying day. She took the bad news surprisingly well. No tears; just quiet resignation. Magnus knew his mother was feeling depressed for other reasons, and it simply wasn't fair that she had yet another loss to add to her burden. But there was nothing anyone could do about it. He offered her a lift to the Kirk but she had already made other arrangements. They sat in the little kitchen drinking coffee and talking about the dogs they'd had in their family over the years, and discussing where to bury Jess in the garden.

Magnus left her house when one of her friends collected her to go off for the Sunday morning service. He stood at the end of Jo's driveway for a moment wondering whether he should go in and see her. He knew she was scunnered with him but he had to tell her about Jess at least. It was nearly ten and all of the blinds and curtains were still drawn as if Jo hadn't got up yet. But then, she had been up in the middle of the night, she was probably still tired. He started to walk away but Ben had other ideas. He ran up the drive of Jo's house and barked one short sharp woof and scratched optimistically at the front door. Magnus called him back and the little dog turned round sadly and followed.

A small movement of the curtains at Jo's bedroom window caught his attention. Magnus hesitated, but decided he might as well get it over with now. He might not get time to come back later as he would be on call for the fire service in a few hours.

He opened the door cautiously.

'Jo, are you up? I need to speak to you!' He called up the stairs. He waited for a moment; he could hear movement upstairs and went to the kitchen to wait for her.

He took his jacket off and put it on the kitchen table and sat down on the window seat. He was tempted to put the kettle on and do something useful, but after the incident with Tricia last night he thought Jo might think he was being too intrusive. She seemed to be taking ages upstairs and presumed she was getting dressed. Ben sat on the floor beside him with his head on Magnus' leg. He ruffled the dog's head softly and wondered how Jo would take the news.

At last she came downstairs looking pale and tired, and not entirely pleased to see him.

'How's Jess?' she asked quietly, bending down to stroke Ben who had trotted over to greet her. She straightened up and saw the discomfort on Magnus' face, so she knew the answer before he had a chance to speak. Jo had been preparing herself for this not entirely unexpected news, but even so she had hoped for a miracle. She turned without speaking and ran back upstairs to her room. Ben hurried up the stairs after her and followed her into her bedroom.

Jo lay on the bed feeling like the world had ended. She had only known the dog a short while, but already the house seemed too quiet without her. Having Jess living with her had felt like the start of something good in her life. Losing her so soon brought it home to her that nothing seemed to be working out for Jo at the moment.

Paranoia and grief clouded her judgement and she began to dwell on the fact she had made such a fool of herself. She could not believe she had made such a scene about Tricia. It was excruciatingly embarrassing. She decided there and then to pack up and return to London. She would ring Megan later and suggest they bought a place together after all. She would take her old job back, get a child-minder and do what every other single mother in the world has to do; just get on with it in the best way one can. She thought about all the attractive things about London that she was missing, friends, shops, the hustle and bustle, and her career. She would no doubt feel stupid going back so soon, as it was after all what everyone expected her to do, but surely that was better than staying here and feeling stupid *and* lonely. Her mind was made up.

Magnus walked slowly upstairs to her room. Ben was still upstairs with her and although he could have just whistled for him, he thought it would be rude, and he felt a little guilty at the way things had been left. He slowly eased open the bedroom door and looked at her lying on the bed with her back to him.

'Go away!' She said angrily, turning her face even further into the pillow.

'No, I won't' he replied patiently. 'Not until I know everything's OK.'

Jo didn't reply and didn't move. She lay rigidly on the bed, desperate to be left alone. Magnus sighed. This was no use; she wasn't going to listen to him. He sat down on the bed in despair and when she didn't react he lay down next to her and stared up at the ceiling.

Jo wondered what he was going to do and she remained

perfectly still but alert. She was confident he did not intend any harm towards her, but it was nevertheless alarming to have a man in her bedroom lying on the bed beside her. He clearly had no intention of going anywhere and even Ben had settled down on the floor to take a nap. It was bizarre.

Half an hour ticked by and nobody moved. Jo felt the first stirrings of the baby inside her. She wanted to say something, but she wasn't sure if that was what she had felt. She also felt hungry and thirsty but was too afraid to move. She hated confrontation more than anything else in the world, which was partly why she was here in Shetland in the first place. She had moved hundreds of miles rather than face up to David. And now she was harbouring plans to do the same again, although now as she started to calm down she realised she was being a little hasty. The baby moved again, a soft fluttery feeling, and distracted her from her depression. She shifted round slowly on the bed to face Magnus.

'I'm sorry about Jess,' he said turning his face from staring up at a cobweb on the ceiling, to look at her.

'Me too,' Jo whispered.

Magnus held his arm out to her and she moved closer and rested her head on his shoulder and wrapped her arm across his chest.

'I'm going to miss her,' Jo said.

'I think I'm going to miss *Ben*, he seems to have adopted you now,' Magnus said smiling at Jo, delighted that she was thawing out a little.

Jo sat up and looked over the edge of the bed at Ben who was lying on the floor snoring.

'Maybe I'll just have to come round and steal him from your garden occasionally,' Jo said smiling ruefully.

'Well I guess joint custody is better than nothing. I hope I get out of this divorce better than my last one,' he teased, referring to their running joke about Jo being his wife. He stood up and flicked the cobweb off the ceiling. He knew he would have to go home soon as he didn't get a decent enough paging signal this side of the hill.

'I take it you made me breakfast and a pot of tea while you were skulking around downstairs,' Jo joked as she followed him out of the room.

'I don't skulk. I sat and waited patiently for you to consider whether you wanted to speak to me today,' he said light-heartedly.

'Well I had to consider whether or not to forgive you first,' she teased back and watched as the expression on his face switched from happy to annoyed in an instant.

'That's just the thing Jo; there was never anything to forgive.' He looked at his watch and sighed. 'I've got to get back home, I'm on standby soon.' He picked up his jacket from the table and Ben took this as a signal to leave and clattered across the kitchen floor to the hallway.

Jo watched Magnus put on his boots in the porch. She didn't know what to say. She had upset him again already. He did not smile when he said goodbye and Jo watched him head off over the hill with Ben close to his heals. As she closed the front door she saw Ruby returning from the Kirk service.

Jo ate her breakfast and started thinking about what she should do realistically, and whether she had been wise to move to Shetland. She decided to see if Megan had emailed her back and she would phone her in a while. It was late morning, but Jo knew that Megan was not an early riser on a Sunday, especially if she had been out late the night before.

There was an email from Megan, which had been sent after midnight.

JoJo

What am I going to do with you? Of course this man fancies you! Cultural differences aside, nobody pays that much attention to a woman without there being some kind of connection. Now maybe he doesn't intend to pursue this and given the bizarre circumstances, I don't blame him. I'm sure there must be some kind of social taboo where you don't go chasing after pregnant single chicks, even if she is gorgeous. I think you'll just have to be very patient. Stop worrying about everything so much! You clearly have too much time on your hands these days. I thought you were going to start studying – no time like the present Cariad!

Maybe this time next year it will all be much easier. You have been through so much just recently, don't try and rush in to anything else. George Clooney could end up making his next film up there and then you'll be wishing you were still available! And forget about the blonde (and by the way we're not all slappers!) she is probably ancient history.

It's the closing date for my, hopefully, new job on Wednesday. Keep your fingers crossed for me and I'll ring you when I'm sober again!

Love Megan xx

Jo reread the email a couple of times, noting the slightly impatient lecturing tone. It was all good sensible advice though. She did have too much time on her hands, even more so now without Jess to go walking with.

Jo spent the rest of the morning surfing the net searching for inspiration and later on she rang Megan.

'Thanks for your much-needed advice. I have just sent off my application to study for a degree in Scottish Literature. I hope I get in.'

'Of course you will! Good for you,' Megan said happily. 'You may have finished school at 16 but you are a mature student now so it won't matter about your qualifications. Anyway you had a good job in the Home Office so you'll be used to doing research and writing stuff. I bet you'll find essays a doddle,' she added encouragingly.

'Anyway what's new with you? What did you get up to last night?' Jo said turning her attention to Megan's life, as she was conscious of the fact that they always seemed to concentrate on Jo's problems just recently.

Megan described her night out with two colleagues who were leaving the school in search of better jobs up north.

'That's a shame, still I don't blame them really, it is kind of expensive to settle in London these days eh? What happened with the veggie geek? Has he said much to you since your date?' Jo asked as she took the phone upstairs so that she could lie down on the bed while she talked. She noticed the indentation of where she had been lying down with Magnus and felt a pang of sadness.

'Oh strangely enough he's been fine with me. It's like it never happened, he is back to being all flirty and funny at work again. But he hasn't asked me out again thankfully. But hey, you never know who might replace Allison and John. Hopefully this time it will be single men,' Megan said optimistically, as she watched out of her flat window as a police car emerged from the nearby station and took off down the road with blue lights flashing. Moments later two more police cars took off at speed. It was an everyday occurrence to Megan and she scarcely noticed the noise of the sirens, at least during the daytime. 'What's new with the ferryman? I feel sure you will have some new scandal to report,' Megan teased.

'Oh don't please. It's been awful here the past 24 hours. Jess died this morning. She wasn't very well last night so I took her around to his house to see if there was anything he could do. Anyway that ex-girlfriend of his was upstairs. He said she had just turned up in his bed when he got home from the party, but I don't know what to think,' Jo said sadly staring up at the ceiling.

'Oh, I'm so sorry Jo. That must have been awful. And the poor little dog, I know you'll miss her won't you,' Megan said sympathetically.

'Yeah, I will. But Magnus came round to tell me this morning about Jess and we kind of made friends again, and then I blew it by referring to that woman and he was offended. And then he picked up his coat saying he was on standby and left. But I've decided I'm not going to let this get me down. I'm just going to concentrate on what I planned to do here all along, which is to have a baby and maybe sort out a new career.'

'I think that will be the best bet. Just think of him as a friend and don't try to read too much into everything,' Megan advised. 'Anyway I'm delighted you've made some progress on sorting out your degree course. I've got some study skills books you might be interested in; I'll post them up to you.'

After the phone call Jo stayed in her bedroom thinking about Megan's advice. She was absolutely right of course. Jo intended to concentrate on matters other than Magnus. She made plans to invite Sarah and some of the other mothers around to her house and decided to initiate some kind of breakaway antenatal sessions at her house, involving coffee mornings and gossip. She needed more female friends, not men with their mixed signals and potential for emotional dramas.

CHAPTER TWENTY FOUR

Jo was just dozing off upstairs in her bedroom later that Sunday afternoon, when she heard the front door open. What now? She thought crossly, assuming that it was Magnus coming round to see her again, just when she had decided to play it much cooler with him.

She got up quickly to circumvent him coming upstairs to find her, but when she went downstairs she found Ruby in the hallway.

'Hello, I'm not disturbing you am I?' Ruby asked anxiously.

'No of course not! I'm really sorry about Jess; it must be horrible losing a pet after so long. She was such a lovely dog,' Jo said kindly to Ruby. 'Come inside and have some tea with me. Let me take your coat.'

They went in to the kitchen and Ruby sat down wearily at the kitchen table. She put a carrier bag down on the table and lifted out a cake tin.

'I bought you over a chocolate cake to cheer you up. I knew you'd be feeling fed up too,' Ruby said taking the lid off the cake tin and lifting out a still-warm chocolate sponge cake.

'Oh Ruby, that's so sweet of you. But I should have been coming over to cheer you up. I was going to later, but you're usually out all afternoon after church,' Jo said as she put the kettle on, feeling guilty that she hadn't thought of making such a kind gesture.

'That's OK. I didn't go to Jeannie's today. She's only just got Fraser back home and I thought I'd give them a break from my miserable self,' she said, smiling self-deprecatingly.

'Really! You are *so* not a miserable person, far from it,' Jo replied as she took out plates and mugs from the cupboards and put some teabags into the teapot. She had never bothered with teapots before moving to Shetland but had recently got into the habit of making tea properly after spending so much time with Ruby.

'I have been lately. I shouldn't spend so much time thinking about the past when I still have my family around me. But sometimes it's hard to let go of people you loved. I spend more time going to funerals these days than weddings and christenings, that's the trouble. It gets me down sometimes. It's nearly ten years since George died and it still seems like yesterday,' Ruby said, as she twisted the wedding ring on her finger.

Jo sat down and poured the tea. She didn't know what to say in response, although she could easily understand how hard it must be to live through losing your husband and seeing your children grow up and leave home.

'Life is very hard sometimes, isn't it?' Jo said at last handing a mug across the table to Ruby.

'Oh indeed it is. But I'm not the only one with troubles am I?' she said looking meaningfully at Jo.

'I guess not. Everyone seems to have such complicated lives these days. I came up here for a quiet life and to get away from my problems and all I've done is end up with a different set of problems,' Jo said seriously and deliberately obtusely. She didn't want to discuss her particular brand of problem with Ruby.

Ruby sipped her tea and crumbled up a piece of cake in her fingers, deep in thought. She was thinking about Magnus and how miserable he had looked when she spotted him walking away from Jo's house that morning. Even though she hadn't spoken to him she knew her son well enough to know by the way he walked whether he was happy or not. He had trudged slowly up the hill with his head down and his shoulders hunched over even though it was a fine day. This made quite a change from the way she had seen him out walking during the past few days, when he had been singing to himself and striding along with a spring in his step. She knew it had something to do with Jo. Ruby had seen the blonde woman get off the bus at Magnus' house after the party and brazenly walk in on her own. She obviously hadn't been aware of who Ruby was, or if she had known, she hadn't cared.

She had been woken by the sound of Jo's car in the middle of the night and had seen her drive off. When Magnus came round to tell her about Jess she had put two and two together and realised that Jo had taken the dog around to Magnus and obviously found out about the other woman.

'Jo, I have never been one to interfere with what my children do, but I couldn't help notice that Magnus seemed really miserable when he left here this morning, and it's just that he seems to have been so cheerful recently,' Ruby said to Jo at last, after deciding to get to the bottom of what was troubling her son.

'I expect it was because of Jess,' Jo said in as innocent a voice as possible.' She took a bite of the chocolate cake and hoped this would be the end of the subject.

'No, it was more than that. I can tell. A mother can always tell,' Ruby said, looking boldly at Jo.

'OK, you win!' Jo said in defeat, putting the slice of cake down on the plate. 'I upset him because I mentioned something about his ex-girlfriend who was staying at his house last night. He said there was nothing going on and I guess I didn't really believe him, although it's really nothing to do with me who he sees is it?' Jo explained forthrightly.

'I see, I didn't realise she was his ex-girlfriend; I've never heard anything about her before. She didn't seem like his type at all. Oh well,' Ruby said very sadly, realising that perhaps she had read it all wrong. Maybe he had invited the girl round after all.

'I didn't think so either,' Jo said sympathetically. She could tell that Ruby was unhappy with this news about Magnus. 'She's got a right foul mouth on her. She called me a pregnant tart for throwing herself at your son, as apparently I have been. Although I can assure you I have done no such thing,' Jo added indignantly.

Ruby looked up in surprise. 'Goodness me, she said that to you at Magnus' house? I can't believe he would let someone insult you like that. He's far too much of a gentleman. Honestly I can't believe what's got in to him,' Ruby shook her head in disbelief.

'Oh no, I didn't see her at the house. She said it at the wedding the night before. I heard her talking about me in the "ladies" just as I was leaving,' Jo explained hurriedly. 'Magnus didn't hear what she said.'

'What a nasty piece of work she sounds,' Ruby said wishing she hadn't started this conversation now. It was far more complicated than she realised.

'That's what he said too. Well at least he said that he stopped seeing her because she drank, smoked and swore too much. Apparently he only went out with her for a bit. And he said he didn't invite her, she was just there when he got home. But I don't know what to believe and it's really none of my business,' Jo stressed, pouring out some more tea from the pot.

Ruby leant back in her chair, and took off her glasses and cleaned them on the edge of her blouse while she thought for a moment.

'I think he was telling the truth. I saw her get off the bus at his house last night and I know he was going round to a friend's first. I didn't see them speaking at the party and I can't imagine he would have invited her back and then travelled separately. That's not his style at all,' Ruby said, feeling that at least she could reassure Jo of her son's honesty. She picked up her mug and looked at Jo thoughtfully.

'Oh dear, I really do owe him an apology don't I? Jo said. 'I should have believed him. I was just so upset about everything, having to take Jess round to him when she was so ill. I didn't expect him to have company. I know we're only friends and I don't know him that well, but I was so disappointed to find out he was hanging around with that old slapper,' she added miserably before finishing the rest of her tea.'

Ruby smirked at Jo's description of the woman. 'Well men are funny creatures, but I honestly don't think you have anything to worry about there. I bet he sent her packing on the first ferry.'

Jo got up and walked over to the sink with her mug and plate. She was surprised at Ruby's inference.

'Ruby, there's nothing going on between Magnus and I, we really are just friends. I really appreciate getting to know you, Jeannie and Magnus; it has made such a difference to my life. I thought it would take much longer to make friends up here. But I have never been on the lookout for a new boyfriend and I won't be for ages and ages,' Jo said feeling the baby moving again inside her and reflexively laying her hand on her tummy.

'No, no; I know exactly what you are going through; believe me. I know you're not looking to replace your baby's father, but I think you should still be open to the possibility that people will care for you regardless of whether you are pregnant or not.'

Jo stared at Ruby, wondering what she meant. How could she possibly know or understand?

'Make me some more tea and I will tell you a story. Maybe then you'll understand,' Ruby said mysteriously.

Jo put on the kettle and made another pot of tea while she listened incredulously to what Ruby had to say.

'When I was a teenager, back in the late 1950s I ran around with a whole group of pals from Whalsay. My sister Violet went out with a young man named Lowrie, who she later married and lived here in this house until she died. Lowrie had a brother, George and George was best pals with Magnus. Magnus and I started going out together, and when I was 17 we got married.'

Jo sat down with the teapot and started pouring it out, frowning in concentration, confused by the names. Ruby ignored her puzzled expression and continued.

'I got pregnant nearly straight away after we were married, but unfortunately I miscarried. The next year the same thing happened and we were really upset. Magnus was often away fishing, along with George and Lowrie, so I was quite lonely on my own. Violet already had her first bairn by then. I got a job in the knitting factory along the road, for something to do and to earn some extra money.' She sipped at her tea, pausing to reflect on her memories. 'Anyway after Magnus had been home for a break I got pregnant yet again. Only this time I didn't tell him, I wanted to wait until I was sure I might keep this one. He had been really upset about the first two, and I didn't want him worrying about me while he was away at sea. They used to be away for weeks at a time in those days.'

Ruby fished around in her pocket for some tissues.

'The only trouble is, he didn't come home. The boat got

caught in a bad storm and he was washed overboard and drowned,' she took a deep breath, and took a sip of her tea before she continued.

Jo stared at her in silence, paralysed by the sadness of it all.

'I was absolutely devastated obviously; but what really broke my heart was the fact I hadn't told him about the baby. I was in such a state at the funeral. I felt so guilty. Nobody knew about the baby at that time so my family was surprised and tried to tell me everything would be fine and that at least I would still have someone to care for.' Ruby sniffed and wiped her eyes. Jo felt an uncomfortable lump in her throat and didn't speak.

'I know they meant well, but a little baby is no substitute for your husband. I was only 20 at the time and I had already lost two babies and then my husband. I was living in that tiny house over there, which at that time was only a tiny but-and-ben croft house with no running water or electricity. It was hard work I can tell you. My pals rallied round and my parents came to help when they could, but everyone was busy with their own crofts and families. All except George that is; he wasn't married.' Ruby paused for a bit and drank some more tea.

'Anyway, one day, a long while before the baby was due he came round to see me and asked me to marry him. I was outraged and told him where to go. George and I had been friends since we were bairns, and his brother was married to my sister, but I was so insulted by this. I couldn't believe he would ask his best friend's widow to marry him. He said he was doing it for Magnus, and that just made it worse. I tell you, I didn't speak to him again for ages. But you know, as time went by, George kept coming round and doing things for me, mostly when I wasn't at home. He fixed my roof after a violent storm. He delivered a whole stack of peats for my fire, enough to keep me going the whole winter. I would come home from work and find fish on the kitchen table, or a brace of rabbits. One weekend when I stayed at my parents he came and dug up the vegetable patch and planted out the tatties and carrots for me. When I was at my mother's having the baby he had been painted the house inside and out. But I still didn't speak to him.' She smiled at the memory and dabbed at her eyes again. Jo pulled a sheet of kitchen towel off the roll and wiped her own face.

'That man wore me down with kindness. One day, after lots of nagging from my parents, I decided I should at least thank him for all his hard work, so one Sunday I went over and sat next to him at the Kirk with the baby. And that was that. He walked me home. We sat and drank tea in my kitchen and he played with the baby and when he asked me later that same day to marry him again, I said yes.'

'Oh my goodness, that's so romantic, and sad and oh gosh, I don't know what to say,' Jo said. 'So he became Magnus' stepfather, no wonder he looks different to Jeannie,' she added thinking she had it all worked out.

'No, sadly that wasn't the case. My baby was a little girl called Marie. George and I got married a few months after he asked me and he became the perfect stepfather to Marie. He was absolutely smitten with her and would have done anything for her or me. But when she was nearly four years old she caught measles and died. It broke both our hearts. I have never seen a man so brought to his knees in grief. It was a dreadful time for us both, and we hadn't had a baby of our own yet. But then a few years later along came Magnus. We named him in memory of my first husband. I know that sounds a bit strange but George wanted to; after all he had been his best friend. Then we had Robbie a couple of years after that and then came Jeanne.'

'What a story! You really have been through it haven't you?' Jo said in astonishment, wondering how Ruby had managed to stay so happy and jolly after such a difficult life.

'Yes it's certainly been an eventful life. But that's why I find this time of year so hard. Both Magnus and George died in October, so it always brings back some sad memories. They're buried near to each other and little Marie was buried with Magnus. It makes going to the Kirk both a blessing and a curse. I can't help thinking of them all, and now that I'm getting so ancient I wonder how long it will be before I join them.' Ruby smiled uncertainly and stared out at the window noticing it was getting dark outside.

Jo didn't trust herself to comment on this. It brought home the fact that she wasn't the only person in the world who had faced some sad and difficult situations. She only hoped she would come through the other side with as much grace, dignity and cheerfulness as Ruby.

'So, anyway, the point of this story is, you never know what's going through a man's mind. I would never have expected George to pursue me like that. It turns out he always had a soft spot for me; only Magnus had asked me out first. Apparently they fell out over it for a few weeks.' Ruby laughed a little at the memory.

Jo smiled. 'Who can blame them Ruby? I've seen the photos of you when you were younger. You were quite the babe!'

Ruby chuckled again. 'I don't know about that. But I think in many ways I was very lucky to have been married to such good men. And I had four beautiful bairns too. Who could ask for more?'

'I'll settle happily for one beautiful bairn,' Jo said smiling back at her. 'Speaking of which, I felt this one move for the first time today.'

They talked about the baby for a while longer before Ruby wanted to go back home. Jo helped her across the road and gave her a hug and thanked her for telling her story.

'My pleasure, just remember things aren't always what you imagine them to be. It always pays to let people explain themselves fully.'

CHAPTER TWENTY FIVE

Jo watched TV for a while and when it got to 9 o'clock she got ready to visit Magnus and apologise. She had not wanted to go earlier in the evening when he might be cooking dinner and would possibly feel obliged to be hospitable. Jo intended to go in, apologise profusely, and retreat as soon as she could. She did however take the time to make herself as presentable as possible, putting on clean clothes, make-up and perfume before she left.

As she walked out to the car she noticed the road was frosty and her foot slipped a little on a patch of ice on the drive. But she confidently got into her new 4x4 and reversed carefully out of the drive. The bright full moon and clear sky showed off the stars to perfection. Jo drove along the quarter of a mile to Magnus' house very slowly and parked on his drive.

She opened up the front door after knocking on it hesitantly. She could hear the TV in the lounge and Magnus didn't appear to have heard the knocking. But Ben had, he trotted out of the lounge into the hallway to greet Jo. Magnus was lying down on the sofa and looked up in surprise when she appeared at the door. He picked up the remote control and switched off the TV.

Jo felt her nerves fail her when he didn't speak. She looked away, unable to meet his eyes, and occupied herself with stroking the dog. But after an unbearably long silence she straightened up and faced him. He was staring solemnly at her, with his hands in his pockets.

'I'm sorry I didn't believe you straight away. I really shouldn't have said anything to you about who you had staying over anyway. I know it's no excuse, but my life has been so crap lately I don't know where my brain is these days. Sorry.'

'No problem, it's been a crap day for everyone today,' he replied grimly.

Jo turned to leave, in the absence of any encouragement to linger.

'So, can I get you a cup of tea, or are you rushing off somewhere else? You look like you're going somewhere special,' he said, observing her pretty outfit.

His voice had warmed considerably and Jo was pleasantly surprised to see he was now smiling at her. She hesitated in the doorway wondering how best to reply.

'I know you're stuck at home waiting for the phone to ring, so I thought I'd just brighten up your evening,' she said, opting for a gently flirtatious approach. She leant against the doorframe and waited for his response, still not committing herself to staying for a drink.

'I'm *not* waiting for the phone to ring. I like to avoid going out on call. But you have brightened up my day, like you *usually* do,' he said, as he walked off towards the kitchen.

Jo felt extremely pleased at the compliment, even with the slightly sarcastic delivery, so she followed him and sat down at the breakfast bar. The kettle clicked off just as a high-pitched bleeping sounded from the radio-pager on the windowsill.

'Oh fuck! Sorry, I've got to go. But do me a favour; please will you wait for me. I'm sure it's just going to be something silly like a false alarm with a smoke detector or something,' he said running to the hall and grabbing his jacket. 'Please wait, won't you Jo?' he repeated, as he flew out the door.

'So. It's just you and me then Ben?' Jo said, as she finished making herself a cup of tea. 'How are you my little sweetheart? You've been having a very crap day too, haven't you?' she said, as they went to the lounge and sat down. Ben wasn't his normal bouncy self and he climbed up on the sofa next to Jo, and laid his head on her lap, begging sorrowfully for attention. She doubted whether he was allowed to be up on the furniture, but she felt sorry for him and let him stay.

Jo picked up the remote control and switched on the TV

again. She had no patience for anything serious and sobering, particularly this evening, so she settled down to watch a rerun of *Sex in the City*, despite having seen the episode a million times already.

An hour went by. Jo channel-hopped and found an old movie to watch. She wasn't unduly concerned. Then two hours had passed since she arrived, and she went to the front door and looked out, feeling a little apprehensive. It was frosty cold outside so she shut the door again and went back to the lounge. She considered going home, as surely he hadn't intended for her to stay this long, but decided to give him until midnight. She carried on watching the film but not really paying attention to the plot.

A little after one in the morning, Magnus returned home. He was surprised to see Jo's car still there as he fully expected her to have given up waiting by now. He was pleased though, as he did not feel like being on his own at the moment. It had been the worst job he had ever been called out to, and he desperately needed to unwind. Unfortunately, he was still on duty so he couldn't have a longed for dram of whisky.

He took his boots and jacket off in the porch and tiptoed into the house. He could hear the quiet babble of the TV and crept in to the lounge and found Jo curled up on the sofa fast asleep, with Ben at the other end of the sofa, wide-awake and looking guilty.

Magnus sat down on an armchair and watched her sleep, her face lit by the TV, the only source of light in the room. Her dark curls framed her face and spread out on the cushion she was using as a pillow. He picked up the remote control and muted the TV so that the silence was broken only by the gentle sound of her breathing. Ben didn't move from his comfy spot by Jo's feet, as if he thought that by keeping perfectly still, Magnus wouldn't notice him sitting on the sofa.

Jo looked so peaceful he didn't want to wake her. Magnus stared at her and brooded gloomily about the accident.

A little hatchback containing four teenagers had come off the road in the icy conditions. The car had rolled over, ending up crumpled and destroyed in a ditch on a lonely stretch of road. The two boys in the front had managed to walk away relatively unscathed as they had been wearing seatbelts.

The two girls in the back who had not had the sense to wear their seatbelts had not been so fortunate. Magnus and his colleagues had the gut-wrenching task of cutting off the roof of the car to get to the girls who were badly injured. One of them had screamed hysterically throughout the whole procedure, making herself heard even above the noise of the cutting equipment. But far worse than that, was the silence from the other girl. She had barely moved throughout, and the only indication she was still alive was when she opened her eyes and stared fearfully at him as he helped pull the roof off. Maureen had climbed down into the ditch to get to them and had set up a drip to try and stabilise the blood pressure of the more critically injured girl. She had no obvious external signs of injuries, but her condition hinted at serious internal bleeding. The air ambulance had taken them both off to hospital and the more badly injured of the two girls had been transferred to Aberdeen. Laura remained critically ill and Magnus was waiting impatiently for news.

It was difficult to be professional under such circumstances. Laura was the daughter of two of his friends. He had even briefly gone out with her mother while they were at the High School together in Lerwick. It could just as easily have been his daughter they were cutting out of the wreckage.

All this time later, sitting in the quiet dark lounge staring at Jo, he still felt sickened and angry at the stupidity of the youngsters. The roads were treacherous enough in the ice without driving fast along a narrow road and not wearing seatbelts. There had been far too many deaths on Shetland's roads in recent years, in similar circumstances, and they still weren't out of the woods with little Laura.

Jo stirred and opened her eyes, and jumped when she saw him.

'Gosh, what time is it? I fell asleep,' she said, sitting up feeling dazed and dishevelled.

'It's nearly two. Sorry, it was a very long job,' he said sombrely.

'Two in the morning! Jesus, I really did fall asleep. I'd

better go home.' She stood up quickly.

'Jo, you're not going anywhere tonight, it's too icy,' he said quietly.

'Don't be silly, I'll drive carefully, that's what I've got a four wheel drive for,' she said cheerfully, heading for the door.

'No, I mean it Jo; I've just cut two girls out of a car and I don't want to have to come along and cut you out of yours, thank you!' He snapped, grabbing her arm as she went to walk past him.

Jo flinched at the exasperation in his voice, although she had the sense to see it wasn't directed entirely at her.

'I guess your crap day hasn't finished yet,' she said softly, taking his hand and pulling him back to the sofa to sit down next to her.

'No, it hasn't. I'm sorry; I didn't mean to snap at you. I'm just feeling really stressed out waiting to hear whether they are going to be alright.'

He put his arm around her and kissed her on the top of her head as she cuddled up next to him on the sofa. Jo thought it best not to ask him to talk about what had happened and they sat in silence in the dimly lit room.

After a while Magnus felt guilty about keeping Jo up and suggested she went upstairs to bed. She sat up straight and looked at him intently.

'You need to sleep too you know,' she said gently.

'I don't think that's gonna happen tonight,' he replied looking at his watch, surprised to see it was now nearly three.

'I think someone else is awake too,' she said smiling and touching her tummy, in response to the gentle fluttering movement inside.

'That's good! I'll have someone to talk to while you go to sleep,' he said wryly. 'Come on Jo; go to bed. You can borrow one of my tee shirts or something if you want.'

'OK I will, but only if you come up and sit with me. If you're going to stay awake all night the least you can do is cuddle me. I promise I won't do anything immoral' she joked.

'Yeah, that really would ruin my day, wouldn't it,' he said sarcastically, but managing to raise a smile.

Jo was pleased she had brought a smile to his face at

last and went upstairs to his room and got ready for bed. She helped herself to a tee shirt out of the wardrobe and washed off the rest of her make-up in the ensuite bathroom.

She got into the bed, which she was relieved had the smell and feel of freshly laundered bed linen, all traces of Tricia thankfully absent. A few minutes later Magnus came into the room and lay down on top of the duvet next to her. Jo had an awkward moment when she realised that Magnus might have meant for her to sleep in the spare room, but he didn't seem concerned. He leaned over and switched off the bedside lamp and lay silently beside her while she fell asleep.

Despite his assumption he wouldn't sleep Magnus dozed off next to Jo. He would have been completely at peace with the world if it were not for his anxiety over Laura. He was haunted by the image of the pale and terrified face looking up at him from the depths of the car wreck.

The phone rang at seven thirty. It was Laura's dad ringing to say that she was expected to live, but that she was still quite poorly. He thanked Magnus profusely for helping to get her out of the car and said he would ring again with more news.

Jo woke up when the phone rang and disappeared to the bathroom to give him some privacy. She could tell it was good news when she returned. He had turned the bedside light on and she felt self-conscious at what little she had on so she leapt back into the bed quickly. Magnus discreetly turned his head away when he saw her.

'Thank God for that! Now we can both get some rest,' he said with relief.

'Why don't you get in the bed properly, you must be cold out there,' Jo said as Magnus sat down on the bed and leaned against the headboard with his eyes shut looking shattered.

He opened his eyes and looked at her doubtfully. The only reason he knew he could trust himself was the fact that he was just too exhausted. He turned off the light and got into bed wearing his jeans and a tee shirt. There was no way he was taking any more clothes off with her lying in his bed like that.

They slept late and were only woken up by Ben's insistent whining at the foot of the bed. Magnus went downstairs to let him out into the garden and set out some food for him. He came back upstairs and found Jo sneaking back into bed from the bathroom.

It was broad daylight and Magnus didn't feel comfortable getting back into bed now, despite the exhaustion he still felt. He grabbed some clean clothes and disappeared into the bathroom. Jo heard the shower running and shut her eyes feeling warm and comfortable in the bed. She would happily have lingered in the bed longer, but to avoid any embarrassing confrontation in her state of undress she slipped out of bed, gathered up her clothes and hurried along the hall to the other bathroom. She showered and dressed quickly and helped herself to a new toothbrush she found in the bathroom cabinet and brushed her teeth. She looked clean and presentable again, although without any make up. She shrugged. I don't suppose he'll even notice she thought to herself.

He looked up and smiled when she appeared in the kitchen.

'I thought maybe you'd run away,' he said. 'Would you like some tea and some breakfast?'

'Yes please! I stole a toothbrush by the way,' she confessed as she sat down at the table.

'You can steal anything you want,' he said absentmindedly as he switched on the kettle, and gazed out of the window at the sea.

'How about your heart then?' she teased.

'I thought you took that already,' he said turning round from the sink and smiling at the surprise on her face. She hadn't expected such a flirtatious reply.

'Does this mean we're friends again?' she asked timidly watching him as he crossed the kitchen to the fridge.

'Friends?' he said quizzically. 'Of course we're friends. What makes you say that?' He stood holding the fridge door open and looked at her wondering what she had meant.

'Well I got the feeling you wanted to talk to me last night, before you had to rush off and so I never knew what you wanted to say to me,' she explained looking down at her hands and fiddling with a cuticle.

'That's right Jo. I was about to say, I accept your apology, here's a cup of tea, now never darken my doorstep again.' He shook his head. Women! What went on in their heads, he thought to himself as he picked out bacon and eggs from the fridge.

'I feel stupid now. What I meant was.... I don't know what I mean really; this is such a strange situation isn't it?' she said seriously, walking over to the kettle, which had just clicked off.

'If you're referring to the fact that we are both single and you just happen to be pregnant, then yes I suppose it is an unusual situation,' he said. 'But there's no law against us being friends is there?' he added as he put the bacon and eggs down on the worktop.

'No, it's just...' She stopped mid-sentence, then picked up the kettle to make the drinks. 'Oh never mind... Black coffee for you?'

Magnus cooked Jo bacon, eggs and toast for breakfast and they sat and ate it at the dining table, talking about life and the universe, anything really, other than how they felt. They discussed the poker night and what they would cook and how much money they might raise for the charity. They discussed Jo's plans for a degree course. Magnus told her about his plans to build a new house and sell his existing house or maybe even move to New Zealand. Jo told him about her old job, her house in London and her friends. Jo hadn't felt this relaxed and happy for ages, and Magnus seemed content too.

They took Ben out for a long walk along the beach. Magnus caught her hand while he helped her down a steep slope to the shore and kept hold of it even after she was safely down on the sand.

Ben was running around as usual, having fun, and they stopped and watched him for a while. They walked back up the hill to Magnus' house and unknown to them Ruby watched them from her bedroom window just before they disappeared from view. Even from that distance she could see they were holding hands.

CHAPTER TWENTY SIX

'Jo, I'm on the back-shift this evening, so I'm going to have to get ready and go to work soon,' Magnus said, later in the afternoon. Jo was sat on the floor examining his CD collection, which was vastly different to her own.

'Of course! I'd better go home now anyway. Your neighbours must think I've moved in,' Jo said, as she put down the weird, in her opinion, Country and Western album and stood up to go.

'There's no rush,' he said, not moving from where he was sat crossed legged on the floor by the stereo, and wishing he hadn't swapped shifts today.

'No, really I ought to go. But I really enjoyed myself today. Thanks! I hope you get some more good news about Laura.'

Magnus stood up and walked out to the hall with her. He thought for a moment as she put on her coat to go outside.

'Look I know this is a bit sudden, but I'm going down to Aberdeen on Friday for a long weekend at Robbie's house; we've got tickets for the Aberdeen v Celtic match on Sunday afternoon. Would you like to come along too? I could show you around the city on Saturday and maybe you could go shopping while we're at the match.'

'Won't your brother mind if you bring along some strange girl to stay for the weekend?' she asked doubtfully.

'Why would he think you're strange?'

Jo buttoned up her coat and shrugged her shoulders.

'Anyway you've already stayed at my sister's so what's wrong with hanging out with my little brother too? He's very nice. And they have plenty of room so you can have a spare room all to yourself,' he argued persuasively.

'Are you sure? I would quite like to go back to Aberdeen; I didn't really see it properly when I drove up to catch the ferry to Shetland.'

She liked the idea of getting back to a big city, and it would a good opportunity to look around the shops for baby stuff while he was at the football.

'Of course I'm sure. I'll book a cabin for you on the boat. I know it's quicker to fly, but it's easier to take the boat if you're doing lots of shopping. I'm working Friday morning but I'll get off early so I'll come by and pick you up after lunch. We'll come back again on the Monday night sailing, by which time you'll be so fed up with me, you'll be wanting another divorce.'

'Ha, ha, very funny! I think it will be the other way round,' she said pushing him gently. 'Drive carefully tonight, or whatever it is you do in the engine room.' She stepped outside into the cool grey afternoon.

'Thank Heaven's it's too noisy to sleep in there. I can't wait until I get home to my bed tonight.' He yawned, and patted her on the head in a bizarre gesture, which struck Jo as kind of like the way you might say goodbye to a child.

Jo drove home. It was only four in the afternoon, but she was exhausted. She made herself something to eat and went to bed early, planning to read, but falling asleep almost straight away.

Jo spent the week keeping busy with her new life of antenatal and aqua-natal classes, making friends and shopping. On Thursday evening as she got back from Sarah's house she was just shutting the front door when the phone rang. It was Megan and she was really upset. Jo could hardly understand her for the tears of anger and frustration.

'I haven't even got an interview for that job?' she managed to explain at last. 'I can't believe it. I had everything they were looking for in terms of qualifications, but the Headmaster said they didn't think I had enough management experience.'

'That's not fair! How can they expect you to get management experience if they won't give you a chance at doing the job? Anyway don't you help manage the school's orchestra? Surely that's enough?' Jo said, completely outraged at what she saw as unfair treatment.

'I hoped that's what they would think, but because it has nothing to do with my actual subject, it didn't hold enough weight, and there were loads of other candidates that had everything they wanted,' Megan said dejectedly.

'I can't believe this. They could at least have given you an interview; that's really insulting. Maybe you should look at moving to a different school that will appreciate you more. I bet they just didn't want to have to find someone else to replace you,' Jo said encouragingly. She knew what this promotion would have meant for Megan and how seriously Megan took her job. She worked really hard, both in the language department and in extra-curricular activities, such as the new orchestra and the annual Christmas concerts.

'You might be right, I'm really fed up now; maybe I should get some experience in a different school. I've been there since I graduated so maybe that's what's letting me down. It is tempting to just go back to Wales. Maybe I could just live at home for a bit, especially if my parents are going to be away for six months of the year it wouldn't feel too much of an imposition. I might then be able to save up and add to what Dad's going to give me, and finally buy my own place sometime before I'm forty,' she said, resigning herself to the idea of changing jobs and leaving London.

'I'm really sorry, Megan, but you shouldn't get too down; you're worth much more than that. Get some more interviews and requests for references coming in, that will show the Headmaster that he can't take you for granted,' Jo said militantly.

'Yeah, perhaps I will start looking for something else. That flat I was interested in has sold already. I think I'm going to have to adopt your solution to life and move somewhere less expensive, although perhaps not quite so radical. I hear the Falklands are a great place to go, tax free and loads more men than women,' she said acerbically.

'Yeah, and more sheep than men, just like here,' Jo said laughing, relieved that Megan was attempting to make a joke of her situation.

'So how's your hero this week?' Megan asked cautiously.

'Well you'll be astounded to hear that there is no news since my last email. I haven't seen him since Sunday so there won't be anything to report until after the weekend,' Jo said happily, feeling sure that Megan was getting tired of this subject.

'Well I hope you have a good weekend anyway. I'm going to go and look for a new job now so I'll speak to you soon. Text me and let me know how you're getting on,' Megan said seriously, before she said goodbye.

CHAPTER TWENTY SEVEN

Jo spent ages in the bathroom getting ready for her trip. She shaved her legs, plucked her eyebrows, and applied a hot-oil treatment on her unruly curly hair. She went through all of the preparations she would go through for a first date. At the same time getting annoyed for bothering, and tried to justify it as normal pampering. She checked her weekend bag constantly to make sure she had everything she needed. At the last moment she remembered her digital camera and threw that in too.

She surfed the net to acquaint herself with the delights of Aberdeen city. She was surprised at how much there was to see and do. It was so far north of London that it had been completely off her radar, and she hadn't appreciated what a lively vibrant place it was. It was awash with oil money, and had everything one needed in a High Street. Magnus could spend as much time as he liked at the football, Jo was going to be in consumer heaven.

Magnus picked her up from her house at three thirty and they drove down to Lerwick. Jo noticed he seemed distracted. Paranoia crept in again, and she worried whether he regretted asking her to come along. Jo tried to keep up a barrage of witty repartee, but finally gave up and resorted to asking him why he seemed to be so quiet.

'I was just wishing I had booked flights instead of the ferry; it's going to be a rough crossing,' he said worriedly, staring straight ahead as he drove along the road to town. 'I wouldn't be surprised if they cancel it, the wind is expected to be blowing around force 9. If it gets any higher it might get cancelled.'

Jo gazed out of the window. The stretch of sea they were

passing seemed calm, and it didn't seem to be particularly windy either. The sky was blue, and the few grey and white clouds scudding by seemed fluffy and benevolent.

'It doesn't look so bad,' she said. 'Anyway I'd rather take my chances on a rough sea trip, than flying in a hurricane. At least I can swim,' she said cheerfully.

Magnus smiled at her innocence. They had arrived at the Northlink Ferry Terminal. He parked in the long stay car park, and carried their bags to the check-in desk to collect their boarding cards. They stood for a moment in the reception area on the ferry while Magnus sorted out the tickets.

'This is your cabin. I got you one with the TV and window in case you get bored; 14 hours is a long time to spend in my presence,' he joked.

'What cabin have you got then?'

'Mine's a four berth without a window or TV. I wasn't planning on spending much time in it anyway. I'm going to watch the football in the bar,' he explained.

Jo frowned. It really wasn't going to be a romantic trip away. She was about to reply when a group of men walked aboard and greeted Magnus. Jo stood by, wondering whether he was going to introduce her; apparently not. While she idly browsed the notice board and tourist information literature she noticed a young woman with two children hurrying across to the reception desk.

'Do you have any cabins free tonight?' the woman asked the receptionist hopefully.

'No, I'm sorry; we're fully booked on this crossing. I can keep you on standby for any cancellations though,' the receptionist explained politely.

'Oh please do! I only booked the trip today, as I have to go down and visit my mother in hospital. I'd hate to have the kids sleeping in the lounge all night; I hear it's going to be a bit rough.'

'I'll see what I can do, but I don't think you will have much luck I'm afraid.'

Jo watched the woman walk over to a large leather sofa in the reception area. She told the children to get comfortable, as they might have to stay there all night. They didn't seem concerned at all, as it was only the late afternoon and they were still full of beans.

Jo contemplated the fact that between her and Magnus they had six berths. It seemed ridiculous. She looked over at him and saw he was still engaged in conversation with his friends, holding the cabin key in his hand. Jo decided that if he was going to spend all night in the bar he could donate his cabin to the woman, and he could share Jo's if need be. It's not as if they hadn't spent the night together already, she reasoned to herself.

Jo walked up to him and gently pulled the ticket out of his hand. He turned to look at her, with a puzzled expression, but carried on speaking to his friends. Jo walked over to the mother and two children.

'Excuse me, but I overheard you say you needed a cabin. Here you can have mine. I can share with a friend,' Jo said, handing the woman Magnus' key.

'Really, are you sure?' The woman said, fumbling in her bag for her purse. 'Let me pay you?'

'No, that's OK. It's no problem,' Jo said happily.

'You're so kind; thank you so much. I can't bear the thought of sitting up all night with these two,' she said gratefully, gathering up her bags to take to the cabin. 'Thank you!'

'Don't mention it,' Jo said, turning back to Magnus whose friends had now wandered off to the bar.

'Have you just sold my cabin to the highest bidder?' he asked good-humouredly.

'Nope, I gave it away! She needed it more than you,' Jo said defiantly. 'You can share with me, when you've finished in the bar.'

Magnus looked at her in amusement. He didn't mind the fact she had given his cabin away. He had half heard the conversation and had worked out what Jo was doing and appreciated the generosity of the gesture. He did not however, intend to share a cabin with her.

'I'll just take the bags along and leave you in peace,' he said, as he headed off down the narrow corridor to Jo's room.

Jo felt snubbed and followed him slowly. He turned and waited at the cabin door for her to open it and he stepped inside and put the bags down on the floor.

'Jo, we're going to be setting off soon. It really is going to be a rough crossing, so if I were you I'd get into bed straight away and lie down, it will help you avoid getting sea sick.'

'What are *you* going to do?' Jo asked petulantly, sitting down on the bunk and studying him carefully, as he hovered by the door obviously keen to leave.

'I'm going to the bar. But, listen, I'll take the key, and I'll come and see how you're getting on later. We're going via Orkney tonight so at least there'll be a bit of a break in the journey. Please try and get some sleep won't you,' he smiled kindly, and left the cabin.

Jo shrugged off her coat and hung it up and sat down on the bunk in a huff. This was not what she'd planned at all. She was hoping to sit and chat to him since she hadn't seen him all week. She felt like he was trying to lock her away out of sight of his friends. Maybe he was embarrassed, she thought sadly.

At five thirty sharp the ferry pulled out of Lerwick Harbour. It was almost dark outside, and Lerwick looked pretty with all the streetlights lit up along the harbour. Jo stared desultorily out of the window at the town from this unfamiliar vantage point and then switched on the TV for want of anything else to do. There were complimentary newspapers, tea and coffee, handmade local chocolates and bottled water in the cabin. She was temporarily cheered by the fact that Magnus had booked her a first class cabin, but since he wasn't here to enjoy it, Jo got bored and restless. She contemplated going along to the shop or the on-board cinema but that would mean having to track him down to get the key to get back in. She checked her mobile but there was no signal so she couldn't while away the time ringing or texting anyone. She gave up and decided she may as well just get into bed. She got undressed quickly in case he came back and folded up her clothes and put them in her bag. She put on her pyjamas and dressing gown, took off her make-up and brushed her teeth. While she was standing at the sink she noticed the first rolling movement, as the ferry moved into the open water.

Jo got into bed and sat watching the TV, but the only programmes on this early were boring game shows, and the news. She got up and made a cup of tea and ate the chocolates. She got out a magazine and started to read, but couldn't concentrate, in such a bad mood. She put the magazine down on the bedside table and watched it slide across the smooth surface, as the boat rolled to one side. She picked it up and got out of bed and went to put it in her bag. As she stood up she realised that it was now difficult to walk across the cabin. The boat lurched violently. Sea spray hit the cabin windows and ran down, leaving foamy white trails on the glass. Jo started to get alarmed, and hurried back into the bed, and sat propped up against the pillows, staring blindly at the TV.

She was starting to understand what Magnus had meant. After a while she started to feel queasy. Half an hour later she was leaning over the toilet vomiting. She washed her face and grabbed at a towel to dry it and instantly had to lean back over the sink, retching and gagging. She could hardly stand upright in the tight confines of the bathroom, and banged her elbow on the towel rail, when she was thrown against the wall. She grabbed a sick bag and staggered back to the bunk and fell down awkwardly on it. The TV blared in the background, but Jo was oblivious to it. Her stomach cramped painfully, her throat was sore, and the nausea just would not go, despite the fact her stomach was now empty. She wanted to die. She was sure she was going to.

She lay down on the bunk and pulled the duvet over her, but the violent roll of the boat made it difficult to lie still. She was forced to brace herself against the edge of the table, in order to stay in the bed. She wondered how Magnus could possibly think she could sleep through this. She felt an irrational anger towards him, and imagined him laughing and joking with his friends in the bar. She assumed that he wouldn't be feeling the same effects as her, since he was a professional seaman.

Her misery continued for another three hours, by which time dehydration and low blood sugar levels made her head thump with pain, and her body felt weak and cold. She couldn't remember feeling this ill in her life before. She fantasised about the ship sinking, and even considered that disappearing under the sea and drowning would be a blessed relief.

She became dimly aware that the sea was starting to

feel calmer. Through the cabin window she saw the lights of Kirkwall Harbour appear on the horizon, and steadily grow brighter and closer. She still felt terrible though, and wondered how she could continue all the way to Aberdeen. She was desperate for a paracetamol for her headache. The boat eventually slowed down and moved into calmer water; giving her some respite from the rolling motion. She lay in the bunk shivering, despite being wrapped in two duvets, praying she would last until morning.

She thought she heard a tap on the door, but she wasn't sure, and couldn't find her voice to speak anyway. A moment later the door opened slowly, and Magnus stepped in to the cabin. He surveyed the scene, quickly taking in Jo's deathly white pallor and the unmistakeable acrid smell of vomit.

'Oh Christ! Jo, are you all right?' he asked, rather pointlessly; crossing the cabin swiftly and crouching down beside her. He stroked her hair away from her face gently.

Jo could only shake her head. Her throat burned, and she didn't trust herself to speak, as she just wanted to cry with humiliation and misery.

'That's it! We're getting off,' he said decisively. 'We'll fly down tomorrow morning. I'm so sorry. I should have known you'd feel this bad. Come on, quick, you need to get dressed. We will be docking in a few minutes.'

Jo felt a rush of nausea as she tried to sit up. She dived into the bathroom and hung over the toilet retching up nothing but saliva and bile. Magnus grabbed Jo's bag and pulled out the clothes she had been wearing earlier. He was anxious to get her off the boat before they got stuck on it all the way to Aberdeen. He knocked impatiently on the bathroom door.

'Come on Jo, we don't have much time. The boat's stopped and passengers will be getting off any minute. You need to get dressed.'

Jo opened the door looked at him with a mixture of exhaustion, humiliation and anger. Did he really expect her to get dressed in front of him? He turned away, and picked up one of the Orkney tourist brochures that had been left in the cabin, and started flicking through quickly, looking for hotels. He checked his phone for a signal and started ringing.

Jo dressed in the bathroom as quickly as she could, fumbling with her underwear as her hands were shaking so much. When she came out she sat down on the bunk and leaned down to put her boots on and stood up again feeling dizzy. He turned and saw that she was ready to go and grabbed their belongings and opened up the door for her, bustling her along the corridor to the exit. Most of the people disembarking at Orkney had already left. He knew you weren't supposed to get off the boat halfway through the journey, so he hurried Jo along, hoping the ticket collectors would have gone. Thankfully they appeared to be busy with the passengers waiting to board, so they slipped past into the arrivals lounge of the ferry terminal.

There was one taxi left in the rank and Magnus marched over to it and opened the back door for Jo, who sunk into it gratefully. Magnus got in the front passenger seat and started chatting to the driver.

'St Magnus Hotel please. Is that a new place, I've not heard of it before?'

'Aye, and it's seems very nice, it's quite small but very smart and I hear it has a great restaurant,' the driver said, as he pulled out onto the main road into Kirkwall.

They chatted inconsequentially about life in Shetland and Orkney. Once or twice Magnus turned to look at Jo and smiled encouragingly.

Jo slumped in the back seat silently, feeling drained. It felt like the hangover from hell. She could not imagine how she would recover without some serious medication.

When they got out at the hotel, Magnus carried the bags to the reception desk and filled in the guest book. The porter handed him a key and directed them to a room at the end of the ground floor corridor. Jo followed slowly, she hadn't paid any attention to the transaction at the reception, and so she didn't know whether he had got her a separate room or not. She was beyond caring now.

The room Magnus had booked, which was the only one available after a fruitless search around other hotels, had one large double bed with a separate child's bed in an alcove. There was a large luxurious ensuite bathroom with a spa bath and separate shower, a mini-bar, television, and tea and coffee making facilities, fresh flowers and a basket of fruit on the table. Jo would have found it perfect, had she not felt so close to death.

Magnus looked thoughtfully at Jo. He understood how miserable she was and wondered what he could do to help. He went into the bathroom and started running a bath, putting in lots of bubble bath in it. Jo sat on the end of the bed shivering and lacking the energy to move or speak.

Magnus turned the taps off and came back into the bedroom.

'Don't tell me, your head is killing you,' he suggested kindly, sitting down next to her and putting his arm around her.

Jo nodded slowly.

'I'm so sorry; this is *all* my fault. I should never have brought you down on the boat in this weather. Why don't you go and have a bath, that will help you warm up and relax, and I'll see what I can get to make the pain go away. You're probably dehydrated; it's a classic symptom of seasickness. Just like being hung-over. Only in your case you can't just take an aspirin can you?' he said sympathetically, and helping her to stand up.

Jo walked into the bathroom shutting the door behind her. She took her clothes off and hung them over a chair, and sunk gratefully into the hot sweet smelling bath. She lay back almost fully submerged and cried silently. She felt so humiliated. She knew that even after the pain and physical discomfort had gone, she would always remember the embarrassment of him finding her in such a disgusting and dishevelled state. She could still taste the sour tang of vomit in her mouth. She heard his voice in the other room and presumed he was on the phone, and then she heard the bedroom door open and close and finally silence.

The hot bath warmed her up and eventually she climbed out and got dry. She brushed her teeth for at least five minutes and still her mouth felt disgusting, so she brushed them again. Her throat was sore and it hurt to swallow the tap water. She cautiously opened the bathroom door and looked into the bedroom. Magnus had disappeared. Jo searched in her bag for a clean pair of pyjamas and put them on quickly. She wrapped a towel around her wet hair and climbed into the double bed and lay down. The cool cotton sheets were soft to the touch and Jo stretched out feeling a huge sense of relief to be lying in a bed that wasn't moving. She felt cold though, and pulled the duvet tightly around her, shivering again, as she quickly cooled down after the bath.

A few minutes later Magnus came back into the room accompanied by the sound of clinking china and glass on the tray he was carrying.

'Jo, I rang Jeannie, and she said you were to drink lots of sweet fluids. So I got you some lucozade, some tea, and some hot lemon and honey. I also got you some ice cream. And the night porter said he could make you some toast or a sandwich if you want.'

Jo sat up slowly. Whilst wishing the ground would swallow her up, she did appreciate the fact that she needed a drink. She tried to smile her appreciation, but ended up crying instead. Magnus put the tray down on the bedside table, and leaned across the bed and hugged her tightly. He pulled the towel away from her hair and dropped it on the floor and sat stroking her hair and let her cry.

'Come on,' he said eventually. 'Try drinking something, it will help you feel better.'

Magnus opened the bottle of lucozade and poured out a glass. She sipped it slowly feeling the bubbles crackle away in her mouth, and scratching her throat as she swallowed. But the sweetness took the nasty taste away for a while. Magnus picked up the dish of vanilla and strawberry ice cream and handed it to Jo.

'It's not Ben and Jerry's, sorry!' He said apologetically, smiling at her as she took a cautious mouthful. Jo managed a hesitant smile back at him.

'Oh thank God, I thought you were never going to smile again,' he said lying back on the bed in a theatrical gesture of relief and gratitude.

'That's the last smile you're gonna get.' Jo whispered hoarsely.

'And now you're speaking to me too,' he said happily, and got off the bed and made himself a cup of coffee.

He sat down on a chair by the desk and watched Jo eat the ice cream. She was still having difficulty swallowing, but she was savouring the coldness that was doing wonders for her throat. Jo finished the ice cream and set the bowl down on the table beside her. She sunk down under the duvet shivering with cold.

'Does your head still ache?' he enquired.

Jo nodded and shut her eyes.

'Drink some more then. It's the only way it's going to go away. You need to drink at least a couple of pints before you try sleeping.'

Jo opened her eyes and sighed. She sat up again, and reached for another glass of lucozade. She sipped the cold, painfully fizzy drink staring reproachfully at Magnus the whole time. She wanted him to go away now and leave her in peace, but he wasn't taking the hint. He supervised her for the next half hour making sure she drank all of the drinks he had fetched for her, and even made some more tea. After a while Jo started to feel the headache recede a little. She wanted desperately to go to sleep now, and perhaps wake up on another planet, or better still, back in her old life.

It was well after midnight before Magnus was satisfied that Jo was on the road to recovery. She got out of bed to use the bathroom and while she was out of the room he got ready for bed. When she came back into the room she found him lying down in the child sized bed in the corner. It would have been too small for a twelve year old and he looked ridiculous with his feet sticking out at the end.

'It was either this or the dog-house,' he said, as she crossed the room to get back into bed.

In spite of her misery she returned his smile.

'I'm cold. The least you could do is keep me warm,' she said pointedly, but smiling a little as she jumped back into bed.

Magnus looked thoughtfully across the room at her, as if he was weighing up his options. He got out of bed and walked across the floor and climbed into the double bed. Jo switched out the light and turned her back on him. He moved up closer to her and put his arm around her and held her tightly. She tensed up momentarily, but after a while she relaxed and fell asleep.

CHAPTER TWENTY EIGHT

Magnus was in the shower when Jo finally woke up on the beautifully calm Saturday morning, after the nightmare ferry crossing. She stretched out in the warm bed still feeling tired and sore. She had slept fitfully during the night, having frequent bad dreams about the boat sinking, and being washed up on a deserted island.

He emerged from the bathroom looking cheerful, energetic and slightly damp. He reminded Jo of how Ben looked when he got caught in a wave and would shake himself dry on the beach. Jo slid under the duvet out of sight. Despite the warm comforting intimacy of cuddling in the bed all night, Jo had misgivings about her behaviour. Twice now she had invited him to spend the night with her, and whilst there were extenuating circumstances on both occasions, she was starting to wonder what he thought of her. Megan was right; there was some unwritten, unspoken, social taboo that precluded pregnant women from behaving like she was.

'I'm just going to the reception to use their Internet access; I need to sort out our flights to Aberdeen. It might take a while, so you can get dressed in peace,' he said kindly, but with an edge of efficiency in his voice, which made Jo feel obliged to get up straight away.

She brushed her teeth while the bath was filling up. Her mouth was dry and she still had a revolting taste in her mouth. She thought about how kind and helpful Magnus had been, despite her ruining the start of his weekend away. Jo decided that a damage limitation exercise was needed. She could still recover the situation if she promptly fell back into carefree platonic buddy mode. She got ready to face the day as quickly as possible, resolving from this point on to be cheerful, upbeat and a pleasure to be with. With any luck no more catastrophes would befall her.

Jo was just packing up her bag, squashing the rather nasty smelling pyjamas and dressing gown that she had been wearing on the ferry, into a hotel laundry bag, when there was a knock on the door. Jo opened it thinking it would be Magnus. Instead a young woman in a uniform was standing there with a breakfast tray.

'Your husband asked me to bring you this. He said he'll be back soon, he's just gone out to pick up the car.' The waitress put the tray on the desk and turned swiftly to leave the room.

Jo thanked the waitress, frowning with confusion. She guessed the girl meant that Magnus was sorting out a taxi to take them to the airport. He must have got them on an early flight. Jo sat down and quickly poured out some tea. Her breakfast consisted of fresh fruit salad and a bacon roll. She smiled at his thoughtfulness, and ate quickly, not wishing to delay their journey any more.

Just as she was finishing Magnus came back to the room. He looked very pleased with himself.

'I hope you don't mind, but there's been a slight change of plan. I couldn't get us on a plane to Aberdeen until tomorrow afternoon, which means I would miss the football, so I decided to scrap that idea. We'll just stay here instead if that's OK with you? I didn't think you'd want to continue the journey by boat just yet,' he announced, sitting down on the bed and grinning at Jo.

'Oh, but what about your brother? Won't he be disappointed that you can't go to the match with him?' Jo asked anxiously, feeling the guilt piling back on.

'Nah, one of his mates is gonna go instead. Anyway he just told me that he's managed to get a trip back up to Shetland in time for the poker night, so I'll see him then,' Magnus replied reassuringly.

'Are you sure, I feel really bad about you missing your game?' Jo said doubtfully, as she stacked up the plates on the tray. 'So what are we going to do instead?'

'I've just collected a hire car so I thought I'd take you on a magical mystery tour of Orkney. I think you'll like it. I've been meaning to come back over here myself for ages.'

Jo psyched herself up to sound positive. She didn't expect Orkney to be much different to Shetland, and she was a little disappointed that she would not get to do any serious shopping this weekend.

'That'll be fun,' she said brightly. 'Does that mean we are staying here again tonight?' she added nervously.

'Er, yes, unless you want to try somewhere else instead,' he replied, wondering whether she was disappointed with the hotel.

'No, it's fine; in fact it's lovely. And thank you for my breakfast by the way. It was nice, thanks,' she said, trying to sound grateful. She was in truth very grateful, but she didn't know how to express it properly. She had expected them to be flying on to Aberdeen and putting the whole sorry episode behind them.

Jo grabbed her coat and handbag and followed Magnus out to the car. He had rented a little Volkswagen Polo and it seemed tiny by comparison to his Mitsubishi Warrior.

'Are you going to be OK driving this little thing? Remember it uses petrol, not testosterone,' Jo joked, as she got in to the passenger seat.

'Are you having a go at my pick-up again?' he said, raising an eyebrow at her. 'What has it ever done to offend you?'

'Oh nothing, it's just it's so butch and kind of exaggeratedly macho, especially compared to this little car,' Jo replied, as she put her seat belt on.

'And don't you think it goes with my image then?' he teased. He turned on the engine and pulled out of the car park. 'Or do you think this car suits me better?'

'No that's just it, you kind of look out of place in a normal car,' she said thoughtfully, looking at his long skinny frame sat behind the wheel.

'I'm not sure if that's a compliment or not,' he said, as he drove along the road, taking the first turning off the main road, leading away from the town.

'Me neither actually!' Jo stared out of the car window at the road ahead trying to work out where he was taking her.

In some ways Orkney appeared to be similar to Shetland, the omnipresent sea, for example, and the open landscape largely devoid of trees and hedges. The architecture was similar too, but as the road opened up away from the edges of Kirkwall she could see that Orkney was a softer, mellower version of Shetland. The rugged and heathery peat covered hills exchanged for the rolling fields of good quality grazing. In this late October sunshine it was beautiful.

'Jo, what's wrong? You seem a bit distant,' Magnus asked her after a long spell of silence. 'Aren't you feeling any better?'

'Nothing's wrong, I was just comparing Orkney to Shetland. I thought they'd be more similar for some reason,' she said truthfully, but skilfully passing over her real thoughts. 'Where are you taking me?' Jo asked, after an enjoyable spell of watching out of the window.

'Someplace very special,' he said mysteriously. He carried on driving confidently along the winding road, which occasionally passed by little clusters of houses.

Jo leaned back in her seat enjoying the ride and the change of scenery, but couldn't get away from the nagging feeling that she was in the wrong place at the wrong time. When she had agreed to this trip it had seemed a reasonably normal thing to do with a friend.

Jo and her openly tactile friends in London were constantly bestowing hugs and kisses upon each other, amid flirtatious banter and affectionate name-calling. But this felt different. Magnus had not done anything that Jo could wholly interpret as being anything other than friendly or neighbourly. But still it felt different.

The only thing that could account for how she felt was to assess her own feelings towards him. She shifted slightly in the seat and stared at a point just past his face as if she was looking out at the view. But she could discreetly observe the shiny dark auburn hair, the suntanned face dappled with freckles, and laughter lines etched deeply around his eyes. She looked at his hands on the steering wheel tapping out a rhythm on the wheel, not with impatience, but as if it was in time to some unheard song. He had long fingers that might have been elegant at one time, but hard physical labour made them firm and strong. Magnus was wearing black jeans, a white tee shirt and a black and red fleece with a sailing logo on the chest. Jo unkindly considered that he looked quite normal for once, and then hated herself for thinking that. Why did she care that most of the time she saw him he was wearing an oily old boiler suit, or a survival suit complete with internal buoyancy aids. It was more appropriate to either the weather, or what he was doing at the time after all. She thought about David. She had once thought that he always seemed so well dressed, polished and perfect. David was good looking in a very classic way. He was tall with dark brown, well-groomed hair, blue eyes and the kind of perfect skin that comes from a regimen of expensive and regular skin care, and studiously avoiding the sun. He now seemed drab and ordinary by comparison to Magnus.

She tried to imagine David driving her around Orkney instead of Magnus. He would have rented a larger car; even if there was no need of the additional space. He would have driven faster, and would have tutted in frustration at the tractors and slower vehicles that held them up on the winding country lanes. She thought about the ferry journey. David would not have helped Jo if she'd been seasick. The one time she had come home the worse the wear for drink, and spent the night in the bathroom, David had fumed for days about it. He had no tolerance for Jo's weaknesses or faults, and could not bear to be around someone when they were ill.

What had she been doing with David all those years, she thought to herself? He didn't appreciate her cooking. He didn't like spending too much time with her friends, particularly Megan. He looked down on her dull career choice. And although he often said that she was pretty, he would sometimes follow it up with a comment about her unruly hair or the fact that she looked too pale and should wear more make-up. Naturally these criticisms hadn't appeared all at once or he would have been shown the door a long time ago. But Jo realised sadly that she had let his meanness creep up on her, and he had often changed things around with a skilful turn of phrase that meant that Jo felt guilty or responsible for his moods. She wondered what it was about her that he had appreciated, and it all boiled down to the fact she was financially secure and too trusting. She had willingly cast aside her doubts about him just because, theoretically at least, he seemed a decent man and a good catch.

What Jo decided to herself, after analysing her relationship with David and this burgeoning friendship with Magnus, was that she was a hopeless judge of both characters and situations. She really would have to play it cool from now on, as her misplaced attraction to Magnus was probably not reciprocated.

Magnus was tempted to put on the radio to counteract the silence and wondered whether he had done the wrong thing in changing his plans to go to Aberdeen. She didn't look impressed with Orkney so far. She was looking out of her side window and hadn't yet seen the huge Stone Age monument he wanted to show her.

Finally Jo looked up and started paying attention to the view.

'Is that where we're going?' she asked staring at the huge stone circle in the distance. 'What is that place?'

'It's the Ring of Brodgar, it's a Neolithic stone circle, older than Stonehenge. I thought you might be interested in seeing it. We don't have anything quite as big as that in Shetland.'

Magnus stopped the car in a car park next to Harray Loch, a short walk from the stone circle. Jo got out and looked around. It was a beautiful setting with swans gliding along on the water a few metres away from them. They crossed the road together and walked up the hill towards the monument. There was nobody else around.

'I can't believe you don't have to pay to see this,' Jo said, as they walked along the well-worn footpath to the site.

'Do you like it?' Magnus said proudly, almost as if he had built it himself.

'I love it!' Jo replied enthusiastically. They walked around the large stone circle. It was a huge site with an earthen-work outer henge and a ring of towering stone pillars. Jo ran her hands over the stones that had been in place for so many thousands of years. It was hard to get her head around the concept of how they been set there without JCBs and cranes. It made Jo feel small and insignificant, and her problems meaningless in the grand scheme of things. It was both comforting and unnerving to think that so many people must have walked around this site admiring the handiwork of their ancestors.

Jo was impressed by how knowledgeable Magnus was about the archaeology of the site and the surrounding area. He had obviously read quite a bit about this subject, and brought it to life for her far more than she remembered from school when they had studied the Stone Age.

Jo was in no hurry to leave, but Magnus wanted to show her something else, which was quite close by. They drove a short distance to a large dark stone Mill House that had been converted to an information centre for Maes Howe. They bought entrance tickets for the site, and were escorted over to the huge grass covered dome in an otherwise innocuous looking field. They had to crouch down low to enter the long narrow passage inside the chambered cairn. The guide explained that tomb was older than the Egyptian pyramids and pointed out the Viking graffiti that had been carved into the walls of the tomb when it had been raided hundreds of years ago. The tomb was well lit inside and therefore lacked the expected spookiness. Jo was fascinated; she had never been inside a burial chamber before.

'I think this is better than going to Aberdeen, don't you? I can go shopping anytime, but I've never seen anything like this before. It's brilliant,' Jo said cheerfully, smiling at Magnus who was drinking a cup of black coffee, in the café they stopped in for lunch after leaving the tomb.

'I'm glad you're having a good time. I thought you seemed a bit fed up with me for changing our plans,' he said, putting down the cup and leaning back in his chair, and stretching his arms above his head, feeling slightly lethargic after sitting down for a while.

'Oh no, that wasn't why I was quiet. I was just feeling guilty for ruining your weekend by being so ill. I feel so stupid,' Jo said, looking down at her feet, noticing that her boots were a bit muddy and hoping nobody would see them under the table.

'I don't think you're stupid, and there is nothing to feel guilty about. Honestly; I'm enjoying this,' Magnus said reassuringly.

Jo decided to accept this at face value and changed the subject back to the tourist sites of Orkney, of which she was keen to see more of. After lunch they set off on a longer drive down to the south of Orkney across the man-made causeways joining up a series of smaller islands to the mainland, which Magnus explained had been built by Italian prisoners of war. Jo hadn't appreciated that Orkney and Shetland had played such a large role in the two world wars. To her these Northern Isles seemed so impossibly remote and lacking in interest as a possible German conquest. She hadn't realised that these islands were like a busy junction between Europe and the US, and that Orkney had an unusually deep and sheltered harbour; perfect for providing a stop off point for the Allied forces.

Jo was even more impressed with the Italian chapel. It was built by some of the prisoners who were determined to live a civilised life despite being in the middle of a war. The prisoners had utilised all manner of salvaged materials to turn an old army Nissan hut into a beautiful chapel complete with fresco walls and fake marble altar.

'Do they still use this for church services?' she asked, looking at the painted walls that looked almost as good as they must have done fifty years ago.

'Yeah, sometimes, especially for weddings and christenings,' Magnus said, as he looked at the tourist information leaflets on a table inside the door.

'I can't make up my mind whether this would be a romantic place to get married or not. In some ways this place represents the triumph of faith during a time of crisis. And yet, if people really did believe in all of this religious stuff why were they fighting in the first place. It's kind of strange isn't it?' Jo said, turning round to see what Magnus was doing. He looked up from the leaflet he was reading and shrugged.

'Maybe, but I don't think it was all about religion. Perhaps people who are taken away from where they live find it necessary to bring a little of their own culture with them. I think this chapel represents a little piece of home, not just a desperate need to go to church,' Magnus sat down on one of the seats in the chapel, still reading through the leaflet.

'What would you miss about Shetland if you had to move?' Jo asked, as she stood near the altar admiring the fresh flowers.

'People, music, landscape, peace, wildlife, lots of things really,' he said, reeling the list off quickly as if it was something that he thought of frequently. 'Why, what do you miss about London? He asked, looking up at her with a serious expression on his face.

'I don't know really. I miss my friends, and sometimes I miss the anonymity of the place, which I never expected. I feel like I'm living in a goldfish bowl up here. It's nice to have friendly neighbours and everything, but I feel like I stand out, and that's never happened to me before.' Jo sat down across the aisle from him as she spoke.

'I guess it must be hard for you. Sometimes it's hard for everyone in fact. But I think the good things about the place outweigh the bad. Don't you?' Magnus asked, before standing up, as if he was ready to leave.

'Yeah, definitely! But it's kind of funny isn't it, that before I moved here I didn't appreciate how different the culture would be here. I was just wondering what would be my equivalent of this chapel, and all I can come up with is a Marks and Spencer's Food Hall. How shallow is that?' Jo said self-deprecatingly.

They left the chapel and set off on another drive around the countryside. Magnus pulled the car over in a lay-by and looked up at the hill rising up steeply from the shore.

'Here's an interesting little place,' he said, as he turned off the engine. 'Cuween cairn; it's another chambered tomb only there's no guide to show you around, you just help yourself. Let's see how brave you are,' he said mysteriously, as he opened the door and got out.

'I can tell you now; I'm not very brave at all. I don't like enclosed spaces much. Isn't one tomb a day enough for you?' Jo muttered, although loudly enough for him to hear. She got out of the car and looked up at the hill. She could see a small square entrance to the cairn half way up. The sun was low in the sky and it would be getting dark fairly soon and she had no wish to crawl into any more burial cairns.

Jo reluctantly followed Magnus up the hill, which was steeper than it had looked from the car. Jo got out of breath and slowed down. Magnus stopped and waited for her.

'Come on slow coach, it will be dark before you get there!' He took her hand and dragged her the rest of the way. 'This place looks tiny from the outside, but inside it's large enough for about ten people to stand up comfortably. It is supposedly really impressive inside.'

'Yeah, I'm impressed; can we go home now?' Jo said, in the best spoilt-brat voice she could muster up.

'I came here a few years ago on holiday and never got the chance to see inside this place. I'm going to have a look, even if you don't,' Magnus said, ignoring Jo's reluctance to join him.

The cairn was protected by wire fencing to stop livestock getting inside. Magnus helped Jo over the stile, and then took out the torch from a wooden box next to the interpretation board. In the daylight the torch looked dim but at least it worked.

'Are you coming inside?' Magnus asked hopefully.

'You've got to be joking! I'm not going in there with just that feeble looking torch for light. It looks too scary,' Jo said, as she crouched down and peered into the pitch-black darkness at the end of the passageway, which was so long and low it would require visitors to crawl through.

'Go on, I dare you!' Magnus challenged.

Jo just shook her head resolutely. Magnus shrugged and switched on the torch and crawled inside. She could hear him inside when he stood up.

'Come on Jo, this is really interesting. It's not scary at all; the torch is bright enough to see everything. I promise!' he called.

Jo bent down and looked inside. She could see a dim light inside the tomb and could make out Magnus's legs blocking the entrance. He must think I'm such a coward, she thought. A pathetic, useless creature, that can't cope with sheep on the roads, bad weather, rough seas and now the dark. I'll show him, she thought irritably.

'Shine the torch down the passage so I can see what I'm crawling on,' Jo shouted down the passage, steeling herself to not be afraid, and finding that this was a little bit easier given that she had something to prove. She took off her coat so that it wouldn't get dirty and slung it over the stile.

She was surprised at how dry and smooth the paved entrance was. She shuffled along quickly trying her best to ignore the growing feeling of claustrophobia in the tight confines of the passage. She got to the end and Magnus reached down and helped her up. Jo stood up and grasped his arm and clung to him. Even with the torch it was dark.

'You need to let your eyes adjust to the dark, then you'll be able to see better,' Magnus said encouragingly. He took her hand and squeezed it, and shone the torch in the direction of the other chambers. She tried to take an interest, but all she felt was an overwhelming wave of panic.

'I've got to get out of here,' she squealed, as she finally lost the battle with the claustrophobia, and dropped down suddenly to crawl out of the tomb. The sudden movement made Magnus jump and the torch dropped out of his hand and they were plunged into total darkness. Jo shrieked, and scrambled along the passage as if her life depended on it and rushed over to the stile and sat down with her head in her hands, taking deep breaths and trying calm herself down. She knew it was completely irrational to feel this way, but she just couldn't help it.

A moment later Magnus emerged from the cairn and stood up. He was doing his best not to laugh.

'I'm sorry, I dropped the torch, I didn't mean to scare you, honestly,' he said sincerely, but Jo could hear the amusement in his voice.

'It's not funny,' she snapped angrily. Now that the fear was subsiding she felt annoyed with herself for being a baby, and with Magnus for finding her predicament funny. She stood up abruptly, picked up her coat and climbed over the stile and stormed off down the hill towards the car. She heard him hurrying behind her so she walked quicker. Then she heard him start running. She stopped and spun round.

'Leave me alone!' Jo felt an explosive irrational rage brewing inside her. She really wanted to be on her own for a while. She felt overwhelmed by the shame of always failing to create any kind of good impression.

Magnus shrugged. 'Go on then! The keys are in the car. I'll see you later,' he said calmly. He sat down on a grassy bank at the side of the footpath and looked at her without smiling.

Jo felt even worse, and turned and walked quickly down to the car and got into the driver's seat. She put on the seatbelt but didn't start the engine. She felt pathetic. She had left London less than a month ago and it seemed as if nothing had gone right. She was still making a complete fool of herself, even when she was doing her best not to, like attempting to fight off a lifetime's fear of enclosed spaces.

It was getting quite dark now, and the fading sunlight shimmered over the sea below the hill. Across the sea was another island and there were lights in the distance. Jo didn't even know which direction the hotel was and it would only compound her humiliation if she did something stupid like drive off without him. She got out of the driver's seat and hurried round to the passenger side and got back in the car.

She saw the shadowy figure of Magnus stand up and stride down the rest of the hill to the car. He got in without speaking and turned on the engine and drove off. She couldn't tell what kind of mood he was in, and was too afraid to look at him. She turned her face to look out of the door window and watched the view, blinking back hot tears. Magnus drove straight back to the hotel and parked the car, but didn't make any move to get out. Jo was reluctant to walk into the bright lights of the hotel reception with her face looking such a mess, so she didn't move either.

Magnus didn't understand why she was so upset, but he could tell she didn't want to talk about it. He made up his mind to go back to the hotel, get himself another room and leave her to it. He was getting a little tired of her unpredictable moods. He shouldn't have asked her to come along for the trip in the first place he thought sadly. It had all gone so disastrously wrong and now she seemed really angry with him. He'd totally blown it. He shouldn't have laughed at her, but it had seemed so comical the way she had shot out of the tomb like a scalded cat. He had not realised how scared she'd been until she lost her temper with him, and by then it was too late. Even so, surely she should have got over that already.

The streetlamp lit up his face and he looked as miserable as she felt. Jo thought about the fact that she had already ruined his weekend by making him miss the football match, and now it was Saturday evening and they had a whole night to get through. She couldn't bear the tension any longer.

'You must think I'm such an idiot, she said quietly. 'Ever since I moved to Shetland I have made such a fool of myself in front of you. I just wish that for once you could see me at my best, instead of someone who can't seem to step outside the front door without some accident or drama happening. Just once I'd like to have a day when I don't have to apologise for offending you, or having to thank you for pulling me out of a car wreck, or looking after me when I've been sick all night.' She folded her arms across her chest and turned her face away from him.

Magnus didn't speak for a while. He sat and thought about what she had said before responding.

'I think I have seen you at your best actually.' He shifted in the seat to face her and put a hand on her arm when it looked like she was about to bolt out of the car. 'Wait, listen! What I mean is, I don't think I see things the same way you do. I see someone that has just got herself out of a difficult situation by moving to a place she doesn't know. Who's been busy making friends, sorting out a new home and making plans for the future. All that, and being on her own with a baby coming... I know you've had a really hard time recently Jo, but what I admire in you, is your ability to get over it with your sense of humour intact. Well until just now I suppose, but that was my fault, I didn't realise how scared you were until you ran off.'

He withdrew his hand from her arm and waited for a response. She was staring out of the window trying to take in what he had said and wondering whether he was just being kind.

'OK,' he continued. 'It's been a long day and we're both tired. Why don't we just eat here in the hotel restaurant? I'll go and get myself another room, and then you can have a rest without me annoying you,' he said kindly, reaching for the car door.

'You don't annoy me. That's just it. I wish you did. It's all just so weird; this whole situation. I just don't know how I'm supposed to act.' She looked towards him questioningly.

'Me neither! Come on; let's go inside. Why don't we get some dinner and talk about it later.'

They walked inside and Magnus took the room key out of his pocket and handed it to Jo. He began to walk towards the reception desk, but Jo grabbed his arm and pulled him along the corridor towards their room.

'What's wrong? I was just going to ask if they had

another room now,' he said, as they went inside the bedroom.

Jo switched on the bedroom light before speaking.

'Look at my face. It's obvious I've been crying, so if you go and ask for another room the receptionist is going to think we've had an argument, and that's just too embarrassing,' Jo said, as she dived in to the bathroom to sort herself out.

'I see, so even though we're not actually married, or even going out, you don't want the receptionist, who you don't even know, and will probably never see again, to think you're about to get a divorce,' he said, from the other side of the bathroom door. He laughed.

'Yes, of course!' Jo replied seriously.

CHAPTER TWENTY NINE

Magnus sat on the child's bed watching the TV. He switched it off and looked up as Jo emerged from the bathroom after a shower. Her face had a fresh, slightly flushed glow and she looked much more cheerful. The huge hotel bathrobe covered her up even more than the clothes she had been wearing earlier, but he guessed she probably didn't have much on underneath. He put the kettle on to make some coffee and tried unsuccessfully to think about something else.

'It's kind of early for dinner still, so what would you like to do?' Jo said, as she reached across to pick up the mug of tea he made her.

The sound of Jo's mobile ringing in her handbag meant that he didn't get chance to reply. She got off the bed and fished the phone out of the bag and answered it.

'Jo, I've just seen David and he knows about the baby,' Megan began breathlessly, without evening saying hello.

'Oh Jesus; how?'

'He's been trying to get hold of you at your office and nobody would tell him anything obviously. But somehow he managed to find out from your personnel department that you'd gone on a maternity break. So he came round here to find you. I came back from the gym and he was waiting near the flats. I don't think he remembered exactly which one I lived in.'

'Oh shit!' Jo groaned in despair. 'What did he say?'

'He was drunk, and started shouting and swearing at me, and demanding to see you. He thought you'd be in the flat, but I wouldn't let him in. He seemed so crazy. I was afraid of what he would do, so I started walking away in the direction of the police station. He followed me across the road, shouting at me that it was his right to know,' Megan explained.

Jo sat on the edge of the bed frozen with dread.

'Drunk? That doesn't sound like him. Jesus, what a mess,' Jo said, in disbelief.

'I know! It was weird seeing him like that. Anyway I refused to tell him anything, and then he grabbed hold of me and hit me and started yelling at me to tell him where you were,' Megan continued, starting to cry as she relived it in her mind.

Jo shut her eyes, leaning forward as she sat on the bed. She swore softly under her breath, feeling so guilty for putting her friend through all this trouble, and powerless to do anything to help from this distance away.

'My God; did he hurt you, are you OK?' Jo asked fearfully, as it started to sink in what Megan had told her.

'No, I'm fine, honest. I didn't really get hurt, it was just more of a shock than anything,' she said, thankful that Jo wouldn't be able to see the painful bruise forming on the side of her face.

'I never imagined he would do anything like this. I can't believe it. He's never done anything like this before,' she said, hardly able to believe what she was hearing. 'So what happened?'

'Well this is the crazy thing, we were right outside Ealing Police station by then, and he hadn't even noticed. Luckily two policemen were just walking out and saw what happened. Before I knew it David had been dragged off me and was flat on the ground being handcuffed. I was taken inside the police station and a police officer came and spoke to me and made me some coffee. She thought it was some kind of domestic, but I explained what it was about. They told me that he had been arrested and charged with assault and they are keeping him in the cells overnight, but they'll probably have to let him go tomorrow, on bail, until it goes to the Magistrates court on Monday.'

'Why on earth would he suddenly get so upset about all this? I don't understand why he now wants to find me when the last thing I heard was that he didn't want me to contact him again ever,' Jo said.

'Well it seems he was asked to leave his job for some reason, and his wife has chucked him out of the house already. He has nowhere else to go, so I guess he was trying to track you down. He didn't believe you'd really left your job or London. But don't worry he still doesn't know where you are, and I didn't say anything else about the baby either.'

'I don't know what to say. This is such a mess. I should have told him in the first place then none of this would have happened. I'm so sorry, I should have listened to you,' Jo said miserably. She had gradually moved off the bed during the conversation, and was now sat on the floor beside it, her face against the side of the mattress, oblivious to the presence of Magnus in the room.

'No, I don't think so!' Megan replied sharply. 'Having seen how crazy he can get I'm glad you're miles away from him. Just supposing he'd persuaded you to stay; you'd now be dealing with his problems. Nobody in his business just gets asked to resign, not unless something odd is going on. It's just a polite way of getting sacked, so this isn't just about you.'

'I don't know. I don't know what to think. Maybe I'd better come back to London and try and sort it out. Jesus, everything has completely fallen apart in my life. I can't believe this...' Jo stopped speaking, unable to control her voice any longer.

'No, don't! Please don't come back yet, at least not for that reason,' Megan pleaded. 'I don't think it would be a good idea to see him. I'm sure nothing else will happen now, especially not if he's going to get prosecuted.'

'But I can't just let you deal with all of this on your own,' Jo argued, snatching one of the tissues and rubbing her face harshly with it.

'Jo, please! I'll be fine. Just let this blow over a bit and we'll see what we can do then,' Megan said, wishing that she had not told Jo about this until she had calmed down about it herself.

After Jo had hung up she sat on the floor clutching the phone in her hand and burying her face completely into the side of the bed. She was upset about what she'd heard but anger was starting to take over. She was furious with David for taking out his frustration on Megan, but she was also angry with herself for running away and leaving this trail of disaster behind her.

Magnus didn't know what to do. He wanted to ask about what had happened, but could see that Jo needed some space. He got up from the armchair he had been sitting in and walked over to the bed, and sat on the edge. He reached down and touched her hair, still damp from the shower. Jo didn't react, and Magnus carried on stroking her hair, winding long curls around his fingers and letting them fall like springs.

'Jo, do you want to talk to me about what's going on? Or shall I leave you in peace?' he asked gently, after a while.

Jo didn't move. She was deep in thought, planning on flying down to London and confronting David like she should have done in the first place. Magnus nudged her shoulder when she didn't reply.

'Please talk to me. Maybe there's something I can do to help.'

'There's nothing anyone can do to help. I have completely screwed up my life. Everything is turning into a complete fecking nightmare,' Jo said angrily, as she stood up suddenly and retreated to the bathroom.

Magnus got up and stood by the window looking down the hill at Kirkwall Harbour. It was a calm and beautiful evening and he considered putting on his jacket and going for a walk, and leaving Jo to sort herself out. Without knowing what was going on it was hard for him to try and help her, and he wasn't even sure that she wanted his help. He heard the bathroom door open and Jo came back into the bedroom, still in the bathrobe. She stood in the middle of the room looking at him, as if unsure what to do or say next. She looked like someone whose world had ended, and before he thought too clearly about how she would react, he walked across the room and put his arms around her

'Jo, please talk to me. I hate to see you this upset,' he said. He held her away from him a little so that he could see her.

'Fine! I'll tell you,' she said at last, removing her hands from her face. She had a feeling that he wasn't go to leave her alone and knowing that since she had already made such a fool of herself so far, she had nothing left to lose. She might as well just tell him and get it over with.

'OK, but before you do, why don't you get dressed? I'll

go and get a menu from the restaurant and maybe we can order something to eat,' he said, gently taking the edges of her bathrobe where it was gaping open at the top and pulling them across her chest.

Jo clutched at the bathrobe and tightened the belt crossly.

'I'm not hungry!' she said, going over to her suitcase to get some clean clothes out.

'I wasn't just thinking about you,' Magnus replied patiently, picking up his wallet from the desk and walking to the door.

Jo turned round and glared at him.

'Fine, you go and get something to eat then. I'm staying here,' she said, as went to go back to the bathroom to get dressed.

'Actually, I wasn't thinking of me either,' he said pointedly, looking in the general direction of Jo's tummy.

Jo blushed and slammed the bathroom door behind her.

Magnus walked down to the restaurant and ordered a whisky and sat at the bar for a while studying the menu. He wondered what the chances were of Jo calming down sufficiently to want to come and eat in the restaurant. He looked around the room with its freshly decorated stylish décor, and large bay window that looked down over the harbour. The menu looked good too; it would be nice to have a meal here. It was now early Saturday evening and the restaurant was starting to fill up. He finished the whisky and picked up the menu to try and entice Jo out of the room, or at least to consider room service.

He opened the bedroom door cautiously. Jo was sat on the bed leaning against the headboard. He walked over and handed her the menu. She took it; resigned to the fact he was going to make her eat something.

'Life just doesn't get any better than this does it?' she said with an edge of sarcasm in her voice. She opened up the menu and stared at the writing without taking any of it in.

'Jo, you're not the first person to have gone through the misery of breaking up with someone. You should have seen me three years ago. You look as cool as a cucumber by comparison,' Magnus said as he sat kicked off his shoes and sat down on the bed beside her.

'What do you mean?' she asked, as she threw the menu down on the bed.

'Lynne didn't actually inform me that she intended to leave; she just packed up, took Ella and left me a note. I was working on one ferry; she left Whalsay on the other. By the time I got home from work she had already boarded the Aberdeen boat. It was the first day of the school summer holidays and she must have been planning it for weeks. She's a primary school teacher.' Magnus got off the bed again and went over to the mini bar and took out a tiny bottle of whisky. He poured out the contents into a glass from a tray on top of the fridge and proceeded to drink.

Jo watched him curiously.

'I went crazy. I had no idea where she had gone. Her parents and sisters refused to tell me, and treated me as if I was some kind of villain who had been mistreating her. And of course she hadn't told them that she had been having an affair for years with an ex-boyfriend – Ella's real father. I didn't go to work for three weeks. I didn't do anything, except maybe drink too much,' he said, as he finished the whisky and put the glass down on top of the fridge. 'One night I was sitting in the house on my own and I got completely pished and miserable, and I decided to go out and visit one of my friends. I got in my car and didn't get even 100 yards down the road before I had driven it into a ditch and wrecked it. I was lucky to get out in one piece.'

Jo stared at him in surprise. She couldn't imagine him doing anything so reckless. Magnus looked at her and smiled briefly before continuing.

'I was lucky there was no policeman on the island that night. One of my friends came by and pulled me out and took me home. He then went back and winched my car out of the ditch and brought the evidence back and hid it in my garage. I would definitely have lost my licence if I'd been caught.'

'Wow, I'm surprised. I never imagined you doing anything like that,' Jo said at last. She was still sat on the bed, hugging her knees up to her chest and staring at Magnus in amazement.

'Well that wasn't the only stupid thing I did. I eventually went back to work and kind of got back to normal, but I was still drinking too much and not eating properly. I started going into Lerwick at the weekends, going to the clubs and hanging out with a crowd of people who drank a lot and took drugs. That's how I met Tricia,' he said, looking faintly embarrassed at the mention of her again.

'I can't say I blame you actually. I think if I hadn't been pregnant when all this happened I could easily have gone off the rails a bit myself,' Jo said sympathetically. She patted the bed beside her, inviting him to come and sit down again. But he chose to ignore her, and walked over to the window and stared out, but not really seeing anything of the view.

'That wasn't all,' he continued. 'I hadn't even found out at this stage that Ella wasn't really my daughter. When Lynne told me a few weeks later, I thought I really would go crazy. Nobody would let me stay on my own for ages. I was just so angry and self-destructive.' Magnus turned round to look at Jo who had got off the bed and walked over to him.

'I'm sorry you had such a hard time,' Jo said quietly, putting her arms around his neck and hugging him. Magnus hugged her back briefly, then sat down on the bed and leaned back against the headboard. He looked tired, as if talking about his marriage had exhausted him. He shut his eyes for a moment but when he opened them he smiled at her.

'OK; now it's your turn. Beat that if you can Mrs Birdseye!'

Jo couldn't help but smile back. She certainly felt a lot more comfortable telling him, now that he had confided in her.

'Right,' she said melodramatically, 'now that you're sitting comfortably, I'll begin.' She strode over to the armchair and sat down facing him and recounted the story about her break-up with David and her impulsive decision to move to Shetland.

'I see, so that's how you ended up here. I always knew it had to be something rather dramatic,' he said, as he went back and sat on the bed, nursing another whisky that he had helped himself to whilst Jo had been relating her account of the last few weeks.

'Yeah, however, that doesn't seem to have solved anything. I should have told David about the baby. Megan tried to persuade me to speak to him before I left London but I refused. Stupid I know, but I just didn't know how to go about it. So about a week after I moved in to my new home I sent him an email just to explain why I had moved. I didn't mention the baby or where I lived, but just said I'd gone away. I kind of wanted him to explain himself a bit first.' Jo stopped for a moment and drank some of her tea. She looked over at Magnus who was still sitting quietly on the bed, listening with interest.

'Anyway he wrote back a couple of days later and said that I'd got it all wrong, that he wasn't an addict, he was a professional gambler, and a successful one at that. He said he had just bought the house we were supposed to be going to buy together, but that now his wife and two sons were moving in with him instead,' Jo continued sadly.

'He was married?' Magnus queried, shocked that Jo would have had a relationship with a married man with children. He drained the last of his whisky and stared at her in unmasked horror.

'Yes, but I never knew that about him either. It came as a complete surprise to me. It's like I never knew anything about him at all,' Jo said, leaning right back in the chair and staring up at the ceiling, feeling drained.

'I see,' Magnus said doubtfully, wondering how someone could keep something like that a secret for so long. 'So what has happened today to make you so upset?' he asked, wondering whether he should get another drink from the mini-bar, but deciding to wait a while.

She described what had happened, feeling all of the guilt and anguish return, as she did.

'So he wants you back then?' Magnus asked, slightly bitterly.

'So it would seem. But obviously not for the right reasons,' she said, all but slamming her mug down on the desk beside her.

'But what really upset me was the fact that he took it out on Megan.' Jo leaned forwards and rested her head on her arms. Talking about it just reminded her about what a dreadful mess her life was in.

'What are you going to do now?' Magnus asked cautiously.

'I'm thinking of going back to London. It's not fair on Megan to leave her picking up the pieces on my behalf; I should have just told him everything before I left.' Jo stood up abruptly as if she intended leave immediately.

Magnus stared at her, not quite wondering what she meant by *going back to London.*

'It's just as well you keep your guns locked up, I could kill the bastard!' she said angrily, still standing in the middle of the room at a loss at what to do next.

'If that's what you mean by sorting out the mess in London, I think you'd better stay here until you've calmed down, don't you?' Magnus said wryly, standing up and walking over to where she stood.

'I don't know what I'm going to do,' she said softly, as he put his arms around her again. She could smell the whisky on his breath as he kissed her on top of her head.

'I don't know either, but seriously, I'm starving now, can we at least get something to eat,' he said as he let go of her.

Jo shrugged wearily, and went into the bathroom to check that her face didn't look too frightful. She still didn't feel like eating but knew she would have to. It was getting late now and the restaurant stopped serving food at nine. They only had a few minutes left to get to the dining room. She spritzed on some perfume as the only contribution to making herself more presentable. Her pale face was slightly blotchy but she deemed it beyond repair in the little time she had.

'You look great, come on,' Magnus said encouragingly, as she he opened the bedroom door for her and stood waiting for her to follow.

'You're just too drunk to notice how awful I look,' Jo replied grimly as she walked passed.

Magnus flinched at the criticism, but chose to ignore it.

'You'll feel better when you've had something to eat. I promise,' he said, as they walked along the corridor to the restaurant.

They took a table by the window and Jo stared down at Kirkwall Harbour that was brightly lit with streetlamps. People were milling about taking advantage of the calm weather and starry skies.

They ordered some food and Jo asked for a jug of water.

Magnus declined the wine list and said he would stick to water too. When the waitress had gone Jo leaned across the table towards him.

'Have a drink, I'm sorry about what I said just now, I know you're not drunk,' Jo said apologetically. 'I'm just feeling ratty. I would give anything to have a large gin and tonic right now.'

Magnus smiled gratefully at her and got up and ordered a whisky from the bar. He came back to the table and sat down.

'It's my last one, honest. Jesus, what a day we're having?' He sipped the drink and put it down on the table and smiled. 'What else can go wrong eh?'

'Oh please; don't tempt fate any longer,' Jo groaned. 'I can think of plenty of things that could go wrong,' she added, staring out of the window trying to avoid meeting his eyes.

Magnus studied her face. Even in the subdued lighting of the dining room she looked pale and tired. Her eyes looked slightly puffy from crying. She wore no make-up and she sat hunched in her chair opposite him, fiddling with a ring on her right hand. He looked at her fingers; they were slim, elegant and neatly manicured with rose pink polish on her nails. He wanted to reach out and hold her hand but he didn't know how she would react so he picked up the whisky instead. He knew he shouldn't be drinking. It was hard enough sharing a room with her anyway, let alone reducing any inhibitions he might have with alcohol. He put the glass down again wondering what to talk about.

'Jo, I don't think you should go to London; what good will that do? You don't want to go back to him, do you?' he asked, after a while of watching her stare out of the window.

'No, of course I don't want him back!' she replied sharply. 'I just want to make sure he never bothers my friends again. I never actually want to see him again, and I wish I didn't have to share a baby with him. It's not fair that I'll always be connected to him.' She crossed her arms petulantly and slumped back in her chair.

'Do you think he's likely to want to stay in contact with you and the baby?' Magnus asked cautiously, not wanting to provoke any anger from her.

'I really don't think so actually. I think he just wants

someone to look after him now he has nothing. And it isn't going to be me, that's for certain,' she said resolutely, looking Magnus in the face, daring him to suggest she should keep her baby's father in her life. 'You probably think I should encourage him to stay in contact don't you?' she added.

'No, I don't actually. Ordinarily I would say a father has equal rights to a part in his child's life. But given these particular set of circumstances I don't. I think he would just try and take advantage of you, and you'd end up getting even more hurt. Maybe he'll sort himself out one day and things will be different then,' he said sincerely, and reaching out and taking her hand at last.

Jo looked down at their joined hands on the table. Her hand didn't feel like it belonged to her. His hand was freckled and tanned and had a small scar on one of the knuckles which Jo had never noticed before.

'I thought you might think I was some awful person trying to deprive a father of his child, especially after what you told me earlier.'

'I don't think you're an awful person at all, and this is completely different to my life.' He let go of her hand as the waitress appeared with their food. He picked up the bottle of mineral water and poured some more in Jo's glass and poured some out for himself. Jo filled the gap in the conversation by helping herself to salt and pepper and taking a sip of water.

'This salmon is nice, but it's not as good as the one you cooked that night when you first came round,' she said, after one mouthful of her dinner.

'That's probably because that fish was pretty much as fresh as you could get. I'm glad you liked it. Your face was such a picture when you saw it,' he said, laughing at the memory.

'That's because I'd never seen one like that so close up before, still with it's head on and all, I didn't know what to do with it. I still wouldn't, so if you bring me anymore, I'd have to get you to show me how,' she replied, smiling at his amusement.

'I wondered if you would, it was all part of my cunning plan to have dinner with you,' he teased.

'Really?' Jo asked in surprise, dropping her knife loudly

on the plate. It clattered on to the table and she picked it up, trying to recover her composure.

'Well kind of; I don't think I really put much thought into it. But I was glad I got to know you better that evening. It was fun.' He picked up the glass of whisky, took a sip, and then put it down quickly, aware it was already loosening his tongue a bit too much.

Jo smiled, by way of acknowledging she had enjoyed that evening, which now seemed like it happened months ago. She watched Magnus drinking the whisky and wondered whether it was a good time to find out what else was going on in his head. She continued eating for a few minutes, thinking about what to say.

'What are we doing here?' she asked after a while, putting down her knife and fork and looking across the table at him.

Magnus regarded her thoughtfully while he chewed a mouthful of steak. He took another sip of whisky before speaking.

'You mean, other than sitting here having dinner?' he replied, double-checking he knew what she was referring to, and stalling for time.

She nodded.

'I don't honestly know!' He picked up a chip from his plate with his fingers, stared at it for a moment, and then put it back on the plate. He was quickly losing his appetite now. 'I've never been in this situation before,' he added quietly.

'What situation?' Jo didn't know whether she ought to pursue this line of questioning or not, but it was bugging her now.

'Being friends with someone I find attractive, but who isn't really available. It feels wrong, but I can't help the way I feel about you.' He shrugged and looked down at the table feeling awkward. He picked up the glass of whisky and finished it.

Jo froze like a rabbit caught in the headlights of a fast moving car. It was kind of the answer she was hoping for, but now that she'd heard it, she was afraid. Because the very next question, screaming to be asked was - now what? She searched around in her mind for an excuse not to have to go back to their room any time soon. She looked out of the window and decided to suggest a walk after dinner. She desperately needed some fresh air. Magnus saw the apprehension register in her face and wished he hadn't been so honest.

'I'm sorry Jo; I didn't mean to offend you. I know you're not ready for a new relationship. I didn't intend for anything to happen between us. I was just happy enough to be friends with you,' he said sincerely.

'I'm not offended. I just didn't think that was how you felt, that's all. You've never done anything to make me believe anything differently.' She replied, looking at him and realising he was just as nervous as she was about saying the wrong thing.

'Well I do have it in me to act like a gentlemen from time to time, even if it has been difficult at times,' he said, winking at her.

Jo blushed and looked down. She felt the baby move and rested her hand where she had felt it. She noticed the baby always seemed to remind her of its presence when she needed it most. She felt out of her depth now and regretted being so forthright.

'I didn't know you were pregnant the first time I saw you,' Magnus said, looking at Jo's tummy. 'When you and your friend first came to see the house I was working on the ferry and I saw you both get out of the car. When you left later that evening I was off duty, and just going across on the ferry to see a friend in town. I was upstairs in the wheelhouse chatting with my colleagues. You went upstairs and sat in the lounge didn't you,' he continued.

Jo nodded and looked puzzled, wondering why she hadn't noticed him.

'You couldn't see me, but the lads had spotted you and Megan on the CCTV. It's not every day you get two such bonny tourists sitting on the ferry, so it caused a bit of a fun. When we got to the other side you walked right past me to get to your car. I thought you looked lovely.' Magnus grinned and leant back a bit as the waitress came over and cleared their plates away.

'Most people notice Megan before me,' Jo replied quietly, wishing she could remember seeing him.

'Yeah, I was in the minority, everyone else was looking

at the tall skinny blonde,' he teased; picking up the dessert menu the waitress had brought back to the table.

'Thanks!' she replied sarcastically. She paused for a moment fiddling with her napkin. 'What did you think when you found out I was pregnant?'

'I thought, that's a shame, as I figured you must be married or something. And when it turned out you were on your own, I still thought there was every possibility some man would come along and claim you back.' He stared at her, and smiled when she looked up at him.

'And what do you think now?' she ventured.

'I think you've been through a really horrible time and you probably don't want to rush into anything too soon. So I figure I'll probably have to wait at least another year before I get to kiss you.' He reached over and squeezed her hand, and let it go as the waitress came back to take their order.

Jo found herself ordering lemon tart and ice cream just to avoid the awkwardness of what to do when they had finished eating. Magnus ordered the same and some coffee.

'I thought you were going to kiss me that night on the beach,' Jo said, in a hushed voice, referring to the time when they watched the Northern Lights.

'I very nearly did,' he said seriously. He looked out of the window disappointed to see rain trickling down the window.

Their pudding arrived and Jo picked up the spoon and twiddled it nervously in her fingers and consequently dropped it on the floor. Magnus reached over to another table and picked up a clean one from where the waitress had just set out clean cutlery for the morning.

'Thanks,' she said, taking the spoon. 'So what stopped you?' she added boldly.

'Well apart from the fact if you'd screamed in horror, my mother might have heard you, which would have been seriously embarrassing,' he paused, as if considering another reason. 'I also didn't want to start something I couldn't finish.'

Jo swallowed some ice cream awkwardly and nearly choked. She took a sip of water. 'What do you mean, something you couldn't finish?' she said, when she was sure she wouldn't start coughing.

'Don't make me spell it out for you Jo,' he said, looking away from her.

'No, really, I don't know what you mean?' Jo asked anxiously.

'It would be very difficult for me to stop there. It's been hard enough spending so much time with you, especially sharing a room with you,' he explained quietly so nobody else would hear, then leaning back in the chair, as if he needed some distance from her.

Jo finally grasped what he meant and looked down.

'I never realised. I'm sorry,' she said, and resumed eating the lemon tart, trying to absorb the fact Magnus did have feelings for her.

They finished their meal more or less in silence. The brief rain shower had stopped already, and Jo thought about going out for a walk, even though it was quite late now.

The waitress came over to the table with the bill. Jo picked up her handbag.

'I'll get this!' Jo said, taking her purse out.

'Can you put it on our bill please; room 3?' Magnus said to the waitress, ignoring Jo's offer to pay.

Jo sat with her purse in her hand, feeling snubbed. She was very aware this unscheduled stay in Orkney was costing rather more than Magnus had perhaps been expecting to pay for the weekend. He had refused to accept anything as a contribution towards the cost so far, and now he wouldn't even let her pay for dinner. She did not want him to feel sorry for her; neither did she want him to think she was just after him for his money. She stood up and followed him out of the restaurant, but only after she had put down a £5 note on the table as a tip.

Magnus opened the door to their room and stood back to let Jo in. He could see she had been annoyed by his action and he was amused by it.

'Jo, honestly, do you really think I'm going to let my pregnant wife pay for my dinner?' he said jokingly, as he went over to the window and glanced out to see what the weather was doing. The rain had returned just as quickly as it had left.

'But I'm *not* your pregnant wife? And I don't need you to pay for everything. I'm quite capable of paying my own way, thank you!' Jo said crossly, as she kicked off her shoes and stomped over to chair and sat down and glared at him.

'OK, I'm sorry, maybe this joke about you being my wife has gone too far,' he said, as he turned back from the window and looked at her. He was still amused by her annoyance and she looked funnier still, sitting in the chair with her arms folded defiantly across her chest. 'I know you're perfectly capable of looking after yourself. I was there, remember, when you hammered down the cost on your new car, and unflinchingly paid for it all on your debit card. For all I know you have more money than me. But I don't give a damn. I can't help being a bit old fashioned about these things, and I don't understand why it matters so much to you.'

Jo's shoulders dropped in defeat and she stood up and disappeared into the bathroom. Magnus switched on the TV and started watching the end of a football match. When she came out of the bathroom he was still glued to the highlights of the Aberdeen v Celtic game.

'I'm going out for a walk.' She put her shoes back on and went to the wardrobe to get her coat.

'It's raining again,' Magnus replied in exasperation, switching off the TV and sitting up on the bed.

'So! My coat's waterproof!' Jo put on her coat quickly, and started doing it up. Magnus got off the bed sighing deeply, and walked over to her.

'You're not going anywhere, it's getting late and you don't know you're way around the town,' he said as he undid her coat and slid it off her shoulders. 'And, we need to talk,' he added meaningfully.

Jo stood in the middle of the room looking down at the floor. She wanted to talk too, but she also felt like running out of the room and down the street as fast as she could. She was afraid of what would happen next. And in some ways even more afraid nothing would happen next. Her heart was hammering away inside her chest, and she wished she could just have a few minutes to herself to gather her thoughts together.

Magnus hung her coat up in the wardrobe and then came over and took her hand and led her over to the bed.

'Don't worry, nothing's going to happen. I just want to talk to you,' he said, as she stood next to the bed looking at him nervously.

Jo sat on the bed cautiously then lay down next to him on the left hand side staring rigidly up at the ceiling. Magnus laughed at her.

'Honestly Jo, what on earth do you think I'm going to do to you? Come here,' he said gently. He scooped his arm around her shoulders and drew her in towards him and held her firmly. Her head lay on his chest just above his heart and she could hear it beating loudly and quickly.

He held her until he could feel her start to relax and trust him. After a while she moved her left arm and wrapped it around his waist. He picked up her hand and brought it up to his lips and kissed it. Jo stiffened instantly, and he gently let go of her hand. This time she put it on his chest almost as if she was preparing herself to push him away.

'I thought you wanted to talk,' she said, after a few minutes of silence.

'I do,' he replied, loosening his hold on her a little and looking at her face. 'But I just wanted to hold you for a while. You seem so nervous all of a sudden. I thought you would have trusted me by now.'

'I do trust you. But this is all so weird. I'm scared,' she said, in a whisper, wriggling away from him to sit up. She sat crossed legged on the bed, with her face in her hands and breathing deeply.

'So am I! I have just as much to lose as you if this goes wrong,' Magnus replied seriously, turning on his side to face her. He noticed she still had her shoes on and he pulled them off while she sat there and threw them on the floor into the corner of the room. Jo stared at him.

'What do you mean? What have you got to lose?' she demanded incredulously, as Magnus lay down again, only this time with his hands behind his head while he stared up at the blank TV screen.

'Let me see; so you're perfectly happy to fight to the death over your right to pay your own way in life, and that's fine. But you don't think I'm capable of getting hurt every bit as much as you if this doesn't work out. What kind of equality is that?'

Jo got off the bed and stood up. 'You're right, I'm sorry. I just can't seem to do or say anything right at the moment,' she said, in exasperation. Once she had stood up she didn't know what to do, she just felt very jumpy and anxious.

'Put the kettle on while you're up,' Magnus said, and smiled broadly when Jo turned to scowl at him. She managed a half smile back, and took the kettle into the bathroom to fill it up.

Jo made some tea and coffee and carried the mugs over to the bed. Magnus put his mug down at the side of the bed and then took Jo's mug out of her hand and set it down next to his. He pulled her gently down on to the bed next to him and held her closely again.

'Can you stop trying to run away from me now and listen,' he said, as he rolled over on his side to face her. He lay propped up on one elbow, looking down at her. Jo burrowed closer into his chest, as much to avoid making eye contact with him. She took hold of his free hand, measuring hers up against his, until he folded his hand around hers and held it tight. She took a deep breath to calm her nerves, and then another, as that clearly failed to work.

Magnus let go of her hand and rested his hand on Jo's tummy. He could feel the small firm swelling of her abdomen and as he stroked his thumb along the top of the bump he could feel her uterus contract. He smiled to himself.

'Can you feel that?' he asked her, as he sat up to get a better look at her.

'Feel what?' Jo asked nervously, feeling uncomfortable at the close attention he was giving her tummy.

'The Braxton Hicks contractions; I just felt one with my hand and wondered what it felt like for you,' he explained, keeping his hand firmly on her.

'Of course I can feel it. But it doesn't hurt or anything so I hardly notice it,' Jo replied, remembering Magnus had been all through this before with his wife and wondering whether he was thinking about her.

Magnus was fascinated by Jo's tummy and when she didn't seem to object, he prodded her gently and expertly trying to locate the baby. Jo squirmed uncomfortably, so he stopped.

'Sorry, I was getting carried away. I sometimes envy my sister doing what she does for a living; this is far more interesting than being an engineer. It's hard to believe there's a little baby inside you isn't it?' he said happily, removing his hand from her.

'Yes, sometimes I find it hard to believe too,' Jo agreed, although feeling that the tiny creature inside her was momentarily the size of an elephant; it seemed to have so much significance to what was going on between them.

Magnus sat up on the bed and moved back so he could lean against the cushioned headboard. He reached over to the mug of black coffee and sipped it, buying himself some time before speaking.

'Jo, if you hadn't been pregnant, I probably would never have got to know you at all, as we would never have met,' he said seriously, watching Jo as she sat up. 'But I'm glad we did meet, and I'm glad you're pregnant too. As far as I'm concerned this baby doesn't get in the way of how I feel about you at all. It doesn't make you less attractive.' He paused for a bit, took another sip of coffee and continued. 'But if you weren't pregnant, I would probably have asked you out, and maybe you would have said yes, and perhaps by now we'd be dating like any other couple.' He stopped. Jo had shifted away from him, wondering where this was going, anticipating a rejection. He reached out and took her hand and pulled her back.

'I didn't do any of that, because I didn't think you'd be interested in me, and I thought maybe you wouldn't be ready to get involved with anyone else and there was a good possibility your ex-partner would come back one day,' he continued. 'I still don't know whether you're interested in me or whether you are ready to get involved with anyone. I still don't know for sure David won't persuade you to go back, but I do want to say this.' He stopped again, trying to summon up the courage to continue.

Jo looked up at his face, noticing the amber glint catching the light from the bedside lamp. He looked so serious. She stared at the freckles on his face and wondered how long it would take to count them. She reached up and ran her fingers through his hair, that was almost the same shade of red as a Red Setter. She pulled his head towards her until he was close enough to kiss, inhaling the sweet mixture of black coffee and whisky on his breath.

That was all the encouragement Magnus needed. He

kissed her; gently at first, with his hand caught up in a tangle of curls. Then he leaned back on the bed and pulled her on top of him. Jo lifted her face away from his and looked at him and smiled. Then she kissed him, holding his face in her hands. Magnus held her firmly, one hand behind her head, still buried deep in her hair, the other grasping her firmly around her waist.

Jo experienced the giddy feeling she used to get when she played on a swing as a child. She pulled away to get her breath back.

'I'm sorry! You were going to say something,' she said. She pulled away from his arms and sat astride him looking down at him and grinning mischievously.

Magnus smiled back at her, catching her hands in his, and pulling her back towards him. He kissed her tenderly and manoeuvred her beside him on the bed and held her in his arms, stroking her bare arm. He pulled away and looked at her, caught hold of a lock of her hair, watching in fascination as the curls sprang back into place when he let go.

'Maybe on this occasion, actions speak louder than words,' he said, grinning shyly.

'No way! You're not getting out of it that easily. What were you going to say?' she said, pushing him away playfully as he went to kiss her again, marvelling at his strength and solidity that resisted her attempts to escape, so effortlessly.

He groaned in mock pain.

'Well.... I *was* going to say I'm crazy about you and I want to be there for you when you decide you're ready to start again. But after this, I've changed my mind,' he said solemnly, laughing when her eyes narrowed with suspicion.

'Changed your mind?' Jo squealed, pretending to be mortally offended. She knew he was joking, but she didn't quite know what the punch line would be.

'Yeah! I aint waiting for you to be ready; I want you right now,' he said, grinning wickedly at her. He kissed her briefly on the lips, amused at the surprised expression on her face. She gazed at him in silence, although her heart was beating so hard, it didn't feel silent to her.

'Jo, you're beautiful,' he said quietly, stroking her cheek and brushing his thumb over her lips. 'I know it feels fast; it *is* a strange situation and it might not be plain sailing for a while. But I want you in my life, permanently. I want to spend every minute of the day and night with you. I want all of you, including this,' he added, moving his hand down to her tummy and caressing it.

Jo was speechless and decided to avoid a verbal response to this bombshell. She pulled him towards her and kissed him. Butterflies flipped inside her and she pulled him closer still, needing something strong to cling to, until the giddiness subsided.

'You're right, actions really do speak louder than words,' she said, when he pulled away at last, leaving her feeling breathless. Magnus narrowed his eyes and stared down at her quizzically, and she laughed. 'OK, OK, I feel the same way Captain Birdseye,' she said, trying to sit up. 'Jesus! I came up here for a quiet life, and now I've ended up with you.'

'I know, it's a tragedy, isn't it,' he said and sat up. He picked up his mug of coffee, but it had gone cold so he set it down again.

'How did this happen to me?' Jo said giggling. 'I moved up to Shetland less than a month ago, and it's been one long series of mishaps, most of them involving you. Even the fact we're here right now in Orkney is an accident. I really wasn't thinking of meeting anyone, and then you come along in your big manly pickup truck, wearing your oily old boiler suit and day-glo jacket, bearing gifts of fresh fish. Seriously, how could a girl resist that?' Jo fell down on the bed giggling like a schoolgirl.

'What about me?' he replied. 'I've ended up with a woman who doesn't know one end of a fish from the other, runs down poor defenceless sheep, can't go out in a boat in a little bit of bad weather, can't dance properly, and probably wouldn't understand me if I spoke normally. What kind of wife would you make?' He leaned over her, about to kiss her again.

'Is that a proposal?' Jo asked grinning, holding him away with her hands.

'Not yet! But I don't think it will take me long to get around to that. Maybe I'll see how you get on at shearing a sheep and then I'll decide whether you're up to the job.' He pushed her arms aside and kissed her, pausing when she started giggling, and waited for her to stop. When she had regained her composure, Jo kissed him back.

CHAPTER THIRTY

Jo stretched out in the bed lazily and opened her eyes, noting the bright slant of sunshine streaming in through a gap in the curtains. She remembered last night and felt a quick hit of adrenaline fizzing through her. Then she realised she had no clothes on under the duvet, and her bathrobe was still hanging up on the inside of the bathroom door. She panicked and wondered how she could get out of bed and dressed before Magnus came back. The shower stopped and she froze halfway out of the bed. She jumped back in and pulled the duvet up over her and waited.

Magnus opened the bathroom door, wearing jeans and a black jumper, wafting steam and the scent of after-shave.

'Good morning Mrs Birdseye. You've finally decided to wake up then,' he said cheerfully, as he sat down on the edge of the bed and started putting his shoes and socks on. He had noted the way she was holding the duvet around her as if terrified he would catch the smallest glimpse of her body. He smiled to himself and remembered how she had insisted on turning off all the bedroom lights last night. He stood up and walked towards the door.

'I take it Madam would like breakfast in bed again,' he said as he opened the door.

Jo nodded gratefully and as soon as he had left the room she shot out of bed and dived into the bathroom, noting again with annoyance the bathroom door did not have a lock on it. She was grateful for the privacy of being left alone, even though she knew it was ridiculous after what had happened between them. She started running the bath and while it was filling up she brushed her teeth, thinking about how they had moved swiftly from kissing to making love. Her tummy still did a loop the loop every time she thought of it. But now in the cold light of day she wondered whether he had any regrets, or whether she had even imagined everything.

She tied her hair up in a scrunchie to keep it out of the water and lowered herself into the deep bubble bath. She looked down at her body, partially hidden by the bubbles, and felt a twinge of anxiety about her appearance. She had always lacked confidence in her body and being pregnant only made it worse. She was only going to get bigger and bigger and it was a scary thought.

She was about to get out of the bath and get dressed when there was a knock on the bathroom door.

'Are you decent? Can I come in?' Magnus asked, from the other side.

'No, I'm in the bath!' Jo squeaked fearfully, and slid noisily under the foam, sending a wave of water over the top and spilling onto the floor.

'Ah, go on, I've made you some tea,' he replied, and to Jo's horror he opened the door and peaked in grinning like a Cheshire cat.

Jo groaned and slid further under the water scooping up the bubbles to cover herself up better.

'Don't be shy, you're beautiful,' Magnus said, as he put the mug of tea down on the vanity unit in the bathroom. He pulled a chair over and sat down on it still smiling with amusement at her discomfiture. He was beaming with pleasure as if he had just won the lottery.

'Oh God, you really are a morning person aren't you?' Jo said in despair. The water was getting cold but she didn't want to get out while he was in the room and he didn't look like he was about to leave.

'I certainly am,' he agreed proudly. 'And I can tell you are a night owl, at least judging by your performance last night anyway,' he added, grinning at the memory. He leaned forward from the chair and flicked some of the bubbles at her face.

Jo felt herself blushing. Despite her discomfort of being undressed in front of him, she couldn't help smiling at him. His happiness was infectious.

'Come on, out you get, you'll get all wrinkled and cold soon,' he said, standing up and taking a clean bath towel from the heated towel rail. He opened it up and held it out, waiting for her to stand up. Jo leaned forward and pulled the plug out and nervously stood up. Magnus wrapped the towel around her and lifted her out of the bath as if she was just a child. He stood for a moment beside her, pulling the towel tightly around her body and covering her up. He took hold of her bare shoulders and bent forward and kissed her lips. Then he pulled at the scrunchie and released her hair from its grip, and ran his fingers through it.

There was a knock on the bedroom door and Magnus let go of Jo and slipped out of the bathroom to answer it. Jo sat down on the chair wrapped in the towel feeling a heady rush of pleasure. She got herself dried and put on the bathrobe and opened the door to the bedroom.

'Breakfast is served Madam!' Magnus said, pointing to the trolley the waitress had delivered to the room. He was sat on the end of the bed waiting for her.

Jo stood looking at the trolley and then looked back at Magnus as if she was trying to decide what to do next.

'If I were you I'd start with breakfast. You're going to need all the energy you can get,' he said roguishly, as he stood up and walked over to the trolley. 'Sit down. Allow me!' He pulled the trolley over to the desk and poured out some fresh tea and coffee. He uncovered a basket of Danish pastries and croissants and a bowl of fresh fruit salad. 'I didn't think you'd fancy a full cooked breakfast this morning,' he added as he pulled over another chair and sat down beside her.

'Are you always this perfect?' Jo asked as she helped herself to the fruit salad first. She speared a cube of mango and put it in her mouth. The fresh sweetness was exactly what she had craved for breakfast.

'I wouldn't be divorced if I was perfect would I?' he replied seriously, as he ripped open a croissant and liberally spread butter over it.

Jo shrugged. She couldn't imagine why anyone would have chosen to leave this man. She couldn't imagine ever wanting to leave him. If she had her way she would take up residence with him in the hotel room and stay there happily for the rest of her life.

Jo ate her fruit, trying to look into the future.

'Where are we going to live?' she asked after a while, watching him while he pulled apart a Danish pastry and ate it, and licking his sticky fingers afterwards.

'I think it is a bit soon to be talking about that, don't you?' He picked up his coffee and drank it and then poured out another cup from the cafetiere on the trolley.

Jo flushed with embarrassment and regretted she had said anything. She picked up her tea and drank it quickly, wishing she had said something less presumptuous.

'Jo, I didn't meant it like that,' Magnus said, as he realised he had upset her already. 'Of course we're going to live together. But I would like to have a few more weeks of trying to be like an ordinary couple. I'd like to take you out on normal dates, and get to know you properly. And also, you need to find your way around Whalsay and get to know people without me getting in your way,' he explained kindly. He took her hand as he spoke and squeezed it when he saw her relax and smile.

'Sorry, I just started wondering whether I'd imagined it all,' she said gratefully, and picked up a pastry to eat.

'Don't be sorry, and you certainly didn't imagine it. It's real, very real. I love you and I want to be with you,' Magnus said firmly. He stood up and kissed her on her forehead. Then he walked over to the TV and switched it on and proceeded to watch the news and weather.

Jo absorbed the fact that he had just casually mentioned that he loved her as if it was no big deal, when as far as she was concerned it was the biggest deal ever. She stood up followed him over to the bed and sat down next to him wondering whether she should reply. He put his arm around her shoulder, not taking his attention away from the news. She cuddled up next to him feeling at peace with the world. When the news had finished he switched off the TV and turned to her, eyeing her up in her bathrobe, and smiling lasciviously.

Jo laughed and pulled away from him and ran over to her suitcase to grab some clothes. Magnus stood up suddenly and chased after her and caught her before she got to the bathroom. He picked her up and carried her over to the bed dropping her gently down. Jo shrieked and giggled as he pinned her down. He put his hand gently over her mouth in a playful attempt to gag her.

'Not so loud, you'll get us kicked out,' he said laughing at her as she tried to wriggle out of his hold.

She bit his hand gently. He pulled it away shaking it out as if she had really hurt him. Jo couldn't move under the weight of him straddling her thighs and pinning her down with his arms. She giggled again, turning her face away from his as he bent down to kiss her.

An hour later they were lying in bed together, tightly entwined in each other's arms.

'Am I never going to be able to kiss you without all of this happening?' Jo asked, referring to the passionate way he had made love to her for the last hour.

He stroked his fingers over her tummy and along her thighs, delighted that at last he could see her, half expecting her to cover herself up again. Her skin had a luminous intensity of whiteness. He traced the brown line that was just starting to show on her tummy, another sign of her pregnant state. He was curious about the baby and hoped it would be a girl, and he imagined it being as beautiful as Jo. He had no idea what David looked like, and didn't particularly want to know either. He was convinced the baby would only have the striking appearance of its mother. The happiest days of his life had been when he was a father to Ella. Now the crippling grief and heartbreak of losing her had eased a little, he felt more than ready to be a father again, biological or not.

'Will you have another baby, after this one?' he asked, after a while of studying her body.

'Yes I should think so,' Jo replied. 'I always imagined having two or three,' she watched him looking at her and wondered what kind of father he would be to her first child. She was well aware from her own experiences that not all men take to being a stepfather very well.

'Jo, I promise you, I'll treat all our children exactly the same,' he said as if he could read her mind, kissing her tummy and then moving up towards her face to kiss her again.

They kissed for a few moments more before Magnus pulled away and picked up his phone from the bedside table to check the time.

'It's nearly lunchtime. I think we're lucky not to have

been disturbed by the cleaners,' he said, sitting up on the bed. 'Come on, let's go out and have a walk around Kirkwall; you haven't seen it yet.' He got up and walked to the bathroom and shut the door.

Magnus went to get their coats from the wardrobe. Jo picked up her handbag and looked at her mobile phone, checking for messages or missed calls. She remembered the call from Megan about David and made an instant decision.

'I just have to make one call,' she said, as she dialled David's mobile phone. Magnus looked at her, unsure whether to leave the room or not. Jo shook her head at him as if to say he could stay, so he sat down on the chair and waited.

'David, it's Jo,' she said, as his familiar voice cautiously answered the phone. She walked over to the window and stared unseeingly outside.

'Jo! Thank God, I really need to speak to you. I've missed you so much,' David started.

'So much so you went back to your wife and children I never even knew existed,' Jo interjected coldly.

'I know, I'm sorry, I should have told you about them, but the only reason I went back was because I was so lonely without you. Please can we meet up and talk. I want to know more about our baby,' he pleaded.

'There's nothing to talk about. I only rang you to tell you never to hurt my friends anymore. I can't believe what you did to Megan,' Jo said, restraining the anger from her voice as much as she could.

'But I heard about the baby from your office, that's why I went mad. I sorry about what I did to Megan, really I am, I don't know what got in to me. I just wanted to see you so much. Jo, I really love you, I need you. Please come and see me,' David said. Jo could hear the desperation in his voice and she felt a tiny glimmer of sympathy for him, but she could not forgive his dishonesty and treachery.

'The reason you need me has absolutely nothing to do with love. I suggest you get some counselling for your problems and sort yourself out,' Jo said, as kindly as she could. She looked round at Magnus who was staring at her, wondering where this conversation was going. He fiddled with his watch nervously. Jo turned back to the window, conscious of the scrutiny.

'I know I need help, I'm sorry,' David said. 'I should have talked to you before about it. I thought I could sort myself out, really I did. But if you come back now I'm sure we can work this out. I promise I can give up gambling. Jo, please come back to me. I want you, and our baby,' he begged. He sounded genuinely distressed and apologetic. Jo had to steel herself to reply.

'But David, it isn't your baby. I'm with someone else now,' she lied convincingly.

'What do you mean you're with someone else now? You can't be!' David gasped in shock and irritation.

'Well I am. I'm getting married to my baby's father. I'm sorry about your situation but it has nothing to do with me. I just wanted to say goodbye,' Jo said, looking out of the window and still seeing nothing. She hated doing this to David but could not bear the thought of always being tied to him in some way, and knowing the relationship would always be strained between them. She also felt, since he already had two children of his own he had failed; he didn't deserve another opportunity to screw up a child's life.

'I can't believe this. You're just going to leave me stranded; after all we've been through. You fucking whore!' David yelled down the phone, before Jo cut him off. She remained standing by the window looking down at the phone in her hand and thinking perhaps she should have asked Magnus to leave the room after all. Her hands were shaking; she was still thinking about David's final words to her and the relief of closure hadn't started to sink in yet. She worried about him and what he would do, although she knew he had wealthy parents he could count on for support, so she had to stop feeling the burden of responsibility for him.

Magnus got up slowly from the chair and walked over to her. He put his arm around her and turned her around to face him.

'Are you sure you wanted to do that?' he asked kindly, lifting her chin up with his fingers to look at her face.

'I'm sorry, maybe you shouldn't have been here to hear that,' Jo said regretfully. 'I hated lying to him, but I just don't want him in my life now. He's had his chance with one family already and he screwed it up, I don't see why he should be allowed to hang around and screw up my life and my child's,'

Jo said defiantly, moving away from Magnus, wishing to get away from him temporarily, feeling the saddle of guilt weighing her down.

'Perhaps I'm being selfish, in fact I know I am, but I think you did the right thing,' Magnus said encouragingly. 'The only thing that worried me about hearing all of that, was how calmly you lied to him. That was kind of scary,' he added trying to make a joke out of it, but failing. Jo turned round sharply at the awful realisation of the impression she had just made.

'I'm not like that normally; I don't know what's come over me.' She exclaimed. She sat down heavily on the bed.

Magnus laughed and came and sat next to her and put his arm around her.

'I know you're not. I was kidding. You did what you had to do. Anyone could see that,' he said reassuringly. 'Now, please can we go out now? Unless of course you want to spend the rest of the afternoon in bed.'

Jo stood up suddenly and picked her coat up off of the chair.

'I'll take that as a no then,' Magnus said, smiling at her. Jo grinned back and grabbed her handbag and dived out of the door as he chased after her. She ran along the corridor with Magnus in pursuit and emerged into the bright sunshine of midday.

'Shall we go for a walk around the town now? I know it's Sunday and most of the shops are closed but we might find a café open, and there's always the Cathedral to see,' Magnus said, taking Jo by the hand and walking down the hotel driveway.

'Cathedral?' Jo said mystified. 'I didn't expect Orkney to have a Cathedral.'

'Yes, and it's named after my good self,' Magnus said boastfully.

'That figures! First you take me to the St Magnus Hotel and now we're going to the St Magnus Cathedral. Is there no end to your ego?' Jo replied, as she walked alongside him, feeling the stress of speaking to David melting away. 'Who was St Magnus anyway? The patron saint of annoying boyfriends?' she teased, laughing when he crushed her hand as punishment.

'Where to now?' she asked, after they had spent half an hour wandering around the beautiful red brick cathedral and admiring the stained glass windows.

'There's a shop along here I thought you'd like. Jeannie raves on about it the whole time. In fact if she knew I was going there she would probably demand I bought her something back.' He replied.

'Oh? What kind of shop?' Jo asked, noticing most of the shops along the high street were closed.

'It's a jewellery shop; owned by some local designer called Sheila Fleet. She makes all this silver and gold jewellery and uses coloured enamels in the patterns. It's quite bonny. I think you'll like it,' Magnus explained. 'I hope it's open on a Sunday.'

Jo picked up a pretty gold ring that had an intricate design of strands of gold and diamonds. It was too wide for an engagement ring but she pushed it on to her ring finger of her left hand and admired it. It was really pretty. She took it off and tried on some of the silver and enamel designs, while Magnus was looking at earrings for his sister. When she had finished browsing she picked up a leaflet from the desk, noticing there was a website she could order stuff from.

She followed Magnus out of the shop and linked her arm through his.

'They were pretty earrings, I think Jeannie will love them,' she said, as they walked along towards the harbour.

'Yeah, she'll love them,' he agreed, smiling. 'And then she'll be really pissed off I bought them for you, not her.' He ducked out of Jo's reach, as she had attempted to slap him on the arm, and set off running down the road. Then he stopped and waited for her to catch up with him. 'I'm glad you like them. I knew you would never let me buy them for you if I asked you. And I didn't want another war to break out in the shop,' he said, when she stood in front of him with her hands on her hips pretending to be annoyed with him.

'Thank you! That's very sweet of you,' Jo said. 'Am I allowed to kiss you in public or is that just asking for trouble?' she added, putting her arms around his neck.

'OK, I'll steel myself. I'll think of England or something; that will put me off.' He laughed and looked down at her seriously.

Jo kissed him, before starting to giggle, and taking revenge on him by kicking him gently on the shins. Magnus picked her up and carried her over towards the pier and threatened to throw her in if she didn't behave. Jo shrieked with laughter and struggled to get down. They finally sat down on a bench, exhausted with laughing and playing around, conscious that people had been watching them.

'Oh, God, I feel like a teenager again!' Jo said bending over, trying to get her breath back. She sat up and leaned against him feeling overwhelmed with happiness.

'Me too,' he said, as he pulled her close to him and kissed her hair. Jo was starting to like this gesture, which she had first interpreted as rather paternal. Now it seemed wonderfully intimate.

They sat for a while looking at the boats in the harbour and watching people walking by. A young mother walked along with a pushchair with another small child walking alongside her holding her hand. Around their feet scampered a tiny white puppy. It was a wriggling fluffy ball of energy and as it passed by it jumped up at Jo, and tried to clamber up her legs. Jo laughed and bent down to stroke it.

'Come here Jess. Sorry about that!' The woman said apologetically to Jo, trying to pull the excitable puppy away.

'Oh she's called Jess too,' Jo exclaimed. 'Oh, she's beautiful, how old is she?' She picked up the puppy that had managed to jump up onto her lap.

'She's just twelve weeks old, we only got her last week,' the woman replied, grinning at Jo who was being subjected to the full frenzy of the puppy that was trying to lick her face and hands.

'What kind of dog is she?' Jo asked, putting Jess back down on the pavement.

'She's a West Highland Terrier. I got her from a local breeder. She's adorable isn't she?'

Jo stood up to look into the pushchair. 'Looks like you have two adorable little boys too.'

'Most of the time they are,' the woman said, smiling as she started to walk away.

'Wasn't that puppy cute? I would love one of them,' Jo said to Magnus as she sat down again. 'Isn't it funny she's called Jess?'

Magnus jumped up suddenly and hurried to catch up with the woman with the puppy. Jo watched him speaking to her, but couldn't hear what was being said. She could guess though, and she smiled to herself. When he came back to the seat she took his hand and grinned at him.

'Does that mean you're going to buy me a puppy? She asked happily.

'No, afraid not, that was the last one in the litter. But at least now I know what you'd like for Christmas.'

He stood up and pulled her up by the hand and they set off along the harbour. Jo turned and watched the woman and child disappear from view, the puppy still bouncing along beside them.

They walked around the town for a while and had lunch in one of the cafes. Then Magnus suggested getting the car and going out for a drive. They walked back to the hotel and Magnus opened the car door for Jo.

'I've just got to get something from the room,' he said, and dashed inside the hotel. He came back out a few minutes later looking smug and cheerful. They headed away from Kirkwall, singing along with the radio. Jo saw the signs to Stromness and guessed that was where they were heading. But Magnus carried on driving and only stopped when they got to a farmhouse at the end of a very long lane. Jo assumed he had got lost but Magnus turned off the engine and got out of the car. He came around to Jo's side and opened up her door for her, subserviently bowing as she got out. Jo smiled but was feeling puzzled as to why they were there. She followed him to the front door, wondering whether he knew the owner.

A middle-aged smartly dressed woman answered the door and seemed to be expecting them.

'Come in, come in. They're in the kitchen. Come and have a look,' she said, as Magnus and Jo walked past her and walked into the huge, warm and rather stuffy kitchen. As soon as Jo entered the room she realised why they were there. An adult Westie and her two little black puppies sat in a basket in the corner. Or rather the mother sat in the basket, while her two offspring climbed all over her with the same amount of energy Jo had seen in the little white puppy.

Jo approached the basket and crouched down beside it, not sure whether the mother would allow her near to her puppies. She didn't seem to mind, and Jo tentatively stroked one of them, then picked it up and held it. She turned round and looked at Magnus who looked delighted with himself. He was sat at the kitchen table talking to the owner. Jo didn't really understand everything they were saying as they had slipped naturally into dialect. She listened carefully, recognising that the woman's accent was also from Shetland. She put one puppy down and picked up the other.

'Jo, would you like a bitch or a dog?' Magnus asked her after a while. Jo shrugged as if she didn't really know.

'OK, why don't you just decide which one you like best and we'll see what it is then?' he asked when she didn't reply.

Jo looked at the puppy she was holding and then at the one that was wriggling around on the floor. It was a tough decision. She stood there trying to work out which one was the most lovable.

'Could we take both of them?' Magnus asked the woman.

'Yes of course you can,' she replied. 'It does seem a shame to separate them.'

Jo stood cuddling one of the puppies, looking over at Magnus. She was overwhelmed by his generosity. Too overwhelmed in fact. She thought about the way this whole situation was gathering momentum, and she felt giddy and out of control. Just a month ago she had never met Magnus, and now as she looked at the man she had fallen in love with, she wondered whether she even knew him. The stinging insult from David came to mind and wounded her afresh. This was from a man who she had known for six years, and it turned out she had known almost nothing about him. She stared at Magnus and felt a cold trickle of fear that this relationship might end the same way. He was almost too good to be true, and she'd thought that about David once upon a time.

Jo felt her heart racing and heard a roaring in her ears. She imagined she could smell burning and as she went to put the puppy down, she fainted.

Magnus had seen the way the colour had drained from Jo and had already walked over to her. He caught her fall and held her upright, leading her over to a chair as she came to, a few seconds later. The puppy she had been holding was unharmed and had scarcely noticed the short drop back into the basket.

The woman fetched a glass of water for her and opened up a window, exclaiming about the heat in the kitchen. Jo took the glass from her, hands shaking, not knowing exactly what had happened. Magnus crouched in front of her, looking up at her face anxiously.

'Are you alright Jo? You scared the life out of me,' he asked, taking one of her hands in his.

'I don't know, I don't know what happened,' Jo stammered, trying to drink the water in an attempt to calm down.

'Would you like me to call a doctor?' The woman asked solicitously, looking at Jo with concern, and noticing for the first time she appeared to be pregnant.

'No, I'll be fine, honest, thank you,' she said to the woman, trying to reassure her. To Magnus she turned and said. 'Can we do this another time; I think I need to lie down.'

'Of course, no problem,' he replied, helping her to stand. He told the woman he would be in touch about the puppies before they left Orkney. Then he led Jo out to the car and opened the door for her. Jo sat in the passenger seat feeling shaken and not knowing how she would talk about this to Magnus. There was only person she really wanted to speak to right now and that was Megan.

'I think maybe we should just stop off at the hospital on the way back to the hotel, just to be on the safe side. You really didn't look very well just now,' Magnus said, as he started the car. He patted her leg reassuringly and drove off down the narrow farm lane back towards the main road.

'No, really, I'm fine. Really I am,' Jo said, looking away from him and staring out of the window. She was trying to work out why she had felt so upset back in the farmhouse. She realised it was partly because nobody had ever been so generous towards her and she simply did not know how to respond. And whilst David had bestowed a variety of gifts brought home from his travels, the only thing of value he had given her was the diamond engagement ring, and Jo was starting to wonder whether that had even been real.

The two little puppies would have been the most perfect and generous present Jo had ever received, and all this from someone she hardly knew. Despite their protestations of love and commitment to each other over the past 24 hours, Jo saw the puppies as the first tangible evidence this was all real. It wasn't a dream, and she hadn't even told her best friend what was happening. She felt a fresh wave of panic and opened the window to get some fresh air, wishing the roller coaster of emotions she was currently riding would slow down. She was aware Magnus was watching her as he drove and she felt the car slow down and come to rest in a lay-by overlooking the sea.

'What's wrong? You look like the world's going to end?' Magnus asked seriously. He turned to look at her, but kept his hands on the steering wheel, not knowing whether he should touch her or not.

'I don't know. I really loved the puppies and I really wanted to buy them, but all of a sudden I panicked. It all seemed so fast, you buying them for me....' She paused and turned her face to look at him. 'I don't really know you do I? It just seemed like such a big step,' she continued. Magnus nodded in understanding, but waited for her to carry on. He picked up her hand and held it in his and looked at her, wondering whether she was changing her mind about everything.

'It's so crazy, I mean, we've talked about love, marriage, the future, children, everything. And I want all of that, I really do,' Jo said earnestly stroking his hand and then grasping it firmly. 'But when I saw you were going to buy me the little puppies I just felt overwhelmed. It's like it's all too good to be true, and I felt dizzy, and kind of like I wasn't in control any more. Does that make sense?' She looked into his eyes hoping he had understood her.

'It makes perfect sense. It's my fault I shouldn't have try to surprise you like that. I think you have probably had a few too many surprises just recently.' He smiled at her and squeezed her hand.

'Oh, no, it was a lovely surprise. I'm just not used to people being so nice to me, it feels weird,' she said quietly, and looked down at their hands. His hand still felt alien to her, even though it was warm and strong and comforting to hold.

'Well, you'd better get used to it! Because I intend to spend the rest of my life being nice to you,' he said, pulling her towards him and kissing the top of her head.

She smiled and looked up at him. 'Are you afraid to kiss me properly?' she asked flirtatiously.

Magnus looked round the car as if he was sizing it up. 'Definitely, this car's way too small for any passionate encounters.'

Jo started laughing. Magnus smiled with relief and sighed, leaning back in the seat.

'I love the way you laugh,' he said. 'And I love the way you make jokes to cover up your nerves. I've seen you doing that a lot lately,' Magnus became serious for a moment. 'It's OK to feel the way you do. It is all happening fast, and it's a lot to take in. Three months after Lynne left I was still getting drunk and being an idiot; I would never have been ready for all this,' he said lifting her hand up by way of illustrating their relationship. 'So don't be too hard on yourself if you freak out every once in a while. I understand.'

'See, that's exactly what I mean!' Jo said, in mock frustration. 'You are just too perfect. I can't even have a minor nervous breakdown without you being caring and considerate and just plain perfect.'

'There's absolutely no way I'm perfect. Believe me!' Magnus said, shaking his head despairingly at Jo. 'Onywye, whit aboot da twa peerie dugs den?' he asked, slipping into his normal accent.

'Can we just get one of them?' Jo asked.

Magnus nodded. 'Of course! Which one would you like?'

'I don't mind, but do me a favour, chose one for me, I can't decide. I can't go back in there and make that kind of decision and I didn't know which was male or female anyway,' Jo explained.

'OK, I'll have a good look at them and choose the fittest and best natured. How's that?' he suggested. He shifted in his seat as if he was going to drive on. 'There's just one problem, my peerie jewel, if we buy a puppy we'll definitely have to get the ferry back home as we won't be able to take it on the plane. Is that OK?'

'Of course!' Jo said smiling. 'I'm sure I can stay here

until the summer, when the weather improves.

Magnus laughed and started the engine. 'The forecast is fine for the next couple of days.' He said reassuringly.

EPILOGUE – ONE YEAR LATER

As Magnus had predicted it had been a Godless whore of a night, and Jo hadn't slept much as a result. Now the storm had passed by, leaving a soggy and exhausted landscape, with weak and watery sunlight filtering through the curtains. She stretched out her arm to the other side of the bed. It was empty and cold. She sat up and looked over at the cot in the corner of the room. It too was empty. She glanced at the bedside clock; it was nearly eight. Jo jumped out of bed and hurried into the bathroom. She would be late for college if she didn't get a move on.

A few minutes later she went downstairs in her dressing gown and walked into the kitchen. Magnus was sat at the window seat feeding Freya her breakfast. Minx was hovering underneath the high chair, waiting for the inevitable spillage of baby porridge. Ben sat in his usual spot by the radiator, ignoring everyone, as he had already eaten his breakfast.

'Here's mummy at last!' Magnus said. 'We thought she'd never get up, didn't we?' He laughed conspiratorially with Freya as he popped the last spoonful of porridge into her mouth, and then gave her the little plastic spoon to practice with. She decided it had served its purpose as a spoon, and it would be much more fun to bang it on her table instead.

'I'm sorry; I feel so tired. I shouldn't have stayed up so late writing that essay,' Jo said, going over to kiss her husband. They stood cuddling in the kitchen for a few minutes. When Jo yawned, Magnus directed her into a seat and put the kettle on to make her some tea.

'Well it's just as well you got it finished last night, as you're not going to have much time this weekend,' he said, handing her a mug of tea and then picking Freya up out of her high chair. He held the little girl in his arms, making faces at her until she giggled.

'I know, but it will be fun though. I think Megan and Aiden make a good couple don't you?' Jo said, looking up at Magnus and Freya, and noticing how her daughter's face lit up when he smiled at her. Jo stared past them and looked at the calendar hanging up on the wall. She had put a star on today's date and she wondered if Magnus would remember what day it was.

He saw her looking and smiled at the memory.

'Can you really believe it was a year ago we went to Orkney? So much has happened since then.' Magnus said; kissing the top of Freya's head and passing her over to Jo, so he could make some breakfast.

Jo sat cuddling her very precious daughter thinking about the past year. Freya Georgia Inkster was born in mid-March, a trifle early, but otherwise without any drama. Not long after she was born Megan applied for the post of Modern Languages teacher at Whalsay High School and had moved up to Shetland in May. She was now going out with the gorgeous Aiden, an Irishman who taught English at the same school. Megan was renting Magnus' house and was trying to decide between buying it, or having her own house built and taking advantage of the first time builder's grant. A dilemma she couldn't get her head around, after her years of renting dingy flats in London.

Jo and Magnus had married in August, on the beach below her house in a small Civil ceremony, but with a more traditional reception at the hall. A few weeks later Jo started her degree course at Shetland College, and was enjoying it immensely. Ruby looked after Freya while she was at the college, if Magnus was working. Jo and Megan had reinstated their Thursday night ritual of meeting up. Only this time, lacking any wine bars on the island, they went to each other's houses, and Jeannie and Sarah usually came along too.

Jo sometimes found it hard to believe how much had happened since she moved to Shetland. She was happier than she had ever been in her life. Magnus had turned out to be the perfect partner, and although he hadn't been there at the start of Freya's life, he was certainly making up for it now. He was the perfect dad.

'Here's your tea. That'll wake you up,' Magnus said, as he put a mug down on the table. 'What ferry are you going out on this morning?' he added, as he walked over to the fridge to get some butter for the toast.

'The 10.30, my lecture is at 12.00 and then I'll be back on the 2.45,' Jo said, as she picked up the tea. She took a sip and wrinkled her nose in distaste. 'Is this milk off? The tea tastes funny.'

Magnus picked up the container and looked at the date, and then he took the top off and sniffed it. 'No, it's fine,' he replied. He turned to look at Jo who was attempting another sip of tea. She pulled another face and put it down in disgust.

'Yuk! It must be me. I feel a bit icky today, it must be the late night,' she said, turning her attention to Freya and stroking her dark wispy curls, and then wiping a tiny speck of porridge away from her cheek.

Magnus stared at them thoughtfully for a moment, and then started grinning to himself. He looked at the calendar trying to work out something in his mind, then picked up the plate of toast and carried it across to Jo.

'Well then Freya, what would you like? A baby brother or a sister?' he asked, as he ruffled the baby's hair. She lifted her head to grin at him, drooling from the corner of her mouth.

Jo looked up at Magnus, not quite focused enough to work out what he was saying, or rather what he was implying. Finally it clicked.

'Oh my God' she exclaimed, as she stood up with Freya in her arms. 'I'm pregnant, aren't I?'

Magnus put his arms around his wife and daughter and kissed them both.

'I think that's a distinct possibility,' he said, smiling broadly at Jo who looked stunned and delighted in equal measure. 'Looks like we will be having a double celebration this weekend.'

The End

ABOUT THE AUTHOR

Frankie Valente is studying for a Masters in Professional Writing with University College Falmouth. She has lived in England, Wales, Scotland and Ireland and is married, with two sons. She is working on a novel about loss and reconciliation, called *Peace Lily*. She is also writing a screenplay for her dissertation. It is called *Fostering Hope* and it is set in the Child Protection Office of a Social Work Department in England. She has recently moved back to Shetland after 18 months in Ireland, and is enjoying being back amongst friends, even if the weather is a tad cooler, wetter and windier! In her opinion Shetland is a little bit of Heaven on earth. If you've haven't been there yet, make sure you put it on your "bucket list."

You can follow Frankie Valente on Twitter and she has a website: www.frankie-valente.co.uk and for more information about Shetland go to: www.visitshetland.com.

CPSIA information can be obtained at www.ICGtesting.com
Printed in the USA
BVOW071428160412

287792BV00001B/271/P